The Urbana Free Library

To renew materials call
217-367-4057

SO-AGH-218

Freeze Me, Tender

*Other Five Star titles
by Michael A. Black:*

A Killing Frost
Windy City Knights
The Heist

Freeze Me, Tender

Michael A. Black

Five Star • Waterville, Maine

First Edition
First Printing: February 2006

Published in 2006 in conjunction with Tekno Books and Ed Gorman.

Set in 11 pt. Plantin by Myrna S. Raven

Printed in the United States on permanent paper.

Library of Congress Cataloging-in-Publication Data

Black, Michael A., 1949–
    Freeze me, tender / by Michael A. Black.—1st ed.
      p. cm.
    ISBN 1-59414-471-0 (hc : alk. paper)
    1. Rock musicians Fiction.   2. Cryonics—Fiction.
  3. Journalists—Fiction.   4. Memphis (Tenn.)—Fiction.
  5. Las Vegas (Nev.)—Fiction.   6. Musical fiction.
  I. Title.
  PS3602.L325F74 2006
    813'.6—dc22   2005028669

For Julie . . .

Thanks

Acknowledgments

The path a writer walks is often arduous and fraught with unexpected twists and turns. Writing this book was no exception, and I owe a debt of gratitude to many who helped me along the way. I couldn't include everyone, but here's a partial listing of some of those people who helped me make *Freeze Me, Tender* a reality.

But before I begin, I need to clarify a few things. I've taken quite a bit of artistic license with this novel, which falls somewhere between the time-honored traditions of a roman à clef and a picaresque farce. All the characters contained herein are fictional, as are some of the places. Not only have I slightly reshuffled and augmented the geography of the Las Vegas strip, but I have also extended those liberties with the Las Vegas Metro Police Department. I felt all this was a necessary evil, since I am writing fiction, after all.

Now, on to the copious words of appreciation. In no certain order, I would like to say thanks to the members of my writer's group, the Southland Scribes: Helen Osterman, George N. Kulles, Sherry Cole, Sandi Tatara, Lydia Ponczak, Ralph Horner, Linda Cochran, Jane Andringa, Ryan S. O'Reilly, and Joan Marie Poninski. Thanks also to my north side writing friends, David Walker, Mary Harris, Libby Fischer-Hellmann, Michael Allen Dymmoch, Eleanor Taylor Bland, Gordon McIntosh, and Lisa Kartus. Both groups gave me valuable insight into my writing when I was crafting the book. Special thanks to my first readers, Len Jellema, my friend and mentor, J. Michael Major, whose wise counsel has helped me immensely, and Big Dave Case, my brother in blue and fellow cop-writer. Thanks to Joe

Tartaro, his daughter, Peggy, and all the folks at the Second Amendment Foundation who funded my first trip to Las Vegas, and thus allowed me to capture the spirit of that wonderful city. My appreciation to Torrey Johnson, "the real CSI," and head of the Las Vegas Metro Police Department's forensic unit. (Any mistakes I've made with LVMPD's procedures were entirely intentional!) To my peerless editor and advisor, Debbie Brod, who did her customarily fantastic job of trimming my adverbs and pointing out places where my writing needed a bit of spit and polish. Thanks to Mary Smith, Tiffany Schofield, and everybody at Five Star, for their continued support and for believing in me. Thanks to Martin Greenberg and Big John Helfers and all the people at Tekno Books. Thanks to my best friend, Ray Lovato, whose friendship has endured numerous decades and several thousand miles separation. Thanks to Patricia Pinianski, who personified for me the definition of courage with her astonishing grace under pressure. (To her father, Walter, as well, who was a good guy.) Thanks to my unofficial publicist at the PD, Melody Froncek, and my friend and supporter, Marg Murphy of Otsego, Michigan. Thanks to Peggy Check, for bidding on a walk-on part in my novel at the Toronto Bouchercon. And thanks to Rob Kantner, author of the Ben Perkins series, who helped me with my fledgling prose so many years ago. Thanks to Andrew Vachss, Mike McNamara, and Zak Mucha, my modern day "wolf pack" buddies, and all the men and women at the MPD, who stood with me all those times when our backs were against the wall. And sincere thanks to Julie A. Hyzy, my special friend and writing partner, without whose help this novel would never have been finished.

There are certainly many more deserving of mention. Until next time, take care.

Prologue

The faraway lights from the city glowed like a distant star, in sharp contrast to the darkness of the desert night as the car sped along the solitary ribbon of highway leaving Boulder City. The row of mountains in the backdrop had merged with the velvet sky. A big green sign flashed by, and she glanced at it momentarily as her headlights washed over the reflective metal.

LAS VEGAS 75 MILES

A moan broke the silence inside the car as the hulking figure, covered with a blanket in the passenger seat, rolled slightly and snorted something indecipherable, his voice a rickety groan. Marjorie Versette reached over and laid a comforting hand on the man's shoulder, squeezing it with practiced ease. The sonorous breathing seemed to lessen, and the movements ceased. She patted his arm once more, then checked her watch before returning her hand to the wheel.

"Easy, easy," she said. Then, after looking at her face in the mirror, added, "You know, don't you? You can sense it. We're almost there."

The skin around her eyes crinkled, sending faint skeins along her fat cheeks. She reached up and wiped away a solitary teardrop. The man beside her stirred again, as if straining to emerge from a troubled slumber.

"Maybe a little music will help relax you," Marjorie said, reaching across and flipping on the radio. The voice of the disc jockey came on, glib and fast.

". . . so all of you out there who remember, and all of you out there that don't, come on by to Vegas, the city of bright lights to help celebrate the most solemn anniversary we know. Two more days and it'll be the tenth anniv—"

"Never you pay no mind to that," Marjorie said, pushing the edge of the tape into the slot. "Just never you pay no mind."

The tape player activated and then the voice crooned on in mid-song, unbothered by the previous interruption, hitting all those ridiculously wonderful notes and sounding like no other voice ever had . . . just like he'd never stopped.

Almost like an echo, she thought, turning up the volume. Like he's right here with us. With us!

She looked across the seat again and smiled.

And in a way, she thought, he is.

Chapter 1

Just Business

T.J. "Big Daddy" Babcock poured himself another two fingers and paused to admire the amber liquid before replacing the bottle in his liquor cabinet. It would be his last one before the flight, he decided, as he felt the slow burn of the blended whiskey sear down his esophagus. Older whiskey, faster horses, younger women, more money. . . . Or something like that. Too bad he didn't own the rights to that song, but, hell, he had to leave some of the pie for those other saps, didn't he?

Shoulda added fine cigars to those lyrics, he thought as he withdrew one of his hand-rolled Havanas from a silver case and looked for something sharp to slice off the tip. He moved to his desk and sat in the padded leather swivel chair. The top was a clutter of papers, coffee cups, CDs, and old magazines. The new computer, which sat amid the disorder, hummed slightly. His pudgy fingers rummaged through the detritus for a cutter, but found none.

The front doorbell rang, and Big Daddy decided the hell with it and just bit off the end, spitting it onto the floor next to the wastebasket. Anybody notices, I'll just say it was the maid's day off, he chuckled, not bothering to pick it up. He patted himself for a lighter, a book of matches, anything, but came up empty.

The doorbell rang again.

Snorting, he glanced at his watch and then managed to raise his considerable bulk from the chair. He wore a light gray suit, the pants of which neatly covered the tops of his shiny black cowboy boots, which were inset with a lattice-work design resembling fine silver and gold. The hand-tooled leather made creaking sounds as he walked out of his study and across the living room toward the front door.

It had to be the driver. An early bird. He'd asked the agency for Sharon, that pretty, long-legged blond girl from the last time.

Anxious bitch, he thought. Hell, she must have me confused with a big tipper, Big Daddy thought. The house was sumptuously furnished, with thick, forest green carpeting and sky blue walls. Numerous paintings of horses and landscapes adorned three walls, hanging strategically at each center. On the fourth wall, which extended into the hallway, was a double row of photographs, both color and black and white, of himself and Colton Purcell at various stages of his career. Green floors, blue walls, and the white-capped vaulted ceiling always gave Big Daddy the illusion that he was walking outdoors, even if he wasn't. But if there was one thing he'd learned from his years in show business, it was that perception was reality. This he knew.

His faint smile faded as the doorbell rang again. A double ring, sounding even more insistent. He stepped around his two packed suitcases.

"I'm a-coming, goddammit," he yelled, glancing at his watch. An eager beaver, he thought. The damn plane isn't due to take off for more than four hours, and I'm getting picked up by a gal with ants in her pants. But maybe she'll have a light. Big Daddy paused at the mirror in the hallway. In his light colored suit he looked like a slightly shopworn version of Burl Ives in *Cat on a Hot Tin Roof*. He adjusted his string bow tie and smoothed out his mustache and goatee, thinking that maybe there'd be some time for a little hanky-panky.

He opened the door and immediately felt his gut sag. It was a man, and this guy was huge. He looked like a pro boxer or maybe one of those massive wrestlers they had jumping around flexing their muscles on cable these days. The guy was dressed in a black leather jacket and wore a dark, peaked cap.

"You from the limo service?" Big Daddy asked.

"Yes, sir."

"Where's Sharon?"

"She couldn't make it," the man said. "My name's Corrigan." He raised his eyebrows slightly and moved forward. Big Daddy moved aside and gestured toward his suitcases sitting on the floor.

"Them there's the bags. Ah, you got a light, by any chance?"

Corrigan nodded and reached in his pocket. He was wearing thin, black leather driving gloves. The lighter, a plastic disposable model, looked like a sliver in his hand. He flicked the wheel and held out the bluish flame. Big Daddy leaned forward, twirling the end of the Havana in the fire and puffed prodigiously to get it started. Blowing out a grayish cloud, he straightened up and said, "Thank ya."

Corrigan pocketed the lighter.

He moved well too, like some kind of big jungle cat. The son of a bitch had the biggest hands Big Daddy had ever seen, at least on a white man. He thought about telling him that, but decided not to. After all, this was the "New South," and you just never knew when you were going to run across a transplanted Northerner. Or even worse, a liberal white Southerner, like that idiot Jimmy Carter. An ex-president going north to help a bunch of do-gooders build houses for low-income families.

Big Daddy snorted at the thought, then looked up to see the other man watching him.

"You're kinda early, ain't ya?" Big Daddy asked, canting his head to blow the smoke upward.

The guy seemed set to answer when a ringing started. Big Daddy looked around, then saw the driver reaching into his jacket pocket. The huge mitt came out with a cell phone.

"Hello," he said after pressing the button. Big Daddy took another drag on the cigar and looked at the size of the man's biceps, which seemed to stretch the upper arms of the jacket.

"Yeah, I'm with him now," Corrigan continued. "Un huh. Yes, sir."

Politeness, thought Big Daddy. A rare commodity in today's youth, although this massive son of a bitch was no kid. He looked to be in his mid-thirties, with a hardness about him. No sugar in his gas tank, that was for sure. When he'd terminated the call and slipped the phone back into his pocket Big Daddy looked at him and said, "Like I told ya, them there's my bags."

Corrigan nodded again, then reached in his other pocket, glancing around. His gaze swept over the array of Colton photos covering the wall.

"I've heard about you, sir," he said. "You were Colton Purcell's manager, weren't you?"

Big Daddy smiled. A fan. Why hadn't he recognized the big bastard's reticence as adulation? He stuck the cigar into the corner of his mouth and flashed his practiced grin.

"Yep, that was me," he said, holding his left hand toward the photos. "As you can see, we were together from the time I discovered him right after he got outta the army."

He pointed to a picture of a sullen-looking young blond

man standing next to an obviously younger Big Daddy, wearing the same style gray suit and string bow tie. Big Daddy's smile looked frozen, and the young man's upper lip curled slightly in a crooked smile.

"Took him from being a poor hillbilly singer to the king of rock and roll," Big Daddy continued. He gestured down the wall at the other pictures, which showed Colton's evolution, getting more slicked back, more sophisticated with each new photo.

"This one here was for our first gold record album," Big Daddy said. "Things was vinyl in them days, before the CDs took over." He gestured with the cigar. "Our first movie. That there's Sonny Proper, Colton's best friend. They grew up together, dirt poor."

He pointed a finger at a broad shouldered, heavyset man with slicked back hair modeled after Colton's. But in contrast to Colton's sleek, blow-dried look, Sonny's looked coarse and thick.

"Him and Colton started playing at hayrides down South," Big Daddy continued. "Of course, it was Colton's voice what made 'em special. I seen that right off. Sonny couldn't carry a tune in a picnic basket." He brought the cigar up to his lips and took a few copious puffs. "Colton kept him on, though. Personal assistant and bodyguard. That Sonny was one rough son-of-a-bitch. Ex-marine."

Big Daddy licked his lips as he withdrew the cigar.

"This one here," he said, pointing to a color photo of Colton in a fancy tuxedo holding a slice of wedding cake up to a stunning brunette's face, "was when he got himself hitched to Ladonna."

"She looks like a real babe," Corrigan said.

Big Daddy grunted a quick laugh. "Me and Sonny called her Ladzilla behind her back. A real bitch. Gave him a nice daughter, though. At least until she growed up and started looking for love in all the wrong places."

Corrigan smirked.

"There's little Melissa Michelle," Big Daddy said, indicating a shot of a prepubescent girl, solemn-faced and fair in black and white, sitting on Colton's lap. "Always her daddy's little girl. Trouble was, he always wanted a son." He drew heavily on his cigar. "She'll be eighteen this year. Time does fly. Stands to inherit the bulk of the estate then." He blew out a cloudy breath. "Gonna be worth a pretty penny, yes siree." He grinned broadly. " 'Cept that I still own fifty-one percent of all the profits from the recordings." Big Daddy puffed proudly as he grabbed his lapels. "Controlling interest. Colton dying the way he did turned out to be a very profitable career move. He's bigger now than when he was still singing."

Corrigan stepped down toward the last of the pictures. Big Daddy followed, explaining the significance of the various poses. He stopped in front of the last three suspended frames.

"That's him in his last movie role. He always wanted to play a cowboy, but we figured he was raking in so much from his concerts at Vegas, so why not just make a movie about that?"

One of the final two pictures showed a bloated Colton Purcell in a red, white, and blue jump suit, complete with cape, his sharp chin jutting from a dollop of blubber. The other showed a solitary Big Daddy standing next to a huge metallic cylinder that dwarfed him in size.

"Man, he really blew up at the end, didn't he?" Corrigan said.

Big Daddy nodded. "Yeah, he was a real walking pharmacy by then. Caused a big split between him and Sonny.

16

He tried to get Colton to give up the drugs." Big Daddy shook his head. "Prit near broke his heart when Colton told me to fire him, after all them years together. But I told Sonny, it wasn't nothing personal. Just business is all."

"Just business. I like that."

"That there's our last public appearance together," Big Daddy said, indicating the picture with him and a huge metallic cylinder.

Corrigan moved to the last hanging frame, which had a white silk scarf displayed artfully under the glass.

"That there's the custom-made scarf he wore at his last concert," Big Daddy said. He chuckled. "Shit, he used to have a whole box of 'em on stage with him during a performance. He'd go grab one, wipe his face, then throw it to some gal in the audience. In the old days Sonny and I used to laugh about it. Call 'em come-quickly scarves. Them little gals would be lined up at the hotel afterwards, just itching to take off their panties. Don't know why he thought that cryogenic thing was what he wanted, though."

Corrigan reached out, removing the framed scarf from its position.

"Now what in the hell do you think you're doing?" Big Daddy asked, momentarily taken aback at the other man's audacity. Corrigan reached in his pocket and removed a folded piece of paper and a pen.

"If you wouldn't mind, sir, I'd like your autograph," he said holding the frame with the scarf toward Big Daddy. "Here, you can write on this."

Big Daddy smiled, but it was forced. He was beginning not to like this bastard Corrigan very much. He accepted the frame, brushing his hand in a dismissive gesture toward the proffered pen. He reached inside his jacket and removed a fine, gold-plated writing instrument with his name etched on it in block letters.

"Colton gave me this one," Big Daddy said, holding up the pen. "One thing about that boy, he never did anything cheap. Liked to give people things." He gripped the display, his thumb pressing down on the shiny glass, and signed his name, T.J. "Big Daddy" Babcock, with his customary flourish. As he replaced the pen in his pocket, he felt Corrigan gently pulling the frame away. But instead of hanging it back up on the wall, he held the paper outward.

"Here," he said. "Check this out and see if it's okay."

Big Daddy's brow furrowed. What the hell was this son of a bitch talking about? He took the paper and unfolded it, reading the three typewritten sentences above his signature.

"What is this?" Big Daddy asked, looking up.

Corrigan began stripping the heavy cardboard backing off the rear of the frame.

"Hey, boy, what in the goddamned hell you think you're doing?"

Corrigan pulled the silk scarf out of the glass encasement and laid the empty frame on the hallway floor. He looked down at the other man and smiled. It was a feral-looking smile and Big Daddy suddenly felt like someone had reached inside and grabbed his bowels in an iron fist.

"Like you told Sonny," Corrigan said, "nothing personal. Just business."

Chapter 2

Regencies

"Holy shit," Tim Stockton muttered as he glanced at the flashing television screen showing a close-up of the CNN news babe. But what had attracted Stockton's attention wasn't the comely newscaster, but the fleeting block-letter headlines that scrolled across the bottom in teletype fashion. He grabbed his coffee cup and took a quick swig, then punched several numbers into his desk phone. It rang numerous times as Stockton's eyes kept scanning the screen, hoping for a replay of the headline.

"The cellular customer is not currently available," the computerized voice said. "Please try your call again later."

Stockton hung up and dialed Harry's apartment. The phone continued for at least a dozen more rings before Stockton slammed down the receiver and took a deep breath. He swallowed some more of the bitter coffee, and glanced at his watch. Eight-oh-five. He hoped that Harry was on his way in, maybe trapped in a slow moving elevator somewhere, instead of, God forbid, dead drunk and passed out at home. In desperation, Stockman dialed in Harry's pager number, then punched in his own phone with a 9-1-1 behind it.

Oh God, Harry, he thought, why did you have to pick today of all days to be late for work? Today of all days, especially with that headline. He began scanning the electronic images again, watching the block letters scroll across the bottom. It was showing sports news now.

Come on, come on, he thought. He moved the cursor of

his computer to the Internet Explorer and then to news headlines.

The phone rang, jarring him like an electric shock.

"*Regency Magazine,*" he said, hoping it was Harry. It wasn't, he realized a second later, looking down at the LCD to see it was an inner-office call. "Stockton speaking."

"Where the hell's Bauer?" the gruff voice on the other end asked.

"He's out at the moment, sir," Stockton said, hoping he sounded convincing. He heard a snort from the other end.

"Tell that washed up asshole to get his drunken ass down to my office as soon as he rolls in, understood?"

"Yes, Mr. Bishop. I will, sir."

"Or better yet, you get down here now. I've got an appointment scheduled shortly."

The phone went dead and Stockton looked at it dumbly for a few seconds before replacing it.

Jesus, Harry, he thought. Are you in big trouble now.

Harry Bauer dropped his last bit of change into the street musician's upside-down hat on the sidewalk as he passed. The insistent beeper chirped again on his belt and Harry regretted that he'd once again left his cell phone in his apartment. But at least he'd managed to stay off the booze for another night.

One day at a time, he thought. One fucking day at a time. I wonder if it works for women too? Ex-wives.

Harry continued walking down Michigan Avenue, glancing at the ubiquitous traffic and legions of work-bound pedestrians. He had a tall, rangy build, and an unruly crop of brown hair. It had been too long since his last haircut and it showed. It had been too long between changing clothes, too, and he hadn't had time to get to the cleaners yet. But what the hell, he figured. All I have to do today is put the finishing touches on the article and sign the divorce papers.

The street musician's mellow saxophone continued to follow Harry, and he recognized the melody. An old Chuck Mangione tune called "Feels So Good."

God, that has to be from the early 80s or maybe even before that, he thought. An oldie, but goodie from way back when . . .

He let his mind drift back to high school, when he and Karen had been sweethearts. Dancing to the tunes at the prom, going away to college, dropping out, enlisting in the marines, going to Saudi, coming back, finishing school, getting hired at *Regency Magazine*, working his way up, marrying Karen, Lynn's birth, his book shooting to the top of the heap, living the good life. . . . The writer's life.

Too good, he thought. It always seems good before it falls apart.

Things fall apart, the center cannot hold.

He wondered where he'd heard that. Yeats maybe? It summed up his life lately, that's for sure. Everything was going to hell in a handbasket.

No, that wasn't a good metaphor, he thought as he pushed on the revolving door at the entrance to the building. Everything's getting flushed down the toilet, he added mentally. A real big toilet.

"Jesus, Harry, where the hell you been?" Stockton jerked up from behind his Spartan-like desk. Harry waved dismissively and went to his own work space, a big gunmetal gray desk awash in papers, assorted paper coffee cups, old magazines, newspapers, an electronic spell-checker, a couple of books spread out on top of more papers, and a computer monitor rising from the center like a monument. He pulled out his chair and plopped down. Stockton was already up and moving toward him.

"Did you see this?" the kid asked, handing him a paper with an article printed on it.

"How the hell could I have seen it?" Harry smirked. "I'm everybody's favorite mushroom, remember? They keep me in the dark and feed me shit." He liked the kid. If he hung around long enough, he was going to develop into a top-flight journalist. Of course, he probably wouldn't. Not if that son of a bitch Bishop had his way. One of his favorite quotes was that Harry "wasn't the kind of person to mold young minds." As if that prick Bishop was. As if he'd know anything about "molding" except slipping his hands around someone else's wife.

Harry set the paper on the pile in front of him and grabbed an old paper coffee cup.

"You got any java around here?" he asked.

"Dammit, Harry, you'd better read that. I just finished running interference with Mr. Bishop for you."

"Oh?" said Harry, standing. "And what's on the great one's mind this morning?"

Stockton pointed to the paper he had given him.

"Big Daddy Babcock's dead," he said. "Looks like he killed himself."

Harry's brow creased and he snatched up the copied news story. It was from the *Memphis Gazette*.

T.J. Babcock, Former Colton Purcell Manager, Found Dead

T.J. "Big Daddy" Babcock was found dead yesterday afternoon in his palatial home, an apparent suicide victim. Babcock,

71, was found hanged to death by a limousine driver who had arrived to take him to a Las Vegas ceremony honoring the tenth anniversary of the death of his most famous protégé, Colton Purcell. Babcock was credited with finding the young Purcell performing at local music concerts in the South, and parlaying the dynamic young singer into the number one act in show business. Over the years much has been said about Big Daddy's purported domination of the singer's royalties, of which he owned a substantial percentage. "I never met a dollar I didn't like," Babcock was once quoted as saying. Police are continuing an investigation, but Captain Vern Grimes said that "Suicides are not uncommon on the eve of certain dates that mark the passing of a loved one." Funeral arrangements are pending.

"Did he seem suicidal when you interviewed him last month?" Stockton asked when Harry set the pages down.

Harry shook his head. "Not at all. I should go down there and follow up on this."

"That's what I been trying to tell you. The boss *wants* you to follow up and then amend your article." Stockton licked his lips and looked down. "Then he wants you to go to Vegas to cover the big celebration." He held up the travel voucher.

"Yeah," Harry said, his mouth twisting into an ugly scowl. "And I bet I know why, too. So he can wine, dine, and tuck my soon to be ex-wife into bed."

"Ah, Harry, I'm also supposed to ask you if you signed the papers," Stockton said.

"Why? They worried I'm going to sue them for adultery at this late juncture?"

Stockton shook his head, then resumed looking at the floor.

"They're getting married this weekend," he said. "The

whole staff's invited, well, almost the whole staff." He looked at Harry's face, as if to gauge his reaction.

Harry feigned a smirk, but the words hit him like a couple of gut-punches. "Sounds like a good weekend to spend in Vegas," he said, picking up the voucher. He swallowed the imagined lump in his throat. "Who knows, maybe I'll even find a reason to stay out there."

Chapter 3

Mi Amada Dulce

The Latina dancers bumped and ground to the beat as the svelte figure at the center of the soundstage moved his pelvis to the rhythmic syncopation. He turned, clapping his hands, lip-syncing words the huge speakers were blasting out, then whirled around as the cameramen strained to catch every twitch. Eric Vantillberg stuck an unlit cigarette between his lips and watched the take. His gaze drifted to his left where Melissa Michelle Purcell bounced and twisted to the percussive beat, clapping enthusiastically as the sound of "Pablo" continued to emanate from the speakers. She wore a buckskin-like vest over a lavender halter top and jeans cut so low that they barely concealed her panties and framed her pierced navel.

A thong, Eric thought. She's gotta wear thongs. He smiled at the thought of this, but his momentary joy evaporated as his glance took in Melissa's mother, Ladonna, sitting off to the side staring at Pablo with a look of utter contempt.

Shit, he thought. Looks like the old lady still hates him.

Eric swallowed with a little difficulty, removed the cigarette from his lips (Ladonna hated them), and slipped it back into his pack. Brushing back his fashionably long brown hair, he sauntered over to her, carefully stepping over numerous cords in the semi-darkness.

Pablo was shaking his processed geri curls and singing one verse in Spanish, then the following one in English. "Mi ammaaaada dulce . . ." he wailed. "My swweeeet lover.

. . ." His long, glittering earrings snapped and danced with each jerk of his head.

"It's going pretty good, don't you think?" Eric asked. He cracked a crooked smile, trying to look sexy and cool.

Ladonna glanced over at the soundstage, then back to him. Her lips compressed and she said nothing.

Eric shrugged, trying to achieve a self-deprecating gesture. Damn, she was hot for an older broad. Her dark hair was short and feathered back from her face like a helmet. He couldn't help but appreciate the delicate curve of her jawline, the artful design of her eye shadow. In contrast to her daughter, Ladonna was dressed in a sleeveless black satin top and dark jeans. A delicate necklace hung suspended around her neck. Too bad she was such a fucking bitch.

"I mean, he's no Colton Purcell," he said, quickly adding, "Hell, nobody is, but he's got something, doesn't he?"

Ladonna's eyes moved toward the stage again. Pablo was leaning back, his left arm whipping backward above his head, his right hand gripping the mike. She looked back to Eric, smiled benignly, and crooked her finger at him.

Buoyed, he leaned closer, until her lips were by his ear. He felt her fingers grasp the front of his collar, then his tie, pulling it tight.

"Listen, you greasy fuck," she said in a harsh whisper. "You'd better give me a certified letter showing that little faggot doesn't have AIDS before I leave my daughter alone with him even for one second."

She released him suddenly, pushing away. Eric stumbled backwards, but managed to regain his balance. He rotated his head fractionally and readjusted his necktie knot.

No sense trying to talk to her when she's like this, he

thought. Although he felt like pimp-slapping her, he knew that would be a mistake. A real big mistake, since her body-guard/boyfriend, a big two-hundred-forty pound Samoan hulk, was standing about ten feet away. He settled for a weak smile and nod as he retreated.

Some day, he thought, I'll have the control to show her. Once I have the rights to the music, she'll be lining up to kiss my ass. He looked at her again and smiled wickedly, his imagination slipping onto overdrive. Among other things, he mentally added.

The large Samoan straightened up from the wall and stared with a look that implied menace. For a second Eric wondered if the big fucker could read minds, but knew that was silly. Still, he shifted his gaze back to his protégé, saun-tering around under the hot lights. Huge circles of sweat were starting to form under the arms of Pablo's royal blue shirt. He raised his arms as if to proudly display the wet half-moons, then his hand sunk down and he grabbed his crotch.

Shit, thought Eric. I wonder how that's gonna play on MTV?

He saw Ladonna pointing at him, then felt a slight vibra-tion next to his chest.

"Your pocket's ringing," Ladonna said. "Go answer it. I don't want to have to sit through another take of this crap."

Eric tried to smile again, looking nonchalant as he re-trieved the cell phone from his pocket and glanced at the screen.

Out of state area code, he thought. Better take this one outside.

He pressed the button as he headed for the door and said, "Hold on a minute."

Eric walked briskly through to the hallway and then toward the door at the end that led to the parking lot. On the way he fished out his cigarettes and stuck one in his mouth, slapping his pockets for a lighter.

"Okay, talk to me," he said, stepping out into the bright California sunshine. He blinked twice and flicked the lighter, drawing the smoke down into his lungs.

"It's Corrigan," the deep voice at the other end on the line said.

"Yeah?" Eric said, taking another quick drag. "Did you get it done?"

"Not quite."

"Whaddya mean, 'not quite'?" Eric asked, his voice cracking slightly at the end of the sentence.

"Big Daddy's done. Gonna need some time for the other one."

"Huh? I thought the fucker was supposed to be in some nursing home?" He drew in on the cigarette and blew out a smoky breath.

"He was, but not when I got there. They think some crazy nurse ran off with him."

"Nurse? What nurse?"

"Her name's Marjorie Versette," Corrigan said. "I'm looking into the matter."

"You're looking into it . . ." Eric said, letting the derision creep solidly into his tone. "You know, they told me you were the best. Now I get this shit." He waited for a response, but got none, and he suddenly was glad he wasn't within grabbing distance of the big son-of-a-bitch. "Well, you got any leads on where they're at or anything?"

"I'm waiting to pay a visit to her apartment now. Had to lay low for a bit. Ran into some complications."

Eric decided it was better not to ask what that meant. Ashes from his cigarette fell off the butt and clung to the front of his jacket.

"Okay," he said, trying to sound businesslike as two studio technicians strolled by. "Keep on top of things and keep me posted. Understood?" He moved to the side of the building and leaned against it, standing in the shade.

"I will," Corrigan's distant voice said, "but don't push it. Just remember, I ain't the one that owes the big man two-hundred and fifty G's. And you ain't my boss."

Eric was searching for something more to say. A quick comeback, something that would end the conversation with a hint that he was in charge, but then he thought of the size of Corrigan's hands. Suddenly he heard the doors push open followed by an angry female voice. Ladonna's. She strode forward, taking brusque steps with her long legs, yelling into her cell phone. Her left arm whipped in the air with gesticulations as she spoke.

"What the fuck do you mean, *'missing'?*" she said, hissing with the pronouncement. She paced some more, up and back, listening. Eric flattened against the side of the building and drew on his cigarette.

"I gotta go," he whispered into his cell phone.

"Montgomery, how in the fucking hell could something like this happen?" Ladonna said into the phone. Her voice had regained some of its usual control. "I mean, Christ, he's been in that place for years."

Montgomery? Montie Spangler? Eric wondered.

"No, *you* listen," she said. "I want this handled immediately. We're talking damage control here." She smacked her forehead with the flat of her palm. "Christ, if this gets out at all, much less this close to the goddamn anniversary." She listened some more. "No, I don't want the police involved. Hire somebody private to find him. And do it quick, understand?" She stopped, bending forward slightly with the phone. "You're the fucking mouthpiece."

Eric nodded to himself and took another drag. She was talking to Spangler. Good. Keep it in the family, he thought. Her back was to him now, and he stole another quick look at her ass moving inside the tight jeans.

"Somebody private, got it? I don't care who," she said. She slammed the phone shut, leaned forward placing her hands on her knees, and vomited.

Eric's lips stretched into a big smile as he let the smoke seep out from between his teeth.

Things were definitely looking up.

Chapter 4

Freeze Me, Tender

Harry Bauer watched as the seemingly unending stream of men in red, white, and blue jump suits sauntered down the center aisle of the plane, each with his hair slicked back in a dark pompadour with long, flaring sideburns. He closed his eyes and leaned his head back, ruminating over the past seventeen hours: from the office in Chicago to the airport, down to Memphis on some half-assed rinky-dink airline . . . so rinky-dink that the stewardess didn't even serve drinks, just the customary Pepsi and a bag of salted pretzels.

But maybe that was a blessing in disguise, Harry thought. At least I didn't have to worry about being tempted.

He was entering his fifth week of sobriety. Five and a half, really, counting the in-patient stay. All that talking, life-prioritizing, and promising. It'd be a shame to let it all go down the drain simply because he found out his ex-wife was getting remarried. But not just remarried, she was marrying a prick who also happened to be Harry's boss. A bad combination, to say the least. Harry grinned and opened his eyes, still smiling. At least now, he told himself, it's going to be her problem. But who am I trying to kid, he thought. It'll be hers *and* my daughter's.

He sighed and spread open the notebook on his closed laptop. The interview with the Memphis detective had been as confusing as it had been enlightening. His finger traced down the page to the last two words he'd written before he'd left the police station: *The note.* What was it that kept

31

gnawing at him? Hell, a lot of things.

"Sheeit, Mr. Bauer," the detective had said. His name was Tucker, and he looked like an unctuous version of Garth Brooks gone to seed. He was leaning back in his chair with his fancy boots crossed on the top of his desk. "We're up to our armpits in homicides 'round here. I just got back from one this morning at a sanitarium. Of course they call it a special living center, or something nowadays. Graceful Valley, it's called. Right nice place, too, for a nut house. Or least-wise, was. Head nurse found dead in an office." Tucker removed a toothpick from his mouth and held it up. "Somebody done snapped her neck like this." He demonstrated, bringing his thumb forward to break the wood. "Day before that, looks like one of the nurses run off with one of the loonies." He paused to take out another toothpick and insert it between his lips. "Anyways, I got a whole shitload of suspects out there, and you're here taking up my time asking questions about a solid suicide?"

Harry forced a quick smile.

"It just seems so incongruous," he said, trying to figure out a way to broach the subject without offending the southern cop. "I mean, I interviewed Big Daddy last month, and he didn't seem despondent at all."

"Well," Tucker said, taking his feet off the desktop and leaning forward, "sometimes that in itself can be a sign. Especially around sad anniversaries. My mama's cousin, Shadrock, went to church one Sunday morning, normal as can be, saying hello to everybody up an' down the pews, smiling and laughing, then went home afterwards and took a gun to himself." Tucker shook his head. "Messiest scene I ever did see. A twelve gauge'll do that."

Harry's mouth dropped open a bit. He coughed and cleared his throat.

"So you say you found a note?" he asked.

Tucker's eyes narrowed slightly.

"What was the name of that there magazine you said you write for again?"

"*Regency*," Harry said. "*Regency Magazine.*" He pulled out one of his cards. One that said, *Harry Bauer Staff Writer Regency Magazine.* "I'm also writing a book about Colton Purcell's life," he added quickly. "I might have a section where I could use a quote from you."

Tucker's eyebrows rose. He didn't look like he had the mental dexterity to raise just one. The cop swallowed, then ran his tongue over his teeth.

"I don't suppose it'd do any harm if I let you have a look-see," he said, taking out a manila envelope and un-bending the clasps. "These here are Polaroids. The regular thirty-five millimeters won't be ready for a spell." He held the photos out toward Harry who took them. The first showed the slumping figure, back arching to form an ex-tended U-shape, the enormous gut sagging toward the floor, the long, purplish tongue distended.

Harry flipped to the next one, which was a close-up.

"What we conjecture he did," Tucker said, suddenly lapsing into a semi-professional tone, "was to tie that there scarf around his neck like this." He stuck his hand around the front of his own neck. "Then he tied that to a length of phone cord, tied the cord around the doorknob, and looped it over the top." Tucker raised his fist above his head, as if to indicate he was holding a hangman's rope. "Then it was a matter of him leaning forward to hang himself."

Harry flipped through the rest of the Polaroids.

"You'd be surprised how many times something like this

happens," Tucker continued. He rolled back in his chair, opened his desk drawer, and removed a thin box. "Got a bunch like it of scenes I been to." His lips twisted into a sly smile. "Lot of 'em are them auto-erotic things. Ever seen one?"

Harry nodded. He debated whether to ask for a copy of Big Daddy's demise.

"And you said you found a note?" he asked again.

Tucker nodded, sorting though the envelope again. He withdrew a piece of paper and handed it over. "That there's a copy. The original's already been to the crime lab. Checkin' for his prints."

"Can I call you about the results?"

Tucker smiled again and shook his head.

"I know what you're a trying to do," he said, his grin widening. "You're trying to insinuate that there's some kinda conspiracy here, ain't cha? Like one of them stories of how Colton Purcell really ain't dead, but someplace fakin' it?"

It was Harry's turn to smile. He studied the copy of the note. Three typewritten sentences along the top portion read, *Can't go on anymore. Nothing left for me here. Maybe I'll see Colton soon.*

T.J. "Big Daddy" Babcock was scrawled across the bottom section in a large, flourishing script.

"This signature doesn't look too despondent," Harry said.

Tucker shrugged. "Hell, how do you know how he signed his name?"

"What are these lines here and here?" Harry asked.

"Them's where the paper was folded," Tucker replied. He licked his lips and looked around. "You know, I might be able to part with a few items here . . . if the price was right and you could guarantee me a quote and maybe a picture in that there book you're writing."

The price had been fifty bucks for a copy of the Polaroids and the note. Harry also had to pose for one standing side-by-side with Tucker, the cop's arm draped over Harry's shoulder. Cheap at twice the price, he thought.

Now, more people waddled down the plane's center aisle as Harry scribbled a note to look up Robert Sawyer, a reporter for the *Las Vegas Mirror* whom he'd known a long time. Sawyer had been one of Harry's early influences when he'd gotten out of the marines and started writing. Robert, or Buzzy as he liked to be called, had been a marine as well, a generation before in Vietnam, and had then become a reporter. He'd encouraged Harry to write about his experiences in the first Gulf War.

It'll be good to see him again, Harry thought.

Someone said, "Excuse me, sir," and Harry looked up to see a beefy man in a stunning jumpsuit trying to squeeze in front of him to the window seat. Another equally good-sized jump-suited figure was already lowering himself into the aisle seat to Harry's right.

"I'm Lance Fabray," the big guy on the right said, extending his hand toward Harry, who shook it. "That there's my first cousin, Powell Fabray. We're heading to Las Vegas for the big Colton Purcell look-alike contest."

"Pleased to meet you, sir," Powell said, his voice a pretty fair imitation of the original's. Harry shook hands with him and introduced himself.

"Cousins with the same last names, huh?" Harry said, trying to be sociable, and subsequently realizing he'd just made his first mistake. "The sons of two brothers?"

Lance smiled crookedly, again, in a fair imitation of the original's.

"Actually, sir, my real name's Clyde D. Bonner," he said. "I just figured Lance Fabray sounded more like a singer."

Harry's mouth gaped slightly and he was hoping the stewardess wouldn't come along and offer them drinks. He might just be beyond abstention this time.

"Now Powell there," Lance continued, "his name's even worse than mine. Go on, tell him, Powell. Tell him your name."

Powell just affected a haughty look, his lip curling back slightly.

"Mess with me, and you're messin' with trouble," he said in a husky tone.

Harry was taken aback.

Lance slapped his leg.

"See, don't that beat all?" he asked. "That's one of Colton's best lines. From *King Rebel*. Where this young guy who works at a bar becomes a singer."

"Oh yeah," Harry said. "I think I saw that one."

Powell was twitching one side of his face now.

"Mess with me, and you're messin' with trouble," he repeated.

Lance slapped Harry's leg again.

"Don't he do that good?" Lance asked, pointing his finger. "But I'm still gonna tell him your real name if'n you don't."

Harry looked toward Powell again, who continued to twitch.

"It's William Runyon Outhause," Lance said. "Get it? Willy runnin' to the outhouse?" He guffawed again, and then added, "So I figured, since we both sing like Colton, that we could call ourselves The Fabulous Fabray Boys. Sure beats the other'n, don't it?"

Both of them started to guffaw, and Harry joined in, afraid not to.

The inmates are running the asylum, he thought.

"So what is it you do for a living, Mr. Bauer?" Lance asked.

"I'm a writer," Harry said, realizing moments later that he'd just made his second mistake.

"Oh really? What kind of stuff do you write?"

"I write for *Regency Magazine*." He automatically pulled out a group of his Staff Writer cards. "We're doing a story on the anniversary of Colton Purcell's death." Mistake number three, he thought. But maybe it would give him some sort of edge with these two nutcases.

"Well, ain't that something?" Lance said, grabbing one of the cards. "You think you could put us in it? We're real, what you call, photogenic."

"I can see that," Harry said, adding mentally that he'd have to make sure they used a wide-angle lens.

"That's why we're all dressed up like Colton," Powell said. He snatched a card for himself, too. "Our manager worked it out so they're gonna film us getting off the plane. Get us some advance publicity. We intend to win that contest."

"Contest?" Harry said. "You mean the. . . ." He intentionally let his voice trail off.

"The Colton Purcell Best Imitator Award," Lance finished for him. "Fifteen thousand dollars for first place. That's gonna be ours, all right."

"I'll bet it is," Harry added.

"Shucks, my Aunt Louisa says that the only way we won't win is if Colton himself shows up in person," Powell said.

Lance leaned close to Harry.

"Don't say nothing to Powell," he said in a husky whisper, "but he thinks Colton's still alive. Just been in hiding all these years."

"He is," Powell said, his voice suddenly losing all the acquired resonance of the original's. "And don't you say different, neither."

Lance smiled the crooked, half-smile and leaned back.

"Freeze me tender," he began singing in a deep baritone, "freeze me blue, never let me out. For it's there that I belong, 'cause I don't want to melt."

"You better stop that, C. D.," Powell said, balling his hands into ham-sized fists. "You better stop that right now."

"For, my darling, you froze me, and I just want to chill."

Harry sensed a tense movement on his left and turned just as Powell's arcing fist sailed from the far seat toward the warbling Colton imitator. Suddenly, Harry felt a jolt to his jaw and a myriad of bright lights exploded against a field of black velvet.

The damn place looked like a shrine to Colton Purcell. Corrigan scanned the selection of pictures, all framed lovingly in those huge plastic jobs you could buy at discount stores. Each had little typewritten tags indicating dates and locations, but most of them looked like they'd been clipped from magazines. Not like the ones hanging on Big Daddy's wall. Those had been the real McCoy. Corrigan was suddenly sorry he hadn't taken a couple. Probably could have used them as bargaining chips if he had to play let's make a deal for some information with some of these Purcell geeks. They were fanatical, that was for sure.

He removed one photo of a rotund, middle-aged broad

standing next to a slender Colton Purcell clad in his customary red, white, and blue jumpsuit. The woman had a dumb smile on her face, clutching her fingers together in front of her like a schoolgirl. The flat look to Purcell's face made it obvious that she was standing next to one of those life-sized cardboard cut-outs.

Corrigan stripped that picture from its frame and put it in his pocket. He removed another one, this one showing the same woman in a starched white uniform, holding some type of gold nursing pin. He noticed something else, too. Her watch. It was on her right wrist, unless the negative had been reversed. He pulled out the other picture and studied it. No, the watch was on her right arm in that one also, her hands clasped in front of her, with the right one overlapping the left. What did that mean? That she was some kind of non-conformist or just left-handed. He pocketed both of the pictures for future reference.

Who knows, he thought. They could help. Idiosyncrasies were important when you were tracking someone.

He stepped lightly for a big man, moving past the walls of photos to the bedroom. More Colton Purcell photos on the walls there too. Some appeared to have been snapped at a concert of some sort. The figure on the stage looked like a tiny doll, completely unrecognizable.

Pathetic, he thought. He began checking the dresser drawers, starting with the bottom ones first to save himself time. That porker's been gone for almost ten years and this bitch is still carrying a torch. No wonder she latched onto—

He heard the doorbell ring, and then a knock.

He moved noiselessly to the door and stooped to look out the peephole, his hand reaching inside his jacket for his piece. On the other side the oval face of an older lady stared upward expectantly.

"Marjorie, is that you?" the old lady asked. "Did you get back already?"

Corrigan glanced at his watch, then out the peephole again. This one looked like the type who'd call the police if no one answered. And he wasn't even close to finding his first clue as to where the nurse had gone. He sighed and slipped the pistol back into its holster and took his spare wallet from his jacket pocket, affixing the gold colored shield. He was still wearing his clear latex gloves.

When Corrigan swung the door open the old broad looked shocked.

"Who . . . who are you?" she asked quickly. She moved back a step toward the stairway.

Corrigan debated giving her a gentle little shove to help send her on her way, but decided against it.

"Detective Southerland," he said, holding up the phony shield. "Police Department. We had a report of a burglary to this apartment."

The old lady's lips formed an "O" and she immediately brought her hand up to cover it.

"Mercy," she said. Her head canted to the side and she appeared to try and look around Corrigan to see into the apartment. "Is anything missing?"

"We're not sure," he said. "We can't seem to find Ms. Versette. Would you have any way of contacting her?"

"I'm Mabel Crawford," she said. "I live directly below. I just got back from the store and heard the sound of someone walking upstairs and figured Marjorie was back."

Corrigan affected the look of a bored public servant.

"But I had no idea that something like this happened." She tried to peer around his huge form and into the apartment. "Is anything missing?"

"Like I said, ma'am, we're not sure. Do you know when

40

Ms. Versette will be back? She works at the nursing home, doesn't she?"

Mabel looked up at him. "Why, yes, but she gave me a key the day before yesterday . . . or was it earlier than that?" She shook her head. "Anyway, she asked me to look in on Colton and Clayton for her."

"Colton and Clayton?"

Mabel smiled. "Her two goldfish." A look of alarm spread across her face. "Are they all right? I'd hate to have anything happen to them on my watch." She tried to look inside again.

"The fish are fine," Corrigan said, hoping that would get rid of her. "Now, I'm afraid no one is allowed in here until I'm finished investigating." He tried a quick smile. "But I suppose you could come in to check on Colton and Clayton. Just don't touch anything."

Mabel smiled and walked past him as he turned with his arm extended. She went immediately to the long buffet in the dining room. Two stunning goldfish flipped their fins in peaceful tranquility.

"Thank heavens they're all right," Mabel said. She grabbed a box of fish food and sprinkled a tiny bit on top of the water. "Colton . . . C.W.," she cooed. "Come get your din-din."

"When was the last time you were in here?" Corrigan asked.

"Why, I believe it was last night about seven. I came up to check on them," she gestured toward the bowl, "and then went down to watch a rerun of Lawrence Welk."

"This must have happened after that." He canted his head. "So do you know when Ms. Versette is coming back? Where is she, by the way? Vacation?"

"Why, she's in Las Vegas," Mabel said. "For at least two

41

weeks. She was going to call me if it looked like she'd be gone longer than that. That's why I was so surprised to hear someone up here."

Vegas, he thought. That's a start. This old broad was a gold mine.

"Where's she staying in Vegas?" Corrigan asked. "What hotel?"

"I'm not sure. She didn't say, but I'm sure it's got to be someplace nice. It was a very special event."

"She likes to gamble, I take it?" he asked.

"Well, we do go to bingo at the church on Thursdays," Mabel said. "But that's not why she went." She paused, then added, "She said she was getting married."

Chapter 5

Legitimate Concerns

Eric Vantillberg stared out the floor-to-ceiling window of Montgomery Spangler's elegant fourth floor office at the darkening California twilight. It was obvious Ladonna had clout to keep a lawyer like him working this long past the cocktail hour. Spangler's round, paddleboard face looked like it was showing the strain, too. His small chin seemed tucked on top of his slack fleshy neck. To Eric's left, Pablo Stevenson stretched his legs out, which were still encased in the same tight black polyester that he'd worn for the video shoot. The shirt was the same, too, and the sweat stains under the arms now looked crusty white around the edges. He fiddled with one set of his dangling gold earrings. His massive bodyguard, Theophis Gant, leaned against the far wall dressed in all black and looking like a pillar of carved ebony.

Eric sighed and took out a cigarette. How the hell did he let himself get into this mess?

"Don't even *think* about it," Ladonna Purcell said. She was sitting on his right, and Melissa Michelle was next to Pablo, holding his slender fingers in her own.

Eric shrugged and stuck the cigarette on top of his ear.

Ladonna turned to her lawyer, and compressed her lips.

"Well?" she asked.

Spangler flipped up the last page of the document he was reading and then took off his half-glasses.

"I think the contract's very clear," he said. "Upon his death, Big Daddy's share of the stock in Colton Purcell Enterprises reverts back to Colton's heirs, which are you and Melissa."

"See," Melissa Michelle said. "We came all the way down here for nothing." Her voice was a petulant whine.

Ladonna ignored her.

"All right," she sighed. "We've got to get back to Memphis tomorrow. Can you have someone take care of that? We've got to go home and pack."

"No way I'm going back there," Melissa Michelle said. "Not in a million fucking years."

Ladonna looked over at her, her brows furrowing.

"We have to make an appearance at the funeral," she said. "And don't use that kind of language."

"I can say anything I fucking want."

Ladonna stood, walked over to Melissa Michelle, and grabbed her daughter by the upper arm. From the way Ladonna's fingers sank into the tanned flesh, Eric knew the grip was hard.

"Let's go," Ladonna said gutturally, her teeth showing behind her lower lip. She glanced toward Spangler. "Look over that damn prenup like I told you. Go over it with a fine tooth comb, understand?"

She began to pull at Melissa Michelle's arm, but the girl bent forward to plant a kiss on Pablo's puckered, proffered lips.

Ladonna seemed to cringe at the sight.

When the two of them separated Pablo looked up at Ladonna and smiled.

"You know, Moms, you shouldn't get your pantyhose in an uproar," he said. His voice was a high tenor. "That prenup ain't worth shit since we're already married."

Melissa Michelle bent to kiss him again, but Ladonna gave her daughter's arm a wrenching jerk.

"That was in Mexico, asshole," Ladonna said. "And we had that annulled. It was never consummated, remember?"

Pablo's thin lips stretched over his sparkling capped teeth.

"How do you know?" he said.

"Yeah," Melissa Michelle parroted. "How do you know?"

Ladonna stared down at Pablo for several seconds, then said, "Believe me, I can tell." She pulled her daughter to her feet and began heading for the door, stopping as she gripped the knob.

"That other matter I spoke to you about," she said to Spangler. "Have you taken care of it?"

Other matter? thought Eric. She has to mean crazy Willard.

Spangler raised his hands, palms outward.

"Working on it," he said.

Eric tried to gauge Ladonna's expression, but she was stonefaced.

"Call me as soon as you know," she said. "And don't forget to make the flight arrangements."

She pushed Melissa Michelle out the door just as the nubile teen was waving and saying, "Bye, Pablo."

Eric swung his chair back to face the lawyer. He took the cigarette from its place on his ear and held it up.

"May I?" he asked.

"By all means," Spangler said, smiling.

Welcome. McCarran Airport, Las Vegas, Nevada, the sign said. Below it were a cash station machine, a bill changer and a couple of slot machines. The massive baggage tray wheel kept revolving, making Harry Bauer's acute headache ten times worse. Another suitcase came through the

45

hanging rubber flaps. A blue Samsonite this time. Not his. He shifted the strap of his carry-on case, and pressed the bag of ice to his face. The stewardess had given it to him right before he deplaned. It had been his fourth. She'd offered to get him a special, free martini after they woke him up, but he'd been too groggy to accept. His counselor at the clinic would have gotten a chuckle out of that one. A couple of aspirins, a bottle of water, and three hours of suffering later, they were circling in the glow of the purple Nevada sky waiting for a landing opening. But that wasn't the worst part of it. When the plane had banked he'd caught a glimpse of the lighted strip and thought how, a dozen years ago, when he and Karen had come here on their honeymoon, she'd pressed against him to look out the window at the sea of white and pink neon. Déjà vu. All over again.

Twelve steps be damned, he thought as he glanced over at the bright neon signs advertising refreshments with an arrow.

Refreshments, he thought, picturing a swirl of Johnnie Walker Black in a glass with some ice. Yeah, it was so damn hot here, he'd have to have ice. Even in this manufactured coolness he could sense it. The desert in August. Maybe he'd have a double. Hell, he'd even settle for Red. He gingerly felt the swelling on his jaw and wondered how he looked. The hinges made a faint clicking sound when he opened his mouth.

Christ, I hope that big clod hopper didn't break anything, he thought, testing his jaw again and feeling the corresponding pop. At least they got kicked off the flight. No fifteen grand for them. What will old Aunt Louisa think? He grinned at the thought and immediately regretted it. Two more suitcases flipped through the flaps and another Colton

Purcell imitator in his brightly colored jumpsuit grabbed the luggage.

"Shit," he muttered.

"Excuse me, sir," a voice behind him said.

Harry turned. A slender kid, maybe twenty-five or so, stood next to him, his hand outstretched.

"I believe these belong to you," the kid said. He held a dozen or so business cards. Harry's cards. Harry patted his pocket, shrugged, and accepted them.

"Where'd you get these?"

"I was sitting across the aisle and one row back," the kid said. He had light brown hair, swept back from his face with a bit of mousse, moderately long sideburns, and hazel eyes. Harry picked up a vestigial Southern accent. Maybe Louisiana or East Texas.

Gotta be another one of those imitators, he thought. Making the trek to the promised land and hoping to leave with fifteen thousand clams. Another sucker with stars in his eyes.

"When that guy hit you these went scattering. I picked them up, but you looked really out of it, and then there was the commotion when they kicked those two fellas off." He smiled shyly. When he did that he kind of looked like the original.

Harry stuck the cards in his pocket, nodded a thanks, and turned to look at the rotating tray again.

"Are you a really a writer, sir?" the kid asked.

Harry looked around, holding the ice bag as conspicuously as he could, and said, "Yeah." He turned back as another suitcase and a guitar case rotated by. The kid reached out and grabbed the guitar.

Figures, Harry thought. Everybody's but mine.

He glanced again at the refreshments sign and could almost feel the familiar taste washing over his tongue, slipping down his throat, and then hitting his belly with a fanning heat.

"Ah, sir?"

It was the kid again.

"What?" Harry asked.

"Are you really doing a book about Colton Purcell?"

Harry nodded. That was a mistake. His temples felt like they were going to burst.

"Well, I wonder if I could talk to you about something?" the kid asked.

Harry's head throbbed, his jaw hurt, and when he heaved a sigh it was obvious he was in no mood to be bothered by some wannabe.

"Look, kid," he said. "I've had a real rough day. No, make that a real shitty day. I had to sign my divorce papers this morning, my wife took me to the cleaners, she got custody of my daughter, I got punched in the jaw on a fucking airplane, and I hate to fly. So if you'll excuse me." He turned back to the conveyor belt and saw his suitcase on the far edge.

Finally, he thought.

"Sorry," he heard the kid say.

Harry switched hands on the ice bag and started to reach for his suitcase. He swayed slightly and straightened up. As his luggage started to go by the kid reached out and grabbed it.

"Here, sir, let me get that for you," he said, setting the case down by Harry's feet. The kid turned and retrieved a shoddy-looking, green nylon suitbag with duct tape patches on both ends. He picked up the guitar case, nodded to Harry, and began walking away.

Harry watched him walking, thinking that there was

something almost familiar about the way this guy moved. Glancing down at his suitcase, Harry looked over at the refreshments sign, then called out.

"Hey, kid."

The young man turned.

"What's your story?"

The kid stared at him, his head tilting to the right slightly.

Damn if he doesn't sorta look like the original, too, Harry thought.

"I don't want to put you out, sir."

At least this kid was polite, thought Harry.

"Don't call me 'sir'," he said. "I work for a living." Harry stooped, still holding the ice bag with one hand, and picked up his suitcase. "Come on, I'll buy you a drink."

"Well, sir, that's very kind, but I'm afraid I don't drink."

What is this, weirdo's week? Harry wondered, but still. . . . He sighed.

"You know, neither do I anymore," he said. "How about a cup of coffee then?"

The kid smiled. Harry stopped next to him, set his suitcase down, switched the ice bag to his left hand, and held out his right.

"I'm Harry Bauer, by the way."

The kid set the guitar case down and shook Harry's hand.

"Gabriel Freeman," he said.

"Nice name for a musician," Harry said, nodding at the instrument case. "You here for the big imitator's contest?"

"Yes and no," Gabriel said. "I'm here to see some people, I hope, and to get some things set straight."

Harry picked up his suitcase and started walking.

"I think there's a little restaurant over this way," he said.

49

They passed a row of brightly lit slot machines. "Who you looking to see?"

"Ladonna Purcell. Melissa Michelle, too."

"Looking for a hot date?" Harry asked.

Gabriel shook his head.

"No, sir."

Harry glanced over at him, sighed, then asked, "Well, what then?"

They walked a few steps further, avoiding an old lady bringing a bag full of coins toward one of the ubiquitous slots.

"I need to see them," Gabriel said. "You see, sir, Colton Purcell was my daddy."

It had been a long conference going over the terms of the prenup with Spangler, and Eric was feeling the strain of having to listen to all of Pablo's attempts to be cool during the proceedings. Finally, they had things pretty well mapped out and Eric figured he could grab a quick drink in the back of Pablo's limo on the way to dinner, then grab his own car on the flip-side. Gant pushed the glass doors open and glanced up and down the street, but no throngs of screaming fans awaited. The afternoon heat had not subsided with the onset of evening.

"It's clear," Gant said.

"No fans?" Pablo asked, primping his hair.

Fans? We'll be lucky if we don't get stoned, Eric thought. Stoned? Maybe that would be in order tonight, too. He grinned to himself, but then heard someone call his name.

"Mr. Vantillberg."

Eric heard the voice again as he began walking down the sidewalk. When he turned and saw Jack Moran, he felt a familiar tightening in his gut.

"Hey, Jack," Eric said, trying his best to sound cordial. Maybe if he pretended hard enough . . .

"Mr. Casio wants to see you," Moran said. He was medium height, but thick through the arms and shoulders, like a guy who worked out a lot. He wore a thin gray sport coat, no tie, and dark slacks. Despite the lack of sunshine, he had on wrap-around designer sunglasses. The bristles of his dark beard formed a burgeoning mustache and goatee.

"Okay, great," Eric said. "Just let me get my car and I'll be right with you."

"Uh-un," Moran said. "I'm supposed to drive you." He cocked his head toward a Lincoln with tinted windows idling at the curb. Eric could see another figure behind the wheel.

Oh no, he thought. He sent two tough guys for just one of me.

Thoughts of what this possibly could mean, none of them good, raced through his mind.

"Ahhh, look, Jack, I'm parked in this place that charges an arm and a leg. . . ." He let his voice trail off and punctuated the sentence with a quick smile.

Moran cocked his head toward the Lincoln again. "Let's go."

"Is this guy causing problems?" Pablo said, moving between them.

"Pablo, it's okay," Eric said. "I know this guy. He's a friend."

"He don't look like no friend," Pablo said. He was up on his toes, prancing a bit, the golden loops in his ears bobbling as he rotated his head. "Listen, greaseball. This is my manager and we have important business to discuss."

Oh no, Eric thought. He's playing this like one of his damn music videos.

51

Moran looked at him, his mouth still an unruffled line.

"Hey, Gant," Pablo said. The big man moved next to his diminutive boss, his wide nostrils flaring, and fixed Moran with a menacing stare.

"Heeeey," Moran said, drawing out the word as he took off his sunglasses with his left hand, smiling slightly. He raised the glasses upward and when the giant's eyes followed the movement, Moran's right fist shot into the bigger man's gut. Twice. Gant sagged forward, bending at the waist, his mouth wide open sucking in air. Moran pushed the bigger man's head down with his left hand while his right whipped back and forth across the back of Gant's head, making a hollow thumping sound each time. The giant grunted and collapsed to all fours, his big chest and belly sagging down like an overloaded bladder. Moran stepped to the side and kicked the distended cavity hard. It sounded like a man splitting a watermelon. Gant squealed in pain as Moran kicked him again. Gant rolled over on his side, the big welts on the back of his head dappling the sidewalk with bright crimson spots. The dark leather sap dangled from Moran's right hand momentarily before he dropped it in his side jacket pocket.

"You didn't have to hurt him, you big creep," Pablo screamed, kneeling down and protectively covering the prostrate bodyguard. The blood was pooling under Gant's head.

"Back off, short eyes," Moran said. He turned to Eric, replaced his sunglasses, and said, "Now, let's go."

Eric flashed another nervous smile and nodded, reaching into his pocket for his cigarettes.

"Sure, Jack, sure. No problem. I mean, what's a little parking tab, right?" He followed Moran toward the car, looking over his shoulder to say, "Pablo, I'll call you later, okay?"

He could see the singer's thin fingers tracing over the bigger man's skull.

Moran opened the rear door of the Lincoln and motioned for Eric to get in. Eric nodded.

"Say, how's Rocky?" he asked.

"He's still in rehab," Moran said, and slammed the door.

Chapter 6

Giving the Devil His Due

Harry watched the kid sop up the rest of his gravy with the last piece of the biscuit. He was a country boy, all right, ordering meat loaf and mashed potatoes with gravy. "Lots of gravy, ma'am," he said to the waitress. She looked to be bleached blond and all of thirty-five. Probably made her day, that's for sure, Harry thought. But there was a certain, southern-style charm about this guy Gabriel, or Gabe, as he mentioned he liked to be called. They sat in the booth near the corner of the airport restaurant and Harry rubbed his sore jaw, getting a small measure of vicarious pleasure watching the kid eat.

"So how'd you come to find out you had such a famous father?" Harry asked, picking up his coffee cup. It had long since cooled off and the waitress was nowhere to be seen with a freshening pot. Probably in the ladies' room redoing her make-up after that "ma'am" crack, Harry thought as he swallowed a mouthful and wished he had some more aspirins.

"My mama was a backup singer on *The '82 Comeback Show*," Gabe said, shifting the biscuit to the side of his mouth. He held up a finger and continued chewing. "You familiar with that one?"

"Yeah, that was the big TV special that renewed Purcell's popularity." Harry smiled. "I watched it. When I was a kid."

"Yeah, well, that's where they met." Gabe reached for his own coffee and suddenly the waitress appeared with the

54

pot and a high-wattage smile saying, "Here, let me warm that up for you."

Harry held his cup up too, but she poured his as an afterthought.

After another "Thank you, ma'am," Gabriel continued.

"It was back when she was first starting out," he said. "Back in the early eighties. Colton's manager, Big Daddy Babcock, seen her at the Louisiana Hayride shows." He emptied another sugar packet into his coffee. "My mama was the star of the Hayride, too. Patti Jean Love, she called herself. Her real last name was Freeman, same as mine, but Love was the name she used on stage. He was looking for local acts to give the TV special a real Southern flavor and signed her to sing a gospel number with Colton."

Harry nodded. "Was she good? A singer, I mean."

Gabriel smiled. "She had a few records. Country tunes, mostly. Some gospel. Taught me how to play the guitar, too. I been playing since I was around six." He pronounced it "gitar," just like the original.

"What's she say about all this?" Harry asked.

Gabriel's face twitched.

"She passed last year," he said.

"I'm sorry."

Gabriel nodded and continued. "You see, I never knew Colton was my real daddy till mama got sick. I grew up wondering, but by that time she'd already quit show business altogether and married my step-daddy. He was a nice enough guy, but we never got real close, you know? Maybe it was because I always kept my own name."

Harry nodded again.

"Yeah, step-dads can be rough," he said, thinking about Lynn and hoping she'd keep her name Bauer rather than change it to Bishop. She was only nine and that was a crucial age. But Bishop could try to adopt her somewhere down the line, and Harry made a mental note never to let that happen while he was still breathing.

"Then last year, when we found out mama had the cancer," Gabriel said, "she called me into her room all alone and give me a key to this safety deposit box. Told me my name was on it too, and said to go look in it and I'd know who my real daddy was." His nostrils flared suddenly. "She said she hoped I'd understand why she kept it a secret for so long."

He took a deep breath.

"Well, sir, when I went in that little-bitty room with the box, I didn't know what to expect." Gabriel stared down at the slick Formica, rotating his cup slowly with both hands. "Finally, I got up enough nerve to open it, and found three things: a photo of my mama and Colton when she was real young, a copy of my birth certificate, and an envelope." He looked up, his eyes misting slightly. "Inside the envelope was this letter. I could tell my mama had wrote it a long time ago 'cause the paper was so yellow. It was addressed to me, and explained how they'd met and fallen in love and all. It also said that after she got pregnant, Big Daddy gave her a cashier's check for a lot of money on the condition that she terminate the pregnancy and make no more mention of it. Ever. Obviously, she didn't and she kept the money to make a new start for herself." He smiled wistfully. "For both us, actually. Right after I was born Mama used the money to put a down-payment on a nice house, and met Paul Kincaid. He's my step-daddy. Well, this was back in 1983, and they got married. She never tried to contact Colton Purcell while he was alive. There was some kind of secrecy clause attached to her taking the money. Plus I think she was scared of Big Daddy. She said she had to give the devil his due. But Colton's listed as the father on my birth certificate." He reached inside his jacket, removed a long nine-by-twelve manila envelope, and unclasped the metal fasteners. With the utmost care Gabriel removed a discolored Photostat and handed it across the table. It said Certificate of Live Birth across the top, and listed Patricia Jean Freeman, 23 Nov 1959 as the birth mother. In the space marked Birth Father, Colton Gabriel Purcell, 14 Feb 1949, had been neatly typed.

Harry raised his eyebrows. "This never surfaced before?"

Gabe smiled. "I grew up in the South. Little-bitty school where they never even checked, 'cept to see if I was acting up."

"That's quite a story," Harry said, handing back the paper. "You tried to contact anybody in the Purcell estate?"

Gabriel nodded. He carefully replaced the certificate in the envelope.

"A couple of times," he said. "After I read the letter I went to Memphis and took the tour of his house. I tried to ask somebody how to contact Ladonna and Melissa Michelle, but I just kept running up against stone walls."

"Sounds like you need the services of a good attorney," Harry said.

Gabriel shook his head.

"They'd just think I was after some money, and that ain't it at all." He looked Harry straight in the eyes. "I just gotta find out who I really am, Mr. Bauer. Can you understand that? I ain't after no money that ain't mine, and I can earn my own way anyway. But if I am Colton Purcell's son, then that means I got some more family that I ain't never seen. Melissa Michelle's my sister."

"You'll need her to give up a blood sample for a DNA test to prove anything," Harry said.

Gabriel nodded.

"And that's why I came to Las Vegas, sir. There's this newspaper man that I wrote to awhile back. I sent him copies of my mama's letter and the birth certificate. He called me back saying that he'd like to do a story on it. Sent me money for a plane ticket even."

"Oh yeah?" Harry said. "What's his name?"

Gabriel shifted to the side and pulled out a well-worn wallet. He withdrew a dog-eared business card from the billfold section and handed it across the table.

Harry accepted the card and looked at the name.

Robert "Buzzy" Sawyer

Reporter

Las Vegas Mirror

(702) 555-9741

Well I'll be, Harry thought, his lips stretching into a large grin. Small world.

Ricardo Casio lay face down on top of a pristine white gurney, a towel covering his lower extremities. His upper body, which was bare, was covered with a fine layer of coarse hair, most of which had turned from dark black to light silver. A buxom blonde clad in tight beige shorts and a bikini top labored furiously, kneading the olive skin of Casio's shoulders. Jack Moran pointed to the side of the gurney and Eric stopped there. He could smell the liniment the masseuse was using, and he caught a pungent whiff of his own body odor, too, which reminded him how wet his armpits felt underneath his sport coat.

Casio adjusted his head, still looking away from where Eric was standing.

"That's good for now, Ingrid," he said.

The blonde traced her fingers over his back in a finishing

flourish, grabbed a towel, and walked away. Casio turned his head toward Eric and regarded him without changing his expression.

"Jack, let's all get some steam," he said. He sat up, swinging his hairy legs off the gurney. Eric knew the guy was in his mid-sixties, but he still looked like he could take care of himself in a fight. Jack Moran was suddenly at Eric's side, grabbing his elbow and pointing.

"That way," Moran said.

Eric went with him, going into a small room on the far wall. It was a combination of bright yellow tiles and a series of shower stalls opposite a row of metal lockers. The house was so big he felt lost inside it. They'd come in through the back doors, the servant's quarters, past a tough-looking guy who would probably shoot you first and say he was sorry later. Moran had led Eric upstairs, down a long carpeted hallway, and into a large room with a panoramic view of the ocean. Beyond the huge window Eric could see the banister of an extended balcony. He hoped he wouldn't go sailing over it. They were high up on the coast.

Moran indicated a locker and then began stripping off his own clothes. When Eric hesitated, Moran said, "Put your stuff in there."

Eric nodded and grabbed a metal hanger. Hell, he thought as he slipped off his jacket, I already feel like I sweated through this fucking thing, so what's the difference?

He glanced surreptitiously at Moran who was now shirtless. He had on one of those dago tees, and the huge muscles of his arms and chest danced beneath the taut skin. The guy looked like he'd been chiseled out of solid granite. Moran carefully hung up his pants and looked in Eric's direction. His dark eyes seemed to assess the other man's body, as if gauging the muscularity, or, in Eric's case, the lack thereof. Apparently feeling Eric wasn't much of a formidable threat, he took off his underwear and fastened one of the big white towels around his trim waist. He had several blue ink tattoos rimmed with black on his upper arms, shoulders, and chest.

"Where'd you get tattoos like that?" Eric asked.

Moran just stared back at him.

Eric wished he'd undressed faster as he completed the task under Moran's watchful presence. Conscious that his own thin arms looked like twigs and his belly was as pale as a dead mackerel's, Eric grabbed two towels, placing one around his waist and looping the other over his neck.

"You got any shower slippers?" he asked.

Moran shook his head and pointed.

They walked across the hallway to a glass door wet with condensation. Moran grabbed the elongated metal handle and pulled it open. Wispy vapors swirled momentarily before dissolving into mist. Eric went in and saw Ricardo Casio seated on the taller of two receding ledges. Each ledge was about two-and-a-half feet tall and covered with small ceramic tiles. To the left a shower nozzle protruded from the wall, and opposite a large vented section expelled clouds of hot steam.

"I like to hold all my personal conversations in here," Casio said, motioning for Eric to sit on the lower ledge. The air was so hot it seemed to sear his skin.

"Ain't nobody gonna wear a wire in here," Casio continued. "That's the beauty of it. That, and it feels healthy as hell."

Eric sat down as Moran moved behind him.

"I got it on good authority that the Feds are watching me close," Casio said. "Real close."

Eric nodded, smiling. When Casio glared at him, the smile faded quickly.

"That's why I'm doing my level best to make the proper investments in legit business ventures," Casio said. "I'm the soul of propriety, as they say." He took a couple of deep breaths, then looked down at Eric. "Breathe in. Deep. Do it."

Eric tried to take a substantial breath and felt the heat seize his lungs. He began a coughing fit.

"Ahh, shit," Casio said. "You smoke too much, that's what the problem is." He shook his head. "So tell me about the deal. How's it going?"

Eric struggled to regain his breath. "It's fine," he wheezed. "Everything's proceeding according to plan."

Casio drew in more hot air through his nose.

"I hope so, Vantillberg, for your sake." He exhaled copiously. "I let my son Rocco talk me into investing in your company. Buying all that stock." Casio shook his head. "My Rocco, he's a good boy. Grew up listening to all them stories about how it was in the old days with Frank, Dino, and the rest. So, understandably, he wants to go into the record business. So we acquire your label, Vantillberg. Supposed to be the newest superstar. What's this asshole's name? Pablo?"

"Pablo Stevenson," Eric said. He heard his voice crack.

"Whatever. I go out of my way to pour money into the enterprise. My hard-earned money in a legitimate business venture. Pull some strings to put your boy in one of them fine hotels to do a show. And what happens?" He shook his head again. "He tanks. Christ, I had Wayne Newton imitators draw more of a crowd than that fucking little faggot."

"Well, his fan base is mostly young girls," Eric offered. "Not a lot of them can come to a Las Vegas hotel without their parents, and—"

"Shut the fuck up," Casio said.

Eric felt his throat tighten.

"So this burgeoning superstar, this new singing sensation, gets caught with his pants down," Casio said. His tone was pure derision now. "And who's he get caught with? Not some broad, but an under-aged boy."

"That really was blown out of proportion by the press," Eric said.

Casio slapped him.

"Don't fucking interrupt me," he said. He waited a few beats, then added, "Now give me some good news."

Eric felt the stinging on his cheek where the blow had struck him. It felt hotter than the rest of him. He was covered with sweat, but suddenly his mouth felt very, very dry as he tried to swallow.

"We're getting close," Eric said, talking fast. "The kid's family signed a secrecy agreement after the payoff. That came out of our funds. That nosey reporter's been taken care of too. Pablo's finishing up his latest music video. It'll be released to coincide with the announcement of his engagement to Melissa Michelle. The ex-manager's no longer a factor, so when Pablo and the daughter get married, she'll give him the rights to all of Colton Purcell's old songs. He'll start releasing them as remixes, and the stock will soar." His voice cracked again toward the end, and he hoped he sounded more optimistic than he felt.

"The mother's all right with her daughter marrying that nigger spic?" Casio asked.

Eric winced.

"Well, Melissa's almost eighteen," he said. "Ladonna knows she's just about out of her control. She's having a prenup drawn up, but it's not a problem."

"A prenup?" Casio said. "Get a copy and have our lawyer look it over first."

Eric nodded.

Casio smiled slightly. It was the first overt display of emotion that Eric had seen on the old man's face today.

"I seen that broad, Ladonna, on the news. She's still a looker. No wonder that hillbilly pecker fell for her. How old was she when he knocked her up?"

"Nineteen, twenty."

"So that'd make her what? About thirty-seven, thirty-eight now?" Casio pursed his lips slightly. "That's a good age for a woman."

"She's single, too," Eric said. Then, hoping it would ingratiate him to the old man, he added, "But whaddya expect from some broad that's dating some Samoan prick. That's kissin' cousin to a nigger, ain't it?" But instead Casio slapped him again.

"Keep your smart-ass comments to yourself," he said. "You think it's easy to raise a kid today? My Dorothy did a good job with Rocco, and look at the fucking mess you made outta my boy's life, introducing him to all those Hollywood types, getting him hooked on that shit." He stared down at Eric for a moment. "You know what you are, Vantillberg? You're a fucking cancer. You know what they do to cancers?" He snapped his fingers and Eric suddenly felt a thick forearm snake around his throat. Moran's other arm braced against the back of Eric's head and pushed forward, cutting off his air.

"Say the word, boss and I'll finish him."

Casio sat and watched Eric's effete struggles for a good twenty seconds, then made a dismissive wave. Moran loosened his grip and Eric fell forward gasping, the steamy air providing both relief and torture with each breath.

"If I wouldn't have given you the adjustor to help straighten this mess out," Casio said, "you wouldn't be anywhere near closing this deal. You owe me three hundred and fifty grand, and I want this thing sealed by next week, understand? That means Monday morning."

"Three fifty?" Eric croaked. That wasn't right. It was only supposed to be two hundred and fifty thou. He raised his hand but Moran slapped it away.

"Don't you *ever* raise your hand toward Mr. Casio," he said.

Eric opened his mouth but no sound came out. He tried to explain that the figure was wrong, but his throat felt totally seized up.

"Three hundred and fifty thousand," Casio repeated. "The vig don't stop because you got some shit in the works. And my boy Corrigan don't come cheap. You got that?"

Eric nodded, his mouth gaping open, drawing in huge amounts of the burning air. He saw Casio make a dismissive gesture and then felt Moran's powerful hands pulling him to his feet.

This was hell, he thought. And he'd just been seated at the feet of Satan himself.

Chapter 7

Absent Friends

The bright lights flashed in front of her as she ran down the strip, making the hot night seem almost like a hard-edged, surrealistic day. Her eyes continuously searched the throngs of people. How could she have let herself be so careless? But then again, she hadn't expected him to wake up and walk away from the room. A drunk stumbled out in front of her and they both almost went down in a heap.

"Jesus, lady," the drunk said.

"Sorry," Marjorie Versette answered as she moved on, dashing over to the curb and holding her hand above her eyes to cut down on the ubiquitous neon glare. Several car horns blared in warning, and Marjorie stepped back trying to compose herself.

It had been the phone call to Mabel that had caused it, that was for sure. She should have called from the room, but wanted to use the phone card instead of running up a big bill to pay later. Then Mabel had told her about the burglary, and the police investigator.

"He said he'll be off for a few days," Mabel mentioned. "So it won't do any good to try and reach him at the station. But he's going to call me back to see if you'd called or anything. I'm supposed to get a number where he can reach you."

"Was anything missing?" Marjorie asked.

"Well, there didn't seem to be. But then how would we know, dear? He said for you to check when you got back, but he does need to talk to you." Marjorie heard Mabel's chuckle. "And my heavens, he's a big one. Reminds me some movie star or something. Who was that handsome man who turned out to be gay and died of AIDS? Rock Hudson? Remember how surprised we were? Well, he's that big, but much more rugged looking."

"Are Clayton and Colton all right?" Marjorie asked.

"Of course they are," Mabel said. "Now tell me about the wedding."

The wedding hadn't taken place yet. Detoxification was taking longer than she expected. Plus it was slow work. He was making progress, of course, but she hadn't completely stopped the injections of the sedatives.

Marjorie started to cross the street. A car screeched to a stop and honked. People stared, blank, unfamiliar faces. She felt lost in a world of strangers in this gaudy, artificially lit world. Several men strutted down the block dressed in red, white, and blue jumpsuits. Colton imitators. Maybe she could ask them for help?

"Please," she said, grabbing one of them by the arm. "I'm looking for my fiancé. He walked away from our room."

"Well, shucks, ma'am," the one she'd grabbed said, "Can't say that I blame him. Let go of my arm."

"Please," Marjorie said. "Can you just help me look up and down the strip?"

The man pulled his arm from Marjorie's grasp and shoved her away.

"Mess with me, and you're messing with trouble," he said, sounding convincingly like the original.

"Aww, leave her be," the other one said. Then over his shoulder as they walked away, "Lady, you don't need us. Call the cops."

The police? No, can't risk that, she thought.

A howl from a small club on the right advertising *Karaoke Night* caught her attention, then the familiar melody. Several people stood at the door laughing and pointing. Marjorie followed their gaze and felt relief flood through her body. *Colton Purcell imitators welcome,* the second line of the sign read.

The heavyset man stood on the small stage, his large, distended gut rotating to the music, as he belted out "Way Down" just the way Colton Purcell had done it on *The '82 Comeback Show.* Half the crowd seemed enthralled at this bloated singer with the wild, graying hair, the long side-burns, the same snarling half-smile as the original. The other half seemed to be laughing hysterically. But the singer was hitting all the right notes.

Marjorie slipped through the doors and moved into the crowd. She spied a burly-looking guy leaning against the wall with his arms crossed, watching the stage. The back of his black T-shirt had SECURITY in white block letters stenciled across the top. Marjorie pressed two fingers gently on the man's sloping, weightlifter's shoulder. He turned.

"That's my fiancé up there now," she said over the blaring music.

"Oh yeah? He's pretty good. Knows how to sing, that's for sure. Even sounds a lot like Colton."

Marjorie smiled at that. She cupped her hand next to the guard's ear.

"I'm afraid he's not well," she said. "He's under a doctor's care. I have to get him back to the hotel."

The guard nodded and waved at someone up near the front. Then he turned to her.

"You go out and flag down a taxi," he said. "We'll bring him around from the back."

"But be careful," Marjorie added. "Don't hurt him. He's not a well man."

"Gotcha, lady," the guard said, nodding his head. "We do this all the time. We'll be gentle."

The song ended with the singer throwing himself down on one knee, hitting that incredibly low note. The crowd burst into applause and there were several cries of "More, more!"

The disc jockey put on a version of "Teddy Bear," and the big man launched into that number, his substantial belly bouncing to the rhythm, interacting perfectly with the recorded back-up singers. Marjorie watched enthralled till the song was almost over.

They love him, she thought. They really love him.

Then she turned and pushed her way out the door. Two taxis slowly cruised down the strip and she held up her arm. One of them pulled over. The driver leaned over and opened the rear door.

"Where to, ma'am?" he asked.

"The Lucky Nugget Hotel," she said. "But wait. They're bringing out my fiancé."

As the waitress refilled their cups for the third time, Harry thought something wasn't quite right. The number on the card that Gabriel had given him was no longer in service. Strange. After getting the number for the *Las Vegas Mirror*, he dialed it with as much a sense of urgency as Gabriel's intense stare seemed to indicate. The switchboard operator wasn't much help.

"I'm sorry, sir," she said. "Mr. Sawyer is . . . no longer with the paper."

Her voice had a bit more hesitation than normal.

"Do you know where he went? I'm a friend of his."

She was silent for a moment, then said, "Just a moment."

Harry spent what seemed an eternity on hold. He kept glancing at his cell phone making sure the connection was still open, the battery charged. Finally he heard a deep male voice on the other end.

"This is James Nash. May I help you?"

The timbres of the voice suggested he was African American.

"Yeah, my name is Harry Bauer. I'm a friend of Buzzy Sawyer's, and I just hit town." The voice on the other end was silent. Harry continued. "I thought I'd look him up. I'm a reporter, too, and I might have a lead on a story he was interested in."

"You say you're a friend?" The voice was slow.

"That's right."

More silence.

"I hear he's no longer with the paper?" Harry said.

"In a manner of speaking," Nash said. Harry heard a heavy sigh. "Mr. Bauer, I've got a deadline I'm working under, so I really don't have time for chitchatting. I don't know how well you knew Buzzy, but I'm afraid he's deceased."

"Deceased?" Harry said, stunned. It took him several seconds to recover his composure. "What happened?"

"He was . . . killed." Nash's resonant voice spoke slowly. "It was an apparent mugging."

"A mugging?"

Nash's heavy sigh came over the speaker again.

"Look, Mr. Bauer, is it? I told you, I have a newspaper to get out. I really can't discuss anything with you regarding the matter. Now if you'll excuse me."

"Wait a minute. At least tell me when he died."

"It was nine days ago, Mr. Bauer. Now, I really have to go. Please don't call back again tonight. Good-bye."

Nine days, Harry thought, pressing the END button. He'd been in the rehab program, isolated from newspapers, TV, and radios, busy sharing his feelings with a bunch of strangers while a friend of his had been killed. Murdered. He looked up to see Gabriel's intense hazel eyes staring at him from across the table.

"I guess Mr. Sawyer ain't gonna be looking into my story after all, huh?" he asked.

Harry shook his head, suddenly feeling a tightening in his gut. He needed a drink, but he knew if he started, the floodgates would open. He'd never be able to stop. He swirled the remainder of his cold coffee in his cup and raised it high. It was a half-assed toast, but maybe one Buzzy would have appreciated.

"Here's to absent friends," he said. Then added, "I'm gonna miss you, buddy."

Chapter 8

Freedom of Information

The next morning, as Harry sat in the air-conditioned waiting room of the Downtown Division of the Las Vegas Metro Police Department, he thought how much he needed a drink. The room was all chrome and glass windows, slick tile floors and cool concrete block walls. Locals, he'd been told, called it "The Gym." It looked a lot like the clinic where they spent time waiting for their individual counseling sessions, which he'd always thought of as a jail of sorts. And speaking of jail, he had twenty-three days, sixteen hours, and forty-five minutes of sobriety, and virtually all of that had been the time he'd spent in rehab.

One day at a time, he thought.

He'd almost succumbed last night, when that waitress had walked by holding that tray of cool-looking martinis, the olives bobbling like fish bait. He could still smell a trace of vermouth if he concentrated hard enough.

Twenty-three days, sixteen hours, and forty-six minutes.

Last night he'd thought about Buzzy. The craggy smile when they'd first met. The older, established veteran shaking his hand and saying, "I enjoyed your book. Ex-gyrene to Ex-gyrene," Buzzy'd told him. "I served with the Second Marine Div in Khe Sanh in '68. Wrote some stuff for *Stars and Stripes*. That's how I got started in this business."

Served with them, Harry thought. He'd later found out that Buzzy'd won the Silver Star for carrying a wounded buddy back from a perimeter breach and killed half a dozen

71

VC in the process. But Buzzy'd shaken off any claims of heroics when Harry had brought it up. "Nah, they hit 'em with napalm just as I was carrying him back. I looked over my shoulder and all I saw was a bunch of flaming gooks."

Gooks, Harry reflected. *I wonder if you could get away with calling them that back then.* You sure couldn't now.

After having his cab drop Gabriel off at the cheap little joint he was booked at, Harry had proceeded to the MGM. Might as well stay at one of the best since it's on the magazine's nickel, he thought. But he doubted he'd be able to sleep anyway. The soft-spoken boy from Louisiana had mentioned how tired Harry looked, and he realized it had been a long day. A very long day. And his damn jaw continued to ache. But maybe it was hearing the bad news, too. Harry knew he needed some decent rest if he was going to be able to look into Buzzy's death. It was the only thing that kept him straight going through the casino even after seeing that gorgeous redhead carrying those sparkling glasses with the clear liquid and floating olives . . .

But he'd looked at the slumbering lions in the spacious glass cage, wondering if his image to them looked as confused as he felt. The corridor to the elevators was covered with a cracked mirror design, behind a pane of sparkling glass. Looking totally pristine. Harry had resisted the urge to smear his fingerprints over the smooth surface just to leave a trace of himself in the sterile, surrealistic environment. To make sure he was really there. To make sure this existence was real, and not some strange place where African lions slept in a hotel in the middle of Las Vegas, while his ex-wife was marrying some shitbird in Chicago, and his friend was dead, killed nine days ago in a mugging while Harry was getting in touch with his feelings along with a bunch of other losers.

And let's not forget rock and roll icon Colton Purcell suspended in liquid nitrogen in a metallic tube a few hundred miles from here, he thought as he'd pressed the button.

The elevator doors had slid open with a ring, and he'd taken the car up to his floor, and gone to bed. He'd taken enough aspirins to sink a battleship, but swallowed two more and felt the fatigue wash over him. He was, after all, still on Chicago time.

But actually sleeping became problematic despite his lassitude, almost like that old Hank Williams song where sleep wouldn't come. Didn't Colton do a version of that one? He wondered as he rolled over. *But I'll bet that Gabriel knew it,* he thought as he looked at the red digits spelling out 0327, and yawned till his jaw ached.

Now, much later, in the antiseptic environment of Las Vegas Metro PD, he massaged the lump as he sat there waiting. It seemed bigger than he remembered. A lot bigger. Hurt more too.

Shoulda used more ice, he reflected and looked at his watch. It was close to noon. A couple of bicycle cops in yellow uniform shirts and black shorts led a handcuffed man down the hallway. The man's head was bowed in front of him making him look like a perfect picture of dejection. No hope. No one to help.

Nash, Buzzy's editor, hadn't been very helpful either. In fact, he barely took the time to talk to Harry, much less agree to allow him a look at Buzzy's files.

"You know better than to ask me that," Nash had said. He was a big, bald black man who seemed to be perpetually sweating, despite the coolness of the air conditioning. "That stuff's all classified."

"Look, all I'm saying is maybe I can help. I'm a reporter

myself, and I knew Buzzy."

"Then you know I got a newspaper to get out," Nash's deep voice boomed. "Sawyer was our star columnist. Circulation's down eleven percent since the mugging. But what the hell . . . sometimes you just have to move on and make the best of things."

Nash had, however, given him the card of the police detective investigating the case. Harry looked at it now.

Detective J. Grey

Las Vegas Metro Police

(702) 555-6578 Ext 1543

J. Grey, Harry speculated. John? Joseph? Maybe a former serviceman? *Hey, Joe, old buddy, old pal . . . how about going over some of the aspects of this case with me? Ex-gyrene to ex-gyrene.*

His reverie was broken by the clicking of flat heels along the polished tile floor, and he took time to assess her. About five-five or six, maybe a hundred and twenty-five pounds, but with a lean-looking muscularity to her bare shoulders. Sleeveless pink blouse with brownish colored hair hanging just below her jaw line. It was a strong-looking jaw, too. Her petite features were offset by a pair of rimless oval glasses.

"Mr. Bauer?" she asked, stepping over to him and extending her hand. "I'm Detective Grey. What can I do for you?"

He noticed her eyes drifting over his swollen jaw and he tried a quick grin as he introduced himself. Her eyes were gray, too. Grayish blue.

"I was a friend of Buzzy Sawyer," he added. The blue-gray eyes looked momentarily perplexed.

"Robert Sawyer?" she asked.

"Right. His nickname was Buzzy."

She nodded. He expected her to invite him into her office, sit down behind a large, but neatly arranged desk, and hand him a thick file containing all the pertinent information on the case. But instead she just stood there.

"I'm sorry about your friend," she said finally. "Now, what exactly can I do for you?"

Harry blinked, wondering why she was having a hard time getting it.

"Well, I'd like to know what happened," he said. "Maybe get a look at where you think the investigation is leading."

Detective Grey's eyes seemed to harden.

"I'm sorry, but it's still an open investigation," she said. "I'm not at liberty to discuss it with the general public."

General public? Harry thought. What the hell was she talking about? Didn't she realize he might be able to help?

"Oh, hey, I'm not exactly the general public," he said, taking out one of his cards and handing it to her. "I work for *Regency Magazine.*"

She looked at the card and started to hand it back to him.

"That's okay, you can keep it," he said.

She shrugged and slipped it in the pocket of her slacks.

The awkward silence lasted a few more seconds, then Harry said, "What I mean is, I'm out here on a story, and I just heard about my friend's death. It's been kind of a shock, I guess." He shot a quick look her way to see if her expression had changed any. "I went to the paper, but they couldn't tell me much. James Nash, Buzzy's editor, referred me to you."

Detective Grey took a deep breath.

"Mr. Bauer, I'm afraid I won't be able to tell you much either. As I said, the investigation is still ongoing."

Harry felt the desperation surge within his gut.

"Couldn't I just see the basic case report?" he asked. "You know, I could file a request for it under the Freedom of Information Act."

"I'm sure you could."

He realized it was a mistake trying to be confrontational. He remembered his rehab training. Share your feelings. He coughed slightly and lowered his gaze to the floor.

"Look, Detective." He exhaled slowly, trying to give the impression of grief rather than exasperation. "I'm sorry if I seemed pushy. It's just that, Buzzy was a close friend of mine . . ."

"And you're just now finding out about his death?" She sounded skeptical as ever.

"I am," he began, unsure of what to tell her. "I've been in the hospital for the past few weeks. Plus, I've been going through a divorce. No one contacted me because I was incommunicado, I guess."

The blue-gray eyes softened just a bit.

"Come back to my office," she said, turning and walking down the hall.

Eric watched as the attendants took Ladonna's and Melissa Michelle's heavily laden suitcases from the big Samoan bodyguard and placed them on the cart. Through the large glass windows he could see the maintenance men fueling up the *Melissa Michelle*, and giving the Learjet the last once-over on the small tarmac. Good thing they didn't try to fly out of LAX, he thought. It woulda taken the whole goddamn day. But then, why fly commercial when you have your own private fucking jet?

Must be nice, he thought. Real nice. He smiled slightly, thinking that in a few months, maybe weeks, he'd be sitting in the plane telling the pilot where to go. Hopefully. If all this shit could be handled correctly. But it was like trying to juggle a dozen meat cleavers. One slip and his whole fucking hand could be lopped off. Or worse.

Eric reached in his pocket for his cigarettes, then remembered this was a no smoking area and stuck it above his right ear. He caught Ladonna giving him a sideways stare.

"Looks like things are pretty much shipshape," he offered, trying to work up an ingratiating smile. It didn't work. Ladonna just pursed her lips into a frown and looked away.

God, she's got great lips, Eric thought. I wonder if she has them injected with collagen? The big Samoan, his crossed forearms looking like twin fifty-pound hams, stood a few feet away watching him.

"I still don't see why Pablo couldn't come with us," Melissa Michelle said. "I mean, it's not like there's no room on that fucking plane."

Ladonna turned to her daughter.

"Don't use that kind of language," she said. "Especially in public."

Melissa Michelle made an audible, sarcastic clucking sound and flipped her hair, rolling her eyes at the ceiling.

"But he still *could've* come with us," the girl said, her voice a petulant whine. "Now I won't have nobody to talk to or hang out with."

"We're going to be too busy," Ladonna said. She continued to watch the maintenance men tend to the plane.

"But there won't be anybody there *my* age. How am I gonna have any fun?"

"This is a funeral we're going to," Ladonna said. "You're not supposed to have fun."

"I don't even want to go," Melissa Michelle said,

crossing her arms with a definitive gesture. "I hated Big Daddy anyway. He was never nice to me, and all he ever did was try to look down your blouse."

"Stop talking like that," Ladonna said. Her tone sounded worn, like she was out of patience.

"Look, honey," Eric said, "Pablo had a doctor's appointment this morning anyway. He had to get that blood test so you two can you-know-what in a couple of weeks." He tried one of his high-wattage smiles on her.

Melissa Michelle frowned. "But we already *had* those. Down in Mexico, remember?"

"Well, you'll have them again," Ladonna said. "At least he will." She glanced at Eric with a malevolent look.

"This is bullshit!" Melissa Michelle said loudly. "You are like, totally uncool. This is just soooo unfair."

"That's enough, Melissa!" Ladonna said.

Melissa Michelle canted her head and stuck out her tongue.

"Hey, hey, hey," Eric said, "Pablo'll call you. I promise he will. He should be working on the music video anyway."

"Oh you shut up!" Melissa Michelle snapped. "You're nothing but a big leech anyway. Just like Big Daddy. After me and Pablo get married, I might have him get rid of you."

Eric raised his eyebrows.

Jesus, is this kid a brat and a half, he thought.

"Pablo knows better than that," he said. "Besides, don't you want to wait until I've made you a star, too?" He waggled his extended index finger at her, trying to lighten the mood. "Remember that music video duet . . ."

"Screw you, greaseball," Melissa Michelle said.

Ladonna reached over and touched her daughter's arm. The kid shook away.

"Melissa, just stop it, okay?" Ladonna said. Then,

turning to the big Samoan, "Joe, go see how much longer the plane's going to be."

Joe uncrossed his arms, nodded impassively, and walked toward the doors leading to the tarmac.

Melissa Michelle seemed to take this as a cue and began again.

"I mean, if Pablo and I are gonna be together forever soon, why can't he go? We could rehearse our song together, and hang out . . ."

"I told you, we're going there for a funeral, not a vacation," Ladonna said. Her voice was grating. "Now just be quiet."

"I don't care. I hated Big Daddy. He was mean and fat and—"

Ladonna stood up and grabbed Melissa's upper arm, her fingers digging into the tan flesh.

"I've had enough of your attitude," she said, drawing her open palm back.

"What are you gonna do? Hit me?" Melissa Michelle shot back. "Go ahead, 'cause I'm almost eighteen. I'll just hit you right back."

The words seemed to stun Ladonna.

Go on, hit her, thought Eric. Hit that spoiled little brat right in the chops.

"And pretty soon everything that daddy had will be mine, not yours anymore," the girl added, her mouth twisting into a sneer.

Ladonna hesitated, and Eric saw the mascara-coated eyelashes glisten with tears, then spill over, leaving twin tracks down her cheeks. She released her daughter's arm, brought both her hands to her own face, and began to make a series of little hiccupping sounds. Melissa Michelle watched, too, rubbing her upper arm where her mother had grabbed it, her lips still stuck in a defiant pout.

Ladonna, still cradling her face, turned and abruptly ran for the ladies' room. Her daughter looked after her, mouth drifting open slightly, and then began following at a quick jog shouting, "Mom, I'm sorry, okay? I didn't mean it."

Eric watched her slender, but shapely little ass moving inside the low cut, extremely tight blue jeans as she moved away from him. Just then his cell phone rang. He unclipped it and pressed the button.

"Yeah," he said into the phone.

"Vantillberg?"

It was Corrigan. Eric felt the familiar tightening in his gut.

"Hey, buddy," Eric said. "I hope you're gonna tell me some good news."

"Yeah, here's some real good news, asshole." Corrigan's voice was rough. "Your fucking company credit card was maxed out, so I had to use one of mine to buy my plane ticket outta Memphis. I don't like to do that."

"Maxed out? You sure?" Eric felt some sweat trickle down from his armpits. "I'll have to look into that. It must be some kind of mistake."

"The only mistake you need to be concerned about is not keeping me happy," Corrigan said. "And I ain't your buddy. I ain't *your* anything. I work for Mr. Casio."

Eric swallowed. He could almost feel those big hands around his throat. He pulled out his wallet and sorted through his credit cards, trying to figure out which number he could give to Corrigan. Maybe it was time to open a new account somewhere.

"Look, how about I call you back with a new number in a bit?"

"I'll call you. I'm tracing down the pigeons."

This made Eric feel a bit better.

"You are?" he asked. "You said you left Memphis?"

"Right. I'm in Vegas now. My source told me they were staying at the Lucky Nugget."

"Oh, Christ," Eric said. "They're in Vegas? If something goes wrong and somebody discovers he's alive it'll ruin everything."

"Relax. I got it covered. I'm down the street from the Nugget now," Corrigan said. "In a couple of hours they'll both be laying in some unmarked grave out in the desert somewhere."

Detective J. Grey's desk was neatly arranged with stacks of paper sitting in various plastic trays marked Incoming, Outgoing, File, and Cleared. He noticed she wore no wedding ring. No jewelry of any kind except for a watch and a pair of gold earrings. Harry searched the metallic surface for signs to her personal life. Two framed photographs sat in the center, facing toward her, and out of Harry's view. Boyfriend? Children? Parents? He continued to speculate.

"So you say you knew Mr. Sawyer quite well?" she asked.

Harry cleared his throat. "Well, I'm from Chicago, so we'd kind of lost touch a bit. I met him a number of years ago when I was first starting out. I wrote a book about the Gulf War, Operation Desert Storm, and Buzzy liked it." He flashed a quick smile. "We were both former marines."

Detective Grey nodded. The blue-gray eyes continued to watch him, and Harry realized this was encouraging him to open up more.

"He helped me out quite a bit with my writing," he continued. "He was based in Chicago then, too. We both worked for the same paper. The *Sun-Times*."

She nodded.

"So when was the last time you saw him, Mr. Bauer?"

"Hey, call me Harry. Everybody else does."

"The last time, Mr. Bauer?"

Harry shrugged. "Hard to say. We hadn't really kept in touch since he made the move to Vegas."

She nodded again.

"So, can you tell me a little bit about what happened?" he asked, leaning forward.

Detective Grey canted her head slightly, her lips parting ever so slightly.

"I can tell you that he was found next to his car inside a parking garage at," she opened up a tan filing envelope and read him the address. "His wallet was missing. So were his watch and other personal possessions."

"Other personal possessions?" Harry tried to look expectant. He figured he'd get one shot at this and it was already half over. "Meaning?"

Detective Grey sighed.

"Meaning other personal possessions," she said. "I already told you, it would jeopardize the investigation if I were to reveal too much."

"Too much?" He tried to crack a smile. "This is hardly anything. I could've learned more reading the papers."

Detective Grey shot him a lips-only smile.

"I'm sure the *Mirror* has back copies available," she said.

"Well, can you at least tell me if you think it was a random killing? I mean, Buzzy had kind of a unique view of things. He could be sort of pugnacious. Sometimes people got kind of angry."

Detective Grey smiled again, showing her teeth this

time. She had nice teeth, obviously the result of superb orthodontics.

"That's putting it mildly," she said. "He made Art Bell sound like Alan Greenspan. I used to enjoy his column." She pulled out a paperclipped sheaf of newspaper clippings. "Some of these are hilarious, but I doubt that aliens or black helicopters are responsible, Mr. Bauer."

So, we were sticking with Mr. Bauer, eh? he thought.

She flopped the stack of newspaper clippings on the desk between them.

"You're welcome to go over these, if you want," she said.

Harry removed the clip and began sorting through them, looking at the dates and the titles: "Where's the Real Radio-active Waste Going? (Love Canal was only the tip of the toxic iceberg)," "Black Helicopters in the Nevada Sky. (Can you hear them hovering?)." He flipped through a few others: "What's the Real Story Behind That Unexplained Crash in the Desert? (What they don't want you to know.)" "Who Really Killed Tupac? (And what they don't want you to find out.)" The dates went back about eight weeks, with the oldest one dated about two months ago. The most recent, July 7, bore the headline, "The King Must Be Spinning In His Tank (Of Liquid Nitrogen, that is.)" Harry skimmed the last one, which dealt with the unconfirmed rumor that Melissa Michelle, the only child of dead rocker Colton Purcell, had married Pablo Stevenson in a secret ceremony in an undisclosed location in Mexico where they had been vacationing.

Or is this just a way of creating what they used to call a good old-fashioned smoke screen, with the civil trial being settled out of court concerning the Punky Prince of

Pop-off's unusual "special affection" for the young son of one of his entourage? It smells like damage control to me. Maybe all those Colton sightings aren't so far out after all. Just the thought of that slimy little creep putting his hands on my daughter would be enough to bring me back from the grave.

Harry smirked.

"You know, I'm here working on the Colton Purcell story myself," he said. "About the anniversary celebration and the big imitator's contest. In fact, I just met a young man who claims to be Colton's illegitimate son."

Detective Grey, one hand tucked under her chin, had a look of amused tolerance on her face.

"I'm sure you'll do a very good job writing about it," she said. "But I'm sorry, Mr. Bauer—"

"Harry. Remember?"

She shot him the lips-only smile again.

"I do have some reports to finish." She stood and smoothed her slacks.

Harry got up too, surreptitiously watching how her hair fell around her face.

"Well, I'm staying at the MGM," he said. "Maybe we can do dinner?"

She seemed surprised by his audacity.

"I'm sorry, but I have plans," she said. Then added, "I'm pretty busy. Most of the time I work late."

"Lunch then?" Harry said quickly. "Lunch for you, dinner for me. I'm still on Chicago time."

Detective Grey hesitated several seconds before holding out her hand as she shook her head.

Harry smiled as they shook hands. She was considering it, that much he knew.

"Thanks, but like I said, I'm really very busy lately," she said.

He felt immediately deflated. Missed it by that much, he thought.

Chapter 9

Say It With Flowers

Harry was talking on his cell phone when he saw the sign.

Say it with Flowers.

Hey, why not? he asked himself.

"So what do you want me to send you, Harry?" Tim Stockton's voice asked over the phone.

Harry snapped back to the conversation.

"Look up any news articles you can get by Robert Buzzy Sawyer. He wrote for the *Las Vegas Mirror*. I'm particularly interested in anything he'd written in the last month or so." Harry pulled open the door of the flower shop and heard the chimes ring.

"What was that?" Stockton asked.

"I'm going into a flower shop," Harry said. Over the speaker system Colton Purcell's voice was singing "Mama Loved the Roses." "Tell accounting to get ready for the expense account to end all expense accounts. Or better yet, tell them Bishop's given me carte blanche, and not to worry about it until he gets back from his honeymoon. Where are they going, by the way?"

"The Bahamas, I think," Stockton said. "You really gonna send them flowers?"

"What? No. Not to them." The overpowering mixture of smells assailed his nostrils. "Tim, look up any news reports on Buzzy Sawyer's death, too. He got mugged here in Las Vegas about a week and a half ago."

"Harry, you're there and I'm here. Wouldn't it be easier for you to trace things down from your end?"

"It'll be good practice for you, kid," Harry said, strolling over to the specially chilled glass cases to look at the selection of roses. "For when you start writing features on your own. Besides," he pulled the door open and took a whiff. Perfect, he thought. "I'm meeting a lot of local resistance here. I need someone watching my back."

"Oh," Stockton said. "Is that what I'm doing?"

"You know it, kid," Harry said.

"How's the Colton Purcell story coming, anyway?" Stockton asked.

Harry listened to the warbling end to the song. "I'm working on it. Why?"

"Did you hear he's got a new hit? They re-released 'Don't Ask the Question.' It's one of his old movie tunes." His tone suddenly sounded more excited than conversational. "They did a remix version of it, and it's selling like hot cakes all over the place. It's already at the top of the charts. Gives him more number ones than anybody else in history. More than the Beatles, the Stones, anybody."

"Wow, the comeback of the new millennium," Harry said, trying to muster some enthusiasm. "I'll have to work that into my story. Now get busy and send me those articles. I'll check my e-mail in an hour or so. Bye."

He snapped the phone shut and saw the clerk talking to a big guy wearing a white Panama hat and tan chambray shirt. The guy was huge and the shirt looked like a small tent. They spoke in hushed tones, and the guy was insisting that the female clerk write out the message for him.

"I got terrible handwriting," the big guy said.

The clerk, who looked about twenty-five, started one card, but the big guy growled at her.

"No, no, no," he said. "I don't want any writing with those fancy loops and circles over the 'i'. Write it nice and plain. Clear, like an older broad would write it."

"I'm sorry, sir," the clerk said. Harry could see she was fuming, but afraid to show it. "Now what was it you wanted me to write again?"

"Write, Congratulations on your wedding. Good luck. Mabel," the big guy said. "That's M-A-B-E-L. You spelled it wrong here." The clerk's head bobbled and she wrote it out again. The big guy smiled. "That's better. Now you can have these delivered in thirty minutes to the Lucky Nugget?"

"I'll put a rush on it, sir," she said. "But it'll be—"

The big guy held a bill in front of the clerk's face. Harry couldn't see the denomination, but from the way her eyes widened, he was sure it wasn't just a sawbuck.

"Like I said, it's very important they be there in exactly thirty minutes," the big guy said. "And make sure they're delivered up to the room. The right room."

"Yes, sir," the clerk said, all smiles as she pocketed the bill.

The big guy turned and strode past Harry, slipping on a pair of dark sunglasses, and saying over his shoulder, "Good. I'll be expecting them there then."

Jesus, thought Harry, that guy's hands look like they could palm two basketballs.

The clerk busied herself filling the order, talking on the phone to the delivery man as Harry continued to wait. "Versette," she said. "Marjorie Versette, at the Lucky Nugget." Finally she looked Harry's way and said, "I'll be right with you."

Harry sighed. No sense getting flustered. Looking at the selection before him, he pondered what type to get. Hell, he was on Bishop's nickel, he remembered. Why not roses?

He looked at them through the pane. Yeah, definitely roses.

Stepping closer, Harry considered the options. Yellow? Too lighthearted. Indicative of fun. Red? Too romantic for a first date invitation. Don't want to scare her off. White? Not durable enough. They'd look like waxed paper by this afternoon.

Pink? He stared at the delicate petals. Yeah, pink. A hint of romance, but some distance from red's passion. Perfect.

The clerk was still busily talking on the phone to the delivery service. Harry decided to write out his card, and selected one with a plain floral print.

Let's see, he thought, and wrote *Ms. Gray, I hope you'll reconsider about dinner.* He was about to sign his name, then added, *I promise not to start any conversations about taboo subjects.* Frowning, he crumpled that card and took another.

Damn, I can't even write a simple note without a rewrite, he thought.

He rewrote the message substituting *I promise not to start any conversations about your case.*

Ah, he thought. Much better. And true, too. Well, almost. He grinned and made a mental note not to start any conversations, but to finish any that she might initiate about the case. Just remember, "Don't Ask the Question," he told himself with a grin. Anyway, it wasn't like he had any expectations besides just a pleasant dinner with a pretty lady. Yeah, right. If he even got that. He smelled the spray of roses in the vase on the counter.

No, they'll get her, he thought. They always fall for the flower bit.

"Un un, man, no way," Pablo said, playing with his dangling gold earrings and staring out the windows of Eric's second floor office. "I ain't sending flowers to no bitches. Especially that old one. She dissed me, man."

Eric rolled his eyes as he listened to Pablo's wavering tenor as it lent a ludicrous quality to the "ghettospeak." Even Gant, who was seated against the far wall had a grin stretched across his face.

Oh no, Eric thought. Him and Gant must have been up watching rap videos all night again.

He leaned forward over the table and spoke in a low voice.

"Look, Pablo, I feel like somebody's been dumping on me with an electric shitmaker. I'm trying to do damage control for your career, in case you ain't noticed, and we need this to happen with Melissa Michelle."

"She's cool," Pablo said. "I told you, she my bitch."

Eric groaned again. "You keep that up and you'll blow the whole deal. Now please, just sign the card, will ya?"

Pablo stared across the table, heaved an exaggerated sigh, and plucked the pen from Eric's fingers with a fluttering grace.

"Okay, for you, I'll do it," he said. "What do you want me to write?"

Glad that the "Menace 2 Society" act had vanished, Eric dictated, "I miss you more and more each day," and watched Pablo scribble it.

God, he's got feminine-looking handwriting, Eric thought. He handed him another card.

"And this one's to Ladonna," he said.

"Say what?" Pablo threw the pen down on the desk. "No, no way. If I give anything to her, it'll be a bitch-slap."

The thought of Pablo giving anyone a bitch-slap was about as likely as George Michael jumping in the ring to go ten with Tyson.

"Just do it," Eric said, finally running out of patience. Gant seemed to take notice of Eric's tone and straightened up.

Shit, I don't want him to go after me, thought Eric. But hell, he's probably still sore as hell from that ass-kicking that Moran gave him last night. He smiled anyway.

"Please, Pablo. Do it for me, won't ya?"

Pablo sighed again, but picked up the pen.

Eric dictated a quick, but reverential message expressing sorrow over the death of Ladonna's friend, Big Daddy.

"Satisfied?" Pablo asked, shoving the cards across the desk.

Eric licked his lips. In another two weeks Melissa Michelle will be eighteen, her and Pablo will be married, he told himself. She'll sign over all the rights to Colton's songs, Pablo's remix versions'll shoot up the charts, the money will start rolling in, and I'll be off the hook to Casio. If he could keep it all together. The thought of the juggling meat cleavers came to mind again.

No problem, as long as he could keep tossing them to Corrigan.

Corrigan was standing outside the Lucky Nugget pretending to look at a newspaper when he saw the delivery van making its way up Main Street. He folded the paper just as the van pulled into the loading zone area and watched as the driver began removing the floral display. Corrigan removed a half-pint of whiskey from his pocket, unscrewed the cap, and took a small amount into his mouth. After sloshing it around, like mouthwash, he leaned over and carefully spat it out, replacing the flask in his pocket and recovering in time to hold the door open for the deliveryman. Following him inside, they both headed to the front desk. A male clerk nodded to the deliveryman as Corrigan leaned his forearms on the polished counter without removing his hat or sunglasses.

"May I help you, sir?" another clerk, a female, asked him.

"You have any of those postcards with a picture of the hotel on them?" Corrigan asked, slurring his speech slightly.

She nodded, recoiling from his liquor-laced breath.

"It's for Marjorie Versette and friend," the delivery guy said. "They're supposed to be delivered to the room."

"Just put them there," the male clerk said. "I'll have them taken up."

The delivery guy frowned. "Can you at least call her up and see if she wants to give me a tip?"

It was the clerk's turn to frown, but he went to his keyboard, tapped in the name, and then picked up his phone. It rang several times before he replaced it.

"Apparently not," he said, smiling a quick shrug at the deliveryman.

"Figures," the guy said, and held the yellow invoice forward for the clerk to sign.

Corrigan was busily addressing a postcard to some phony address in New Jersey. He watched carefully as the clerk scribbled a room number on the flower invoice, and turned to the woman next to him.

"Can you call one of the bellmen for me?" he asked.

The woman nodded and went into an adjacent room.

Corrigan moved closer to the floral spray, waiting until the clerk had finished writing.

"You know," he said, "I ought to get some of these for my old lady. Maybe she'll be nice to me then and let me hit the tables more." He grinned. "Whadda ya think?"

He leaned over and looked at the yellow invoice.

"Course, if I win big, she'll be nice enough, I guess." He did his best to imitate an ingratiating, half-drunk grin, expelling another boozy breath as he placed the postcards in his shirt pocket.

The clerk nodded quickly, turning away.

A young black man in a bellman's uniform appeared and removed the flowers as Corrigan stumbled off toward the elevators. The bellman went in another direction toward a set of doors that led into the interior of the hotel. Corrigan watched the bellman's departure, noting his route, then pressed the elevator button. The doors popped open after about a minute, disgorging several people. Corrigan got on along with an older lady. He tipped his hat and said, "What floor, ma'am?"

"Four," she said, and smiled as he pushed her floor button, and then the one underneath it.

The doors opened at three and Corrigan stepped out, eyeing both corridors and jamming one of his massive hands into his pocket. He took out some change, sorting through it slowly and watched over the tip rim of the sunglasses. The gold plaque on the wall indicated rooms 300–325 with a black arrow. Another plaque underneath showed an opposite pointing arrow for 326–350. Two Hispanic women dressed in tan uniforms pushed large white curtained carts past him chatting in Spanish. The bellman suddenly appeared from down the hallway carrying the flowers. Corrigan began walking toward the man, grazing the wall slightly with the look of a purposeful drunk. They passed as the man paused and glanced down at the yellow invoice. He knocked on the door of room 335 and said, "Hotel services," before slipping a card into the locking mechanism. Corrigan continued down the hallway in the direction the bellman had come. He found the adjacent hallway off to his right that led to the freight elevator.

Passkey only, he thought, looking at the metallic plate on the wall next to the door. He took out the half-pint again, swishing a small amount of liquor around in his mouth, then propelling the stream onto the thick carpeting. The bellman came down the hallway a few moments later.

"Shay," Corrigan said, clumsily moving so that he looked like he was trying to hold up the wall. "I need to get to the lobby and this elevator ain't working." He held up his finger and pointed with conspicuous exaggeration. The two Hispanic women reappeared, heading down the hallway again with their carts.

"That's the freight elevator, sir," the bellman said. "Employees only. You got to go down there."

Corrigan nodded and moved past the man.

Okay, he thought. I know where and how. All I gotta worry about now is when.

Chapter 10

Striking Out

Harry's cell phone rang as he was walking down the strip, ogling the throngs of pretty girls interspersed with the constant flow of tourists taking pictures and looking ridiculously pale and frenzied with silver dollar fever. He unclipped it from his belt, hoping it was Stockton with an update.

"Speak to me," he said into the phone.

"Mr. Bauer?" It was Gabriel Freeman.

"Yeah, Gabe. What's up?"

"I was just wondering if you found out any more about your friend." The kid's voice sounded tentative, unsure. He was holding something back; Harry would bet on it.

"Not a lot. He got mugged about a week ago. The cops aren't really saying much more than that."

"I'm sorry to hear that." Harry could hear a car horn blaring in the background.

"Where the hell are you?" he asked.

"I'm on a pay phone outside this market on Fremont," Gabriel said. "I was wondering if we might be able to meet somewhere and talk."

"Sure. I'm on my way back to my hotel. The MGM. Meet me there and I'll buy you lunch."

"Does the trolley go down that far?"

Oh oh, Harry thought. The poor kid's low on cash. Probably hasn't started his singing gig yet.

"Yeah, I think it does," Harry said. "Take your time. Call me when you get there."

Harry watched with relish as the waitress set the array of late-breakfast desserts in front of them. *Old Bishop is gonna shit when he sees the expense sheet on this one,* he thought. *Like I give a damn.*

Just then he saw Gabriel look up.

"I hope this isn't costing too much," Gabe said. "I'll be glad to split the check with you."

Harry shook his head. "I got an understanding with my boss. I got carte blanche for this little excursion."

"Is that so you can find out what happened to Mr. Sawyer?"

"Not really," Harry said slowly. "How did you two hook up, anyway?"

Gabriel smiled.

"It was pretty coincidental," he said.

"Most things were when it came to Buzzy."

Gabriel had his fork poised above a hefty slice of apple pie.

"Want some ice cream on that?" Harry asked.

"No, sir." He chopped off a piece and shoveled it into his mouth.

"Because, like I said, my boss wants me to spare no expense."

Gabriel nodded, chewing quickly.

"I was staying in Memphis, visiting the mansion just about every day, trying to get a chance to see Ladonna Purcell or somebody."

"And did you?"

He shook his head as he ate another bite. "I was playing this little bar called the Silver Mirror. Mr. Sawyer came in there one night and started talking to me between sets." He took a swallow from his coffee cup. Magically, the waitress was there to warm it up. She beamed as he said, "Thank you, ma'am."

No need to worry about service when this kid's around, thought Harry.

"Well," Gabriel continued, "Mr. Sawyer told me he liked my singing a lot. Said he'd seen me out at the mansion on a couple of the tours and that I kind of reminded him of Colton."

Harry could see a striking resemblance too. The narrow, patrician nose, the same high cheekbones, and long, leonine face. The hair color was different, but then Colton had taken to dying his hair jet-black after his initial recording successes.

"So I told him my story," Gabe said. "He seemed real interested, and wrote my information down and give me one of his cards. Said he'd see what he could do to help me." He shrugged. "My gig went sour a little bit after that, and I went back to Louisiana. Didn't hear nothing from nobody until about two weeks ago he called me on the phone."

"Buzzy called you?" Harry asked.

"Un huh. He sounded real excited. Told me he was working on a big story that was gonna blow a lot of people's minds. Wanted me to come out to Las Vegas. I said, sure, why not, and he sent me the plane ticket."

Harry considered this a moment.

"He say what the story was?"

Gabe shook his head. "Just that it was something big."

"What was he doing in Memphis?"

"Don't know that either, sir."

Harry sighed. "I wish you'd quit calling me 'sir.' Makes me feel a hundred years old."

"Aww, shucks," Gabe said, smiling. "You don't look a day over forty. Sir."

"Forty?" Harry grinned. "Gimme a break, will you?" The kid had Colton's smile, too. Dimples on both cheeks.

"Mr. Bauer," Gabe said, leaning forward, "I was gonna ask you if you'd look into finishing up Mr. Sawyer's story on me. I mean, he seems like my only shot right now. I think he had some evidence or something, otherwise he'd a never paid my way out here, would he?"

Harry raised his eyebrows. It sounded like vintage Buzzy. A conspiracy under every rock left unturned.

"I don't know," he said.

"Look, I really need somebody to help me with this." Gabe's tone was almost pleading.

"Buzzy's a pretty hard act to follow."

"But didn't you say you were a reporter too?"

"Actually," Harry began. But the sudden flash of youthful idealism on Gabriel's face stopped him. "Actually," he began again, "I'm more of a features writer." He sighed. "And to tell you the truth, kid, my best days as a writer are behind me. I'm a dried out drunk. Got so I couldn't work without the juice. Needed it for inspiration. To lubricate the wheels." He placed his index finger on his temple. "Fuel for the brain, I used to say. But who was I kidding? I just got outta rehab the day before yesterday. My third time. You know what they say, three strikes and you're out."

"Then you oughta not let that next pitch go by without taking a swing," Gabriel said. His expression was solemn.

Harry smiled. But it was a weary smile.

"Back again, Mr. Bauer?" James Nash said, wiping his barren scalp with a paisley handkerchief. "I thought I told you before that I got a newspaper to run." He held up an expansive hand indicating the groups of people hunched over computer monitors busily typing.

"I remember," Harry said. "This is Gabriel Freeman, Mr. Nash."

Gabriel stepped forward and extended his hand. Nash shook it with an obvious reluctance.

"Why do I have the feeling that you're not just here for the nickel tour, Mr. Bauer?" he asked.

"You must be psychic," Harry said, flashing what he hoped was an engaging smile. "It seems that Buzzy was working on a story involving this young man here. He even flew him out here from Louisiana. He wouldn't have done that if it wasn't something big."

Nash sighed heavily.

"Look, you told me you were Buzzy's friend, right?" Nash said.

Harry nodded.

"Well, then you must know that Buzzy had a lot of stories going." Nash's lips stretched into a wry grin. "That's how he got his nickname. Always something buzzin' around in that head of his. That was the charm of his columns. People ate that stuff up. But he's gone now."

"That's what I wanted to talk to you about," Harry said. "I'd like to look over Buzzy's notes. His files. I'm working an angle too, and I could really use his insights."

"Sorry," Nash said.

"Aww, come on. Can't you help us out a bit? I'll tell you what. You let me review his files, and if I can put together a story out of it, you can publish it posthumously under his byline."

Nash shook his head slowly, looking at the floor.

"Think about it," Harry said quickly. "One last undiscovered column by Robert 'Buzzy' Sawyer. It'd sell a lot of newspapers."

Nash exhaled copiously through his flaring nostrils.

"Mr. Bauer, I told you I can't help you."

"Can't? Or won't?"

"Can't," Nash said. "Even if I wanted to. Buzzy didn't leave any files. He was so paranoid he kept all his stuff on his laptop. Just downloaded his columns here."

Harry's brow furrowed. "His laptop?"

"Right," Nash said. "It wasn't with his body. Whoever killed him took it. Must be either smashed or traded for some rock by some stone junkie by now."

Raucous laughter from an adjacent booth brought Harry out of his reverie and he glanced at his watch. Three fifteen and still no call from Detective Grey. Maybe I struck out again, he thought. Maybe she didn't like the roses? Maybe she thought it was a ruse? That I wasn't really interested in her at all? Maybe she pegged me as a loser? Across the table Gabe was busy sopping up some of his gravy with the hot biscuits. A Colton Purcell song began playing in the background, offsetting the distracting conversations buzzing around them. Harry smiled.

Don't ask the question, he thought, if you don't want to hear the answer.

They'd left the newspaper office after Nash had belatedly let them sift through a collection of Buzzy's old stuff. A pretty little intern named Jenna, who seemed completely enamored by Gabe, had surreptitiously slipped him a disk with the last three months' worth of columns that she'd downloaded.

"It's password protected," she'd whispered. "Just type in my name."

Gabe had flashed her a smile and a wink, and then given the disk to Harry to slip into his laptop.

Harry sighed as he saw the waitress hovering close by, pushed his coffee cup toward the center of the table top, and asked Gabriel to make sure she warmed it up.

"The cup, I mean," he said, smiling rakishly, and scrolled down to the last file on the disk.

In This Corner
By Buzzy Sawyer
Is Colton Purcell Alive, But Not So Well
(And living in a nursing home in Memphis?)

Graceful Valley Nursing Home is set amongst large flowing willows and honey locust trees, back from the hustle and bustle of the main streets and busy highways of Memphis. Established in the 1930's, the home was once a facility for the mentally insane, transforming to a partial rehab center in the 80's, and now to its present incarnation of a multicare living facility. It looks like it was transplanted from Gone with the Wind, with majestic white pillars and a wrought-iron fence. You can almost imagine Rhett and Scarlett roaming the grounds. Instead, there's a uniformed security guard in an SUV, and a closer look makes it clear that this Tara is set in the Twilight Zone.

How I came to stand in front of these majestic pillars is another story.

Harry looked up from the screen and felt a lump in his throat. Dammit, the guy could write, he thought. Always looking for the odd angle, always the maverick. You left us too soon, Buzzy. Way too soon.

He glanced across the table at Gabriel who was wolfing down more mashed potatoes, meat loaf, and grits, fried

Southern style and thought that maybe it wasn't too bad a way to spend a weekend coasting along on Bishop's guilty dime. And maybe, just maybe there was a story in all of this somewhere, pressed between the secret pages of Buzzy's conspiracy theories.

I have it from a very reliable source that something's rotten in Memphis, and it's not the ham-hocks left out of the refrigerator overnight. It involves deceased rocker Colton Purcell, the hillbilly king of rock and roll. Or is he deceased? Inquiring minds want to know.

So I find myself standing in front of this ersatz plantation, seeking information about another era, a month before the tenth anniversary of Colton's last breath on the plush carpeted floor of his mansion. I go in through the gate, where it says VISITORS, and show my ID to still another set of security guards. This place has better security than Fort Knox. When I say I'm here to visit one Willard Younger, the guard looks perplexed, but taps the keys of his computer nonetheless. Soon I'm escorted down a long, winding hallway to a room. A sweet looking middle-aged lady in a white nurse's uniform is spoonfeeding a heavyset man with long grayish hair hanging around his shoulders. A fine-looking guitar leans in a corner and a small CD player is next to an equally small television. The lady looks up.

I subsequently find out that she's Nurse Marjorie, Willard's primary caretaker. She'd be the first to tell you that she has the best and most important job in the world. The other nurses beam when they talk about Nurse Marjorie, who's been there longer, and still does more than all the rest of them put together.

"She's always here," says Ms. Clemmons, the nursing

supervisor. "Her dedication to all our patients, especially the work she does with Willard, is an example for us all."

I give Nurse Marjorie the cover story as to why I'm there, and dance around the question I need to ask as delicately as my reporter's ethics will allow. The whole time the hazel eyes behind the unkempt hair seem totally oblivious to my presence.

Willard Younger is autistic. He lives in a world within ours, experiencing the same stimuli, but processing it differently. Facially, his beard and moustache obscure what seems to be a strong chin. His nose is narrow and straight, his hairline the same as that of the original. But what does it for me is the voice.

I wonder where the hell he's going with this? Harry thought, looking up again. The waitress was refilling his coffee cup while talking to Gabriel, asking if they needed anything more, and let the hot liquid flow over into the saucer.

"Oh, my God, I'm sorry," she said, reaching across to grab one of the napkins.

"No harm done, ma'am," Gabe said, smiling.

She beamed and strolled off.

It's the dimples, Harry thought. I wonder if I could have a pair surgically inserted.

He doesn't say much. But, man, can he sing.

"Won't you favor our guest with a song?" Nurse Marjorie asks.

And for a moment I glimpse it: the shining glint of something behind those glazed-over eyes. She reaches over and places the guitar in his hands, which he expertly begins to strum. Nurse Marjorie then places a CD in the player and one of Colton Purcell's old songs begins to play. I recognize it: "Until it's Time for You to Go."

I watch as Willard Younger's fingers begin to move expertly over the frets, blending with the music from the disc player. Nurse Marjorie gradually turns down the volume, but it's hardly noticeable. Willard's voice has merged with the fading vocals of the CD, his rich baritone hitting every note, the fingers smoothly gliding over the metallic strings to recapture the melody.

When the song ends Willard mumbles a "Thank ya. Thank ya very much," and drops his gaze to the floor once more, like a life-size windup doll.

Nurse Marjorie gently removes the guitar and explains that the medication is making him very tired lately.

I stand there, totally stunned. Could it be? Could it really be?

The words get caught in my throat, but I manage to croak out, "Is he really Colton?"

Nurse Marjorie smiles. It's a crafty smile, full of mystical knowledge and serenity.

"Lots of folks round these parts think so, once they hear him sing," she says, using her forefinger to straighten a lock of Willard's errant hair. "But we know better, don't we?"

She looks at him lovingly.

Yes, I think. We do. Or at least, we should.

I turn to leave. I knew I'd stayed until it was time for me to go.

The piece left Harry with a sense of incompletion. Like there was more to come. He looked up from his laptop to see Gabriel staring at him from across the table.

"So did you find out anything yet?" he asked.

Harry shook his head, scribbling in his spiral notebook.

Something was gnawing at him though. Something he was missing. He just didn't know what. A feeling that the answer was there right in front of him, but he couldn't quite see it. The standard obit and article about Buzzy's death hadn't shed much light on things either, other than saying that nine days ago his body had been discovered in the parking garage near the *Mirror*, the victim of an apparent mugging.

A parking garage, Harry thought. What a lousy place to die. Then he smiled. As if there's a good place.

Anyway, he knew he needed more facts, but it didn't look like he was going to get any more of those at this point. He glanced at his watch again. Three thirty-five.

"Buzzy must have been on to something," he said. "The question is, what? And was it something that got him killed?"

"I thought Mr. Nash said he was mugged?"

"Maybe he was," Harry said. "I'm just wondering why a mugger would take something as easily traceable as the laptop computer of a well-known reporter."

Gabriel considered this. "What if they didn't know who he was till afterwards?"

"Hey, whose side are you on here?" Harry said, feigning anger.

Gabriel smiled, showing his dimples again.

"I guess I just can't help playing the devil's advocate today," he said.

"Is that the name of one of your songs?" Harry asked, his cell phone ringing on its belt holder. He reached down and unsnapped it, then smiled as the number on the LCD surprised him. "Do you ever sing 'Don't Ask the Question'?"

Chapter 11

The Right Moves

Corrigan had to keep moving, ambling up the block a few hundred feet, then coming back past the front of the Lucky Nugget again, his eyes scanning the pedestrians as he did so. The sun beat down and he'd already sweated completely through the tan chambray shirt. His light blue hat was showing an incremental sweat stain too, ascending from the hatband. In the five hours since he'd begun the surveillance, he estimated that he'd probably lost three to five pounds of water-weight. Luckily, there were always throngs of people moving around, so he didn't stand out that much. He would have been more comfortable in his car, but cars could be traced, even rentals, and he knew better than to leave a trail. Taking another swig from his water bottle, he leaned against the front of the building and looked at the people moving past him. Behind the dark sunglasses, he looked up and down the street for cop cars. Nothing. None of those bicycle cops either, and he wondered how hard it would be to knock one of them on his ass.

Suddenly, out of the corner of his eye, he saw them approaching, the woman in the picture, her mottled hair pulled back from her head under a baseball cap, her watch on her right wrist, her left arm intertwined with the guy walking beside her. He looked like a basket case. His tongue hung out as he walked, his movements jerky and uncontrolled, the long gray hair bouncing around his shoulders, his mouth jerking open with sudden abruptness, not making any sounds that were decipherable. They carried a large wooden picnic basket and a camera.

"It's just a little bit farther now, dearie," he heard the woman saying as they walked by. "When we get to the room I'll give you some of your medicine."

Finally, he thought, and began his slow ambling walk toward the hotel. It's show time.

Marjorie guided him toward the fancy gold elevators, scanning the crowd as they went. Happy faces, sad faces, drunken faces all passed them like a parade of masks. But none seemed to pay them much attention, which was good. She pressed the button and waited as the doors on one of the cars popped open. As they stepped inside, she pressed number three. Then she saw a big man in a tan shirt moving toward them, bumping into several people as he walked with an air of intent toward the elevators.

Oh, dear, she thought, that poor fellow's sweated right through his clothes. She reached out to hold the doors so the big man could get in, but he continued past, walking with the stagger of someone who's been imbibing too much.

Just as well, she thought. He'd probably be a bit smelly.

The elevator doors started to close, shutting off her view, when a big hand appeared and smacked the auto-retractor. The doors slid open again and the big man stepped in. Marjorie smiled benignly as he glanced at the lighted floor button, then turned away.

You'd think he'd have enough sense to take off those sunglasses inside, she thought as the doors started to close again.

"Hey," someone yelled. "Hold that car, would ya?"

The huge fellow didn't move, but Marjorie did. Being nearer the panel, she reached up and pressed the OPEN

DOOR button. The closing doors stopped and retracted once more.

"Thank ya," said a beefy-looking young man popping his head inside. "Thank ya very much."

Another similarly built man stepped into the car carrying a suitcase under each arm and one in each hand. He was dressed in blue jeans and a dark shirt, almost identically to the first, and both with their hair greasily swept back into exaggerated pompadours.

"Can you hold this door for a minute, ma'am?" the second one asked.

Marjorie nodded and the first one stepped over to a luggage cart and grabbed an additional four suitcases from it.

"Hurry up, will ya, Lance?" the second man said. "You're keeping these folks waiting."

"Sorry," the first one said. He stepped into the car and stretched his lips into a half-sneering type smile that was a fair imitation of the original's. "Could you press number three for me, please, ma'am?"

"Certainly," Marjorie said, then smiled herself. "Why that's our floor too."

"Shucks, we might be neighbors," the first man said. "I'm Lance Fabray and this is my cousin, Powell. We're here for the Colton Purcell Imitators contest."

"Really?" Marjorie said. "I wasn't aware of such a contest."

"Yes siree, ma'am," Powell said. "We woulda got here yesterday but we got kinda unavoidably delayed."

"Think we got the right moves?" Lance asked, twitching his wide pelvis.

Marjorie smiled and cooed in appreciation.

"I'll say you do," she said.

The doors finally closed.

Freeze Me, Tender

"Press four for me, will you," the big man in the tan shirt said as the car started going up. His eyes were still not visible under the dark sunglasses.

Corrigan watched the doors close behind the parade on the third floor and thought how easy it would have been if those two cracker assholes hadn't gotten in at the last minute. But he'd spent the day thinking things through, and it was time to put his backup plan into play. It was only a slight variation anyway.

On the fourth floor he moved purposefully toward the west stairwell. On one of his many jaunts around the area waiting for the pigeons to come home, he'd memorized the layout of the hotel: front and back entrances, emergency exits, employee entrance, and loading docks. Extrapolating on what he knew from his observations inside, he guessed the employee area was located in the rear, as in most hotels. And so was the freight elevator. All he needed now was a key.

Two keys, actually. One master for the room and one to run the freight elevator to take down his load. As he walked he stopped at a collection of several trays on the floor awaiting housekeeping removal. Corrigan collected a few items from each plate, dumping them into the cloth napkin and then pouring some liquid from a half full glass over it. When he got to the stairwell he stripped off his tan shirt and removed a garbage bag from the inside pocket along with a few other items. Running his fingers through his hair, he combed it straight back. The profuse sweating had already plastered it to his head. Next he took out a partial denture of small, crooked teeth. The interior portion was filled with soft wax that held the partial in place over his real teeth. The final addition was a pair of black-framed glasses. There was little he could do to disguise his massive build and height, but he also knew that people tended to focus on a few outstanding characteristics and forget the rest.

He slipped his hat and sunglasses inside the bag along with his shirt. His T-shirt stuck to his body. Peeling it loose, he worked the collected materials inside the napkin with his hands, mixing it thoroughly then smeared it over the front of his shirt. Puffing some air into the garbage bag, he placed the end of the soiled napkin at the open end of the bag and sealed it with his massive fist. Then he slicked back his hair with his other hand and proceeded down the stairs.

As he came out at ground level he turned and went toward the set of double swinging doors that he'd seen the bellman go through earlier with the flowers. As he pushed through, a man in a navy blue blazer glanced up sharply from a desk by the doors. Corrigan knew immediately the guy was hotel security.

"Some drunk threw up all over the place," Corrigan said, holding up the bag. He looked down and pointed to his stained shirt. "Including on me. I'm taking this stuff to laundry." He pushed the bag in the direction of the guard.

"Oh, Jesus, go ahead," the guard said.

Corrigan grinned and headed down the long hallway. He passed back entrances to the various restaurants and ballrooms, the casinos and kitchen. A huge dishwashing machine labored to his right, with a group of Latinos busily chatting as they set up and wiped down the dishes. He continued, figuring now that he was inside, he'd eventually run into the laundry room. And he did. It was huge with at least two dozen large machines in various stages of their respective cycles. No one seemed to pay much attention to him as he went past and grabbed one of the big carts with the high canvas sides. It was full of freshly pressed sheets. Corrigan pushed it down the hall, stopping at a room adjacent to the laundry with Men's Locker Room on the door. Leaving the cart outside, he pushed through the doorway and went in, checking to make sure the room was empty. A pair of sinks, urinals, and an enclosed commode were immediately inside the doors. The room expanded with rows of lockers and a coat rack along the wall. Several sets of tan and white jackets had been left on hangers. Corrigan sifted through them finding one that was almost big enough for him. A bit tight, but it would do. He stripped off his soiled T-shirt and put on the white one from the rack. He went to the sink and rinsed off his hands, then dropped the T-shirt into the toilet and held down the plunger. The pressurized release of water swept the shirt out of sight.

Corrigan smiled.

Some plumber's gonna be a happy camper, he thought. As he turned back he saw a black guy in a navy blazer come in. This guy was short and stocky, with a fade haircut. He held a radio on his right hand and looked at Corrigan suspiciously.

"Do I know you?" the guard asked.

"I just started today," Corrigan said. "Some dude threw up on me and I came down here to change clothes."

The guard nodded fractionally, his eyes still filled with scrutiny.

"Hotel Security," he said, holding up a silver shield. "Let me see your employee ID."

"Sure, officer," Corrigan said. He pointed to the garbage bag on the sink. "It's in there. Like I told you, this guy threw up on my shirt."

The guard nodded, moving closer to him.

Corrigan pulled the napkin out of the bag, then immediately dropped it. As the guard's eyes followed the movement, Corrigan stepped around him and used his right hand to push the guard forward. Looping his huge left arm around the other man's neck, Corrigan quickly brought his right forearm up and caught the guard's neck in a scissor-like grip. The radio slipped from the guard's grasp as his hands tried to unseal the vise-like hold on his neck. But Corrigan used his superior size and weight to bear down, forcing the guard to his knees, then rolling his massive shoulders until he heard the accompanying snap. The guard went limp. Corrigan let him drop to the floor.

Shit, he thought. Now I gotta deal with three instead of two. Got to put this dude on ice for the time being.

Stooping, Corrigan grabbed the body under the arms and lifted it up, the man's head lolling at an unnatural angle. Corrigan carried him to the commode and went inside, setting the man down on the plastic and porcelain throne. He quickly went through the man's pockets, taking his wallet, IDs, security pass, and master keys. As an afterthought, he unbuckled the guy's trousers and pushed them down around his shoes. Corrigan reached in his own pocket and removed his thin leather gloves. After putting them on, he twisted the locking mechanism and stepped out of the stall, muscling the door closed and wiggling the blue plastic wall until the lock caught.

"Take your time," Corrigan said to the closed door, checking to make sure the feet looked natural from under the bottom edge of the stall. "I'll be back in a flash."

After cracking the door slightly to check the hallway, Corrigan, satisfied that it was clear, stepped out and grabbed the edge of the cart. He pushed it slowly down the hall, trying for that unhurried nonchalance of menial laborers everywhere. The freight elevator was just ahead to his left. Stopping, Corrigan took out the ring of keys and began inserting them into the inlaid brass circle. The long key with the even, thinly ground teeth, fit in perfectly and twisted at his touch. The elevator doors opened and Corrigan pushed the cart in. As the doors closed he replaced the key ring in his pocket and looked at the cart. It was certainly big enough to hold the two of them. It would be simpler to just leave them both in the room, but he didn't want them found. A bit more of a risk, but nothing he couldn't handle. After all, that was why he got paid the big bucks. It called for a bit more artistic license. All he had to do was pile some of the linen on top and move them out the dock. His vehicle, a rented van, was parked only a short distance away in the employee section. This one he'd rented with cash. His own cash, and under an assumed name.

That cheap prick Vantillberg, he thought. When this is done, he'd have to see if the old man would let him rough that pretty boy up a bit. Him and his child molesting Latino prince of pop. They woulda loved that little fairy in the joint. The image brought a smile to his face. The elevator stopped at the third floor.

Corrigan pushed the cart out the door and down the hallway. Luckily, it was deserted and he moved to room 335, pausing to knock and say, "Housekeeping," before he inserted the plastic master key card into the lock. He depressed the knob and the door swung inward.

Harry stood by the big guitar and watched the people coming west on Harmon Avenue. It was close to six and she still hadn't showed. Maybe she changed her mind, he thought. Maybe she decided that I'm a loser, and decided to stand me up. Maybe she thinks I'm just after information about Buzzy's death.

Am I? he wondered, then smiled. Don't ask the question . . .

He took a deep breath and rationalized her tardiness. Even though she'd said five forty-five, she'd also said, "give or take a few minutes." He ruminated on what he could remember of the conversation, running it through his mind.

"I'll meet you at the Hard Rock Cafe," she'd said. "It's on Harmon and Paradise Road. I've got to stop at UNLV."

He'd been delighted when she'd called, not realizing until he heard the musical sound of her voice how much he was hoping she'd accept his dinner invitation.

"Taking classes?" he'd asked.

"No, I have to interview a witness," she'd said. He could almost picture her sitting at her desk, talking to him on the phone, no one else around, one leg perhaps tucked under her as she spoke.

Mustn't forget she's a cop, he'd thought.

He heard the tap of the horn and saw her wave as she drove past. It was a black Dodge Intrepid with four doors. Not your typical unmarked squad car, but then again, this wasn't your typical city. He strolled toward the edge of the street, trying to see where she'd disappeared to, but a cluster of cars obscured his vision.

Did the damn traffic ever stop around here? he wondered.

Then he saw her walking toward him carrying a large purse looped over her shoulder. She wore the same outfit as when he'd seen her earlier, the sleeveless light pink blouse, the grayish slacks, her brown hair bouncing just below her jaw line, but she'd obviously redone her make-up. Her face looked fresh with a hint of bluish shadow enhancing her eyes. And she walked with an aura of confidence, which was appropriate for a lady who probably was packing heat in her handbag. At least he figured it would be in her handbag.

His gaze swept over her slim figure. Not too many other places it could be, he thought. The gray-blue eyes flashed behind her lenses as she seemed to catch him staring.

Harry smiled.

"Hi," he said.

"Sorry I'm late," she said. "The interview took a bit longer than I figured."

"No problem. I've been enjoying your nice Nevada weather," he said, trying to think of something clever to say. "How'd the flowers hold up in this heat?"

"Fine," she said, smiling. "They're so pretty. Thank you. How did you know I liked the pink ones?"

"Just a good guesser," he said, feeling a bit more ebullient.

"If you would have only spelled my name right," she said, "the effect would have been perfect."

Harry felt his jaw sag. Her name? Then had a vision of her card: Detective J. Grey, not Gray, like he'd written. But he hadn't been thinking of names with British spellings.

"Sorry about that," he said. "Guess I should've brought my proofreader with me."

Detective Grey laughed and he began to feel a bit more at ease, thinking that this might be just what the doctor ordered as far as exorcising all the bad memories of Karen marrying Bishop, his worries about Lynn, Buzzy's death, and being out here in the apocryphal desert city where the booze flowed like water at an oasis.

"So what was your interview about?" he asked, pulling open the restaurant door for her.

"A case," she said, slipping past him. She flipped her hair. "I thought your card said you promised not to ask me about business?"

"I meant that for Detective G-R-A-Y," he said, grinning.

As she walked ahead of him, he watched and appreciated the slim elegance of her figure, beginning to wonder what she'd look like without the blouse and slacks. Would he be fortunate enough to find out?

I'd better just be grateful for the company of a beautiful woman for some pleasant conversation on a dinner date, he thought, mentally chastising himself. He'd be lucky to get through just that without blowing it. If any information came up about Buzzy's case, so much the better. But getting back into the dating scene, especially with the specter of rehab so fresh in his mind, was problematic to say the least. He suddenly hoped that Detective Grey was still on duty or something so she wouldn't order a pre-dinner drink. Or an after-dinner one either. So he wouldn't have to explain why he didn't.

After being seated in a non-smoking booth, she surprised him by ordering iced tea instead of a cocktail. He ordered one too.

As long as it wasn't from Long Island, he thought.

She looked at him.

"You're a writer, huh?"

He nodded.

"Don't write about this, okay?" she asked, smiling.

"I wouldn't dream of it." He smiled back.

"So I ordered a copy of your book on eBay," she said, taking a sip from her straw.

"You did?"

"*Moon Over the Euphrates*," she said. "How did you come up with that title?"

"Actually, I wanted to call it *Perched on Hell's Apron*," he said. "But my publisher changed it."

Her eyebrows raised quizzically. "You were in the first Gulf War?"

He nodded.

"So was it pretty rough over there?"

Harry shrugged. "For about a hundred hours," he said. "But it was no *Rambo III*. We just had to learn how to stop worrying and love the Scuds."

She smiled. "Really?"

"Yeah, they were so inaccurate and slow, you had to love 'em. Good old Communist technology. Just be glad we didn't sell old Saddam any of ours before the balloon went up."

"How did yours compare to the second one?" she asked.

"Those poor guys in the second one were sitting ducks." Harry noticed Detective Grey blink twice, then smile. But it looked like a reluctant gesture. "Why all the interest in the Gulf Wars?" he asked. "Thinking about getting some Abrams tanks for the PD?"

She smiled again, more genuinely this time. Then he glimpsed something else in the gray-blue eyes: a liquid-like flash that coalesced into a solitary tear that she quickly wiped away.

"Sorry," she said.

He reached across the table and touched her hand.

"You lost somebody in Iraq?" he asked.

She nodded.

"My younger brother," she said. "He was only twenty-two."

Harry rubbed his fingers gently over the back of her hand.

"I'm sorry," he said. "Wounds like that never totally heal."

He felt her hand grip his momentarily and with the electricity of her touch, Harry suddenly felt the surreptitious reason for his original subterfuge fade almost completely away.

Michael A. Black

★ ★ ★ ★ ★

Eric felt the plane begin to bank slightly and the *Fasten Your Seatbelts* light came on. He was seated next to Pablo, who insisted on having the window seat, even though he kept the damn shade down because he was terrified of flying, and had popped enough ludes to drop a horse. He also insisted on wearing a disguise so no one would recognize him.

"I can't be seen flying commercial," he'd said. "I'll be mobbed."

Eric frowned, thinking that the fake mustache and large-brimmed hat wouldn't fool Patti Duke playing Helen Keller, and the real reason he wanted to wear it was because nobody would give a shit if they knew who he was anyway.

He doesn't want the public to know he doesn't have his own plane, Eric added, massaging his forehead with his thumb and forefinger. But at least he agreed to come to Vegas for the big celebration and get this thing with Melissa Michelle nailed down once and for all. And he hadn't pissed and moaned about not getting to go down south of the border to pick up another child prostitute either. For once, the little creep was all business. Maybe that stint in Vegas where they booed him off the stage scared him.

Gant sat to Eric's right reading a magazine. The big guy had been exceptionally silent after the beating Moran had given him. Not that he was ever very talkative. At least not with me, Eric thought. But that was a hell of an ass-kicking. I wonder if Casio will have the two of them whacked once Pablo and the brat are married? Just so it was after Pablo did the Purcell remixes and the record company stock went back up. Who knows, he thought, grinning and nodding as Gant turned to look his way, it could turn out to be a good career move as long as the masters are in the can.

Eric glanced at his watch, wondering if they'd make their scheduled landing time of seven fifteen. He also wondered if good news from Corrigan would be waiting for him when they landed. Leaning back, he closed his eyes and tried to imagine they were on the *Melissa Michelle*. Ladonna would be on her knees in front of him, sucking him off, and he'd have a king-sized joint in his hand and a tray of coke off to the side.

Shit, he thought, opening his eyes. Fat chance of that happening unless things all fall into place. First, Corrigan had to take care of the Memphis problem. Without a trace. But not until he'd been able to use that as leverage against Ladonna. The bitch was sharp, that was for sure. And she wasn't about to let her little cunt of a daughter stay hooked up with a child molesting creep like Pablo. Not for long. She wouldn't be playing ball at all if Melissa Michelle wasn't jonesin' so bad for the Latino Prince of Popoffs, thinking Pablo was her ticket to a road of superstardom just like her dead daddy's. Too bad that Mexican Holiday thing didn't turn out. If that wedding would've stuck, they'd be on a sound stage now doing a "Don't Ask the Question" remix video. He couldn't afford another fuck-up of that magnitude. But this time he did have something in reserve.

I do got that small piece of dynamite information, Eric thought. That'll turn Ladonna's attitude around real fast, once I lay that on her. He smiled at the thought. Just like playing chess. You had to wait for the right time to knock off the other guy's queen.

"This is the captain speaking," the voice came over the intercom. "We'll be landing at McCarran International Airport in Las Vegas in about twenty-five minutes. I have turned on the seat belt light, if you'd kindly return to your seats and buckle up at this time."

Pablo slumbered in the seat next to him, and Eri reached over to fasten the belt for him.

Christ, the little shitbird slept through the whole trip denying me a chance to see the view of the bright lights o Vegas rising out of the desert.

He glanced at his watch and wondered again if Corriga would be waiting in the terminal with some good new when they got down there. If not, he could try calling him But Corrigan had made it clear he preferred to be the caller not the callee. And Eric didn't feel like doing anything t get Corrigan pissed off. Not if he wanted to see the problems taken care of.

Maybe when we land, he thought, I'll find I'm one step closer to getting near the end of this thing. This big, hairy awful, messy thing. As long as I keep making all the righ moves.

Chapter 12

Reaching Out

After talking about Lance Corporal Thomas Grey, and how proud he was to be a U.S. Marine, and how he didn't make it back from the second Iraq war to claim his yellow ribbon, her eyes brimmed over with tears and Harry got lost in them. But after a quick apology, followed by a trip to the ladies' room, she came back looking fresher and prettier than ever. It was in the subsequent conversation, somewhere between the coffee and the dessert, that Harry learned her first name was Janice, and she'd been on the force for six and a half years. He found himself talking about his own experience in the Gulf, his return Stateside, writing his book, getting the accolades, and beginning what he thought was going to be a stellar career.

"Sometimes reality has a way of catching up with you," he said, smiling in a self-effacing sort of way. "What about you? Gonna be Lieutenant Grey someday?"

She smiled and shook her head.

"I actually kind of like it where I'm at," she said. "Most of the time, anyway."

He watched the way she tilted her head when he talked, as if she were trying to catch every word, every nuance.

Maybe this is the start of something good, he thought.

The abruptness of her cell phone startled them both. Detective Grey rolled her eyes and seemed to swear beneath her breath as she reached down and dug in her handbag. As she opened it Harry saw the butt of a Glock pistol. A 9mm from the look of it. She pulled out her cell phone and pressed the button, answering with an exasperated sounding, "Detective Grey."

Harry could hear the indistinct sounds of the voice on the other end, and from the way she'd answered after glancing at the number, he figured it was official.

"Actually, I'm off duty and I'm right in the middle of a nice dinner," she said into the phone, looking over at him.

The voice on the other end said something. She looked down, her lips compressing momentarily.

"I see," she said. "How long ago?"

She listened some more, her eyebrows rising, followed by an, "Okay . . . I'll be there in," she looked at her watch, "fifteen minutes tops. See if you can get Torrey Johnson and his crew to respond, and tell them to wait till I get there."

When she looked up again he felt the connection. Something was up. Something major.

"Who's Torrey Johnson?" Harry asked.

She smiled. "He's the real *CSI*. The best."

"Big case?"

She nodded. "Unfortunately, I have to go. I'm on call and they usually put a team together for a serious crime."

"Regrettable, but understandable," he said, waving to the waitress. "How about we do this again?"

She looked at him from behind the clear lenses.

Looking back Harry thought, I could gaze into her eyes all night.

"I'd like that," she said. "Why don't I call you tomorrow?"

Harry grinned.

"I know this is the new millennium, but isn't the guy supposed to call the girl?"

"Only if the girl isn't a cop," she said, standing. "We can go Dutch."

"Un un," Harry said, reaching over to put his hand on hers. "And I'm not being old-fashioned here. I'm on an expense account and my boss is a prick."

She laughed.

"Is he now?"

"Of the worst magnitude," he said. "But we have an . . . understanding."

It was only after she'd dropped him at his hotel, on her way to the crime scene, that Harry acted on impulse and hailed a cab.

"Follow that Intrepid," he said, getting in. The driver, a middle-aged white guy who looked like he was hoping to enter the Colton Purcell imitator's contest, nodded and took off northbound on Las Vegas Boulevard. As a driver, the guy wasn't too bad. He kept back far enough that they could see her car without being too conspicuous. Harry hoped that she'd be too preoccupied with her call-out to check if anyone was following. Besides, cabs were ubiquitous along the strip. They continued north toward the Fremont District, cutting over on Main and right on Carson. Finally her brake lights flashed on as she slowed at Casino Center Boulevard.

"Looks like she's going to the Nugget," the driver said. "Want me to stop here?"

"Just drive on past and then let me out," Harry said, slipping the guy the fare and a hefty tip.

He worked his way back to the hotel, pausing to check for her in the immediate area, trying to formulate an excuse if she perchance saw him.

I was in the area and I thought I'd stop by . . .

Nah, too lame, he thought.

I wanted to see if I could be of any assistance . . .

Worse still.

Maybe I should just tell her the truth, he thought. That I saw something flash in those blue-gray eyes when she looked up at me as she was talking on the phone.

Some kind of vague connection had sparked in his mind. His reporter's instincts, the ones that Gabriel had questioned, had stirred. Like someone had touched him unexpectedly. A cold finger on his prostate. This involved him somehow. That much he was sure of, but how?

Several marked squad cars had been pulled in front of the place as well as an ambulance and one of those nondescript white sedans with CLARK COUNTY CORONER in big black letters across the side. So it was a big case. A homicide most likely. A death investigation probably wouldn't merit calling her in off duty. He quickly scanned the crowd. No sign of her. Harry straightened his tie, took his *Regency Magazine* Press Pass from his pocket and clipped it to his lapel.

Might as well see how far this gets me, he thought and pushed through the doors. The yellow crime scene tape had been used to block off a corridor to the left. Several sets of uniformed officers were dutifully recording names, dates of birth, and phone numbers from a long line of people standing in the lobby. Some looked like tourists. Others were obviously hotel employees. A female officer held up a hand as Harry approached.

"Sorry, sir, we've got this area temporarily closed," she said. Her nametag said *P. Check*.

"Is that P for Paula?"

She shook her head. "Peggy."

Harry smiled and raised his press pass with forefinger and thumb.

"For the homicide?" he asked. "You got a room where they're gonna brief the press?"

The cop looked at the pass, then at Harry making sure the picture matched.

"It's me," he said. "A few pounds heavier, a little less hair."

The copper smiled.

"I noticed that," she said, and pointed to an anterior office section enclosed by glass walls to the right. "You can wait in there."

He walked over, smoothing his hair with his fingers. *I noticed that,* he thought. Never too late for another smart ass. Peggy Check. With a name like that, she's got no room to talk.

The room was filled with half a dozen or so people, each quietly chatting on a cell phone while pressing keys on their laptops.

Harry wished he'd brought something to look official. He strolled over to the nearest desk, grabbed a bunch of papers and a pen, and began scribbling notes like he was writing a story.

"Doing it the old-fashioned way, huh?" a voice said to his left.

Harry looked and saw an older guy in a dark blazer sitting behind one of the desks drinking from a Styrofoam cup. His face was grizzled and flecked with age spots. He held out his hand.

"Meger's the name," the old guy said, grinning with a dentures-perfect smile. "Jim Meger. Hotel services."

"Harry Bauer." They shook hands. "*Regency Magazine.*"

"*Regency Magazine*? What the hell *you* here for, then? I figured this would attract the local guys, but hell, not some slickster like you." He scrutinized the press pass. "Where the hell you based out of anyway?"

"Chicago," Harry said. "But I was in the neighborhood.

Besides, I'm trying to impress a local editor. Applied for a job at the *Mirror*."

Meger raised his eyebrows.

"Got the Vegas itch, huh?" He glanced around furtively, then motioned Harry closer. Leaning down, Harry caught a whiff of what was really in the old guy's cup. It looked dark like coffee, but he'd added a lot of special sixty-proof sweetener. He positioned himself so that Harry's body blocked the view from outside and took out a silver flask. After unscrewing the cap, he poured a bit of the amber colored liquid into the cup, then swirled it around. Scotch, Harry knew immediately. Johnnie Walker Red.

Meger held the flask toward Harry, who licked his lips quickly, then shook his head.

"Aww, go on," the old guy said. "It may be hours before they get back to us."

Harry ran his tongue over his teeth, still looking at the flask. He shook his head again.

Meger frowned and replaced the cap.

"Boy scouts," he muttered. "The whole god damned world's filling up with them." He slipped the flask back into his inside coat pocket and sampled the cup.

"You know what happened?" Harry asked.

"Yeah, I know. I know plenty." A venal gleam came into his eyes, and he held up his thumb and index finger, rubbing them together. "How much would it be worth to you to find out exactly what old Jimbo knows?"

"Depends on what you're selling," Harry said. He reached in his back pocket and began to take out his wallet.

Meger hissed quickly, the ends of his mouth turning downward as if he'd just swallowed something sour.

"Ain't you never heard that discretion is the better part of valor?" he whispered.

"Sure I have," Harry said, slipping a twenty from his billfold and conspicuously folding it in quarters. "My friend President Jackson used to say it all the time."

Meger licked his lips and motioned toward a large silver coffee urn and some adjacent stacks of Styrofoam cups on a nearby table.

"Grab yourself one and we'll talk," he said.

Harry went to the table, filled a cup, and returned. He sat on the desk next to Meger, who took a few swallows, rolled his eyes around the room quickly, and reached up to snatch the folded twenty. He motioned Harry to lean in closer. The smell of the booze on the old guy's breath made Harry keep his distance.

"They were looking for one of the hotel security guys," Meger said. "He'd been on a check of the employee locker room after somebody reported a stranger roaming around." He took another sip, obviously getting more sweetness in this one, and exhaled a short, satisfied breath. "They tried calling him on the radio, but he didn't answer. Finally, one of the other guards found him in the shitter, door closed, deader than a doornail."

Harry's brow furrowed. "How'd it happen?"

Meger scrunched up his face and shrugged.

"Hell if I know," he said. But then he raised both eyebrows momentarily and grinned again. "I heard somebody saying that his head was hanging down awful funny. Like his neck was broken." He drained the rest of the liquid in his cup, and held it out towards Harry for a refill. "He wasn't a bad guy. Roscoe Kelly was his name. A lousy place to buy the farm, huh? The toilet of a Las Vegas hotel."

"As if there's a good place," Harry said, jotting down a few notes, before taking the old guy's cup over to the urn. He filled it up halfway, then looked at his own. Going back to the chair, he handed Meger his, and watched him remove the silver flask from his pocket again.

"Say, pops," Harry said, holding out his own cup now. "Lemme see what you got in there."

After helping Gant load Pablo into a waiting limousine, Eric dialed the cell phone number again, and this time he got an answer. He held the flame from the lighter to the end of his cigarette and said, "Hey, bro, tell me the news is good."

He heard nothing but silence on the other end.

"You there?"

"Yeah," Corrigan said. "Where you at?"

"We just got into McCarran," Eric said. He was starting to feel that familiar set of fingers roaming over his bowels. "You get it done?"

"Un un."

"What?"

"They weren't in the room," Corrigan said. "I followed them up there, but there were too many people around. By the time I got back, they'd boogied. Something must've spooked her."

"Spooked her? What kind of bullshit is this?" Eric took a copious drag on the cigarette and exhaled half of it. The residual smoke curled from his lips with each word. "How in the fuck could *that* happen?"

He waited, but Corrigan made no reply.

"Well, how much longer is this gonna take then?" Eric asked. He brought the cigarette up to his lips again and suddenly became aware of a small boy watching him smoke. He turned away from the prying eyes and said, "I thought you were supposed to be the best."

"I am the best," Corrigan said. "But I got to lay low for

a while. I had a complication."

"A complication? What the fuck's that mean?"

"See it on the fucking news, shitbird, and watch what you say to me."

Eric swallowed, thinking he'd better get control of his anger before the big ape came over to the airport looking for him.

"Maybe I can call Casio and have him bring in somebody to help you," Eric said.

"I don't need no help."

"You just said you gotta lay low, didn't you, for Christ's sake?" Eric waited a few beats before he added, "Look, the old man wants this thing wrapped up by the weekend. And there's no way I can do that with these loose ends flopping around."

He could hear the steady pace of the other man's breathing over the phone.

"You do what you gotta do," Corrigan said finally.

Harry stood in the hallway looking at the dark liquid in the cup. He licked his lips, then set the cup on top of an unoccupied slot machine and took out his cell phone. It was eight-oh-five. That meant it was after ten in Chicago. He dialed quickly, pressing the buttons with trembling fingers. But it was a familiar trembling. Like an old friend who'd come back to visit him.

It rang twice, three times, four, and then someone picked it up.

"Al? It's Harry Bauer."

"Harry," the voice on the other end said, drawing the syllables out. "How you doing?"

Harry glanced at the cup and sighed. "I been better."

"Any lapses?"

"Not yet, but I'm looking for a familiar hole to crawl into and hide."

"Don't do it, Harry. Where you at now?"

"Hotel. Just outside the bar." He looked over and saw the yellow crime scene tape blocking off the entrance, and he was suddenly thankful for the flimsy plastic barrier.

"Go outside. I'll come for you. Where you at exactly?"

Harry snorted a chuckle. "No, Al, I'm in Vegas."

"Vegas? Las Vegas, Nevada?"

"Yeah. I'm on assignment."

"Okay, give me your number, go step outside in the air, and I'll call you back in ten minutes. Got it?"

Harry licked his lips. The smell of the Scotch was separating itself from the coffee in the cup. He could almost taste it.

"Got it?" Al's voice boomed from the phone.

"Yeah," Harry said. He told him the cell phone number and terminated the call. The cup, almost at eye level on top of the slot, seemed to call out to him. A gaggle of voices from down the corridor broke his fixation. One of them, a female's, sounded so much like Detective Grey that he grimaced. But it wasn't her. Taking one more look at the cup, he breathed in and exhaled, turning for the main exit. The same female officer who stopped him before gave him a questioning look.

"Gonna get some air," he said, and moved outside. The night air was dry and warm, and he immediately began to feel himself sweat. He looked up and down the street, the neon brightness canceling out the impending darkness. Cars rolled by, people walked past him. A strikingly beautiful woman, dressed to the nines in black stiletto heels, smiled alluringly and asked if he wanted some action. Before he could reply, his cell rang.

130

"Here's where you want to go," Al's voice said. The blinking lights turned the paper green, red, then amber as he scribbled the address and hailed a cab.

He thanked Al who said he'd stay on the line until Harry arrived at his destination. He was ready for the strange, yet ultimately familiar surroundings, rows of metallic folding chairs, a large card table, and plenty of strong dark coffee. As he talked with Al in the cab, Harry could almost see the group of patient, expectant, and drawn faces as he anticipated making the customary introduction: "Hello, my name is Harry, and I'm an alcoholic."

Chapter 13

Don't Ask the Question . . .

Afterwards, Harry had a cab drop him off a few blocks from his hotel and strolled along the strip. His intention was to let the night air clear his head of the stale cigarette fumes that had wafted over him at the meeting. He was glad that he'd never smoked. One addiction was enough for anybody, he thought as he watched an ersatz volcano erupt in front of one of the plush hotels. More like a belch than an eruption, but totally appropriate for a desert mirage with pretty impressive pyrotechnics for a regular feature. Besides that, the night air was hot. Dry, but hot. He felt like he was walking in a sauna.

He passed several more incredibly large hotels, sanitized white mortar set behind dancing fountains. But there was no breeze to blow any of the cool moisture his way, and by the time he reached his hotel he felt thirsty as hell and longed for one of the cold bottles of water that he knew would be upstairs. His laptop was there too, and in it the last of Buzzy's columns. He hoped that somewhere in them a clue waited. Something was bothering him. Some recent bit of information, but it danced just beyond the cognitive reach of his memory. Two matching pieces that he'd failed to connect. But he felt like he was looking at the pieces of this oversized jigsaw puzzle with all the pieces face-down. He needed to review the whole picture. Like Buzzy would have done. Still, this was the place for disjointed things coming together, he figured as he glanced at the sleeping lions behind the glass walls. A false volcano that belched "lava-water" every forty minutes, while some phony pirates stormed a stationary ship down the block, and the king of the beasts transplanted from Africa so he could sleep a few floors under some tourists.

Upstairs he checked his messages and e-mail. Tim had sent him a few more articles on Buzzy's death. He scanned them quickly, but neither gave much more information than he already knew. Standard pieces for a violent death of a regional celebrity. Hardly more than your basic obit, he thought. I guess Buzzy was no Colton Purcell.

After taking another cold bottle of spring water from the refrigerator, Harry flipped on the television to keep him company as he slipped the secret disk the girl at the *Mirror* had given them. Given Gabe, more accurately. That kid had charisma, that was for sure. Maybe, just maybe, he was the illegitimate progeny of a brief fling between a dead icon and his now-deceased backup singer.

"Mess with me and you're messing with trouble," Colton Purcell's voice said from the television speaker. Harry turned. A black-and-white picture of the young singer in *King Rebel*, dark hair askew on his forehead, broad shoulders swept back under a tight leather jacket, the narrow nostrils flaring on the handsome face, the regal head cocked at a slight angle . . .

Harry hit the remote, but another, more sanitized version of Colton came on. One of his post-*Rebel* movies where he was slightly older and played one of the customary youngish, down-on-his-luck drifters who arrived someplace, sang a few songs, broke a few hearts, got into a couple of fistfights, and then walked off the sound stage with the girl at the end. Hardly better acting, but the undeniable charm and charisma came through even on the small screen. In some respects, Harry thought, Colton transcended the sub-standard material he was given.

"His movies woulda sold even if they'd a had numbers instead of titles," Harry remembered Big Daddy saying in that interview. "Folks just wanted to see him perform. To sing. He was something, all right." Now another little piece of the Colton Purcell legend had slipped way with his manager's passing. A suicide, he remembered the Memphis cop saying. But the signature on the note . . .

Could that be what was bothering me? Harry wondered.

It hadn't looked like the final scrawling of a depressed man.

But still, the photos told the tale.

Or did they?

He pulled them out and shuffled through them, remembering the sock on the jaw he'd gotten from those two Colton-imitating idiots. His jaw was still a little bit purple. He wondered if Janice Grey had noticed. She hadn't mentioned it, but then again, their beautiful dinner was cut short by a murder. To a girl used to seeing such violence, a little bruise on the chin was probably small potatoes.

Harry heaved a sigh and hit the remote again. A music video flashed as pictures of Colton from an old movie appeared in conjunction with a bunch of silhouetted modern dancers writhing to the beat of "Don't Ask the Question." He clicked back to *King Rebel*, then moved the mouse on his laptop so he could open the disk and typed in "Jenna," the girl intern's name. A selection of files popped up and he scanned them, seeing some with titles and others just saying fragments, bits and pieces, or notes of interest. He selected one called "King of the Hustlers" and waited while it loaded.

Freeze Me, Tender

In This Corner
By Buzzy Sawyer
King of the Hustlers
(In Them Old Cotton Fields Back Home)

There's something about the way Big Daddy Babcock talks about his most famous protégé, Colton, "The King" Purcell. I can sense a reverence in his tone, as if he were in church and he was some back-woods preacher telling me how he'd been born again after seeing the sun come up over the mountain.

And the room we're in resembles a church a little bit. High vaulted ceiling and teakwood panels, a beautiful stained-glass window along the top, and picture after picture of Colton Purcell hanging on the wall, depicting the singer in virtually every phase of his illustrious career.

"You see, son," Big Daddy tells me in his finely polished Southern drawl. He grips the lapel of his white sport coat with one hand while holding the other toward the last two suspended picture frames. "Most people think that I viewed Colton only as a commodity. An image to be marketed and sold, but nothing could be further from the truth."

He removes a hand-rolled cigar from his pocket and dips it into his mouth, wetting the brown paper before patting his pockets for a lighter.

I take mine out and hold the flame in front of him. He nods a thanks, but makes no offer to give me one of his cigars.

But that's okay. He's already told me they're Cuban, and for an old Communist fighter like me, anathema.

"Actually," Big Daddy continues after taking a couple long draws, "I was his best friend." The old man smiles

nostalgically. "I suppose surrogate father might be a little more accurate. But when I found him doing those hayride shows down in Texarkana, I knew." He blows a cloud of smoke in my direction. "Yeah, I knew, sure as we're standing here, that he was a once-in-a-lifetime discovery."

Big Daddy points to the next to last picture frame. It's a black and white 8x10 of him standing next to a large metallic cylinder. Two handles form a clamp on the top lid, and a suspended chart hangs in the background. The lettering on the chart is too small to read, but I imagine it says, Purcell, Colton G. August 13, 1996. The tank is shiny stainless steel and is filled with liquid nitrogen having a temperature of minus 196 degrees Celsius, or, for you non-metric folks, minus 320 degrees Fahrenheit.

"That's our last public appearance," Big Daddy says. "And he wanted it that way. Them there tanks are big enough to hold four bodies inside, but that one is specially designed just for him."

Fit for a king, I say to myself.

To prepare the bodies for the freezing all the blood is gradually replaced with glycerol to prevent ice formation, and a gradual cooling process is begun. The corpse, or "patient" as the folks at Cryogen Life like to call their cadavers, is then submerged in a vat of silicone oil, temperature minus 79 degrees Celsius, and slowly cooled down for a period of five days in liquid nitrogen. Then they're ready for their cylinder for the next hundred and fifty years or so. Long enough, many who've undergone the procedure believe, for medical science to perfect a cure for what killed them in the first place. There's another scheme propagated by the Cryogen Life folks about growing a "new" body, but that's a whole other story.

"But this here is my most prized possession," Big Daddy says, holding his palm toward a white silk scarf pressed behind pristine glass. There is no discernible dust, no unseemly fingerprints, just the white scarf on black velvet behind a clear sheen of brightness.

"It's from Colton's last concert," he explains. "After he died, I had it mounted here. I like to look at it and remember what he was."

Harry stopped reading and took a swig of his bottled water.

Most prized possession, he thought. He picked up the Polaroids of the Babcock suicide again and shuffled through them until he found the one displaying the ligature. Would he use something like that to hang himself? Maybe he wasn't thinking straight . . . or maybe he didn't really care as much as he pretended to. Harry went back to the screen.

Big Daddy continues to look wistfully at the framed scarf.

"Maybe you could find a new singer," I offer. "I'm sure there are a lot of talented young kids who would jump at a chance to have you as their manager."

The old man turns to me, looking genuinely shocked.

I try a weak smile, but why do I feel like I've just accidentally asked the Pope to bless a condom in my wallet?

"Sir, you forget yourself," he admonishes. "I already have a job, you see." He turns and looks back at the white scarf, suspended forever behind a pane of crystal clarity. "I represent Colton Purcell."

Next: Dealing with the truth.

I wonder what that means? Harry thought, raising his

eyebrows as he closed out the document. It almost had the feel of an ongoing series. He remembered at least two other articles on Purcell that Buzzy'd written. One on how they found the bloated Colton collapsed on the floor of his bedroom with a couple of vials of prescription meds in his hand, and another one on that little creep, Pablo, and Purcell's daughter. Something about some shenanigans in Mexico. But that one had come out a few weeks before. Plus, Buzzy'd titled this column "King of the Hustlers." That didn't sound much like homage. Could that have been the reason he'd been killed? Or did he simply get caught up in a random act of violence?

He went back to the file lexicon and checked to see what columns he had left to read. Two more: "The Frosty Truth," and "Beyond a Doubt." He yawned. Despite the coffee he'd had at the meeting he felt a wave of fatigue roll over him.

Harry realized the movie had ended and a series of local commercials began blasting. He picked up the remote and changed the channel.

Colton Purcell's image came back on singing, "Don't ask the question, if you don't wanna hear the answer."

Chapter 14

Beyond Any Doubt

Slats of midmorning sunlight filtered in like probing fingers through the openings in the several sets of long Venetian blinds suspended in the large picture windows. The bright light looked almost like sets of bars on the cool, brown floor tiles. Corrigan was slipping another forty-five pound plate on the Olympic-sized bar when he saw the guy come in the door of the gym. There was something about him that looked imposing. Tapered build, jet-black hair, wraparound sunglasses. The guy was wearing a navy polo shirt that showed off his muscles. It looked like he was strong and quick. He leaned over and spoke to the babe behind the desk, who looked around, then pointed over in Corrigan's direction. That's when Corrigan figured, beyond any doubt, that it was him.

He slipped another plate on the other side of the bar and moved around to the bench. Corrigan's gray sweatshirt, which had the sleeves chopped off to accommodate his large vein-covered arms, was soaked with the sweat of a long, continuous workout. But the anger welling up inside him that Casio would dare send somebody to check on him, that the old man would think for a minute that he wasn't totally capable of handling things, that they'd have the unmitigated gall to send him a "helper". . .

He felt the surge of adrenaline and knew he would get a good pump from this set. The guy in the polo shirt stopped in front of him. Corrigan was at least half a foot taller and took some pleasure in being able to look down at the other man.

"You Corrigan?" the guy said. He made no effort to shake hands, which was good. For him, anyway. The way Corrigan was feeling he probably would have forced him down to his knees if they did.

"Yeah," he said, pausing a few moments more, extracting what psychological advantage he could from his superior height. But the other man seemed unfazed.

He took off his sunglasses, folded them, hooked them into the opening of his shirt, and said, "I'm Jack Moran."

Corrigan nodded and sat down, lying backward and sliding under the suspended bar.

"Give spot, would ya?"

Moran nodded and moved behind the bench. He stood over Corrigan. Now it was his turn to look down. Corrigan grabbed the bar with the classic weightlifter's grip, fingers and thumbs curled around from the same side.

"Need a lift off?" Moran asked.

Corrigan snorted. "Nah. It's only three fifteen. I'm just warming up."

With that said, he hoisted the bar from the two metallic supports and began doing his reps, making sure that he lowered the bar almost touching his chest each time. He did a quick set of five and then set the bar back in the holders.

Moran stepped back.

"Good set," he said. "You didn't even need me."

Corrigan sat up, thinking, *Yeah. And I don't either.*

"You look like you do some lifting, Moran. Want to try a set?"

Moran shrugged and held his hands indicating his clothes.

"I ain't exactly dressed for the occasion," he said.

"Yeah, I can see that. But I don't let nobody watch my back till I checked them out. Personally." Corrigan stood and slapped the bar. "This too heavy for you? Want me to strip a few plates off?"

Moran stared at Corrigan for a moment, then shook his head. He carefully removed his sunglasses from their perch on his shirt, and then took off the garment, folding it in quarters before setting it on a nearby stool.

Corrigan looked appraisingly at the lattice-work of blue and black tattoos covering the other man's upper arms, chest, and shoulders.

"Where'd you serve your time?" he asked.

"Here and there," Moran said, sitting down on the bench and sliding into place. "Soledad, Stateville. Did some Federal time, too." He gripped the bar as Corrigan moved around to the spotter's position. But Moran was already pumping out reps. He did five with accomplished ease and replaced the bar with a precise metallic click and sat up.

"Soledad, huh?" Corrigan asked. "You know old Danny Forbes?"

Moran regarded the other man without so much as a change in his expression.

"We mighta bumped into each other," he said. Then he pointed to the bar. "You gonna put some real weight on that thing?"

Corrigan exhaled through his nose, nostrils flaring. Stooping, he grabbed another forty-five pound plate, indicating for Moran to do the same.

Corrigan took a few deep breaths, staring intensely at the wall, then resumed his spot on the bench. Slowly, he adjusted his position under the bar, curling his fingers around the cross-checked sections of the handles. He wore no gloves, but the skin on his hands was thick and tough, with a layer of heavy calluses. After two more quick breaths he snatched the bar from its holders and held it above him. Lowering it slowly, he arched his back as he forced the weight back upward. He lowered and raised it again. After the third rep Moran's hands hovered close to the bar's center.

"Come on," he said, "two more."

Corrigan's face was reddening as he lowered the bar again and raised it with more difficulty this time. "One more," he said, his voice a muffled growl.

He lowered the bar to his chest, then began his final rep, the veins seeming to pulsate as he pushed upward, his arms freezing in place right before the final completion. The bar remained frozen for a moment, then Moran gripped it with two fingers.

"Come on, you can do it," he said. "Push."

Corrigan straightened his arms and Moran helped him guide the bar back into place.

"Good set," he said.

Corrigan sat up, massaging his biceps. He looked at Moran and nodded.

"You gonna try it?"

Moran moved around to the front of the bench without speaking. He sat down and positioned himself, gripping the bar in similar fashion, but taking a slightly wider grip than Corrigan had. After pumping a few deep breaths in and out, he snatched the bar from the metal rungs and began his routine. He did the first one easily, then the second, and the third rep came with measured difficulty, and he held the bar with his arms locked for a moment, as if contemplating replacing it in the holders. Corrigan moved forward, hovering above him and looking down at the other man's face.

"One more," he said. "I got you spotted."

Moran lowered the bar so that it barely touched his chest, then his whole body seemed to writhe as his back arched. The bar rose upward steadily, slowing as he reached the end of his push, freezing at virtually the same point that Corrigan had. Corrigan held his extended index fingers under the bar using miniscule effort to help raise it. Moran grunted heavily and managed to finally straighten his arms, his triceps bulging in bas-relief, letting the bar slip back in the resting place.

He sat up and took a few breaths.

"Not bad for coming in cold," Corrigan said. A hint of grudging admiration was in his voice. "I had you figured for a body-builder. All show and no strength."

Moran nodded, standing. A trickle of sweat rolled down between well-developed pectoral musculature.

"Well, things ain't always how they look," Moran said, reaching for his shirt. "Now, if you're through playing, we can go somewhere and talk about business."

Corrigan grinned back. The adversarial tone was back in his voice when he said, "Sure we can. Just let me hit the showers first."

Eric watched the disappointment spread across Melissa Michelle's face as her head turned from side to side, surveying the crowded waiting room of the airport. He reflected that she had her mother's looks, all right. More like her than her old man, he guessed, which was good for a chick. Still, only a few of the other people showed any indication that they recognized her or Ladonna. Celebrity without sacrificing anonymity, he thought.

"Where's Pablo?" Melissa Michelle asked as she approached Eric.

Ladonna, followed by the hulking Samoan, brought up the rear.

"He couldn't make it," Eric said, trying to effect a sympathetic expression. He watched the brat's face pucker.

"What?"

She seemed genuinely wounded.

"Yeah," he continued, shooting her what he hoped looked like a commiserating look. "He had to go to the doctor. Rhinoplasty problems."

"Huh?" Melissa Michelle asked.

"Rhinoplasty," Eric said, touching his nose. Actually, he was only telling sort of a white lie. They'd had to force a hose up Pablo's nose and down his throat to pump his stomach. He'd insisted on slamming down some Ritalin after they got to the hotel to counteract the ludes he'd taken for the flight. Then he'd been up all night surfing the web for kiddie porn sites, until he decided to take some more downers to catch a nap. When Gant was unable to wake him, after he fell asleep eating a Brazil nut, they were afraid he'd choke. Luckily, they'd been able to get a doctor to discreetly respond and do the old stomach pump. God, it was horrible to watch. The doc squeezing the suction bulb and the yellowish bile and capsules squirting out of the tube and into that plastic basin.

"His nose?" Melissa Michelle said. "He's got some problem with his nose?"

"You don't really think it got that way naturally, do you?" Ladonna said, intruding into the conversation. She brushed off Melissa's "Oh, Mother please," and continued walking by, saying to him, "Make sure our luggage gets to our hotel, will you?"

Like she's some fucking queen, Eric thought.

He watched her take out her cell phone, punch in an

eleven-digit number, and place the phone by her ear.

"Montgomery Spangler, please," Ladonna said into the phone.

That piqued Eric's interest. He quickened his step so he could catch snippets of this side of the conversation.

"Tell him it's Ladonna Purcell," she said as she walked.

Eric was almost even with her now, and he glanced over his shoulder to see where the big ape bodyguard was. Satisfied that he wasn't paying much attention to him, Eric focused on listening and extrapolating on the one-sided conversation.

"Montgomery, it's Ladonna. Did they find him?" She slowed slightly, but kept moving toward the exit doors. Eric hoped they'd have to wait for a taxi.

"What do you mean, 'not yet'?" she asked, her tone redolent with irritation. "I thought I told you to put somebody good on it."

She stopped cold, listening. Eric caught a glimpse of her face, which was pinched tight. He felt a little tickle in his gut.

"Montgomery, that's not acceptable," she said. "I want him found now. Do you know how long it's been?" She listened again. "How could something like this happen? I thought that place was supposed to be the best? It costs enough, for Christ's sake." She paused, listening. "Well, you do that. Now. Call me back as soon as you find out anything. I've got to know he's safe." Before she terminated the call she added, "And this has got to be kept quiet, understand?" She stuck the phone back in her purse.

Eric caught the same strained expression on her face as he moved alongside and asked, "Everything okay?"

She glanced at him, pursed her lips, and then continued

walking as the automatic doors slid open and they were out on the sidewalk.

Maybe, just maybe, before this is over, Eric thought, hailing a cab, I'll have a chance to try out those lips.

He grinned and did a quick two-step so he could open the door of the taxi for Ladonna. The big Samoan slipped into the front seat and Eric made a move to get in the back. Ladonna glared at him, letting him know that wasn't a good idea. "I'll call you later," she said, brushing him off like he was nothing more than the hired help. The stuck-up bitch. But he could tell she was still worried. The strain was getting to her.

So, he thought as he stood there watching the cab drive off, that crazy fucking reporter must've had the straight scoop after all.

"So did that nice Detective Southerland get ahold of you yet?" Mabel's voice asked from the other end of the line.

Marjorie glanced around at the mention of the policeman's name. As if the walls in the small hotel coffee shop had ears.

"No," she said. "And, Mabel, I have to ask you something."

"What is it, dear?"

"Did you send any flowers to us at the hotel? A dozen roses? With a card?"

"Oh, mercy no," Mabel said. "I mean, I intended to give you a card when you got back, of course, but I'm on a fixed income. I couldn't really afford to send anything that expensive."

"That's all right," Marjorie said quickly. She'd figured as much. Her mind raced, unsure of how much to confide in her friend.

"Did someone send you roses, dearie?"

"Yes, but. . . ." She let the sentence trail off, thinking how an alarm bell had gone off in her head when she'd read the inscription on the card. These must have cost a small fortune, and Mabel was, as she said, on a fixed income. It had seemed much too extravagant a gift to actually be from her friend. And the inscription, *Congratulations.* Marjorie knew someone as old-fashioned as Mabel would have specified, *Wishing you much happiness.*

"Well, who was it?" Mabel's voice intruded. "Who sent you the flowers?"

"Never mind," Marjorie snapped, regretting seconds later that she had sounded short with her friend. She sighed. "I'm sorry. It's just that things have been . . . kind of hectic."

She heard Mabel's chuckle.

"That's okay, dearie. You should have been around me back when my Henry asked me to marry him. I spent the whole day practicing writing Mrs. Henry Crawford. Oh, lordy, I was a wreck—"

"Mabel," Marjorie said, again more sternly than she intended. "I may need your help, okay?"

"Certainly, dear."

Marjorie sighed, glancing over at the table where he was sitting eating his soup. He'd been doing so much better since she'd started weaning him off the stronger medications.

"We're not staying at the Nugget any more," Marjorie said. "And if that detective calls back, tell him you don't know where we are, okay?"

"Is something wrong, dear?" The old woman's tone became serious.

"I may be in a little trouble at work," she said. "That's all."

"I see."

"Anyway, we had to leave that hotel and we're staying at another one now. I'll call and give you the number later."

"Marjorie," Mabel's voice sounded concerned. "Is there anything more I can do?"

"No, not now," Marjorie said, sorting through her wallet for the card. She found it, took it out, and looked at it. "I think I know someone here who can help me."

"Mr. Bauer," James Nash said, a frown creasing his expansive forehead as he held out a big hand.

Harry shook it and flashed a smile trying to warm the other man up. But all Nash did was heave a sigh.

"If this keeps up, I just might take you up on that offer to go on-staff here," Nash said. Before Harry could reply, the other man turned and bellowed out instructions to someone to get moving on that latest Colton Purcell imitator contest. "We need profiles of the first group of imitators. I'm sending a photographer over there at three."

"Okay, boss," an anonymous voice called out.

Harry caught a glimpse of the cute little intern, Jenna, as she walked past clutching a sheaf of papers to her chest like a schoolgirl.

But after all, he thought, that's what she is, right? He grinned at her and got a quick, lips-only smile in return. Probably was hoping that Gabe was with me, he thought.

Nash scratched his neck and turned back to Harry with the residual frown.

"Now what can I do for you *this* time?" he asked.

Harry took a deep breath.

"Mr. Nash, I know I've been sort of a pain in the ass," he began.

"You have a talent for understatement," Nash said, his lips stretching into a half-smile.

Harry laughed slightly. This was getting off to a better start than the last time.

"I've been going over some of Buzzy's old columns," he said. "I'm convinced he was onto a big story involving Colton Purcell. He left this incomplete column called 'Beyond Any Doubt.'"

"Say what?" Nash said in mock surprise. "Pardon me while I yell 'Stop the presses.'"

"Look, I know this may seem kinda far out, but I'm not totally convinced that Buzzy's death was a random mugging."

The frown returned to Nash's face.

"Mr. Bauer, I spent a lot of years putting up with Buzzy's crackpot theories about a conspiracy behind every corner, nothing being what it seemed, and black helicopters in the skies." He pushed his glasses up higher on his nose and crossed his arms across his massive chest. "But he was one of my star columnists here. People read him, liked him, and if it meant putting up with a little bullshit to sell papers and keep circulation up, so be it. But you, on the other hand, I owe nothing to. Absolutely nothing."

"All I want to do is find out more about what he was working on. Maybe I could develop it into something."

Nash looked away, snorting and frowning again, then back to Harry.

"Haven't we already done that?" He glanced over and squinted in Jenna's direction. "I heard about the disk, and I didn't say nothing. But like I told you before, I'm sorry about Buzzy's death, but at some point you have to bury the past and move forward."

"Hey, boss," someone called. "There's a lady on the phone wanting to talk to Buzzy. What should I tell her?"

Nash rolled his eyes. "How the hell she get through? Tell

her he ain't here no more."

"Can't I at least look through his desk? Maybe he left something behind that might be significant."

"Clues?" Nash asked skeptically. "You been reading too much Nancy Drew."

"So you're saying you won't help me then?"

"Boss," the reporter called again. "She says it's real important and that she has one of his business cards. It's about what really happened to Colton Purcell."

"Tell her to go to—" He compressed his lips, exhaled heavily, and said, "Put her on hold. I'll speak to her in a moment." He turned back to Harry. "See what you started?"

Harry grinned. "Maybe I should talk to her?"

Nash's eyes widened and he smiled slightly.

"Maybe," he laughed. "Since you are hanging out here so much, I should put you to work."

Chapter 15

Password Protected

After renting a car, again on the magazine's dime, Harry took a combination of south and west streets until he arrived on Green Valley Parkway in the suburb of Henderson. From there he followed the route James Nash had described to the little yellow stucco house with the patio roof extending off to the side covering two cars: a beat-up '93 silver Buick Skylark and a beige Honda Civic. Not the kinds of cars he'd have thought Buzzy would be caught dead in. But then again . . .

Harry stopped in front of the house, slipped on his sport coat and adjusted his tie. Christ, it was hot. As soon as he'd stepped out of the air conditioning he began to sweat. Even the sidewalk seemed to radiate heat. He was grateful that the door was in the shade. He rang the bell and listened. Inside he could hear the sound of a vacuum cleaner. He rang again, hoping it would lead to a passage out of this furnace. So much for the vaunted "dry heat" of Nevada.

The sound of the vacuum cleaner ceased. The inside door was opened by a young woman with her blond hair tied back in a pony tail. It made him wonder if he had the right house. Through the screen a bit of frigid air drifted toward him, teasing in its icy coolness.

"Mrs. Sawyer?" he asked.

She nodded, her eyes wary.

"My name is Harry Bauer." He paused, then continued. "I was a friend of Buzzy's. I just heard what happened."

"Bauer?" she said. "Just a minute." The door closed and

Harry found himself sweating even more profusely. He thought about ringing the bell again. Not just ringing it, but leaning on it. Anything to get out of this heat, he thought. It was either that or go and sit in the car.

But the inside door opened again, and the woman was there, holding a book. She had the pages flipped to the front and the back cover open in her hands. Harry blinked and through the screen saw a picture of a younger version of himself in desert camouflage on the back flap. ***Moon Over the Euphrates***.

"It's me," he said. "A few pounds heavier and a little less hair."

She looked at him, then back at the photo and nodded.

At least she didn't say, "I noticed that," like that smart-ass cop, he thought.

"Come in, Mr. Bauer," she said, unlocking the screen door and opening it.

Grateful, Harry smiled and thanked her.

The inside of the place was almost Spartan-like. No pictures on the walls, a small TV in one corner on top of a large cardboard box, two chairs with sheets thrown over them, and more boxes stacked in the corner.

"I'm Linda Sawyer," she said. "Pardon the mess. I'm moving, you see, and trying to get everything packed up." She gestured at the vacuum cleaner. "We were only renting, so if it's clean, I'll hopefully get the security deposit back." She sat on one of the sheet-covered chairs and gestured toward the other one.

Harry sat down, his eyes still surveying the small, but tidy room.

"Pretty crummy, huh?" Linda Sawyer said, when his eyes came back to her. "It sure wasn't much, but me and Buzzy were kind of happy here. For a while, anyway."

Harry wondered what that meant. But he didn't ask. Instead he cleared his throat and said, "My deepest sympathy on your loss."

She nodded and stood up.

"How rude of me. Would you like something to drink?"

"Water would be fine," Harry said. "You have any ice?"

She smiled and walked past him. Her lithesome figure told him that she had been a lot younger than Buzzy. He heard the sound of ice dropping in a glass, then the fizz of a faucet. She came back and gave him the water, then sat back down, tucking one leg under the other.

"Buzzy used to talk about you," she said. "That's why I knew about your book. He said you were a good writer."

Harry smiled.

"Not as good as him."

"That's sweet," she said, smiling. The smile slowly faded. "So what can I do for you, Mr. Bauer?"

"Please, call me Harry."

She nodded again, the inquisitive look still in her eyes.

"I'm in need of some assistance," he said, deciding that maybe the most direct route was the best. "You see, I'm working on a story. Similar to the one Buzzy was working on. About Colton Purcell."

Linda Sawyer rolled her eyes.

"That's putting it mildly," she said. "Buzzy was living that story. That's all he talked about, playing the man's CDs all the time. He was a method reporter, all right. Believed in immersing himself in his subject matter."

Harry smiled again. "That's what made him so good."

Linda stifled a yawn, then shook her head. "Sorry. My sleeping's been all screwed up since it happened. Trying to get the funeral over with, shipping his body back east for burial. Trying to deal with the rest of his family."

Harry looked questioningly.

"Oh, he wanted to be buried at Arlington," she said. "Had his spot reserved and everything. He was a war hero."

"Yeah, I know."

"Anyway," she continued, "I'm number three. Number one was his college sweetheart. Waited for him to come back from Vietnam. They had two kids. Then number two. She's kind of a bitch. Lives in Chicago. One daughter, fourteen. She got more of his paycheck each week than he did. Alimony, child support. I was still working night shift at the hotel to make ends meet."

Harry tried to nod in commiserating fashion. From her expression, he failed.

"I'm boring you, right?" she said, more self-consciously than angrily. "Sorry. I haven't had a chance to talk much lately."

"That's okay. I understand. Sometimes it helps to share your feelings."

Linda smiled.

"Did Buzzy leave any notes or anything here?" Harry asked. "Could I maybe sneak a quick look at his desk? I know it's asking a lot, but if I could find something to work up, I'd gladly give Buzzy credit for the article."

Linda raised her eyebrows and straightened her legs.

"I don't think he left much, but you're welcome to look," she said, getting up and motioning for him to follow. "The police have already been through everything."

They went down a narrow hallway to a small room on the left. A single narrow window was on the far wall with a pillowcase taped across the frame rather than curtains. A small wooden desk was against the opposite wall, and on it a computer monitor and speakers. The cords hung over the front of the desk. Several cardboard boxes sat in the middle of the floor.

"He didn't do a lot here," she said. "Mostly he worked from his laptop, and I don't know where that disappeared to. It could be at the paper somewhere."

Harry didn't want to mention that Nash had told him that it had been taken during the mugging.

"I was going to box all this up and send it to his son," she said. "He works on Wall Street."

"Do you mind if I plug in his computer and check out the hard drive?" Harry asked, suddenly feeling excited.

Linda Sawyer shook her head and said, "Actually, the police detective took that. A female detective. She said she wanted to take it in the chance that there might be some clues on it, just in case."

That's my girl, Harry thought. Checking out every angle, even if I didn't know about it.

Running her fingers over the monitor, Linda looked wistful for a second. "I told her that Buzzy was pretty secretive about things. He kept it all password protected. He wouldn't even tell me what it was. Still, I thought it would be nice for his son to have the monitor. Those too." She gestured toward the wall. A large frame held a picture of a very young Buzzy, dressed in olive drab jungle fatigues and holding an M-16, surrounded by an impressive array of military ribbons, and a bright red, white, and blue patch. Below it was written: Khe Sanh, '68. 2nd MarDiv.

The Second Division, U. S. Marine Corps, Harry thought. Buzzy's outfit in 'Nam.

Linda walked over to the desk and opened the drawer. She removed a shoebox and held it out toward him.

"You could take a look at this, I guess," she said. "It was the personal effects he had on him when. . . ." She glanced over at the picture and smiled wanly. "When they found him."

Harry looked inside. A set of keys, three pens, cigarettes, a disposable lighter, comb, handkerchief, a few coins, and a plastic CD case displaying a picture of Colton Purcell. He opened the case. Colton's Greatest Hits was printed in blue across the top of the disk.

"You can have that if you want it," Linda said. "If I never hear another Colton Purcell song, it'll be too soon."

Harry nodded and pocketed the CD.

"I want the dog tag, though," she said.

He saw the flat silver colored aluminum attached to the key ring and gently brushed the keys out of the way.

It read:

SAWYER,

R. C.

2109113 A

USMC M

ROMAN CATHOLIC

"He always carried it," she said. "Ever since Khe Sanh. He used to say that it was the turning point of his life."

"Yeah," Harry said. "Once a marine, always a marine."

As he drove over the top of Hoover Dam, Harry saw the twin tower sections. The first one showing a blue-faced clock with white hands and numbers and a sign under it saying, "Nevada Time." He went about a hundred feet farther and saw the second tower with an identical clock that was labeled, "Arizona Time." He remembered the tour guide's voice from so many years ago explaining the state-line, time-zone division. That had been a lot of years ago, now, back when he and Karen had been here on their honeymoon. Now, appropriately, he was there alone, passing over the same spot, as the final machinations of their divorce were completed.

A lot of water under the dam since then, he thought with a cynical smile. But maybe time for a new beginning. Plus, he had one whopper of a story to run to ground. If he still could. If he still had what it took.

Welcome to Arizona, the purple and yellow sign on the side of the road advertised.

Guess I'll find out soon, he thought as he steered around the curve and looked at the craggy mountainside.

He continued southeast on Route 93 watching the dry landscape of the Mojave, with its sandy brown hills and ubiquitous cactuses, on either side of the black ribbon of asphalt. The temperature gauge on his dashboard continued to climb . . . 110 . . . 114 . . . 123, and he prayed that the rental's air-conditioning system would stand the strain. Still, he'd survived Saudi, so he should be able to go the remaining forty-five miles to a place called Resurrection, Arizona.

The arid landscape kind of reminded him of the Gulf, though, and thoughts of the long build-up of the Shield, followed by the protracted bombing runs of the Storm occupied his mind. The hot sand blowing over everything during the day, coupled with the enveloping darkness of the nights as they strained to keep watch for snipers and incoming Scuds. He'd seen flashes of combat after the ground war had started. But one hundred hours later it was over, except for a few final skirmishes, the overrated opponents surrendering by the thousands. Technology and tactics had made the difference. Nothing like the siege on Khe Sanh, which had lasted for months.

That had been Buzzy's war, Harry thought, imagining the daily terror of the numerically superior NVA forces dumping artillery and mortar rounds on the isolated marines.

Technology had made the difference back then, too, with the air support and planes dropping in supplies and ammo. Whoever has the best toys wins, he thought. But then again, that wasn't totally correct, was it?

We may have won all the battles and lost the war, he thought, but what Buzzy did superseded all that. The Silver Star. You didn't get those for handing out Girl Scout cookies.

Harry thought about the irony. Living through hell halfway around the world only to die in some deserted parking garage thirty-six years later. But Buzzy had been a tough guy. A good marine, or at least an ex-marine.

He grinned at the thought. No such thing as an ex-marine, he told himself. USMC. Uncle Sam's Misguided Children.

So how could a mugger take him out like that?

Sure, Buzzy'd been on the wrong side of fifty, but he was a big guy. And he'd faced death before, against incredible odds, and survived. A mugger . . . the guy must have taken him by surprise. With a weapon, no doubt. A gun. It had to be a gun. Even against a knife, Harry convinced himself that Buzzy would have put up one hell of a fight. Maybe he did. That was something he'd have to check into. But that matter was more delicate than it had been.

The radio station he'd been listening to went to sudden static as the reception faded in and out.

Steering with his forearm, Harry managed to pop open the plastic case of the CD of Colton Purcell's greatest hits that Linda had given him. He pressed the disk into the lips of the groove on the dash and thought about Detective Grey's eyes.

The CD player lit up, but no sound came out. Harry fiddled with the volume, but heard only silence. He hit the eject button and the loudness of the static shocked him.

Damn rental car, he thought and he replaced the disk in the plastic case.

The ringing startled him, and then he realized it was his cell phone. Unclipping it from the catch on his belt, he pressed the button and answered it without looking at the number on the screen.

He was surprised when he heard her voice.

"I thought I'd check in with you and see if we could resume our dinner conversation where we left off," she said.

"Yeah, sure. I would have called you, but I didn't know when you'd get in." He quickly added, "But I left a message on your voice mail. You get it?"

"Un huh. That's why I called. Where you at?"

He realized the signal was fading in and out so he pulled to the shoulder, glanced in the mirror, and executed a U-turn until the stronger reception returned.

"Actually, I'm on the road," he said. "On my way to a place called Resurrection, Arizona."

"What? Why are you going there?"

"It's where Colton Purcell's body is at." He grinned. "At least that's what people say."

"We've been getting enough sightings these past few days to make me skeptical," she said, laughing.

He liked the sound of her laugh.

"So did you solve your homicide case from last night?"

The silence on the line made him wonder if he'd lost the signal. Then she said, "How did you know it was a homicide?"

Oh oh, he thought. Recovery time.

"Well, I was just hoping," he said slowly. "I mean, I hate

to think you'd cut short an evening with me for anything less."

He heard her short laugh again and figured he'd covered his gaff.

"Actually, it was a homicide," she said. "A hotel worker was found in the male employee's locker room."

"Wow, that could give the place a bad name. Any suspects?"

Again she hesitated.

"Just a sketchy report of a big guy with buck teeth, dark hair, and glasses that was seen walking around in a maintenance outfit," she said. "Nobody could find him to talk to afterwards. They're working on a composite now, so you'll probably see it on the news tonight."

"Ah, the old police sketch artist, huh?"

This time she laughed out loud. "Hardly. It's done with a computer now. You look at various features and put them all together."

"So, technology eliminates another tried and true aspect of good old-fashioned police work, eh?"

"Not really," she said. "There's still a lot of leads to track down, witnesses to interview, people to see . . ."

"And vhat's your take on de rehst scene of zee crime, Miss Holmes?" Harry said, mimicking a foreign accent.

The beep of a low battery interceded.

"Say, Janice," he said in his normal voice. "My battery's going out. What time can I call you? I'd really like to finish our dinner tonight, if that's okay."

"Call me when you get back," she said. "Here's my cell number. You ready?"

Harry began scrambling for his pen and notebook, then realized the number would be in the memory of his own cell.

"Okay," he said. "Go ahead. I've got a photographic memory." He glanced at the number on the LCD screen as she repeated it, and thought about how nice it would be to talk to her later. Technology made the difference once again.

As the young couple moved to the adjacent booth in the restaurant, Corrigan glared over at them and said, "That's reserved."

Moran looked over at them too, and the two young lovers got up and left quickly.

"Now, where were we?" Corrigan asked.

"I think I'd just asked you to give me a heads-up as to who we're supposed to be looking for and why."

Corrigan snapped his fingers and pointed to his coffee cup. The waitress immediately scurried over and refilled it. She held the pot toward Moran who shook his head.

As she sashayed away, Corrigan made a point of watching her ass.

"Moran, huh?" he said, looking over at the other man. "Funny, you look more wop than mick."

Moran sat impassively.

"I take after my mother's side," he said.

Finally, after taking a long sip of the coffee, Corrigan set the cup back on the saucer and said, "So tell me again, why should I give you anything?" He grinned.

Moran shrugged. "I don't know. Maybe 'cause you fucked up so bad that the old man sent me here to tighten things up?"

Corrigan's smile faded.

"Look," Moran said, holding up an open palm. "Casio sent me here for a reason. He wants this thing done fast. He said we should work together. You want me to tell

161

him that's not possible?"

Corrigan sighed heavily.

"Bring me up to speed," Moran said. "Sometimes two heads are better than one."

"That's fucking original." Corrigan shifted his gaze to the tabletop momentarily, then said, "How much do you know so far?"

"Just that Casio's kid got mixed up in this recording business shit because he'd seen *The Godfather* too many times. He invested money in Cornucopia Records, and the stock tumbled when their number one star got hit with that child molestation suit."

Corrigan nodded. "How long you been with Casio?"

"About three years."

"Then you know what a royal fuckup his boy Rocky is."

"Yeah. I personally took him to the rehab clinic."

"All right," Corrigan said. "That shithead Vantillberg is into Casio for three hundred and fifty grand. That's the vig. The sorry fucker borrowed the money, trading Rocky's record stock, to pay off the boy's family in that Pablo's civil suit." Corrigan smirked. "Now old man Casio wants them to make good. Vantillberg figured that if they could do something to offset the short eye's image problem, everything would be jake." He shook his head.

"The trouble is," Moran said, "nobody realized how fucked up that Pablo asshole is, right?"

Corrigan nodded. "They've had me going across the country trying to clean up this mess. I had to ice two people in Memphis, for Christ's sake." He looked across and saw a flash of something, which he took for admiration, in Moran's eyes.

"Oh yeah?"

"Plus, you heard about the fiasco down in Mexico?"

162

Moran shook his head.

"Vantillberg found out that Colton Purcell's daughter had the hots for Pablo." Corrigan frowned. "Why, I don't know, but she slipped him some kind of love note at this concert she was at. So Vantillberg figures the way out of his financial mess is to have Pablo marry her. The publicity would defuse the child molesting scandal thing, and give them access to the old porker's money fountain." He shook his head. "You know how much money that fucker's estate makes by him being dead? Something like a hundred million a year."

"Go figure," Moran said.

"Anyway, Vanshitberg thinks Pablo can release remix versions of all Colton Purcell's big hits once he's part of the family. He finds out the brat and her old lady are vacationing in Mexico. They fly down there and he has Pablo go sweep the chick off her feet. They snuck away and got married. I mean, blood tests, license, the whole nine yards. Then Ladonna tracks them down, slaps Pablo across the chops, and gets it annulled." He smirked again. "Naturally, it was never consummated."

Moran smiled.

"So now the brat's set to turn eighteen, and once she does, she inherits the bulk of the estate," Corrigan said. "They sent me to Memphis to take care of a couple loose ends so it'd be smooth sailing."

"What loose ends?"

Corrigan looked at Moran again, studying him.

"Colton Purcell's manager, Big Daddy Babcock," Corrigan paused, raising his eyebrow slightly.

"Yeah," Moran said. "I heard he did himself."

"He had a little help. That cracker owned fifty-one percent of everything connected to Colton Purcell. They wanted him out of the way." He drank some more of his coffee. "Then I was supposed to ice some crazy fucker in a nursing home."

Moran's brow furrowed.

"I ain't following you."

"I don't know who the guy really is, except that he's some kind of blood relative to the brat. Hell, he could really be her daddy for all I know. He's there under the name of Willard Younger, but that ain't his real name. He's been in this place called Graceful Estates or something a long time. Vantillberg said if it came out that this guy was still alive, it could mess up the brat inheriting the whole pie." He shrugged. "It sounded like an easy gig, so I went there."

"And?"

"And I find out some crazy fucking nurse abducted the son of a bitch," Corrigan said. "I ended up icing some night-supervisor broad who walks in on me going through the files finding out where the nurse lived. I had to beat feet, but I traced them out here to Vegas." He sighed again and finished his coffee. "Almost had 'em, too, at the Lucky Nugget. If that damn nigger security guard wouldn't have gotten in my way . . ."

"She was spooked?"

Corrigan nodded fractionally. "How, I don't know 'cause I had it all set. But by the time I set that shine I killed on the shitter, and went up to the room, she was gone. Checked out."

"Anybody see you at the hotel?" Moran asked. "Maybe we could go back and find out how she paid. If we can get a credit card number, I can maybe trace it to see where it's been used."

Corrigan shook his head.

"Too dangerous," he said. "If they see a guy my size

164

nosing around after what happened, somebody'll put two and two together. This whole fucking town is crawling with cops and security." He reached into his pocket and took out a security badge and ID. "That reminds me. I got to get rid of these."

"That from the dead guy?"

"Yeah," Corrigan said, his voice suddenly wary again. "Why?"

"Let me use them," Moran said. "Maybe I can get into the hotel and check their records. If anybody stops me I'll say I'm district security or something."

Corrigan considered this, then licked his lips.

"You sure you can find the old broad if we get a card number?"

Moran smiled. "Trust me."

Corrigan hesitated a moment more, then grabbed a napkin and carefully wiped each smooth surface of the badge and ID card. Holding them by the edges, he set them on the table and spread the napkin over them.

"They're all yours," he said. "And if you get caught with them, they're gonna have your prints, not mine."

Moran secured the items inside the napkin and placed the whole thing in his pants pocket.

"Like I said, you gotta start learning to trust me."

Corrigan grinned at him. It was a feral grin full of warning and implied menace.

"Listen, I don't gotta trust nobody," he said. "I been to the joint twice, and I ain't never going back."

Chapter 16

Stone Cold Love

Harry glanced at the concrete facility set against a sloping hill in the middle of a large asphalt parking lot and reflected on how lost he felt. Not literally, but figuratively. He had no idea what he hoped to find here, or even why he'd come. His instinct had told him to keep tracing Buzzy's story, and this is where it led him. He had to find out what Buzzy knew. Buz must have had something more substantial, but, then again, he hadn't been playing catch up.

Better get started, Harry thought, remembering the big signs he'd seen at the hotel advertising the times and departures for the shuttle buses bringing the faithful out to Resurrection for a solemn ride-by. He had to avoid those idiots.

The overpowering heat washed over him as soon as he slid out of the still cool interior of the car. He felt like running to the entrance, like he was trying to escape from an oven. But running wouldn't do any good. The brutal heat was all around him. There was no escaping it in any direction. Not until somebody opened a door and let him back in the air conditioning. Just like everything connected to this crazy story. It was all topsy-turvy, upside down and backwards.

But at least I'm moving forward, he told himself.

Or so he thought, until he heard the voice.

"Hey, look, Lance," he heard someone say. "It's that reporter feller."

No, Harry thought. It couldn't be.

But it was. He glanced over his shoulder and saw the two

166

burly Fabulous Fabray Boys, clad in identical khaki-colored outfits, their dark pompadours sprayed to helmet-like stiffness, moving on an intersecting course from the right.

"Well, I'll be darned, it is him," the garrulous one, Lance, said. He thrust his hand toward Harry. "What you doing here, Mr. Bauer?"

"I'm here to see the king," Harry said, reluctantly shaking the bigger man's hand. He paused to shake Powell's outstretched hand too.

"Well, shucks, so are we," Lance said. "Figured we'd beat the crowds, you know? Unn, how's your jaw?" He reached out and put his fingers on Harry's cheek, turning it slightly. "See what you done and did, Powell. Tell the man you're sorry now."

Powell turned his sullen gaze toward the asphalt, which seemed to be radiating heat like the griddle of a big frying pan.

"I'm sorry, sir," he said.

"No problem," Harry said quickly. He was starting to sweat really bad now, as were the two Fabray boys. He noticed that a drip of dye-laden, black sweat was streaking down Lance's forehead. "Say, we'd better get in here before we melt."

"You got that right," Lance said. "Come on."

They moved toward the door of the facility. It was solid-looking metal painted an aquamarine blue. A tan button was in the middle of a metallic plate with the instructions, *Ring For Service*. Harry began to pray that they'd get in. Being trapped out here in this heat was bad enough, but with the Fabray Boys he felt like he was poised on the edge of hell's basin.

Maybe the devil will be kind today, he thought.

He got there a step ahead of the others and rang the bell.

After what seemed like an interminably long time, a voice emanated from a second metallic plate above the door. This one was perforated by a circular design of small holes.

"May I help you?" the voice said. It sounded distant and unfriendly.

"We're here to see the king," Lance called out. "Let us in outta this heat. It ain't fit for man nor beast out here."

Harry grimaced. If these two big shit-kickers kept him from getting into the air conditioning, they wouldn't have to worry about losing the Colton imitator's contest. He'd kill them both.

"Do you have an appointment?" the voice asked.

"Excuse me," Harry said. "I'm a reporter with *Regency Magazine*. I'm doing a story on the big anniversary celebration of Colton Purcell's death." He paused. Each breath in the heat felt like a dry scalding. Choosing his words carefully, he added, "I'd like to put a positive spin on your facility for the feature."

He waited in silence, praying. Finally, the voice said, "Just a moment, please."

The "please" part sounded promising. At least he hoped so. Turning to the Fabray boys he said, "Look, let me do the talking, okay? I don't want to take the chance of coming all the way out here and having them shut us down."

"Shit, us neither," Lance said. He turned to Powell. "You hear the man? Don't mess with nobody."

"Mess with me, and you're messing with trouble," Powell answered.

Lance's face cracked into a crooked smile, showing his dimples.

"Now don't he do that good?" he said. "That's from Colton's movie, *King Rebel*."

"Yeah, I remember," Harry said.

But the beefy imitator didn't miss a beat in his explanation. "And these outfits, which we had made special, are just like the ones he wore in *Hawaiian Holiday*. You know, the one where he played a helicopter pilot?"

Harry nodded. "One of my favorites."

The steel door opened and a man in light blue uniform scrutinized them. The white patch on the top of his sleeve said, SECURITY.

"We normally don't allow anyone in without an appointment, unless they have a loved one here," he said.

"Well we loved Colton," Lance said. "Don't that count?"

Harry rubbed his hand over his face. It came away wet with sweat.

"Can you please let us in out of this heat?" he asked. "If I can talk to whoever's in charge, I'm sure I can straighten this out."

The security man looked from Harry to the two imitators.

"We're with him," Lance said.

Powell cocked his head to one side and affected a sullen stare.

"Yeah, we're with him," he added.

God help us, Harry thought.

Eric was hot-boxing his third cigarette and glancing at his watch every thirty seconds or so as the solitary sliver of sunlight shone in through the closed drapes of the hotel room. In the background Pablo continued his high-pitched, keening moan, punctuating it with, "Ohhh, what's taking him so long?"

How did I ever get mixed up with this little piece of shit? Eric wondered. He blew two streams of smoke out his nostrils.

"Er-ric," Pablo moaned, drawing out each syllable. "You know that smoking irritates my vocal cords. Why are you doing it?"

Eric felt like going over and giving him one of those "bitch slaps" the little creep was always talking about after he'd spent the night with Gant watching rap videos. But he knew better. Pablo would scream to Gant when the big buck got back with the meds, and Eric didn't want to deal with that prospect. He drew deeply on his Marlboro and grinned. *I smoke, therefore I am,* he thought, mentally mimicking Pablo's whining tenor.

"I mean, can't you *puhleese* put that damn thing out?" the tenor whined for real.

Eric took one last puff, drawing the ash down to the filter and stubbed the butt into the tray.

"Satisfied?" he asked, with a sarcastic lilt.

"That's the least you could do. Now go get me another ice pack," Pablo said, holding out the dripping white cloth.

Eric sighed and snatched it, walking to the kitchenette section to fill the towel with ice from the refrigerator.

"And don't give me that look, either," Pablo said. "If you wouldn't have let that quack stick that thing up my nose, none of this would have happened."

Eric pressed the ice button, caught the dropping cubes in a glass, then transferred them to the towel. In a way, he realized that Pablo was right. The doc had done the stomach pump the old-fashioned way, but only because of Pablo's semi-conscious state. Since he'd almost choked on a Brazil nut, the doctor had been reluctant to put the tube down the throat cavity. So he took a little detour and went down to the stomach through the nose. The only problem was he happened to dislodge one of the implants that had been previously inserted to change Pablo's original Negroid nose into more of a Caucasian one. The resulting pain, when the original shot of Novocaine wore off, had sent the Latino Prince of Pop into a tizzy, moaning and screaming when he woke up, until Eric had managed to get hold of one of Pablo's staff of doctor "Feelgoods," who called in a Vicodin prescription to a Las Vegas pharmacy. Eric looked over and saw Pablo's chocolate brown eyes staring up at an oblique angle, obviously trying for his best "wounded" imitation look. But Eric knew it was as phony as his nose. Latino Prince of Pop, he thought. Prince of fops. He strode back over to the sofa and handed Pablo the ice-filled towel.

"No," Pablo said, holding up his palms and twisting his head away. "I need a clean one. This one might have germs."

"Germs? If there are any, they're your fucking germs, so what's the difference?"

Pablo pursed his lips.

"I'm going to tell Gant how mean you were to me," he said. "Melissa Michelle too. Remember, she and I have no secrets."

"Yeah, I'll bet," Eric said, telling himself how much he still needed the little son of a bitch to keep this whole plan from coming apart at the seams. And Eric knew if the plan came apart, so did he.

He went into the bathroom and snatched the last of the hand towels from the rack.

Great, I'll have to call room service again, he thought. How the hell did I ever get mixed up with this bastard? He glanced at his watch again. Where the hell was Gant?

The phone rang and Pablo moaned again.

"Ohh, answer it. Hurry. Maybe it's Gant about the prescription."

"Yeah, yeah," Eric said, reaching the phone in three

strides. He hoped it was that motherfucking attorney, Montgomery Spangler, finally returning Eric's call of several hours ago. He was going to have to remind that prick just how much shit he had on him. The censure committee would love to see the little group of videos of the good counselor doing line after line of cocaine at one of Eric's parties, wouldn't they? He grabbed it from its cradle and barked a sharp "Hello."

The voice was precise and polite and Eric knew immediately that it was the faggot at the front desk.

"Mr. Vantillberg, I have a delivery of a fruit basket down here, compliments of Mr. Casio. Would you like it brought up, sir?"

"Yeah, go ahead."

"The delivery man is requesting to bring it himself, sir," the voice asked. "Is that all right?"

"Whatever," Eric said, and slammed the phone down.

Fruits for a fruit, he thought. Appropriate.

But no, this was no ordinary fruit. This was a twisted little sick fucker, whose façade was starting to melt, just like his false face. A rotten fruit . . . no, a wax one, with an empty plastic shell on the inside. And I gotta steer him into marrying the dead king of rock and roll's only daughter.

He took out another cigarette and placed it between his lips.

To hell with the little fucker, Eric thought. If he don't like the smoke, he can kiss my ass. He snapped the button on his disposable lighter but got only a spark. He did it again, with the same result. After playing with the adjustments a few more times, he frowned and tossed the lighter at the wall.

"Eric, you're not going to smoke again, are you?" Pablo asked, his tenor masked slightly by the overlapping towel.

"Would I do that?" Eric said, moving toward the door of the suite to answer the knocking. Maybe the bellman would have a light.

He opened the door in a huff, glanced at the slim figure standing in front of him, munching on one of the red delicious apples from the ornately fashioned wicker basket, and wasn't even cognizant of the unlit cigarette dropping from his gaping mouth.

Corrigan shifted into drive as he watched Moran walk confidently into the main entrance of the Lucky Nugget Hotel. The fucker had balls, all right. He'd give him that. And he was cool, always wearing them shades so you couldn't see his eyes. But could he parlay the stolen badge and security ID into a position to get a look at the old broad's registration? That was the million-dollar question.

He checked his mirrors, then did a slow pull out into the lane, carefully watching for any oncoming cars. Once in the traffic lane, he merged with the rest of the northbound cars on Main Street, continued down to Ogden, and turned right, moving fast enough to blend in, but slow enough not to attract any attention. He couldn't afford any overzealous cops pulling him over and maybe recognizing him from some kind of description. Still, he didn't know for a fact that he'd been burned, but he didn't want to take the chance. That's why he was secretly kind of glad to let Moran carry the ball on this play.

Moran, he thought. There was something about that guy. He couldn't put his finger on it, but he knew it was something. He sighed and turned left at Casino Center Boulevard and began his trek back southwest. He'd just keep driving in overlapping circles until Moran signaled him for the pickup. A simple plan, but a decent one. That guy not only had balls, but he was smart, too. Tactical, Corrigan thought. Keeping all the angles covered. But if the son of a bitch thought that when it was time to collect the paychecks, they'd be anyway close to even, he'd get a big surprise all right. There was no way that Corrigan was going to split anything with anybody, and if they didn't like it . . .

He thought back to their earlier conversation.

"How's getting the credit card number of the old broad's account gonna help us?" he'd asked.

"I got somebody that can trace it," Moran had said. "We get the number, find out where it's being used, and we know where they're at. Simple, huh?"

"Simple if it works. How you know you can trust this guy?"

"Relax," Moran said.

"I don't relax until I get the job done. You better remember that. Now, how do you know you can trust this guy?"

Moran popped some gum into his mouth.

"He owes me," he said. "Big time."

Corrigan waited.

"We were inside together," Moran said. "The guy's a geek. But brilliant with computers. He can hack into the fucking FBI's data base if he wants to, believe me."

"So?"

"So I kept him from being somebody's bitch. Now, whenever I need something looked up. . . ." He let the sentence trail off.

Corrigan nodded approvingly.

"Where'd you meet the guy at? Soledad?"

Moran shook his head.

"Un-un," he said. "This was back east. Ryker's Island."

"You were in New York?"

"For a while."

"Nice town," Corrigan said. "That where you're from?"

"I'm from Chicago," Moran answered, obviously growing irritated. "Now if you're finished playing twenty fucking questions, get me over to the Nugget without getting in an accident or getting us pulled over, would ya?"

The guy was all business and no play, Corrigan thought, recalling the scene as he headed back in a northerly direction again. He hated to admit it, but he was beginning to kind of like this guy Moran. Not like they were going to become bosom buddies or anything, but as a professional, Corrigan appreciated competence. He even hoped he wouldn't have to kill him once this was all over.

Using his turn signal to change lanes, he felt a chill run up his spine as a motorcycle cop fell in behind him. He immediately checked his speedometer and eased off the gas. He was doing a few miles under the limit, but he wasn't causing an obstruction or anything. He felt the weight of the .38 snub in his breast pocket. He preferred automatics, but he didn't want to have to worry about picking up ejected shells.

They slowed for a light and Corrigan looked in the rearview mirror. The cop was talking into his radio mike. But this was rental, so it wouldn't come back hot or anything. The light changed to green and a kid in a souped-up Mustang next to him took off kind of fast, squealing his tires. The motorcycle cop swung from behind Corrigan and glided into the other lane, following the speedster.

Good, Corrigan thought, pulling by the stopped Ford and watching the flickering red and blue lights of the motorcycle fading in the side mirror. Thank heaven for young punks with hot cars.

His cell phone rang twice. That was Moran's signal. He pressed on the accelerator, anxious to get back to the hotel and find out how it had gone.

Man, that was quick, he thought. The guy's even slicker than I gave him credit for.

He cut through the traffic quickly, angling back to Main and pulling up in front of the hotel approximately ten minutes later. He saw Moran's glance and followed him to the corner. All told, it had taken less than fifteen minutes.

"Shit, that was quick," Corrigan said and the other man got into the car. "You get it?"

Moran nodded, holding up a fuzzy, black-and-white copy of a Tennessee driver's license and hotel registration card.

"This her?" he asked.

Corrigan nodded.

"Good," Moran said. "Let's head over to the Mirage and I'll see if I can get ahold of my friend. But in the meantime, we got another problem."

"What's that?" Corrigan asked, glancing over at Moran and wondering if he ever took off those wrap-around sunglasses.

"Rocky's out of rehab."

Harry was glad to see the signs for Hoover Dam and Lake Mead flash by on the side of the road. He couldn't wait to get back to Nevada and the Mecca in the desert. The Fabray boys had made the visit to the cryogenics facility less than optimal. After waiting outside for the security guard to contact his supervisor, and watching more of the dark drops of sweat descend down the two ersatz Coltons' foreheads, they had finally been admitted. The supervisor had been impressed with Harry's credentials, and obviously wanted to get some positive publicity out of the deal. He was a short man in his mid-to-late fifties clad in a light blue blazer and charcoal pants. His build resembled a pear: a set of narrow shoulders tapering outward to a rotund waist.

"I'm Mr. Winthrop," he'd said. "How may I help you?"

"We're here to see the king," Lance Fabray had shouted. "Now what you doing leavin' us standing out in that god-awful heat so long for?"

Mr. Winthrop looked a bit shaken. He wasn't a very big man, and looked more than just a few pounds over his fighting weight.

"Shucks, we done sweated right through our nice khaki outfits here," Lance continued, holding his right arm upward and pointing to his sopping armpit with his left.

Mr. Winthrop's chin seemed to go slack at the sight.

"We had these made special, sir," Powell said, doing a fair imitation of the original's voice. "They're the same kind that Colton wore in *Hawaiian Holiday*, you see."

Harry glanced at the look of frozen horror on the supervisor's face and cleared his throat loudly. It seemed to snap the other man out of his trance-like state.

"You were saying that you could arrange for us to have a tour of the facility . . ." Harry prompted.

"Oh, yes," Mr. Winthrop said. He eyed the two Coltons suspiciously. "What function do these two gentlemen have at the magazine?"

"They're part of the story I'm doing," Harry said, shooting a complicit glare at the Fabray boys and hoping they'd both keep their mouths shut for once. "I believe my colleague, Mr. Buzzy Sawyer, was here originally?"

"Ah, Mr. Sawyer," Winthrop said. Then his eyebrows rose and his lips formed an "O" shape. "But didn't I read that he'd met with foul play?"

Harry nodded.

"Yeah, I was a friend of his. I've been temporarily hired by the *Las Vegas Mirror* to complete the feature he was working on."

This seemed to satisfy Winthrop, who held out a prissy palm directing them toward a row of elevators.

"The cryogenic cylinders are downstairs," he said. "We feel it's a safer atmosphere down below."

"Way down, huh?" Lance said, reaching out to press the colored button inside the plastic arrow. "That was one of Colton's songs." He began to sing the chorus and Powell joined in for harmony.

Winthrop's lips compressed, but he nodded politely.

The elevator bell rang and the doors popped open, ending the impromptu tune. They got inside the car and Winthrop pressed the button marked "B."

"So let me ask you something," Lance said, sidling up to Mr. Winthrop like they were old buddies at a hog barbeque. "Is this *really* the king of rock and roll inside this here metal coffin?"

"I assure you it is," Winthrop answered.

"But how can you be sure?" Lance continued. He placed his hand on the smaller man's shoulder. The time they'd spent outside waiting for admittance had taken its toll on all of them, but it was particularly evident in the enclosed space of the elevator car that of the four of them, Lance's deodorant had failed him badly today.

Mr. Winthrop's nostrils seemed to flare as he canted his head away from the beefy rocker.

"You heared about the twin theory, ain't ya?" Lance continued. "My cousin Powell here believes it like it was taught to him in Sunday school." He grinned broadly, showing two stunning rows of capped teeth.

"You better watch your mouth, Lance," Powell said, his voice a husky Colton-like whisper.

To Harry it was déjà vu all over again.

"Guys," he said. "The bruise on my jaw, remember? This is how you got kicked off the airplane in Memphis."

"Yeah, you got yourself a point there, Mr. Bauer," Lance said. He leaned in close to Winthrop, encircling his arm around the other man's narrow shoulders and placing the expansive sweat stain directly on the back of Winthrop's blue jacket. "But don't take no offense now if Powell here starts crowing about this really being Colton's dead twin brother in there instead of the king, okay?"

Winthrop nodded nervously.

"You better quit messing with me, Lance," Powell said.

Harry could see him balling up his fists.

"Powell, chill out," he said.

"Mess with me—" Powell started to say.

"And you're messing with trouble," Harry said, finishing it for him. He stepped in between the two big hillbillies and shoved Powell against the wall.

"If you two guys blow this for me I'll kill you," he said, pointing his finger in the other man's face.

The elevator slowed to a stop and the doors slid open.

"I don't know," Lance said, his arm still around Winthrop's shoulder as they walked out. "Maybe we should change that sayin' to 'Mess with Harry, and you're messin' with trouble.' " He grinned again. "Come on, Powell. Let's go see the king."

Luckily, he'd been able to part company there, after listening to their "graveside renditions" of "Mama Liked the Roses," "How Great Thou Art," and "Stone Cold Love," which was Lance's favorite. He intended, he informed them, to use that for his solo song in the contest, once he made the finals. In the echoing chamber of solitary stainless steel vats, the only accompaniment was the quiet, unending hum of the refrigeration units attached to each cylinder. Colton, who had one of the massive units all to himself, had a gold plaque affixed to it that simply said, Colton Gabriel Purcell 1949–1996.

Harry left not knowing why he'd decided to go there, and equally unsure of why Buzzy had.

If I could just figure that out, he thought, then I'd be close to figuring out the method to his madness.

He began passing over the dam again and felt good that he was back in Nevada. The answer to everything lay before him now, he was sure. Somewhere, the answer waited behind a closed door in the brightest of all cities in the desert.

Chapter 17

Chasing the Dragon

Eric sat at the table and took one of the three cigarettes left in his pack and offered one to the thin, waspish looking man by the fruit basket. The man plucked another apple from the arrangement, placed the old one he'd been eating among the untouched fruits, and took a bite of the new one. He grinned as he accepted the cigarette with his other hand.

"So when'd you get out, Rocky?" Eric asked. He started to offer his lighter and then remembered he'd thrown it against the wall.

"You're not going to smoke anymore in here, are you?" Pablo said, his tone plaintive and whining. "I have to save my voice."

Rocky slipped a lighter out of his own pocket, lit his cigarette, and then held the flame out toward Eric.

"I split last night," Rocky said, chewing on the apple as he exhaled the smoke through his nostrils. Glancing around, he nodded in approval. "I remembered you told me you guys always stay at The Emperor's Palace. So here I am." He smirked and took another drag on the cigarette. "I don't even have a fucking dime on me right now, believe it or not. As soon as I got dropped off, I came here to find you. I ripped off this basket of fruit from some wedding reception." He took another small bite and then tossed the apple away. "Pretty smart, huh?"

Eric watched the partially eaten fruit roll over in front of the refrigerator.

Great, he thought. I can either go over and pick it up, or

take the chance of slipping and falling if I step on it.

He decided to leave it.

"Christ, you got any idea how fucked up it is to sit around in that place?" Rocky said, walking over to the window and pulling the drapes open.

"Ooooohh," Pablo moaned. "Please close them. The light hurts my eyes."

Rocky smirked, continuing his monologue. "No TV, no radio, no newspapers. Just special counseling sessions where we'd all sit in a circle and discuss our 'inner feelings.' " He held up his hooked fingers to indicate quotation marks, then shook his head. "And then we'd meet with some asshole quack who'd go over our 'specific goals for defeating our addictions.' So I managed to sneak a call from one of the shrink's offices. Had one of my boys pick me up. Had to jump out the fucking window."

"Sounds like fun," Eric said, suddenly feeling the creeping sensation in his bowels again.

Rocky looked at Pablo.

"Hey, Pee, what kind of stuff you got?" he asked.

Pablo rolled over, hooking his arm over his eyes.

"Will you please close those damn drapes?" he moaned.

Eric pursed his lips in disgust. "Damn drapes. . . ." The little son of a bitch sounded worse than a broad on the rag.

"Come on, Pee," Rocky continued. "I been jonesin' all week long thinking about scoring here. Thinking about chasing the dragon."

The weakness in Eric's bowels suddenly lurched upward to his stomach. He grabbed his abdomen and held himself. Casio's words of displeasure in the hot steam room about Eric helping to fuel Rocky's proclivities suddenly came back to him. *"I ever catch you giving drugs to my kid again, I'll fucking kill you.* " He inhaled another lungful of smoke, before he spoke.

"Look, Rocky, you just spent the last month getting clean, right?" Eric tried to smile, but even he knew it looked false. "You don't want to start up with that shit again, do you?"

"I'm cool," Rocky said with a dismissive little wave. "I can handle it now." He brought the cigarette up to his lips and puffed on it quickly. "I couldn't before, that's all."

"My man Gant's coming back with some Vicodin," Pablo said. "He should be here any minute. Now will you please close those drapes?"

At the mention of the painkiller, Rocky seemed to perk up. He reached up and tugged the drapes partially closed, but a large wedge of sunlight still filtered through the gap in the middle.

"I figure I got maybe a day or two before the old man tracks me down," he said, slapping his hands together. "So it's party time and broads till then. What else you got, Pee?"

"Ritalin, Valium, some Codeine-four pills, and the Vicodin ES when Gant gets back," Pablo said, adjusting the ice pack on his face.

"That'll do for starters," Rocky said, his eyes getting that faraway look in them now. "You got any syringes? With all that shit, it'll be better to do a special mix and just shooting it."

Or shooting me, Eric thought. 'Cause once the old man gets wind of this I'm as good as dead.

Harry repeated his practiced spiel in his head while the irritating cycle of Muzak played over the phone. *Hi, I'm Harry Bauer. I work at Regency Magazine. I'm doing an ar-*

*ticle on Colton Purcell. I interviewed Ladonna about a month
ago regarding her opinions on the great Colton Imitator's Contest here in Vegas. I wonder if I could get a few additional
quotes?*

So far, all the spiel had gotten him was a series of endless
morons in her publicity department who kept putting him
on hold. He needed an edge. Something with a bite to it.
Something to gain a foothold so he could get past the
bottom layer of screeners.

"This sure is a nice room, Harry," Gabe said, looking at
the high ceilings complete with a suspended chandelier,
arched windows, and an ornate coffee table. "Puts mine
over by the club to shame, that's for sure."

"Yeah, well, my boss wanted to be extra nice to me,"
Harry said. "He told me to get the very best."

Gabe nodded appreciatively. "Must be a pretty nice
boss."

Harry smirked. "He's tops all right." He went back to
waiting.

Gabe had strolled over to the small table by the television set where Harry had dumped his notebook, laptop, and
various other articles. The square plastic box containing the
Colton Purcell's Greatest Hits CD that he'd gotten from
Buzzy's widow sat prominently on top of the notebook. Gabriel picked it up and opened it, turning to Harry.

"Mind if I play this?" he asked, holding it up.

Harry shrugged and pointed toward the built-in DVD
player under the huge television screen. More lulling music
played in his ear from the Memphis connection. Anything
to counteract this would be most welcome.

"I'm sorry to keep you waiting, sir," a woman's voice
suddenly came on the line. It sounded grating and harsh,
and scarcely an improvement over the Muzak. "Ms. Purcell

is not available at this time. I'm told she's away from her office."

"I already know that," Harry said, trying to imbue some cordiality and patience into his tone. "But I'm facing a deadline here, and if I don't get a suitable quote, it could adversely affect the tone of the article."

"I'm sorry, but there's really nothing I can do, sir."

"Aww, come on. This is a national magazine and we're really devoting a lot of space to this feature."

"Just a moment, sir." The voice said. Before he could say anything, he was placed on infinite hold again, the Muzak chiming in his ear once more. This time it was an instrumental version of "Love is Blue."

Swearing, he looked over at Gabe who was pressing button after button on the DVD remote, but no sound was coming out. Harry walked over to where Gabriel was standing and cradled the phone on his shoulder. He held out his hand and Gabe gave him the remote. He pressed a series of buttons, turning TV on, and going to the video, blue screen mode. Then he pressed Menu.

NO FUNCTIONS AVAILABLE the white lettering across the top of the screen flashed.

No functions available, Harry thought, remembering his frustration with the rental car's CD player. It was the same thing, only he had a viewer screen now. He quickly pressed the eject button on the remote and removed the disk as the drawer slid open. Going to the table, Harry picked up his laptop. After powering it up, the screen went through the normal slow series of stages until the final screen saver, a bright blue sky with an array of beach-goers soaking up the sunshine, gradually appeared.

Harry pushed the disk into the slot in his laptop.

The hourglass sprang up, and then the sound of the machine's internal mechanism racing as it scanned the disk. The menu appeared moments later listing the icons for several files. Harry gazed at them quickly, moving the mouse to the one entitled Notes on LP interview/the truth about Mexico.

LP, he thought. Ladonna Purcell?

He clicked to open it, but another rectangular box loomed up informing him that the file was password protected.

Of course, Harry thought. Buzzy wouldn't have left his most secret files accessible. But what could he have used for a password?

He was biting his lip when the woman's shrill voice came back on the line.

"I'm sorry to have kept you waiting, sir," she said. "But Ms. Purcell is away from her office at the present time. I'm not sure when she'll be available."

"I see."

"If you want to give me any specific questions that you had in mind," the voice said, "I'll be glad to forward them to her, but I can't guarantee when that will be."

"Yeah? That's mighty kind of you," Harry said, a smile stretching across his face. "Well, if you're going to get a message to her, tell her it's very important. And if you don't, believe me, she'll be very upset." He paused, but the woman gave no indication that she'd been rattled.

"Just tell her to call Harry Bauer ASAP," he said, repeating his cell phone number with exquisite slowness, and then adding his hotel information. "And make sure you mention that it's in reference to an interview she did with reporter Buzzy Sawyer of the *Las Vegas Mirror*." He paused again, choosing his next words carefully. "Tell her I'm picking up the story where he left off. Tell her . . . tell her that I know all about what she talked about with Buzzy, and the Mexico connection." He waited for two more beats. "I suggest you contact her immediately. She'll really want to know."

Marjorie looked at her watch again, mentally calculating how much longer she could rely on the Seconal to keep him knocked out and asleep in the room, as the cab swung through the busy streets, avoiding throngs of pedestrian and vehicular traffic. They wound their way past the pyramid and the ersatz sphinx, the dancing fountains, the volcano, and the battling pirates. Finally satisfied that no one was following her, Marjorie gave the cabbie instructions to take her to the *Las Vegas Mirror*.

"The newspaper office?" he asked.

"Yes," Marjorie said. "And please, make it snappy."

The cab driver shrugged, muttering, "It's your dime, lady," and immediately turned right.

They went by a few more sights, but her thoughts were still on him in the hotel. She checked her watch again, then compressed her lips. His system had been so overtaxed with so many drugs for so many years, she certainly hated to use any more right now, but what choice did she have? She couldn't afford a repeat of the karaoke episode. She had been lucky to find him so quickly. Especially not now, when she felt that the law must be on their trail. She whispered a silent prayer that she could get him detoxified and back to a state of relative normalcy before they were found. Let me get this straightened out first, she thought. Let me get him back to his rightful place. So the Seconal was a necessary evil right now. Plus, as his nurse for so long, she was very familiar with the dosages and probably knew his tolerances even better than Dr. Ricola.

The cabbie pulled up to the entrance of the newspaper offices and came to an abrupt stop.

"Here you are," he said. "You want me to wait?"

Marjorie considered the question and then felt it was more prudent to hail another cab. Less chance of being seen. She paid the cab fare and allowed herself a slight smile, feeling a bit like Rita Hayworth in one of those old spy movies. Then, pausing to right herself, she marched to the glass doors and yanked them open, resolutely holding Buzzy's inscribed card in her hand. She presented it to the receptionist and said, "I'm here by invitation. Look on the back, please."

The girl, a nice-looking black girl, flipped the card over and read the handwritten note. She then picked up her phone and dialed a quick series of numbers.

"May I have your name, ma'am?" the receptionist asked.

"Marjorie Versette."

The girl smiled a thanks and went back to the phone, her voice a soft purr that Marjorie couldn't quite discern. She did hear, however, the loud, angry sounding exclamations from the other end of the line. The girl moved the phone away from her ear until the noise subsided.

I hope that's not the man who's going to talk to me, she thought. His voice sounded harsh and sharp.

The girl looked up and told Marjorie to have a seat, indicating a series of plastic chairs against the window by the door.

Marjorie looked at them warily.

"Is he going to be long?" she asked. "I don't have a lot of time."

"He's on his way now," the girl said, smiling, but giving Marjorie a chill by the way her eyes looked. She knew something that she wasn't mentioning, Marjorie knew. Perhaps she should just make a quick run for it now, in case the girl had called the cops.

Forcing herself to inhale a deep breath, Marjorie consciously pushed all the negative thoughts and worries from her mind.

I need Mr. Sawyer's help, she thought. And he wouldn't have invited me here if he hadn't believed me and been honest when he'd told me to meet him here in Las Vegas so we could bring out the truth.

She felt a resurgence of righteousness that reinforced her sagging resolve. She went to the chairs, but did not sit. Instead, she stood ramrod straight.

Finally a door opened and an enormous black man emerged with a horrendous scowl across his face.

Marjorie suddenly felt a bit weak in the knees. This man looked big and formidable. But she stood her ground, still clutching the inscribed business card. As the big man drew closer, his face softened slightly, and cracked into a semi-smile.

"Hi, I'm James Nash," the man said. "Mr. Sawyer's former editor. I'm afraid Buzzy's no longer with us."

He was speaking slowly and Marjorie suddenly felt that there was something more he wasn't saying. Something important.

"Well, it's vital that I speak with him," she said, holding up the card. "You see, he wanted me to come here. It's a matter of great urgency. Can you tell me how to get ahold of him?"

Nash smiled again, glancing downward and heaving a sigh before he spoke.

"Ma'am, I'm very sorry, but Mr. Sawyer was . . . is deceased."

"Merciful heavens," Marjorie said, bringing her hand to

her mouth. "He seemed so young."

Nash's heavy lips tightened slightly. He sighed again.

"He was killed about eleven days ago."

Marjorie's eyes widened and she felt an immediate urge to run. She maintained her self-control, however, swallowing hard and looking directly at Nash.

"That's terrible. Was it an automobile accident?"

"Actually, he was mugged." The big man continued to look down at her.

"Well," Marjorie said, her voice sounding mousy now, even for her. "Is there anyone else I can talk to about the story he was working on? I've come a long way to see him and it's a matter of. . . ." She had almost said, "life and death," but figured she'd better keep that to herself for now. A solitary tear trickled down her cheek as she spoke. A tear for Buzzy Sawyer, a tear for Colton Purcell, a tear for herself . . .

"There is someone I can refer you to," Nash said. "Someone who's trying to follow up on Buzzy's stories." His big fingers were fumbling in his shirt pocket. Finally, he extracted a business card and smiled broadly. "The man's name is Harry Bauer."

"Did you know that Colton Purcell was a twin?" Harry asked as he tried another password on his laptop.

"Yeah, I did," Gabe said. "Colton G. and Clayton W. Purcell." He had a pen and tablet in his hand. "Which one was that now?"

"Uncle Sam's Misguided Children," Harry said, watching the rectangular box spring up telling him once again that the enclosed file was password protected.

Gabe scribbled it down.

"Then how come I didn't know it?" Harry asked.

"Christ, I just finished a story about the guy, detailing his life and loves, and I didn't come across squat about him being a twin."

"It's not a well-known fact," Gabe offered. "Clayton, his twin brother was supposed to have died a long time before Colton did."

"How much before?"

"Don't rightly know." Gabe looked up from the paper. "What one you gonna try next?"

Harry shrugged, thinking. "We tried silver star yet? I wish Linda would call back. Maybe she'll be able to give us some ideas."

"Otherwise, it's just like looking for a needle in a haystack," Gabe said, smiling and showing Harry the dimples.

I gotta get some of those someday, he thought, then grinned himself.

The phone rang and they both jumped. Harry sprang to his feet and reached it in two strides, picking it up with an anxious "Hello?"

He'd hoped it was Linda, but it wasn't. The voice on the other end sounded timorous and old.

"May I speak to Mr. Harry Bauer please?" the voice said.

"You got him."

"My name is Marjorie Versette. I was referred to you by Mr. Nash, that nice colored gentleman at the newspaper?"

"Yeah, I know him," Harry said. He realized his voice conveyed the disappointment and frustration that seemed to be overwhelming him. To soften it, he added, "What can I do for you?"

"Mr. Nash said you were following up Mr. Sawyer's story on Colton Purcell?"

"That's right."

"Well, I have some very important information about it," she said. "Mr. Sawyer invited me to come out here with a friend . . . so we could . . . discuss it more fully."

Her words were hesitant, evasive. Harry was sure she was hiding something, the way she was dancing around with the answers. It couldn't hurt to at least hear what she had to say.

"Okay, maybe we could meet for coffee somewhere?"

The line was silent for a number of seconds, and Harry suddenly wondered if she'd been disconnected. But then the voice came back.

"Mr. Bauer, I'm not at all sure I can trust you. You see, I'm charged with a very special responsibility right now. I'll need some kind of assurance that you are who you say you are."

Oh great, Harry thought. Another conspiracy buff.

He thought about blowing her off with an imitation of the old Popeye phrase, "I yam what I yam," but thought better of it. Instead he tried a quiet reassurance.

"Well, Marjorie, I can show you my press pass if you want. You can also call *Regency Magazine* headquarters in Chicago and ask for Tim Stockton. He can vouch for me. Plus, Mr. Nash from the newspaper wouldn't have mentioned me if my intentions weren't honorable, right?"

"That remains to be seen," she said. "In the meantime, I will contact your employer. What's the phone number?"

Harry rattled it off with rote precision. She asked him to repeat it, and then the line went dead abruptly.

Another fruitcake bites the dust, he thought, hanging up and trying Linda Sawyer's number again. The phone rang five times, then went to a recording. He left another message to call him back regardless of the time. After hanging up, he turned to Gabe and asked, "Okay, what

192

was the last one we tried?"

"Silver Star."

Harry nodded, hunched back over the laptop, and then exhaled slowly. Gabriel was wrong. This wasn't as bad as looking for a needle in a haystack, it was much worse. Plus the reward, Buzzy's hidden files, continued to dangle out there in front of him just out of reach. It was maddening.

We need a hacker, he thought. But where in the hell am I gonna find one?

Suddenly he was jarred loose by the phone ringing again. He started to reach for the hotel phone, when he realized this time it was his cell. He grabbed it and pressed the button, answering without looking at his caller ID.

"Mr. Bauer," the woman's voice on the other end said, "this is Ladonna Purcell."

Chapter 18

The Unusual Suspects

Eric answered the phone with a nervous hello, still watching the scene that was unfolding before him like a slow-motion train wreck. Rocky was slumped over next to Pablo, who had just ingested some of the Vicodin and Tylenol-fours. Rocky wasn't looking too good.

"Vantillberg?" a voice asked on the phone.

"Yeah, who's this?" But he knew who it was. And the familiar feeling was seizing his bowels again.

"It's Moran," the voice said. "What room you in?"

"Jack," Eric said, glancing over at Rocky who was leaning back against the sofa with a stuporous look on his face. "What's up?"

"What room you in?" Moran repeated.

Christ, thought Eric, if they come up and see Rocky here like this . . .

"Five seventeen. Why?" He swallowed hard.

"Stay put. We'll be right up."

The line went dead.

He'd said "we," Eric thought. Oh my God.

He ran over and checked Rocky's pupils. Oh sweet Jesus, they were dilated to the max.

"What the hell's wrong with him?" Eric yelled, slapping the lolling face trying to revive him.

"He's got the nods," Pablo said. "He mixed up some shit and shot up."

Eric saw the lighter, the blackened bottle cap, and

the dismantled capsules. Rocky'd used his necktie for an arm ligature.

"When the fuck did this happen?" he screamed.

"While you were in the bathroom," Pablo said. "What were you doing in there?"

Eric had been doing a couple of lines of powder. His own private stash that he didn't want Pablo to know he had. And now the cocaine was racing through his system, making everything seem hyper.

He took a deep breath and grabbed Gant's meaty shoulder. This caused the big man to fumble the blunt he was trying to pack. He looked up at Eric with one of his menacing "don't fucking touch me" stares.

"Get him outta here. Quick," Eric said, removing his hand from Gant's shoulder but continuing to gesticulate wildly.

"Do it yourself, motherfucker," Gant said, going back to his blunt.

"What? Are you nuts? Do you know who's on the way up here?"

Gant ignored him, pausing to pack more of the crushed sinsemilla between the brown folds of the cigar paper.

"It's those outfit guys," he said, the incipient panic edging into his voice. "You don't understand. They'll kill us all if they see him like this."

"They can try," Gant said. He twisted the end of the blunt.

"You stupid shit, these guys are probably armed to the teeth. They're the same ones who beat the shit out of you last time."

Gant's lips drew into a tight line.

"Good," he said. "I been wanting to get another crack at that motherfucker."

Eric felt the tugging in his guts. He was suddenly afraid he'd crap his pants. He tried to swallow, but couldn't.

"Pablo," he said.

The Latino Prince of Pop's chin was trembling slightly.

"Gant," he said. "Just do it."

The big African American snorted disgustedly, stuck the blunt in his shirt pocket, and stood up.

"What you want me to do with him?"

Eric looked around. They were probably in the hallway by now, for Christ's sake. If they saw him . . .

He ran to the door, opened it, and glanced up and down the hall. Empty.

He motioned with his hand, saying, "Bring him over here. Now!"

Gant pulled the semi-conscious Rocky to his feet, lifted him erect, and stooped under him as he fell forward, straightening up with the recumbent man over his shoulder like a bag of potatoes. Gant walked toward the door.

Eric was still watching the hallway.

"Go down the stairway," he said. "Go up one floor and wait for me there."

"Up one floor? Carrying this motherfucker?"

"Okay, down one then. You got your cell phone?"

Gant nodded. Eric guided him out the door and watched as he waddled down toward the stairway.

"I'll call you," Eric yelled, and shut the door. His mind raced. Suddenly an idea came to him. It would be tricky, but he might be able to do it. He ran to the hotel phone and punched in the number for the front desk. Each unanswered ring was exquisite torture.

"Front desk. Don speaking. May I help you?"

"Yes, yes," Eric said, consciously willing himself to sound calm, cool, and collected. By the time he spoke again his voice sounded just a tad next to normal. "This is Mr. Vantillberg in room five seventeen." He swallowed. "I'm with Mr. Pablo Stevenson's party."

"Yes, sir," the hotel clerk said. He sounded impressed.

"We've had some unexpected guests come by," Eric said, "and we need another room immediately."

"I see," the hotel man said. Eric could hear the clicking of keys on a computer. "Just let me check my availability . . ."

Eric jumped when he heard the knocking on the door. It had to be them.

"Just a minute," he called, after covering the mouthpiece with his hand.

The clicking on the other end continued, but little else. Eric forced himself to take deep breaths. The knocking sounded again, louder this time. Much louder.

"Hold on," Eric called, covering the mouthpiece again. Then he spoke into the phone. "I am in a bit of hurry here, Don."

"I'm sorry, Mr. Vantillberg. We're just booked so solid due to the big Colton Purcell celebration . . ."

Shit, thought Eric. The porker's reaching out from the grave to mess with me.

The next series of knocks literally shook the door. He knew he had to do something.

"Look, I'll have to call you back," Eric said.

"No, I'm sorry. Here, I've got it. We've got another empty room on your floor. Do you want smoking or non-smoking?"

"On my floor? No, it can't be . . . don't you have anything else?"

"Well, let me see," Don said, sounding hurt and confused. "I have some on the third floor . . ."

"Fine. That'll do," Eric said.

"All right, may I have the name of the party who'll be staying there please?"

"I'll get that to you later," Eric said. He glanced toward the door as another series of solid knocks seemed to shake the door jamb. "Right now, just put it on Mr. Stevenson's corporate account."

"Very well. I'll send room service to prepare the room."

"No," Eric said. "I'll just send someone down for the key, understand?"

"Yes, sir, I guess I do."

"Great," Eric said. "What's the room number?"

"Three twenty-seven."

Eric hung up and was running toward the door. He jumped into the washroom and flushed the toilet, then moved to the door and opened it. What he saw froze his blood: Moran and Corrigan stood on either side of the door jamb.

"What took you so long?" Moran asked, the space between his brows furrowed. His eyes scanned Eric for a moment, then looked past him. "Who else is here?"

"Nobody," Eric said, trying to seem nonchalant. "Just me and Pablo. Sorry it took me so long to answer the door. I was a . . . taking a crap."

Moran pushed past him, moving into the room like a big cat. Corrigan, ursine-like, followed. Moving to the window, Moran thrust open the drapes, sending volumes of brightness spilling into the room.

"Ooooh, do you have to do that?" Pablo asked. "I like it dark."

"I'll bet you do, short eyes," Corrigan said, walking over to the sofa. He glanced down at the small, wispy figure, then turned away. Moran was already systematically searching the rest of the rooms in the suite.

"What's going on here?" Eric asked, feigning ignorance.

"We're looking for somebody," Corrigan said.

Eric nodded.

Moran came back into the main room and shook his head.

"Anybody else been here?" he asked, looking down at the assortment of drug paraphernalia on the coffee table.

Eric shrugged. "A few people. Who'd you have in mind?"

Moran didn't answer. Instead he reached in his pocket and took out a cell phone. After punching in a number, he put the phone to his ear and waited.

"Yeah, boss, it's me," he said after a few moments. "We're here at Vantillberg's room. No sign of him." Moran listened, his face showing no sign of what the other party was saying. He nodded, replied in the affirmative, and terminated the call.

"Jack, what's up?" Eric asked. He ran his fingers through his hair, hoping like hell he looked sufficiently disinterested. "You gonna tell me, or what?"

Moran looked at him for a few more beats, then said, "Yeah, Rocky's out of rehab. You seen or heard from him?"

Eric let his mouth droop open hoping it would give him a few more seconds to formulate the proper response. This was touchy. If he lied and said no, it could be bad. But if he told the truth and said yes, it would no doubt be worse.

"Huh-un," he said quickly. "He done with the program?"

"In a manner of speaking," Corrigan chimed in. He grinned and leered down at Eric, looking like he was considering twisting the other man's head off.

"Well, that's good, right?" Eric said.

"How about you?" Moran said to Pablo. "You seen Rocky around?"

"Moi?" Pablo said, placing a delicate set of fingers on his chest. "I'm recuperating from an injury." He brought the fingers to his nose and touched it. "I've been here all day and Eric's been with me."

"What? One of your kids close his legs too fast?" Corrigan said, smirking.

Pablo pursed his lips but said nothing.

"I have to go to the john," Eric said, moving toward the washroom.

"I thought you just went?" Moran said.

"Have to go again," Eric answered. "I've got a spastic colon."

"I knew a guy with one of those once," Corrigan said. "He shit his pants right before I broke his neck."

Eric slipped inside the bathroom and slammed the door, twisting the knob-lock. He pulled out his cell and dialed Gant's number. It rang twice before he answered it with his typical grunt.

"It's me," Eric said. "Take him down to room three twenty-seven."

"It's open?"

"No, you have to go down to the desk to get the keys."

"And what am I supposed to do with this motherfucker in the meantime?" Gant's voice was angry. "*You* go down and get the motherfucking key."

Eric licked his lips. "Gant, I can't, believe me." He took another deep breath and patted his pocket for his cigarettes. He took his last one out of the pack and remembered again that he didn't have his lighter. "Look, just leave him there in the stairwell, okay, and go down to get the keys. Tell them I sent you for it. Then take him to the room and wait there till you hear from me. Got it?"

Gant grunted and the line went dead. Eric felt a slight rush of relief. There was a chance that this would turn out okay, so long as he kept his cool in front of them. He looked at himself in the mirror, flashed a quick practice smile, and flushed the toilet. When he went out he went immediately to the coffee table, walking past Moran, and grabbing Rocky's discarded lighter.

"So what's the latest on our other problem?" he asked, flicking the wheel and holding the flame to the end of his cigarette.

Corrigan's big fingers plucked it from Eric's mouth.

"I don't allow nobody to smoke around me," he said, smiling ruefully as he crumpled the white cylinder of tobacco and crisp paper. "I'm on a health kick lately."

"That was my last one," Eric said.

Moran ignored him, his eyes seeming to scan every nook and corner.

Eric went to the kitchen and opened the refrigerator.

"You guys want a drink or something?" he asked, trying to sound cordial. He was praying that Gant was on his way to the lobby, picking up the key.

He has to be by now, Eric thought. That's one thing about him, he's dependable. Like a big robot. Not much imagination of his own, but as long as you tell him what to do, he does all right.

"Not while I'm working," Moran said.

"I wouldn't mind something to eat," Corrigan said, stepping next to Eric and looking over his shoulder. "What you got?" He frowned and turned, grabbing a red delicious apple from the fruit basket on the counter. Eric took out a ginger ale and noticed the cap was missing. It must have been the one Rocky'd used. He swallowed hard and poured some of the yellowish liquid into a plastic glass, then carried it over toward the wet bar.

"Got a bunch of booze in that, huh?" Corrigan asked. He took another copious bite of the apple. "All the comforts of home. All you need is a plastic blow-up doll of a fourteen-year-old for the little pervert over there."

Pablo's lips curled up, then drew together. He looked about ready to say something, but remained silent.

Corrigan stared at him and nodded.

"Wise decision," he said, taking another bite.

Eric's cell phone rang and the jangling startled him.

This will be Gant telling me everything's all right, he told himself. He purposely let it ring twice more before he took his time answering it.

"Eric Vantillberg," he said with an assured smile.

"We got a problem," Gant's voice said. It was imbued with urgency.

"We do?" Eric said, forcing himself to sound light, airy. But his voice cracked slightly as he said, "So talk to me."

"I left this motherfucker in the stairwell when I went to get the key, and when I come back, he done fell down the stairs." After a moment Gant added the words that chilled Eric's bones. "He look bad, too."

Harry was, as Sinatra would have put it, dressed to the nines. He wore a grayish sport coat, a lightly printed lavender and gray tie, complete with a little gold chain tie clip, a light blue shirt, and dark slacks. He'd also given the shoeshine man in the lobby a generous tip to buff his shoes to an uncustomary high gloss. He figured if he didn't impress Ladonna Purcell, it would still pay dividends when he met Janice Grey later for their dinner date. He adjusted his tie as he walked into the restaurant/bar where she'd agreed to meet him. He carried his notebook in a leather case he'd purchased in the hotel gift shop.

Feeling that he looked the part of an all-knowing, professional journalist was a start, and starting was half the battle.

Start twice and the battle's over, he thought, smiling to himself. 'Cause heaven knows I got little else.

The bar was on the right as he went in. A long, darkly stained piece of polished mahogany that curved out to form a sharp wedge at the center. The subdued lighting came mostly from ornately fashioned lanterns on the walls. It was hardly crowded, but then again, it was still early afternoon. He scanned the booths near the wall. The third one, she'd said. But it was empty.

After he seated himself a cocktail waitress ambled over and he ordered a club soda.

She went away without a word and the smell of redolent booze began to waft its way over toward him. Maybe it hadn't been such a good idea to agree to meet here after all. He stole a glance over at the bar. Rows of bottles of the good stuff lined the back wall, like sentinels against loneliness, their sculpted ridges and smooth curves reflected solemnly in the adjacent mirrored backdrop. Harry licked his lips.

Not a good idea at all, he thought. Not at all.

Just as he was starting to feel himself sweat, she walked in. If he hadn't known it was her, he would have still thought she was a stunningly beautiful woman. A swarthy, hulking guy was at her side as she stood in the doorway and he watched her count one, two, three to the third booth. To him. She was wearing sunglasses and a beige, nondescript coat, but it barely concealed her elegance as she whispered something to the big guy and he stayed stationed at the entryway. As she strode purposefully over to the booth Harry noticed that she was taller than he expected. He rose as she got closer, but her perfect lips formed one word: No. Waggling her fingers, she indicated that he should sit down, and then slid into the seat across the table from him.

"Hi," she said. "I'm Ladonna Purcell." She removed her sunglasses and he noticed her eyes were a deep shade of blue, in contrast to her dark hair. "I believe we talked on the phone?"

"Yes, I'm Harry Bauer, *Regency Magazine*." He waved to the waitress and Ladonna immediately turned her face slightly away. "Do you want something?"

"Some ice water," she said, still looking away.

Harry made the order.

"Actually, we talked before," he said. "I interviewed you over the phone about a month ago. Remember?"

She smiled showing him her perfect teeth. The lipstick she wore gave her lips a moist, wet look.

"I'm afraid I get a lot of requests to do interviews. Especially around this time of the year."

Harry smiled. So this was how it was going to be, eh? She wasn't giving him anything. Probably planned to wait to have him show his cards first. Too bad he didn't have any. It was time to bluff or die.

"So, Ms. Purcell." He paused while the waitress set the glass in front of Ladonna and discreetly left. "I appreciate you agreeing to meet me on such short notice."

She sipped her ice water.

"Like I mentioned earlier," he said, feeling the awkwardness of the moment growing. "I'm following up on a series of features that Buzzy Sawyer was doing for the *Las Vegas Mirror*."

The blue eyes scrutinized him, but she still said nothing. She was a counterpuncher. Harry decided to wade right in. It was the only way.

"Let me get to the point," he said.

"Yes," she said finally. "Why don't you?"

He took a deep breath.

"I have Buzzy's notes. All of them."

She raised her eyebrows.

"Then it'll probably be pretty easy for you to finish his story, won't it?"

For a southern girl, her words were remarkably free of any telltale accent.

"I could," he said. "But I wanted to talk to you first."

Something seemed to click behind her perfect features. Like a familiar musical chord had been struck. Her mouth tugged at one corner into a slight smile.

"You believe in being direct, don't you, Mr. Bauer?"

"Of course," Harry said. He suddenly felt like he'd changed lanes on a dark highway and had lost his headlights.

"Well?" she said.

He cocked his head attentively.

"Why don't you lay it out for me?" she asked. She brought the water to her lips again.

As Harry was getting ready to speak, his cell phone rang.

It jarred both of them. The ringing continued, insistent. Her eyes widened slightly and she looked away.

Harry plucked the phone from his belt clip and answered it.

"Hi, Harry, it's Tim," the voice said.

"Tim, I'm right in the middle of an interview. This better be important."

"Well, I just figured I'd call and let you know, it's official. They're married now."

"Fine. Great. Is that it?"

"Not quite."

Something tweaked at Harry's heart.

"Is Lynn okay?"

"Huh? Oh yeah, sure," Stockton said. "Me and her just kind of hung out together at the church. I'm taking her to the reception tonight."

"What? She's only—" He stopped short, looking across the table. "She's too young to go to something like that, dammit."

"Relax, Harry, that's why I'm going there." Stockton's voice sounded placating. "I'll look after her."

"You'd better."

"Anyways," Stockton continued. "The reason I called you was this woman kept calling here saying it was an emergency and asking to speak to me. They finally got ahold of me and patched me through."

"Let me guess. Marjorie Versette?"

"Yeah. She said you told her that I could vouch for you?"

Harry smiled. "Well, did you?"

"Un huh, and she said you need to get ahold of her ASAP. Said she had info, big info, on the Colton Purcell story."

"Her and a million other people," Harry said. "Look, like I told you, I'm kind of busy here. She give you any indication of what she wanted to tell me?"

"She just said it was very important to Buzzy Sawyer and anybody who wanted to find out what really happened."

"She said that?"

"Un huh, and that she could give you the straight scoop on someplace called the Graceland . . . the Graceful . . ."

"The Graceful Valley Nursing Home?" Harry asked. Out of the corner of his eye he saw Ladonna jerk noticeably.

He'd struck a nerve with that one. "She leave a number?"

"No, she wouldn't. But I gave her yours. Your cell. Was that okay?"

"You did great, kid," Harry said. "Now one more thing. Make sure my daughter stays away from the cake and ice cream after seven thirty. Too much sugar will give her nightmares. And who's she staying with tonight?"

"Karen's sister," Stockton said.

"Okay, tell her that her daddy loves her, and that I'll call her later." He terminated the call and slipped the phone back onto his belt. "Sorry about that."

"That's okay. How old's your daughter?"

"Nine, going on fifteen and a half."

Ladonna smiled.

"Mine's seventeen, going on twenty-five. Or so she thinks."

"Yeah, I heard that she almost tied the knot earlier in the summer down in Mexico." He paused. "But we both know how that turned out."

Ladonna's guard came up again.

"All right, Mr. Bauer, where were we?"

"I think I'd just asked to hear your side of it."

Her brow furrowed slightly as she took a long drink of water, looking to the side, to the mirrored backdrop, and the reflection of them sitting in the darkened booth. When she turned back to him, her eyes were glistening.

"I'm not so sure I'm ready to go through this again," she said.

"Go through what?"

"Paying out money." She canted her head. A tear rolled down her cheek. "That's what you want, isn't it?"

"Not really," he said. "I'm actually after the truth."

"Aren't we all?" She sighed. "So am I going to have to

pay out more money to him too?"

"Him?"

"Your friend Mr. Sawyer. I thought he agreed to back off permanently?"

The question stunned Harry.

"You don't know?"

"Know what?"

"Buzzy's dead," Harry said. "He was killed."

Now it was her turn to look stunned. The blue eyes widened for an instant, the pained lips drawing back showing a flash of white teeth like a glimpse of bone through an open wound.

"No, I hadn't heard." She took another sip of her water, but Harry thought it was more a stalling gesture than from thirst.

"Ah, when did this happen?" she asked.

He shrugged. "About two weeks ago I guess. He was mugged."

This seemed to stun her further. The reaction was muted, but he still caught it. She stood up cocking her head. "I can't deal with this right now." The big guy was at her side in a flash, his flat face staring down at Harry.

"I'll have someone get in touch with you," she said as she turned and walked away, the monster lumbering beside her, occasionally glancing back over his shoulder. Harry watched the subtle sway of her hips in the tight pants as she walked, thinking, Yeah, I managed to touch a nerve somehow. If I only knew with what.

Chapter 19

Intimate Convolutions

It was a much more intimate setting than the last time. Soft lighting and arched windows veiled with gossamer curtains. The tablecloths were fine white linen, and light jazz from the piano player was anything but intrusive. Harry knew he had to figure out all the angles of Buzzy's story, why his comments and the news of his death had affected Ladonna so, and put it all together in the very near future. But he also knew the value of the subconscious and letting things percolate. Besides, he was far too interested in the present at the moment. He had a date with an angel. An angel who seemed interested enough in him to call him back after a shaky start. He looked up and saw Janice Grey come in, look around, and then smile as their eyes met.

"Hi," he said, standing and reaching out to touch her hand. She smiled and gave his a reciprocating squeeze.

"Been waiting long?" she asked, sitting as he held the chair for her. She was dressed in a sleeveless white blouse and dark slacks. Like perhaps she'd just come from work. He was about to ask if she had, when the waiter appeared out of nowhere. He gave them menus as Harry sat. She ordered white wine and he caught the flicker of interest as he asked for club soda with a lime twist.

Maybe honesty is the best policy, he thought. Probably better to get it out in the open rather than leave it for later.

"I don't drink," he said.

"No?" Her eyebrows lifted slightly, but she was obviously following his lead.

"Actually, I just got out of rehab," he said, holding up three fingers. "For the third time."

She sat there for a moment, then a lips-only smile crossed her face.

"Well, then," she said, "let's hope the third time's the charm."

Placing her palm over the receiver of the telephone, Ladonna yelled for Melissa Michelle to turn the volume on the TV down a bit. In the other room of the plush suite, the old MTV video of Britney Spears continued to blast away, and Ladonna brought her hands up to her ears. She yelled at her daughter again and the racking beat subsided slightly. But only slightly.

"Ladonna, it's Montgomery Spangler," the voice on the other end of the line finally said. "Sorry to keep you waiting."

"It's about goddamned time," Ladonna said, then added, "Hold on a minute." She walked to the bedroom door and slammed it shut, muttering under her breath. "Have you found him yet?"

"Not yet, dear." The lawyer's tone was conciliatory. "But we're closing in. We have good reason to believe they're in Las Vegas."

"That's saying a lot. I'm in Vegas, for Christ sake." She held the receiver so tightly that her fingers were starting to go numb. "I may have a lead on where they are myself."

"Really? Tell me what you've got and I'll pass it along to our investigator."

He sounded eager. Very eager.

She stared at her reflection in the mirror above the credenza. "Montgomery, what happened to that other matter with that reporter? What was his name? Sawyer, or something?"

"Why, as we discussed, he was paid the agreed upon amount to cease and desist," Spangler said, but she could detect the fluster in his voice. He was lying. She knew it. "Why do you ask?"

"And you arranged the payoff? Personally?"

"Well, I'd hardly call it a 'payoff'." His tone was jovial, but had enough hesitation in it to set her on edge. "I prefer the term kill fee. That's what they call it in the business when a writer is paid although his feature story is dropped."

"Kill fee?" she said. "How come you didn't tell me he's dead?"

"Dead?" Spangler's tone had a touch of surprise. But it wasn't enough to sound convincing.

"Don't lie to me, goddammit. Now tell me, what happened?"

"It's . . . my . . . understanding," Spangler said, taking his time between words, "That . . . he was . . . mugged." He gave a nervous lilt to the last word.

Ladonna felt a shiver travel down her spine. She said nothing for several seconds. Neither did he, but she could hear his sonorous breathing.

"Oh my god," she said. "How could you get us mixed up in this kind of thing? Montgomery, how could you?" Her voice broke and she felt the hot rush of tears down her face. "I trusted you."

"Ladonna, pull yourself together," he said, his tone sounding firm and secure. "First of all, let me assure you that any decisions I make will always have your and Melissa Michelle's welfare at heart." She heard him take a deep breath and exhale. "Secondly, we don't have any indication that Mr. Sawyer's demise was anything other than a standard, run-of-the-mill robbery. You're reading too much into this thing."

"What kind of people are we dealing with here?" she asked. "I want my daughter protected, Montgomery. Do you hear me? Get this mess settled and get us away from here."

"If that's what you want, that's what we'll do," he said, his tone that of the cajoling, comforting attorney again. "Now tell me about this lead you have on Willard."

"Who have you got working on finding him?"

"I told you, they're the very best. Now . . . ?"

She sighed, trying to figure out what to say. The thumping beat from a new video permeated the bedroom now.

I've got Melissa to think about, Ladonna thought.

"Another reporter," she said. "His name is Harry Bauer."

Even the redolence of the alcohol from her glass didn't tempt Harry at this point. He'd become intoxicated by her instead. Her grayish-blue eyes, with the irises dilated slightly in the restaurant's cozy ambience, the way she tilted her head when he spoke, the way her lips drew back in a smile that showed her strong white teeth. . . . Their conversation had never once drifted to work or any related things. All at once, Harry felt as if he'd known her all his life. Or at least for the only portion of it that mattered.

The bus boy came and removed their plates. Another attendant poured them more coffee and asked her if she needed more wine.

She looked at him.

"Do I?" she asked, then added with a punctuating giggle, "Or am I drunk enough now for you to have your way with me?"

He laughed too, and marveled at how they'd each become part of this wonderful mood. All their residual problems and concerns suddenly seemed as far away as the dark side of the moon.

For some strange reason Harry suddenly thought about the moon and wondered if it was full. He longed to go for a walk under the desert sky, looking up at the celestial heavens. But he knew the sidereal view would be overshadowed by the gaudy brightness that never stopped shining in this anomalous city. He caught her looking at him.

"What were you thinking just now?" she asked.

He smiled slightly.

"Just wondering if you'd like to go for a walk under a velvet sky and look at the stars."

She laughed. "You're joking, right? You can't even see the stars around here. There's too much interference from everything."

"Maybe we could if we drove into the desert," he said. "I'd have to drive, of course, seeing as how you've been imbibing . . ."

"Oh, right. I could see us getting pulled over with you driving an unmarked police car."

"I'd be on my best behavior. Scout's honor."

Now it was her turn to smile. She stared at him intently for a moment, then brushed some errant hair back from her face.

"You're staying at the MGM, right?"

He nodded, hoping that he was reading the signals correctly. This almost sounds like she's . . . interested, he thought.

"You know," she said slowly. "In all the time I've worked Vegas PD, I must have been called to every hotel but that one. And it's so big."

"It's humongous. You should see the lions."

She compressed her lips.

"So, I've been wondering what it's like inside . . ." she said. "Is your room nice?"

"It's fabulous." He watched her carefully for another sign. When her head canted and her eyes widened ever so slightly, Harry added, "Want to come see for yourself?"

Ladonna held her hair back with her right hand and finished throwing up into the toilet. The sour taste of bile corroded her throat and esophagus. She flushed the commode and went to the sink, rinsing her mouth with cool water, but it did little to wash away the taste of the bitterness. Looking at her reflection in the mirror she realized she'd have to redo her eyes in case anybody happened to see her. The driving beat of a video suddenly seemed to worm its way into her skull and she thought she was going to retch again.

What kind of people did he get us mixed up with? she wondered, feeling the tightness start to compress her stomach. She leaned over the bowl, but this time nothing came out.

I've got nothing left, she thought.

Swallowing, she straightened up and rinsed out once more. Then she splashed cold water over her face and patted it dry.

She knew there was only one option left. She had to call him, and soon.

As she walked out she saw Melissa Michelle mimicking the dance moves on the TV. Christina Aguilera twisted, bumped, and gyrated to the Latin beat.

"Pablo likes this one," Melissa Michelle said breathlessly. "Maybe we'll do it as a duet for our first video."

Ladonna strode over and shut off the television.

"What'd you do *that* for?" Melissa whined.

"Because I'm fucking tired of not being able to hear my-self think," she said. Her expression told the girl all she needed to know. Instead of arguing, she simply drew her lips together tightly.

Ladonna stared at her daughter a moment more, then turned and went into the bedroom again. She slammed the door and waited. After a few moments she heard the sound of the television resume, but greatly subdued. Closing her eyes, Ladonna reached for her cell phone and checked the battery level. Satisfied that it was almost fully charged, she pressed one, and then the remaining ten digits and listened for the once-familiar rings.

He answered after only four.

"Hi," she said. "It's me."

Silence, then he said slowly, "Howdy, darlin'. What's up?"

"I . . . I'm in Las Vegas," she said haltingly. "I've got some trouble." She waited for a reassuring inquiry, but none came. Finally, after more interminable silence from the other end, she asked, "Do you think you could come here? This is a big mess. I need your help."

Chapter 20

Defining Moments

It began to grate on Harry as she drove them to his hotel. Here he was, on his first real date in he couldn't remember how long, and the girl was driving. Girl, he thought, sneaking a glance at the pertness of her profile. She was probably a good six years younger than he was . . .

Who am I kidding? he thought. I've got a decade on her if it's a day. Well, maybe not a whole decade, but close. She'd said she'd been a cop for six and half years, so that would make her at least twenty-seven or twenty-eight.

He exhaled slowly.

What I wouldn't give to be on the right side of thirty again, he thought, smiling as the cool air rushed in the windows. Even on the right side of thirty-five.

It got worse for him as they parked and walked across the lighted bridge toward the bright gaudiness of the fountains and the massive golden lion at the front entrance. They held hands, like young lovers out for a stroll, but as they headed for the elevators, pausing momentarily to look through the glass wall at the captive lions, Harry suddenly was caught by a feeling of commiseration with the big cats. He felt suddenly very nervous instead of elated.

Performance anxiety?

He wondered how it would all play out, him feeling anything but sure of himself at the moment. He was thinking of how long it had been since he'd been with someone. Someone who mattered.

As if on cue, the big cat raised his head and fixed Harry

216

with a feral yellow iris bisected by a vertical slash of black pupil. The tawny eye blinked once, then looked away.

Do you know something I don't, pal? he thought.

"Maybe he's hungry," she said, smiling. "We'd better get out of here."

As they walked along the hallway past the cracked mirrors, he heard the pinging of the elevator doors. Several people got out, laughing and jostling toward the casino to lose more money. But at least they were having a good time, he hoped.

Tentatively, they stepped into the elevator and the doors slid shut leaving them alone and together. She glanced at him with an inquisitiveness and he realized he hadn't pushed the floor button.

I'm a real suave and debonair kind of guy, aren't I? he thought.

The elevator car rushed upward making a sudden chill go up his spine. Or was it anticipation? Harry swallowed as the doors opened and they went down the hallway still holding hands, him fishing in his jacket pocket for his key.

He slid the card into the slot on the door, watching the red light turn green, and pushed.

"Wow, this is really neat," she said.

"Yeah, isn't it?" he said, feeling the tightening in his neck, trying to remember the last time such a splendid opportunity had presented itself to him.

She turned then and set her purse down in a nearby chair. He wondered if her gun was inside. From the size of the bag, he guessed it was.

Something else suddenly occurred to him.

He hadn't thought that this trip would afford any opportunities for intimacies, and he hadn't prepared. He imagined his childhood Boy Scout leader standing before him in stern admonishment. But to no avail. Condoms, the crucial staple of every modern dating ritual since the 90s, were nowhere to be found in his room. But how to broach this delicate subject when they were already here, and things were going so well.

He cleared his throat.

"It's got a really great view from the windows," he said, his hand on the small of her back, guiding her across the room, past the huge king-sized bed. He wondered what she was thinking.

Pulling open the drapes, he exposed the myriad points of light as the panorama of the cityscape spread out before them. His arm was around her waist now, and her hand found its way to his hip, her head on his shoulder.

As he started to speak she reached up and gently brushed his lips with her fingers. Then turning, put both her arms around his neck, kissing him.

Oh great, she's taking the lead again, he thought. It's a good thing we're not dancing. But he could hardly complain. Their lips parted slightly, then more hungrily, as she pressed against him.

"Janice," he said.

"Call me Jan."

"Jan, there's something I need to mention here."

She paused, drawing back slightly with a wicked looking smile.

"What? You're gay?" She pressed closer. "Hmm . . . no, I don't think that's it."

He smiled too.

"No, but it's close," he said. "Un, I wasn't expecting any romance, so I neglected to bring a certain box of items. . . ." He let his voice trail off.

She kissed him again, lightly flicking her tongue over his.

"That's okay," she said, whispering into his ear. "I've got some."

"And, unnn . . . it's been kind of a long time for me . . ."

She touched his lips softly, then kissed him again.

"It's just like riding a bicycle," she said softly. "Once you learn, you never forget how."

"Doc, what are you doing?" Eric asked, panicking as he saw the doctor lifting up the phone and punching in some numbers.

"Calling an ambulance," the doctor said, pausing to give his nurse, a hefty woman in a gaudy sports outfit, some instructions about adjusting the cervical collar and oxygen mask on the supine Rocky.

Eric patted his pocket and took out his cigarettes. The only way he'd been able to get away from the Mutt and Jeff of organized crime was to beg a moment to go down to get a new pack of smokes. He'd used the time to slip into the third floor room and check how things were going.

"Yes, this is Dr. Edwards, I need paramedics and an ambulance to room three twenty-seven immediately please." He looked over to Eric and snapped his fingers, shaking his head. "No smoking, please. Oxygen here."

Eric looked at the cigarette, frowned, and put it back into his pack. Then he looked at Rocky. Gant had been right. He didn't look good. The man's thin chest rose and fell sporadically, and his color had a grayish tint to it. Eric swallowed hard and asked the question.

"Is he gonna be all right?"

The doctor ignored him, speaking more instructions into the phone. He was saying something about immediate transfer to a hospital and to make sure the paramedics brought stabilization equipment. "We have a possible injury to the cervical area," he added. When he hung up, he leaned over, peeling back one of the slumbering man's eyelids.

"You say he fell down the stairs?" he asked.

Eric looked to Gant, who was slumped in a chair watching TV.

"Gant?"

"What?"

"Did he fall down the stairs?" Eric asked, his voice cracking slightly.

"Yeah." He held up the remote and raised the volume. Two gangstas shot a couple of honky cops and a judge on the screen while a rap soundtrack blared, "Justice for one, justice for all. All the crackers going to fall."

"How many stairs and where?" Dr. Edwards asked.

Eric waited, then said, "Gant?" again.

The big man turned his head, showing Eric a placid, flat face.

"Maybe one floor." He shrugged. "What's that? Maybe ten, twelve steps? Don't rightly know."

"You shouldn't have moved him, you know," the doctor said. "There's evidence of significant trauma to the cervical vertebra, and the medulla oblongata is possibly affected as well."

Eric winced as if he'd been hit.

"Doc, in English?"

"He quite possibly has a fractured neck," the doctor said. He looked up at Eric over his sagging glasses. "There may be injury to the spinal cord as well. In these cases, moving the patient before stabilization can have disastrous consequences."

"So what are you saying?" Eric asked. "That he could be paralyzed or something?"

The doctor shrugged. "We'll know more when we get a CAT scan and MRI."

Eric rubbed his hand over his face, then looked at his watch.

Oh, Lord, oh, Lord, he thought. Get me on the first plane outta here. He turned to Gant.

"You gotta go with him to the hospital," he said.

"Huh?" Gant said, his face crinkling in distaste. "What the fuck am I gonna do there?"

"You're going to get him registered under a phony name, that's what," Eric said. "That'll buy us some time."

Gant's mouth gaped open slightly, but he said nothing.

"Mr. Vantillberg," Dr. Edwards said. "I'm afraid I cannot be part and party to any duplicity involving this patient."

"Okay, you're fired then," Eric said. "Just get him to the hospital, that's all. We'll take it from there."

Dr. Edwards frowned and turned away.

Eric squeezed the bridge of his nose, like he was trying to stop an impending nosebleed. His eyes were crushed shut.

Think, think, think, he told himself. If he gets checked in to some hospital, then there's no way to trace it back to me. That way, no matter what happens, the old man'll think he came to Vegas looking to score and ended up on the wrong side of the dollar.

Yeah, he told himself. It could work, as long as I can play it cool in front of Corrigan and Moran. He took a deep breath.

"Okay, you got it? Get him checked into the hospital and then call me with the info." He glanced at his watch and went to the window. He could see the set of rotating red lights winding its way down the strip through the maze of lights. That had to be the ambulance.

"I gotta get back upstairs," he said, pointing at Gant, then to Rocky. "Call me, okay?"

The black giant nodded.

Once they'd shed their clothes in two separate heaps by the bed, and had settled in under the sheets, Harry's initial nervousness had vanished. He was struck at how delicate, yet supple her body looked. She'd insisted on leaving the drapes open but the lights off. In the moonlight that filtered in through the window, he traced the outline of her face first, then each subsequent curve of her form. Their love-making had been unhurried, almost in slow motion, each caress a painstaking anticipation of what was yet to come. Finally, as they made love, first with him on top and then switching so she straddled him, he watched in fascination at the breathless movements of her face, her shoulders, her waist.

Afterward, they lay together with her head tucked in the crux of his shoulder.

"I have a confession to make," he said.

She leaned her head back slightly so she could look up into his eyes. "What?"

"That was a lot better than riding a bicycle."

For a moment he was afraid he'd read her wrong. Misjudged her cop's sense of humor. Then he saw the white flash of her smile and felt the rush of breath from her laugh.

"Are you always this funny in bed?" she asked.

"I hope that's a compliment."

She snuggled closer. "Mmmm, it is."

He felt her hot skin against his and thought in that instance there was no other place on earth he'd rather be. Nor no one else he'd rather be with.

He told her that.

"Isn't that supposed to be my line?" she asked softly. "Since you did such a marvelous job of sweeping me off my feet?"

She was the one who'd done most of the sweeping he thought. But he said, "I just wanted to be totally honest with you."

Her fingers traced over the hair on his chest.

"That's a refreshing change from what I'm used to," she said. Her head raised off his shoulder. "Anyway, you were wonderful. I'm glad I gave up the chance to work overtime tonight to be with you." She giggled.

"Wow, now I really feel fortunate," he said, smiling. Her laugh was infectious.

"So when you go back to Chicago, will you remember this as one of your defining moments?"

Defining moments, he thought. And something clicked inside his head, like the cartoon of someone turning on a light switch.

She must have sensed his reaction because she asked, "What?"

"Just what you said just now. 'Defining moment.' I've been trying to break the password code on one of Buzzy's disks all day long. And now I suddenly realized what I think the password is."

"Defining moment?" she asked. "Isn't that kind of long for a password?"

"No, it was something to do with one of his defining moments. His wife mentioned it to me."

"So I suppose you want to get up and try it, huh?"

"Not a chance," he said, squeezing her shoulders.

"Well, I have to get up," she said, reaching across him and pulling back the sheet.

He watched as she padded, naked, to the bathroom, her

skin looking like pale opalescence as the ambient lighting washed over her back. As he lay there alone his mind raced back to the puzzle. He couldn't help it. Something had been gnawing at his subconscious all day, perhaps longer. It was something that he'd remembered hearing that had seemed vaguely familiar. Something that he was struggling with now to set into place. The proper place. But what?

Reviewing all his activities of the day in his mind, one by one, he tried to sort it out. Getting the runaround from Nash, driving out to meet Linda Sawyer, her telling him Buzzy's defining moment, the trip to Resurrection, the call from Jan, the tales in the crypt with the Fabray boys, the CD discovery, the Ladonna interview, and then this . . .

He smiled at the most recent memory.

He heard the toilet flush.

Something had jarred Ladonna during their talk. Him saying that Buzzy'd been murdered? No, she'd been affected before that. During his phone interruption. Who was it? Marjorie Versette. The name stuck in his mind . . . Graceful Valley Nursing Home . . . Nurse Marjorie. Buzzy's column. That much he remembered. But there was something else. Something more that still wasn't quite clear.

The lights snapped on and she was jumping next to him on the bed.

"Turn over," she said, her mouth twisting into a mock-evil grin. "You're under arrest."

"Shouldn't we close the drapes first?"

"Screw 'em," she said. "We'll give somebody a show." She flipped him on his stomach, with some assistance from him, straddled his hips, and began a soothing massage of his back and shoulders. "You looked tense. This will relax you."

It did. Her fingers were like velvet rubbing over glass.

224

She traced his spine up to his neck and began kneading the flesh there. That's when it came to him.

"The neck," he said.

"Too hard?"

"No, Graceful Valley Nursing Home. The head nurse was found with a broken neck."

She stopped her kneading and leaned over close to his ear.

"You'd better tell me what you're driving at before I really do slap the cuffs on you."

Harry felt the immediate need to sit up. She stretched out beside him and shot a questioning look his way.

Harry licked his lips and said, "Bear with me a minute. This has been bothering me for a couple of days. Let me tap into your expertise."

The questioning look continued, but she used her hand to prop up her head and listened intently.

"Could you tell the difference between a strangulation and a death by hanging?" he asked.

"You certainly know how to sweet talk a girl after you've been to bed with her."

"No, I'm sorry, but really . . . this is important. Could you?"

She sighed. "I suppose an autopsy might disclose it. If the hyoid bone was broken. But death by hanging, unless it's done execution style, where the person's neck is broken, is really asphyxiation."

"Exactly," Harry said. "And that security guard the other night died of a broken neck, right?"

Her eyes widened, then narrowed. Her stare was intense.

"How did you know that?"

"Never mind," he said. "I just heard it, that's all. But listen to this. Back when I was in Memphis, I talked to a de-

Michael A. Black

tective about the death of Colton Purcell's old manager, Big
Daddy Babcock. He supposedly hanged himself."

She looked guarded now. "So?"

"So, I told the detective that I'd interviewed Babcock
about a month ago, and the old boy sounded anything but
suicidal or depressed."

"People are sometimes good at masking their emotions,"
she said, lapsing into her professional tone now.

He was losing her, he realized, and sought to tie it up
quickly.

"But I looked at the signature on the alleged note,"
Harry said. He was talking fast now. "It was too flamboyant
for a man about to kill himself."

"Really, Dr. Freud?"

He smiled and touched her arm lightly, holding up a
finger with his other hand.

"But the guy said they were knee-deep in homicides, including the head nurse of the Graceful Valley Nursing
Home, who died of a broken neck."

Janice Grey's brow furrowed, but he kept talking.

"And it just so happens that Buzzy'd interviewed this
woman, named Marjorie Versette, who took care of this old
guy who was rumored to secretly be Colton Purcell, at the
very same Graceful Valley place. And she's now here in Las
Vegas trying to get ahold of me." He held out his arms,
palms up. "Don't you see? It all ties together somehow.
Don't you think so?"

Her face grew solemn.

"More than you know," she said, sitting up and tucking
the sheet over her bare breasts. "Do you remember the
name of that detective in Memphis?"

Harry nodded. "I'm sure I have it in my notes somewhere.
He scammed me out of fifty bucks." He grinned. "Why?"

"I think I'd better call him," she said. Her lips compressed into a thin line, then she touched his arm. "When I got called away last night for that homicide, it was because the MO was similar to one of the cases I've been working." She paused.

Harry looked at her expectantly.

"Your friend Buzzy," she said. "He also died of a broken neck."

Chapter 21

All Roads Lead to Rome

Harry heard her in the shower and glanced at his bedside clock. The red numbers spelled out 5:03 AM. He thought about getting up to join her but heard the water being shut off. Better to let her preserve her modesty, he thought, and stretched out under the sheet. After a few minutes she came out with a towel wrapped around her and sat on the edge of the bed.

"I was wondering if you needed your back scrubbed?" he said.

Her hair was still damp and dripped water onto her shoulder. Taking the towel from around her, but still with her back to him, she dried her neck.

"I didn't want to wake you," she said. "I have to get home and change clothes for work." She slipped on her underwear and fitted herself into her bra.

As she stood his eyes followed her, traced over the body that he'd come to know so well the night before.

"Well let me buy you some breakfast, at least," he said, kicking his legs out from under the sheet.

"No," she said, then placed her palm gently on his shoulder. "I really have to get going. I'll grab something on the way."

"Oh yeah, I forgot about what they say about cops and donuts."

She smiled.

"What about dinner?" he asked.

"I'm on call tonight. Might be a long day." She was but-

228

toning her blouse now, and he watched her fingers fasten each button. "Do you have the name of that Memphis detective for me?"

"Oh yeah," Harry said, standing and slipping into his underpants. For some reason, despite their night of intimacy, he felt slightly uncomfortable being naked when she was almost dressed. He walked to the desk and paged through his spiral notebook. "So much has happened to me since then . . ." He turned and smiled. "So much of it good, that it seems like ancient history now." He found the envelope in the notebook's pocket. The Polaroids of the Big Daddy Babcock crime scene and the detective's card were tucked inside.

"The guy's name is Roger D. Tucker," he said, handing her the envelope. "His card's in there. There are some photos too."

"He gave you these?" she asked.

"Actually, I bought them. With a stipulation that Roger D. has a walk-on part in my book about the whole thing."

She stuffed the envelope into her purse, looked at him, and smiled.

He felt a twinge of embarrassment at being clad only in his briefs.

"What?" he asked.

"I was just wondering what part I'll occupy in your story."

He grinned.

"Let's hope the best of that part is yet to be written," he said.

Ladonna finished stripping off the rest of her makeup and twisted her hair into a ponytail. Glancing in the mirror, she figured she looked sufficiently dowdy, and slipped on a blue T-shirt which she let dangle over the top of her jeans. She set the baseball cap on her head, looping her ponytail over the plastic strap in back before snapping it in place and slipping on a pair of dark sunglasses. When she tried to slip out of her room, Melissa Michelle was suddenly looming in the hall in a bathrobe, her hair damp from the shower.

"Mom, where are you going?" She recoiled slightly. "And looking like *that?*"

Ladonna inhaled sharply and moved past her.

"I have to go out and meet somebody. Stay here until I get back."

"What? No way," the girl said. "I need to get a new outfit for tonight, remember? And I want to see if Pablo can meet me for lunch. And then I have to get my hair done. Remember?"

Ladonna stopped and turned. She was about to start yelling but thought better of it.

"Melissa, I don't think that's a good idea."

"What? Going shopping or seeing Pablo?"

Ladonna closed her eyes.

"Look, I don't have time to go into this now," she said. She took off her glasses and rubbed her eyes. "But we have to sit down and have a real serious talk, okay?"

Melissa Michelle pursed her lips.

"Oh, Mom, you're so old-fashioned." She began stomping off toward her room. "I'll see you when I get back."

"I told you to stay here."

Melissa Michelle made a face and stuck out her tongue.

Ladonna strode down the hall after her daughter.

"I'm sick of your shit!" she screamed, grabbing the girl's arm and spinning her around.

Melissa Michelle winced and tried to twist away, but

Ladonna's grip was too strong. She put her index finger in front of the girl's face.

"Now you listen." Her voice was a sharp hiss. "You're not to go out at all, understand? And I don't want to hear anything more about Pablo."

"Mom, you're hurting me."

Ladonna's stare seemed to cut into her daughter for a moment, then she released her and started to cry.

"Mom?" The girl's voice was imbued with obvious concern. "What's wrong?"

Ladonna continued to shake for a few moments more, then she wiped her cheek with the back of her hand and looked into her daughter's eyes.

"I know you think I've made some mistakes," she said. "And I have. I know I have, believe me. But I'm just trying to spare you the problems I've been through."

"Mom, you were my age when you married daddy."

"I was eighteen," Ladonna shot back. "And it was a mistake. A big mistake."

Melissa Michelle seemed to recoil.

"So am I a mistake too, then?"

Ladonna reached up to try and stroke her daughter's hair, but the girl turned her face away.

"No, honey, you're the only good thing that came out of it." She caressed the girl's cheek slightly, then said, "Please, don't go out anywhere until I get back. I won't be long, and I want Joe to go with us, okay?"

Melissa Michelle's mouth was still pulled together in a haughty pout.

"Melissa, please."

With an exaggerated huff, she said, "Okay, Mom."

Ladonna wiped her face again, then put the sunglasses back on. She was out the door and dialing her cell phone as she walked. The other phone rang twice after she pressed the SEND button.

"Hi, darlin'," he said.

"Hi. I'm on the way down now."

"I'll be a waiting."

Harry whispered a prayer as he typed in Khe Sanh in the box provided for the password. Seconds later the words disappeared and PASSWORD PROTECTED reappeared. He swore and punched the bed.

Back to square one, he thought, standing up and grabbing the list of previous attempts. He scribbled the latest try and reviewed the selection.

He'd been so sure that it was Khe Sanh. The defining moment comment gave him the idea. Linda had said that Buzzy still talked about it. About its effect on him. What else could it be? What would a paranoid ex-gyrene like Buzzy use to safeguard his information?

Harry dialed Linda's home number again and heard it ring three times before her answering machine switched on.

He left still another halting message for her to call him on his cell or hotel phones, and that it was a matter of the utmost urgency. Just as he was hanging up her voice came on the line.

"Harry?"

"Linda. I thought you were out."

"I was, but I just came in as the machine picked up. What's going on?"

Harry thought about how to phrase his request.

"I got a few of Buzzy's files from the paper," he said, figuring he'd better keep the disguised Colton Purcell CD that she'd given him a secret. "But I can't open them."

He heard her laugh.

"What did I tell you?" she said. "Password protected, right?"

"You got it." He sighed. "Any ideas? I've tried everything I could think of."

"I really don't know what to tell you," she said. "You can read me the list of the ones you've tried, if you like."

So he did. She laughed at most of them, gave him a few suggestions, then lamented when they came up wrong.

"You obviously knew him a lot better than I did," Harry said. "What's your best guess? Would he have used numbers or letters or a combination?"

He heard her sigh.

"It's hard to say," she said slowly, "but he wasn't always real good at remembering numbers, but he did say that a numbered code would always be harder to break."

"Numbers, numbers, numbers," Harry repeated, trying to mentally come up with a list of possibilities to run by her.

"Look, Harry, I don't think there's much hope in pursuing this. Buzzy was kind of fanatical about his privacy. He wouldn't have picked something that anybody else would have been able to figure out."

"Yeah, I guess you're right."

After an appropriate goodbye, he hung up and sat staring at the laptop's screen. The picture of the file with the oblong box designating the secret impediment seemed to stare back at him in mocking fashion.

Defining moments, he thought. Something that would be easy for him to remember, but impossible for anyone else to figure out.

He thought of his own passwords, which were mostly combinations of letters and numbers. Letters and numbers, he thought, and suddenly another idea that he hadn't tried struck him. He grabbed the phone, quickly punching in the numbers and silently hoping that if she did pick up she wouldn't think he was some kind of intrusive nutcase.

"Hello," Linda's voice said.

"It's Harry," he said, wincing as he heard her audible sigh in response.

"Yes, Harry."

He figured from her tone he'd have one and only one shot at this now. Trying to sound as unobtrusive and conciliatory as possible, he asked the question.

"Look, I know I'm being a real pest here, but if I could ask you one more favor . . ."

He let the question sort of drip off into space until he heard her reply.

"Ask away." Her voice sounded patient, but he knew it was probably masking residual anger.

He felt a surge of relief, then hoped like hell that this wouldn't be yet another false hope.

"Do you think you could give me Buzzy's service number?"

Corrigan watched the slow mid-morning shuffle of dejected losers heading into the bar from the casino as he sipped his coffee. He'd taken his customary seat with his back to the door, and was delighted to find it meant that he could also see the TV that was mounted above the bartender's station. But he wasn't interested in the talk shows and told the guy to switch it to the local news show so he could keep an eye on any possible composite drawings of the suspect from the hotel murder. He loved seeing how far off those things invariably were. But so far, there'd been nothing. He sipped more of the hot liquid and waited. Finally he saw Moran come through the archway.

Corrigan nodded and Moran came to sit opposite him.

The waitress came and Moran ordered a coffee, black, also.

"You find them?" Corrigan asked.

Moran shook his head.

"I started nosing around, but the place is crawling with cops."

"Shit," Corrigan said. "What we gonna do now?"

"My source is sure that her credit card was used last night at that hotel. They gotta be there. Only thing we have to figure out now is which room."

Corrigan blew out a slow breath.

"Easier said than done." He looked at Moran. "Why would the place be crawling with cops? Uniforms?"

"Both," Moran said. "At least I saw one in uniform talking to a plainclothes guy and a woman. I had 'em pegged for the heat right away anyway."

"You hear what they were talking about?"

Moran shook his head. The waitress returned, set the coffee cup and saucer on the table, and filled it. Moran smiled at her.

"Maybe I can call that old broad in Memphis again," Corrigan said. "Use the Detective Southerland routine one more time."

"I thought you were worried about getting burned?"

Corrigan shrugged.

"I mean, it's possible she caught on to that one," Moran said. "Maybe that's why she booked up from the last place."

"Yeah, I guess I shoulda whacked that old broad in Memphis instead of trying to play secret agent man. Guess I'll have to go back and take care of that when this little gig here is finished."

"Whack her? An old lady? For what?"

Corrigan shot him a suspicious glance, surprised at what

possibly could be a soft spot in Moran.

"To tie up any loose ends," he said. "You got some scruples against whacking old broads?" He watched the other man's reactions closely.

Moran shrugged noncommittally. "Not really."

"Does that mean I'll have to do the old nurse when we catch her?" Corrigan asked. He was thinking that it'd be just as easy to dig three graves in the desert instead of just two.

Moran shrugged again, taking a sip of his coffee.

"Give me a break," he said. "Anyway, we got to catch her first."

The waitress came by and warmed up both their coffees.

When she'd left, Corrigan was about to ask him what his master plan was now when Moran's cell phone rang. He answered it and Corrigan affected an air of disinterest as he listened to one side of the conversation.

"Yeah, boss," Moran said. "Un un, we still ain't found him yet . . . un huh, I know . . . okay, we will . . . yes, sir . . . I understand . . ." Corrigan could hear the voice on the other end yelling, although he couldn't discern the words. But he knew it had to be Ricardo Casio. Moran muttered a few more apologies, and then ended the call. He shook his head and drank some coffee.

"That the old man?" Corrigan asked.

Moran nodded. "Yeah. He's been driving me nuts with this Rocky crap. Been calling me every thirty minutes asking for updates." He shook his head. "You'd think the guy was a thirteen-year-old kid, or something, for Christ's sake."

"Nah, if he was thirteen, we'd have an easier time," Corrigan said. "All we'd have to do would be to go up to Vanshitberg's room. That fucking Pablo would probably be breaking him in."

Moran smirked, just as his cell phone rang again. He picked it up, rolling his eyes.

"Moran," he said.

Corrigan studied the other man's reactions. From the relaxed expression, he knew it wasn't Casio this time.

Moran muttered into the phone and then asked, "So lemme ask you, you seen Rocky around at all?"

"Okay," Moran said. "Well, that sounds like good news." He listened some more, then added, "All right, get back to me when you know more."

"Guess who that was?" Moran said, his lips tightening into a slight smile.

Corrigan just stared at him.

"It was Vanshitberg himself," Moran said. "He says he got a call from Spangler, Ladonna's attorney. They got a lead on where the nurse is hiding out. She's been trying to contact some reporter named Bauer."

"Reporter?"

"Yeah. But the sweetest part is Vanshitberg's gonna set up this meet so that we can step in and grab 'em."

Corrigan raised his eyebrows.

"That'd simplify things. If he can deliver."

"He says he's getting it all worked out. Gonna get back to me, but he assures me it's a done deal."

Corrigan snorted. "That'll be the day, with that fucking shithead. He'd mess up a one-car funeral."

"Well, if he comes through," Moran said, "all we have to worry about is finding Rocky so the old man quits driving me nuts."

Something that caught Corrigan's interest flickered on the television screen above the bar. It was an ancient looking black-and-white photographic mug shot of old man Casio, complete with a booking number under his chin.

Corrigan waved to the bartender and yelled, "Hey, turn that up."

Moran turned to look.

The bartender grabbed a remote and the dotted volume line gauge appeared. The audible sound simultaneously followed. The picture of Casio faded and the reporter's voice began talking as a picture of a Las Vegas hospital filled the screen.

". . . was admitted sometime last night suffering from an undisclosed illness or injury. Rocco Alphonse Casio is the son of reputed mob boss Ricardo 'The Hammer' Casio as well as the former manager of the Roman Holiday Hotel and Casino. The elder Casio, who once owned the establishment, until the loss of his gaming license in 1989, is still purported to own a significant amount of stock in the hotel, although this has not been confirmed." A quick flash of the Roman Holiday filled the screen, then faded as the camera showed a lone reporter standing in front of the emergency entrance of the hospital. "Doctors would not comment on the extent of Rocco, 'Rocky' Casio's injuries, and would only say that he is in 'guarded' condition."

"Looks like we found him," Corrigan said.

Moran nodded, taking out his cell phone.

"Yeah, the Roman Holiday is where they're hosting that big Colton Purcell imitator's contest tonight," he said. "That's where Vantillberg is supposed to deliver the nurse and her charge." He punched in the numbers and said, "Let me speak to the boss right away." He paused, and then turned to glance back at the television set. "All roads lead to Rome, I guess."

Chapter 22

Man in Demand

Buzzy, you were one goddamn paranoid son of a bitch, Harry thought ruefully as he watched the PASSWORD PROTECTED letters pop up in the block again. He'd thought for sure that the service number would do it, but no luck. He tried reversing it, and then transposing some of the numbers. But nothing worked. He thought about calling Linda again but decided not to. She'd sounded about at the end of her patience with him.

Something else had occurred to him also. The string of broken necks extending from Memphis to Vegas. Obviously Buzzy had tapped into something. Something big. And if his gut had been right about Big Daddy Babcock's suicide not being kosher, that meant that whatever it was involved Colton Purcell, or his estate. Harry thought about the earlier columns Buzzy'd written and Linda's comment. *He'd been obsessed with Colton Purcell lately,* she'd said. And Ladonna had been acting funny at their meeting, too. She'd alluded to some kind of payoff. Could Buzzy have been on the take? Or maybe he got another kind of payoff for getting too close to whatever it was. Ladonna . . . was she part of it too? He suddenly realized that he'd have to be very careful from here on out. He made sure he had Jan's cell phone number in the memory of his phone.

I hope she knows how to use that gun she carries, he thought. Then after remembering how strong her hands had felt last night he figured it was a good bet she did. Any girl who carried a Glock and drove an Intrepid had to be capable. Maybe he should just turn everything over to her and just ride out the next forty-eight hours or so and head back to Chi town? But there was something else too. He hadn't even thought about wanting a drink since he'd been trying to run this story down. Not even when she'd sipped the white wine in front of him. Maybe this story was his lifeline back. But back to what?

He was blowing out a slow breath when his cell phone rang. The number was one he didn't recognize. His caller ID listed it as a local Las Vegas call. He pressed the button and answered it with a grunting hello.

"Mr. Bauer?" the male voice said. It had an unmistakable Southern sound.

"Yes."

"I'm an associate of Ladonna Purcell," the voice said. "She wanted me to get ahold of you and work out some details about your conversation yesterday."

Harry was wary. He wondered if Buzzy had received such a call too.

"I'm in Las Vegas," the voice said. "I can come over to your hotel if you like."

"I'd prefer someplace else," Harry said. "Someplace a little more public."

He waited for the other man's reaction, but the voice just said, "You name it then."

Harry's mind raced. He didn't want to call Jan and ask her to accompany as bodyguard on what might be nothing. Still, he needed someone to watch his back.

"There's a little place called the Winston Room on the old strip," Harry said. "You ever hear of it?"

"Yep, I know the place."

Harry was surprised. Gabe had described it as a hole in the wall. Maybe this guy was more than he seemed.

"You do? You're sure?"

"Hell, I knew Vegas back when it was all wise guys and hookers," the voice said. It had a distinct Southern quality to it.

"I'll meet you there in an hour," Harry said.

"Good enough."

"Wait, how will I know you?"

"I'll know you," the voice said, and hung up.

Welcome back to the big leagues, Harry thought, remembering what it was like to walk on the Devil's Basin.

Harry's cell phone rang again in the cab on the way over to the Winston Room. He'd left right away, figuring it would be better to set up and wait to make sure his adversary didn't do it first. Plus he'd called Gabe right away and enlisted his assistance in case trouble came a calling. Not that he wanted the kid to do anything more than call Jan and 911 if it looked like an emergency. After all, this wasn't a Colton Purcell movie where the bad guys would fold after a few well-placed punches.

He answered the phone.

"Mr. Bauer?" the woman's voice asked.

"That's me," he said. The voice sounded vaguely familiar and Harry knew he'd talked to her in the past few days.

"My name is Marjorie Versette. I spoke with you yesterday about a story that Mr. Sawyer was doing."

Harry identified the voice as soon as she mentioned her name.

"Yes, ma'am. What can I do for you?"

"Well, I do need to speak to somebody about what I know. I had hoped to come see poor Mr. Sawyer. He was such a nice man, and I was sorry to hear about his passing."

"Yeah, I was too." He figured she was another nut case, just like Buzzy. Birds of a feather . . . "Look, Ms. Versette, I'm a little busy right now. In fact, I'm on my way to meet somebody."

"Goodness gracious, is it about the Colton Purcell story Mr. Sawyer was working on?" The alarm in her voice was palpable.

"Yeah, it is," Harry said, sorry a moment later that he'd told her. But he suddenly remembered another bit of information that he'd read in one of Buzzy's columns. "Say, are you the nurse from that nursing home?"

"Graceful Valley?" she said. "Yes, that's me. But I have to be careful. There are people after me. I'm sure they're the same ones who killed poor Mr. Sawyer. He was getting too close. They'll stop at nothing, you know."

"I believe it," Harry said, reassessing her possible worth as an interview. If nothing else, maybe she could give him and Jan some background about the woman who'd ended up with a broken neck. "Look, Ms. Versette, like I said, I'm on my way to an appointment. But I'd really like to talk to you. Is there a number where I can reach you?"

"Oh, I'm sorry, but I can't give that out. I've already changed hotels twice since I've been here because I don't want them to find me."

"Who's 'them'?"

The line was silent for a moment, then she asked, "How much did Mr. Sawyer tell you?"

Harry thought for a moment. If he told her he knew next to nothing, then it might make her think meeting with him was a waste of time. But if he expected her to trust him, he'd better be upfront.

"He didn't tell me much at all," he said. "In fact, I've been trying to sort through his notes and figure things out.

He was a friend of mine."

More silence from the other end. Harry figured he'd blown it, until she said, "I can help you with that, Mr. Bauer. When can I call you back?"

He told her that he'd be back at his hotel in about two hours and to contact him there. He made the offer to pay for lunch as well. After Marjorie hung up, the cab pulled to a stop in front of the Winston Room and Harry paid and got out. Gabe had been right. It was, for lack of a better term, a joint. This was old-Vegas, and it had substantially less glitz than the rest of the city, especially the ultra modern strip. A couple of winos sat across the street by an Open 24 Hours liquor store passing the brown paper bag back and forth. Harry nodded to them as he walked across the street, regretting his smugness about maintaining his sobriety earlier.

Pausing, he took out his cell phone and dialed Jan. The oppressive heat was settling over him, like that first barefoot step on hot sand at the beach. He listened to four rings before her crisp, businesslike voice answered with "Detective Grey."

"Hi, it's me," he said.

Her tone softened.

"Well, hello. How's the tiger man?"

Harry smiled as he talked.

"I don't know. If I run into him I'll tell him you asked."

Her responding laugh sounded like musical chimes.

"So you get anything from my buddy in Memphis?" he asked.

"I'm still waiting for him to call me back," she said. "But I did put out an NCIC message regarding that broken neck MO."

"Mmm, I love it when you talk cop-talk," he said. Then

he grew serious. "Say, I'm meeting a source at this place called the Winston Room. Ever hear of it?"

"Yeah, it's a sleaze pit. What are you doing meeting somebody there?"

"Backup. I've got a friend who works there."

"What? Security?"

"No," he said. "He sings. He's pretty good, too. Or so I've heard. Supposed to be Colton Purcell's illegitimate son."

"Yeah, right. Him and about a million other guys." He could sense the concern in her voice when she added, "Look, I can probably skate out of here for a few minutes and swing over there. I mean, this guy in Memphis is obviously on more than Central Standard Time."

He was touched that she offered, but he declined.

"All I wanted to do was give you a head's up," he said. "If a guy named Gabriel calls and says Harry needs help, you'll send the cavalry, won't you?"

"Gabriel?" she said. "You've got to be joking."

"Nope."

"Well, I hope he turns out to be a guardian angel to watch over you," she said. "Don't let anything happen to yourself, Harry Bauer. Okay?"

He smiled again at the concern in her tone.

"Scout's honor," he said. "I've got too much to stay healthy for now that I've rediscovered the joys of bicycle riding."

He ended the call and grabbed the elongated metal handle. It was attached to a solid wooden door that squeaked noticeably as Harry pulled it open and stepped inside. The air conditioning hit him, as did the wave of ambient booze. The lighting was dim and a haze of cigarette smoke lingered in the air. A raised wooden stage with sur-

rounding dark blue curtains and a shiny chrome microphone stand was at the far end. A few people looked up in
mild surprise at the flash of light from the open door. Gabriel was waiting at the bar, his elbow leaning on the polished surface, his boot resting on the brass rung that ran
along parallel to the floor.

Harry nodded and smiled as he walked over.

"Howdy, Mr. Bauer," Gabe said, holding out his hand.

"What, after twelve hours apart you're back to calling
me 'Mr. Bauer'?" Harry grinned and shook Gabe's hand.
"We've got a few minutes to set up here." He took out his
phone and handed it over. "This is set for my girlfriend's
cell phone. She's a cop and she knows where we're at. Any
sign of trouble, dial her, tell her 'Harry's in trouble,' and
then call 911. The cavalry will be on the way."

"Your girlfriend's a cop?" Gabe said, grinning. "When
did you have time to meet somebody out here?"

"You're not the only one who's irresistible to women,"
Harry said with a grin. They were about to split up when
the door opened again and a heavyset man with grayish
brown hair and a full beard stepped inside. He wore a
short-sleeve tan polo shirt and although he was obviously
middle-aged, his arms still looked corded and thick and his
broad shoulders and barrel chest gave a suggestion of slumbering power. He took off a pair of wrap-around sunglasses
and his large head rotated slowly on a powerful looking
neck. The eyes were surprisingly dark and piercing, even in
the bar's gloominess. He seemed to spot Harry and Gabe
immediately and strode slowly to the bar.

"You Harry?" he asked, holding out his big hand.

"Yeah," Harry said, shaking hands. The guy's grip was a
bit stronger than Harry'd expected, but he managed to
squeeze back without flinching.

"Glad to meet you," the man said. "I'm Sonny Proper."

After swinging by the Roman Holiday Hotel to make sure their entrance and special VIP section was all set up, Ladonna took a cab back to the hotel. She'd stopped in the hotel ladies' room to redo her make-up and comb out her hair so she'd look more presentable. More like herself. More like Colton Purcell's widow, even though they'd divorced before he died. As the scenery shot by she thought about the many times she'd been to Vegas with him before and after they were married.

The first time had been when he was making that movie with that sexpot young actress. Ladonna had known after visiting the set that they were up to something. And it had been her jealousy that had put an end to it. Her tearful ultimatum that she'd leave and go back home if he didn't stop seeing her. Always charming, always glib, Colton had cajoled her into believing that it was all in her imagination. That there was nothing going on. They were just friends.

Friends. The word always had a ludicrous sound to it whenever he used it when he was talking about a woman. And she hadn't been the first starlet to succumb to Colton's considerable Southern charm. His boyish shyness and incredible good looks . . . too bad he didn't marry that one. Maybe they could have made a success out of it. Maybe then I would have been spared a million heartbreaks, she thought. But then there'd be no Melissa Michelle.

The cab pulled to a stop and she thought of calling Sonny before she went up. But he was probably meeting with that damn nosey reporter. She took a deep breath and cursed to herself for letting themselves get into this horrible mess in the first place. But now that Sonny was here, he'd fix it. He always had. She hoped he always would. Maybe it's time, she thought, for both of them to sit down with Melissa Michelle for that heart-to-heart talk. Maybe it would help straighten her out. God knows, she needed something. Ladonna thought about her daughter's current obsession with that creep, Pablo, and the slimeball's equally creepy manager. Maybe she'd ask Sonny to talk to Eric too. He'd be able to handle that little dirtbag, even if he did threaten to expose some ugly little secrets to the press.

Have the talk, and it will take away his leverage, she thought. But how much will be destroyed in the process?

She'd leave it to Sonny. He'd take care of it.

Of course, he has good reason to, she thought as she walked through the front doors, conscious of more than just a few stares. God, she hoped nobody would approach her. With this big Colton Imitator's contest coming up every nutcase south of the Mason Dixon and west of the Mississippi was dressing up for a shot at the title.

Two men dressed in the gaudy red, white, and blue jumpsuits, their hair dyed glossy black and stiffly feathered back into the pompadour and dangling spit curl, passed by, mimicking the familiar refrain, "Mess with me, and you're messing with trouble."

Losers, she thought. In a way it was both sad and funny. Sad because so many people had become enamored with an image and were so desperate to become part of it. Funny because she'd actually been a part of the real Colton's life, of that magnificent image, and would give anything at this moment to get out. To just be herself. Lead a normal life . . . just become herself again. But it was too late. She could never get out of it. That was the only thing she did know for sure. It was too late.

As she pressed the button for the elevator the doors popped open and Joe, looking worried and haggard, stepped out. Stress wrinkles framed his almond eyes, and his forehead was deeply furrowed. When he saw her, he looked stunned.

"What's wrong?" she asked, stepping over to him and placing a hand on his massive forearm.

"It's Melissa Michelle," he said, his voice sounding cracked and broken. "I thought she was in taking a shower and then after about an hour of the water running, I knocked on the door to see if she was, you know, all right." He brought his big hand up to his head and plastered his black hair back nervously. He seemed to have visibly aged.

"What happened?"

He looked into Ladonna's eyes.

"Well, she wasn't even in the bathroom," he said. "She somehow snuck out and gave me the slip."

The three of them sat in a booth near the back, facing the stage. Sonny offered to buy everybody a beer, but Harry ordered a club soda and Gabe got a soft drink. The sight of Sonny sipping the frosty stein made Harry's mouth water a little bit, but he concentrated on the task in front of him. And it would be like playing poker with a shallow hand: a pair of deuces and a couple of matchless face cards.

He looked across the table at Sonny Proper. The man looked hard and fit, just like he had in all those bit parts in Colton's movies where he'd played a tough guy for the willowy singer to clobber in a staged fist fight.

I wouldn't want to be in a real fight with this guy, Harry thought, trying to recall some background information from the article he'd written. A black ink version of the eagle on the globe, with USMC in the middle, graced Sonny's right forearm.

Ah, thought Harry. Some common ground.

248

"You an ex-marine?" he asked.

Sonny smiled.

"No such thing as an ex-marine," he said.

Harry grinned. "Yeah, don't I know that. San Diego or Parris Island?"

"Parris Island," Sonny said. He took a sip of beer. "You?"

"San Diego. I was a Hollywood marine."

Sonny nodded approvingly.

"So you said Ladonna Purcell asked you to speak to me?" Harry asked.

"Yeah, she did." He scratched his cheek, then raised an eyebrow in Gabriel's direction. "Why don't you get lost for a while, boy? Me and him got things to talk about."

Gabe stiffened and he set down his glass.

"Just 'cause you bought me a soda, sir, don't give you the right to insult me."

Sonny seemed to appraise him, then licked his lips.

"I don't think either Mr. Bauer or myself want you listening to the business we've got to discuss." He grinned. "That better? If not, I'll be glad to step out into the alley and show you what a good old-fashioned ass-whipping is all about."

Gabe's mouth turned down at the corners, and he was about to speak when Harry reached across and placed a hand on his arm.

"Hey, why don't you go up and sing a few numbers for us?" Harry said. He held his hand out to show that the place was practically empty. "I haven't heard you sing yet."

Gabriel looked at him, then his eyes shot back to Sonny whose implacable stare seemed both menacing and placid at the same time.

Sonny pointed to a big sign on-stage that advertised:

CopperSnake Playing Nightly—With Bob Park. "That might not be a bad idea, sonny. Looks like Copper Bob won't be on till later."

Gabe stared at the bigger man a moment more, then said, "All right then. Anything in particular you want to hear?"

"How about 'Until It's Time For You To Go'?" Harry said. "I haven't heard that one in a long time."

Gabe picked up his guitar case, popped open the latches, and ducked under the instrument's sling. As he walked away, Harry noticed Sonny watching the boy's departure.

"Glad I didn't have to hurt the kid," he said. Then to Harry, "Now what exactly, or should I say how much exactly, is it gonna take for you to go away too, Mr. Bauer?"

Harry wasn't sure how to play it. This guy seemed within a hair trigger's notch of going off. And from the looks of him, he didn't plan on obeying the Marquis of Queensbury Rules.

"How much?" Harry said, trying to stall a bit. "What makes you think I'm after money?"

Sonny grinned. "Well, shit then, you tell me. What are you after?"

"How about the truth?"

Sonny was about to reply when they both heard Gabe start singing. He'd set the microphone in front of him and was playing the soft melody flawlessly. For a moment, Sonny seemed genuinely moved.

"Well, I'll be damned," he said. "He can sing pretty good, can't he?" He turned back to Harry and raised his eyebrows. "The truth?"

"Yeah," Harry said. "I went to see Ms. Purcell to confirm certain details regarding a story my friend, Buzzy

Sawyer, was writing. Now all of a sudden you people are treating me like a pariah." He paused for effect. "Or are you just running scared? Afraid of what I might print?"

Sonny blew out a slow breath.

"Personally, I don't give a shit what you print in that crummy rag of yours, Harry. But when it comes to seeing people I know and care about get hurt unnecessarily, I take exception to that." He looked at Gabriel again. When he turned back, his brow was furrowed.

"How long were you with Colton Purcell?" Harry asked, hoping to seize the initiative and catch him off guard. Maybe backtracking would make it less confrontational. Less apparent that he didn't have squat and was whistling in the dark.

"Almost twenty years. Longer than that, actually. We grew up together."

"And he hired you to be one of his bodyguards?"

Sonny nodded. "It was a role I was comfortable with."

"But you two had a falling out," Harry said. "What caused the rift?"

"For a man with all the answers, you seem to be asking a lot of questions."

Harry felt that sinking feeling. It was easier to dig out a Michigan wood tick than get any feel for where this guy was coming from. He needed more leverage. Something to gain some purchase with.

"So now you're reassuming your role as the family fixer, huh?"

"I'm here to get you off a very special lady's back. Whatever that takes, that's what I'll do."

The implied menace in the guy's voice was not lost on Harry.

Gabriel finished his song, and Sonny turned to him.

"How about a request?"

"Name it," Gabe said.

" 'Don't Ask the Question.' "

"Yeah, I can do that one." He began singing.

Sonny followed the melody and beat for a moment, then turned back to Harry.

"Where'd you find him?" Sonny asked, cocking his head toward the stage.

"Actually, he sort of found me. Heard I was reporter doing a story on Colton Purcell. He strongly believes that Colton was his biological father."

Sonny snorted, then stopped. Gabriel was hitting every note with perfect pitch. His style was similar to the Colton version, but with enough originality to make it clear he was improvising and not copying.

"So you knew Colton Purcell," Harry said, gesturing at Gabe. "What do you think? Is he?"

Sonny grinned.

"Man, this is Vegas," he said. "If you can't tell the illusion from the reality, just remember, most of the time, there ain't nothing here that really is what it appears to be."

Harry figured it was time to seize the initiative.

"You know a woman by the name of Marjorie Versette?" he asked.

Sonny looked implacable. "Should I?"

"How about Willard Younger?"

That brought a hint of recognition to Sonny's face, but it was quickly replaced by a practiced smile.

"Interesting name."

"It is, isn't it?" Harry said, picking up his club soda and taking a sip. "And what about Colton's daughter marrying Pablo Stevenson in Mexico a few months ago?"

"That was annulled," Sonny said. "Look, we gonna keep

playing games here, or are you gonna put your cards on the table?"

"That's fine with me. I told you, my friend Buzzy Sawyer was writing a story on Colton Purcell. I happen to have come across a lot of interesting information that he had."

"Information that he was paid for not to use," Sonny interjected.

"That remains to be seen, since Buzzy was murdered," Harry shot back. He stared at the other man's face. "He was my friend, and I aim to find out who killed him and why, if I can." He realized the 'if I can' weakened his stance, but he continued looking Sonny in the eye, hoping to see something. What he saw was the appearance of absolute serenity.

"Look, I'm sorry about your friend," Sonny said. "But what you're doing is gonna stir up a lot of stuff that's best left buried."

"Who's Willard Younger?" Harry blurted out. "How's he tied into this?"

Sonny's dark eyes narrowed slightly, then he smiled and sat back.

"You know, I just had me a thought," he said, clasping his hands in back of his head. "I think for a man who's supposedly in possession of a lot of information, you don't really know shit, do you?"

It was Harry's turn to try and look serene. He had the feeling he wasn't quite pulling it off.

"So I'll tell you what I'll do," Sonny said, standing and dropping a bill on the table. He reached in his shirt pocket and removed a folded envelope. "I'll go back and talk to Ladonna and tell her what I think. You can meet us tonight at that Colton Purcell thing." He held up the envelope.

"Here are some VIP passes to get in. Just ask for her table. Bring a couple friends. I wouldn't mind talking to old Willard again. Been a while."

Gabriel was finishing up the number as Sonny walked over to him. He stood in front of the stage and asked, "So who was your mama anyway, boy?"

Gabe played the last few bars of the melody, his eyes two smoldering coals as he stared back at the bigger man. Harry was afraid he was going to jump off the stage and go after Sonny, which in all probability, would not be a wise move.

"Her name was Freeman," Gabe said, his lips twisting into a sneer. "Patricia J. Freeman."

Sonny's face scrunched up momentarily, then he shook his head.

"And how was she supposed to be connected to Colton?"

"She sang with the Louisiana Hayride. Was in *The '82 Comeback Show.*"

Sonny smiled knowingly.

"Patti Jean Love," he said.

Gabe said nothing, but gave a fractional nod.

"Well, don't that beat all?" Sonny said. "I do remember her and Colton spending a lot of time together. A lot of time. She was a little sweetheart."

Gabriel let his guitar drop to the floor next to the microphone and clenched his fists.

"You best not be saying nothing against my mama."

Sonny stepped back, grinning and holding up his palms.

"Looks like you got his temper too, all right," he said. "And I can see your mama done raised you right."

"Her and my step-daddy did," Gabe said, still holding his fists tightly.

"Then remember what they taught you and don't get in

254

over your head," Sonny said, his smile still in place. He turned back to Harry and pointed at Gabriel. "Bring this young firepisser with you tonight, Harry. I want Ladonna to see that maybe Colton did do something in his life that turned out right." He nodded to Gabriel and strode out of the bar, pausing at the door.

"Be there by seven," he said.

"You stay at the fucking hospital and don't move from there until Donnie and Philo get there to relieve ya," Casio yelled into the cell phone as Corrigan drove the van to a loading zone area of The Emperor's Palace. The man in the back seat gave Corrigan a sign that said Hotel Services, and he put it in the windshield.

"And if that fucker shows up there, you grab him and hold him for me, understand? I want that fucking Vantillberg."

Corrigan was silently glad that he, and not Moran, got the assignment to go with the old man to the hotel. It meant that Casio still trusted him, or his ability, more than that wop-looking mick. Not that he wouldn't have minded Moran coming along. The guy had good moves. But Corrigan was craving for action and this would be a good fix. So long as he didn't get burned by anybody looking for the face on the composite drawing of the security guard's killer.

Casio was throwing caution to the wind, hurrying in through the front doors when Corrigan placed a hand on his shoulder.

"Boss, we got to be careful here," he said. "Lots of these places have cameras."

Casio glared up at him, then nodded. He pulled out a pair of sunglasses and a baseball cap and stuck them on, motioning with his head. "You go in first. I'll meet you by the elevators. Freddie, you go in after us and stay in the casino. Keep a lookout for any cops. Anything looks bad, you call me right away, *capisce?*"

Freddie, whose head was about the size of a basketball, smiled and nodded, holding up his cell phone.

Corrigan was about to say that he thought taking the stairs rather than the elevators would be better, but it would wait. He thought Casio might just go totally nuts and blow somebody's head off if they got in his way, he looked so pissed. Seeing his boy Rocky in ICU, lying there in a coma, tubes coming out of his mouth and taped in place, might've sent the old guy off his rocker a little.

Corrigan pushed through the door after slipping on his own glasses and cap. There was no way to disguise his size, so the name of the game was to appear nonchalant. Like just another one of the happy losers who'd come to Vegas to blow a bundle and have a blast.

At the elevators he pressed the button and waited. A car opened almost immediately and Corrigan glanced back to look for Casio. He saw him pushing his way through the lobby.

Jesus Christ, Corrigan thought. Knock a couple people down, why don't ya. It was apparent that Moran had gotten the better end of this deal after all.

Casio moved into the car and Corrigan followed, giving a stern glare to two women who tried to enter the elevator after him.

"This car's reserved," he said, and watched them back away with indignation.

Bad move, he thought, if they complain to management, and they talk to security. He reached over and pressed a button above the floor they wanted. He then hit another for the penthouse suite.

"I thought you told me they were on the fifth floor?" Casio said.

"Yeah, we'll walk down a flight. No sense letting anybody know what floor we got off on."

Casio didn't acknowledge the plan. He just kept staring at the doors, as if he couldn't wait for them to open. Corrigan was beginning to wonder how the old man maintained his icy reserve enough to take care of family business, when Casio let out a deep breath.

"You're right, goomba," he said. "I been going about this too emotional." His lower lip twisted with a slight tremor. "But when I seen my boy all taped up like that . . ." He heaved another sigh. The doors opened and they stepped out, Casio waiting for Corrigan to show him the way.

They went down the hallway to the stairwell and descended to the floor below. Casio paused and took out his cell phone, pressing the redial button. After a moment, he asked, "We're at the room. Any sign of anybody?" He listened to the reply, then terminated the call, sticking the phone back in his pocket. His hand came out holding a chrome snub-nose .38 Smith & Wesson. "You packing?"

Corrigan nodded. "But I'd prefer to use my hands." He grinned, slipping on a pair of thin leather gloves. "Less noise, more fun."

Casio placed the hand with the pistol back in his pocket as they pulled open the door and walked down the hallway. Putting his thumb over the peephole in the door, Corrigan knocked loudly several times. He thought he heard some voices inside, then knocked again. "Hotel security," he said loudly. "Open up, please."

A moment later he saw the door open slightly, a large black forearm across the intervening space. Slamming his body forward, Corrigan heard the crack as the door flew open, slamming into the man behind it. Rushing inside, he saw a large black guy stumbling backward. The guy regained his footing with the aplomb of an athlete and held out his hand, pointing.

"You'd best get your white asses out of here, motherfuckers," he said. " 'fore I call the man."

"Where's Vantillberg?" Casio said, his voice a growl.

"Who?" Gant asked in mock indignation. Then added, "He ain't here."

"Where's he at?"

"I don't know. Now get the fuck out."

Casio stepped back and shut the door, nodding his head at Corrigan. "Take care of him."

Gant's mouth drew open slightly, and he raised his hands into a boxing stance. They were about the same size. The fucker was big, all right, but Corrigan caught the momentary flicker in the other man's eyes. He knew what it was. Fear. The guy looked more like a jock than a fighter, judging from his build and unmarked face. The kind who was probably a ball of fire on the football field, but would turn out to be a big pussy in the yard at the joint. Still, that body slam to the door had been harder than Corrigan had thought, so he figured to do it the smart way.

"Come on, gorilla-man," Corrigan taunted, curling his fingers. "Let's see what you got. Unless you're a fucking fag like your boss."

The epithets had the desired effect, causing Gant to rush forward, his head slightly down. He couldn't sidestep the vicious kick to the knee that Corrigan delivered. Stumbling, his arms flailed outward, trying to regain his balance. Corrigan slapped an open palm against the back of Gant's right shoulder, spinning him around, while looping his long left

258

arm over the black giant's head. Gant immediately lowered his chin to his chest, but Corrigan merely thrust the extended knuckles of his fingers under Gant's jawbone and made a can-opener-like motion, working his forearm around the other man's throat. Corrigan's left palm grabbed his right biceps, and the large right hand slipped up behind Gant's head. From there it was merely a matter of dexterity and physical dynamics. He heard Gant's gasp and grunt, his breaths sounding like snorting wheezes. Corrigan compressed his arms a bit more, careful not to break the neck, but steady enough to ratchet up the pressure. Gant's eyes rolled back in his head, his flailing arms becoming more and more effete in their movement, until finally, his whole body went limp. Corrigan didn't release his grip until perhaps a minute or so more, then he let the heavy body fall to the floor.

Corrigan smiled. Hardly winded, he thought.

"Like I told you," he said. "More fun this way."

"Search the rooms," Casio said. "If that fucker's here, I want him now."

Corrigan pulled out his own gun, a big Colt Python, figuring it would be more expeditious to shoot if Vantillberg suddenly popped up with a piece of his own. But he found nothing until he came to the bedroom, which was locked.

He grinned.

"What we got here?" he said in mock surprise. His gloved fingers closed over the knob and twisted hard. The door held fast. Corrigan took out a long tack puller from his pocket and pressed it between the door and the jamb. Then he jerked on the knob again, forcing the thin metallic shaft the other way. The door popped open and Corrigan immediately crouched and held the gun out in front of him. The room looked empty. He moved inside, going first to the bed and lifting it with one hand and pointing the pistol with the other. Nothing.

A closet door was on the far wall and he moved there next, pulling it open and holding the Python back slightly so no one inside could make a move to grab it before he fired. Two sets of feet cowered behind a hanging array of clothes. Corrigan swept the clothes out of the way and grabbed Pablo by the mane of longish hair. He stuck the barrel to the caramel-colored forehead, then smiled as he saw who else was in the closet.

"Get out here, bitch," he growled.

Melissa Michelle, clad only in a bra and panties, stepped out next to Pablo. Her face held the look of abject terror.

"Where's Eric?" Corrigan asked, pressing the gun harder against Pablo's head.

Pablo, who was wearing some fancy leopard-print undies, and a T-shirt, immediately wet himself.

"He's gone," Melissa Michelle said, crossing her arms over her breasts. "He left a while ago."

Casio was standing at the door now, his gun hanging limply in his fingers.

"Where'd he go?" he asked. His voice was no more than a harsh whisper.

"I don't know, honest," she said. "Please, don't hurt us."

Casio shook his head slightly, so it almost looked like a palsy tremor, as he walked toward them. "We just want him," he said. "That's all. Now tell me, where's he at?"

"I really don't know," the girl said. Her voice was pleading now. "Honest. I just snuck over a little while ago and he wasn't here then. My mom's gonna be coming here looking for me."

Corrigan glanced over his shoulder at Casio.

"That could mean cops," he said.

The old man seemed to consider this momentarily, then nodded. He reached up and grabbed a hank of Pablo's processed locks and doubled it over in his fist. Leaning close to the singer's face, he spoke in a low, guttural tone.

"Okay, short eyes, you're gonna make a call. And here's what you're gonna say."

Chapter 23

Rain Checks

After Gabe had finished stowing his guitar in the back room at the Winston Room, he came back and sat at Harry's table. The boozy ambiance started to get too pervasive, and Harry suddenly felt an overwhelming urge to get the hell out of there. Either that, or have a drink. He stood.

"Let's go," he said. He took out his cell phone and began dialing Chicago.

Gabe looked up at him, glanced toward the bar, and nodded. He called to the bartender on the way out, saying he'd be back later.

"Tim? It's Harry," he said into the phone, talking while they walked. Gabe held the door open for him. "You get any line on a good hacker for me yet?"

"Not yet, Harry," Stockton's distant voice said. "The wedding went fine and Lynn's with your sister, by the way."

Harry frowned. The afternoon heat met him head-on as they left the shady gloom of the bar.

"Okay, thanks. That was my next question." He rubbed his thumb and forefinger over his eyes. "Look, keep trying to find somebody who can break this password code. I'm striking out on these interviews because these characters sense that I don't have all the facts. I need to read the rest of Buzzy's files in order to solve this one."

"Why don't you just go with what you've got?" Stockton asked.

Harry felt like throwing the phone against the brick wall.

"Because there's something here," he said. "I'm not sure exactly what, but it's already cost a couple people their lives. And I'm gonna crack it or die trying."

Stockton was silent for a moment, then said, "All right, Harry. I'll keep looking, but be careful, okay?"

"I will. Just find me a hacker." He ended the call and exhaled sharply. The bright afternoon sunshine was beating down more relentlessly than ever, making just standing a sweaty chore. The heat seemed to reflect up right through his shoes from the asphalt. Harry pointed down the street to a thatch of palm trees.

"Looks like some shade over there," he said.

"Just shade ain't gonna cut it. We need to get in the air conditioning fast," Gabe said.

"I thought you were a southern boy? You know, used to the heat."

Gabe smiled as they walked.

"This ain't just heat, it's purgatory."

"Purgatory's where you wait to go to either heaven or hell, kid," Harry said.

"I know," Gabe said. "And I'm hoping it'll be the former." He scanned the street. "You didn't bring your rental car?"

Harry shook his head.

"No, why?"

"I thought you might drop me at the newspaper office, is all."

Harry's brow furrowed. "The newspaper office? The *Mirror*?"

"Yeah," Gabe said, smiling again. "That little gal, Jenna. She's gonna take me out to see Hoover Dam today."

Now it was Harry's turn to grin. He held up his phone as he waved to a taxi cruising the strip.

"I'll let you call her to say you're on the way as soon as I check in with my lady," he said.

Harry had been standing by the parking area of the MGM Grand watching for her black Intrepid when he saw her pull into a parking space. An appropriate car for a very capable girl, he thought. She made a graceful exit, smoothed out her slacks, brushed back her hair, and adjusted her purse over her shoulder. He corrected himself. Hardly what you would call a girl. A woman, plus she packs a gun. And a badge. She saw him and smiled.

"Thanks for coming," he said as they fell into step together.

"It's been a day of frustrations anyway." She glanced at him. "Your buddy, Detective Tucker, still hasn't called me back."

"He's probably out trying to peddle some more crime scene photos to some other reporter."

She laughed briefly and he caught her hand in his as they walked. He considered asking her to go to the Colton Purcell imitator's contest with him tonight. Maybe meet Gabe and Ladonna Purcell and have some fun, while he put the finishing touches on the story. She'd be good backup to have around, in case things went a bit sour, but most of all he just wanted to be with her. Next week he would, in all probability, be back in Chicago working on his next feature, whatever that might be. Meeting her had been so serendipitous, he wondered when the ride would end. Of course, this was Vegas, and, as Sonny Proper had reminded him earlier, everything was an illusion.

"What are you thinking?" she asked.

He looked quizzical.

"You had the strangest expression on your face just now," she said.

Harry shrugged.

"Just trying to make sense of all this," he said.

"I never asked you, is this your first trip to Vegas?"

Oh oh, he thought.

"I was here a long time ago," he answered, searching for the right thing to say. "Back when it was all wise guys and hookers."

She laughed.

"It's still all wise guys and hookers," she said. "There's just a lot more glitz on top and a few different players."

His cell phone rang as they walked through the long corridor of shops, toward the massive casino, and the restaurant that lay beyond. Harry plucked it from his belt.

"Mr. Bauer," a nervous voice said. "You told me to call you back in two hours."

"Yes, Marjorie. Are you still up for a meet?"

He could hear what sounded like a nervous swallow, followed by a tentative, "Yes."

"I'm having lunch with a very important person in my life," he said, glancing at Jan. She tilted her head and smiled at him. "But I certainly want to make time for you. Is there a number I can reach you at?"

"No, I'll call you back," she said, and the call ended.

"Who was that?" Jan asked.

"The nurse who takes care of Colton Purcell."

She smiled. "You mean, 'Freeze Me Tender' Colton?"

Harry grinned as they approached the buffet. "One of my favorite songs. I'm surprised you know it."

Eric hot boxed the cigarette as he stood across the street from the hospital and watched the main entranceway. He was sure it was Moran talking with two guys in suits. They didn't look like your typical mob muscle, but maybe that was the point. If Moran was there, that meant that Casio knew about Rocky, and the word would be out on him. He hoped that was all that was out on him.

But there's still a chance that they might not associate Rocky's fall from grace with him.

After all, it was an accident, for Christ's sake, Eric thought.

He drew some more smoke into his lungs and let it seep slowly out his nostrils.

I have to think this through, he thought. Think it through and it'll be all right.

He began rehearsing scenarios in his mind, testing the sound of the various lies. *No, I just heard about Rocky on the news,* he heard himself say. *Tragic, fucking tragic.* No, that wouldn't do. Honest, I was out when he came by the room, which was partially true. *I had no idea that he'd relapsed. But it can hardly be considered my fault.*

They all sounded fine, even logical, until the vision of Ricardo Casio's face took their place in his mind's eye. Then logic and everything else went out the window. But he'd have to believe that I had nothing to do with it, Eric told himself. He's got to know what a jonesin' fool his kid was. Maybe he won't blame me at all.

The two guys in suits disappeared as had Moran. Why the hell would they be wearing jackets on a hot day like this unless they were packing heat? He dropped his cigarette and ground it out with his toe as he placed another one in his mouth. After flicking his lighter, Rocky's actually, he dialed the hotel room again and let it ring seven times. Still no answer. When the automatic voice mail recording started, he hung up.

Damn, where could they be? He silently hoped that Pablo hadn't taken Gant and gone cruising the strip for some young prostitutes. That last time they'd been in Tijuana Eric had been sickened by the Latino Prince of Pop's wicked proclivities. He didn't want to mess with cleaning up another mess of that magnitude again. But Pablo was still the meal ticket, at least for now. Let him record some of those Colton songs, release them as remixes, and they'd be back on top. Then maybe I can disassociate myself from this mess and find some new talent somewhere.

He considered Melissa Michelle for a moment. Why not? She wasn't a bad looking kid, as no-talent young babes went. And if it worked for Britney Spears . . .

The cell phone rang and jarred him back to reality. He pressed the button and answered.

"Eric? It's Pablo."

"Where you been? I musta called the room half a dozen times."

"Never mind that," Pablo said, his tenor voice quivering. "You need to get back to the room right away."

"Why? What's up?"

Eric felt the hairs on the back of his neck start to stand up.

"It's Melissa," Pablo said. "She came over here and we started messing with some downers—"

"You didn't give her any of that shit, did you?" Eric screamed. He looked around afterwards to see if anyone was looking at him. No one seemed to have paid much attention. No sign of Moran either.

"Relax, I'll give her some Ritalin and she'll be as good as new," Pablo said. "But you're coming back now, right?"

"I'm on my fucking way," Eric said, and hailed a cab as

he snapped his phone shut. Checking on Rocky and dodging Moran would have to wait.

Ladonna Purcell, still wearing her baseball cap, T-shirt and jeans, marched through the front doors of The Emperor's Palace with her bodyguard Joe, Sonny Proper, and two Las Vegas Metro uniformed police officers, in bright yellow shirts and black shorts, behind her. As they made their way through the casino portion, Ladonna continued her animated gesticulations and conversation.

"I know she's got to be here," she said. "It's the only possible explanation. And I want her out of that little creep's room right now, understand?"

"Ma'am, calm down, would you?" one of the uniformed officers said.

Sonny rolled his eyes in the cop's direction and nodded in commiseration. Ladonna continued marching to the front desk and then said to the nervous-looking Oriental girl behind the counter, "What room is Pablo Stevenson in?"

"I'm sorry, Ma'am, but we can't give out the room numbers of guests without their explicit permission," the girl said.

"Don't give me any shit," Ladonna said, leaning forward.

Sonny placed his hand on her shoulder. Joe, the Samoan bodyguard stiffened slightly, but did nothing.

"Hold on a minute, Ms. Purcell," the closest uniformed officer said. He was a bit older than his partner. "Call your security for us," he said to the clerk. She picked up a phone and spoke into it.

"Now, look," the officer continued, turning to Ladonna, "I know how worried you must be, but unfortunately we can't just run into a hotel and start breaking down the doors to look for your daughter."

"But you don't understand," Ladonna said. She brought her fingers up to wipe at her eyes as her mouth began to tremble.

"I do understand," the officer said. "I have a girl her age myself, and something similar happened to my family. Anyway, once the security guard gets here, we'll go up and check the room if they'll give us permission."

"And if they don't?" Sonny asked. His voice was full of implied menace.

"Let's cross that bridge when we come to it," the officer said.

As two more uniformed security guards and one in plain-clothes moved toward the desk, they almost bumped into a man with a head like a basketball stumbling toward the bar, fumbling with a cell phone.

The cell phone rang in Ricardo Casio's pocket and he answered it with a sharp grunt. Listening intently, Corrigan watched the man's eyes. The window to the soul, he thought, and behind Casio's dark orbs he was sure was the gateway to hell. Casio grunted again and ended the call.

"We gotta get outta here," he said. "Freddie says the lobby's crawling with cops and security. They're gonna be coming up."

Corrigan nodded, his face showing no emotion.

"Want me to take them outta here?" he asked, gesturing at the shivering Pablo and Melissa Michelle.

Casio rubbed the sides of his mouth with his index finger and thumb. He glanced over toward the flap of the leather belt extending down from the top of the closed door.

"That gonna work, you think?" he asked.

"Like a charm," Corrigan said, smiling. "One of my special numbers. I used it back in Memphis a couple of days ago."

"All right," Casio said. "Let's take them out, just like we planned to do. As long as we got this little fuck," he shoved his finger at Pablo, "we can get Vantillberg later."

Corrigan moved over to Pablo and Melissa, placing a large hand on each of their narrow shoulders.

"Okay, pervert, listen up," he said. "You too, missy. We're going over to the stairs, and we're gonna walk up one flight. Then we're gonna take a little elevator ride down to the lobby and go out the back door into the alley. If you try to run, or to call out to anybody, I'll shoot you both in the spine and leave you laying there. Understand?"

Melissa Michelle nodded fractionally, her face tight with terror. Pablo's head bobbled like a ball on a swivel.

"You can let me go," he said quickly, his voice a plaintive whine. "Just keep her, and I guarantee I'll bring Eric to you. I promise. Please. Trust me. Just—"

Casio reached over and slapped his face. The blow silenced the Latino Prince of Pop.

"Shut the fuck up," Casio said, his voice edging toward a low growl. "Is that any way to talk about your bride-to-be?" He waved his gun at the door. "Let's go. Now."

The waitress had just brought their drinks, and Harry had been broaching the subject of her accompanying him to the Colton Purcell Imitator's Contest tonight, when her cell phone rang. She smiled instead of answering his question and reached for the phone inside her purse. He felt like he'd been sucker-punched.

"Detective Grey," she said.

He watched as her grayish-blue eyes narrowed behind the glass lenses.

Oh oh, he thought. Please don't tell me . . .

"Which hotel did you say?" she asked, still on the phone. "Okay." She glanced at her watch. "I'll be there in fifteen minutes. Call an evidence tech and find out what his ETA is." She ended the call and looked across the table, reaching out to touch his hand. "I have to go."

"Duty calls again?"

"Yeah," she said, tossing her hair back slightly. "I don't know what it is, but ever since you came to town, this place has been hopping."

"Another homicide?" he asked, hoping that it wasn't. "Where's it at?"

She looked ready to rebuke him for asking about her work, but then her expression softened.

"The Emperor's Palace. They said it looks like either a suicide or an autoerotic." She paused. "You know what that is?"

Harry nodded.

"Yeah, I know," he said. "Ah, but a man's gasp has to outlast his grasp, or what's a heaven for? Apologies to Robert Browning, of course."

She giggled.

"Robert Browning?"

"He was a Victorian poet," Harry said. "He wrote a poem called 'Andrea del Sarto.' About a monk."

"A horny monk?"

"Actually, he was a frustrated artist."

"I'll have to remember that one," she said as she stood up.

Harry stood up too.

"So will you be long?"

She shot him a quick, lips-only smile, and Harry thought he saw genuine regret in her eyes.

"Could be. The rule is, you have to treat a suicide like a homicide until you know for sure you can close it."

"I'll walk you to your car."

"No, go ahead and eat," she said. "I'm a grown up girl."

He shook his head and smiled.

"I know you are, but the food will keep. I'll get a rain check."

Chapter 24

Best Laid Plans

Just to be cautious, Eric had the cabbie drop him across the street from the hotel. He strolled toward the corner, taking out a cigarette and lighting it with affected ease. As he squinted through the smoke, he glanced over at the front of the Emperor's Palace. Two black and white cop cars were parked in front. The little lighted figure on the walk signal illuminated and the people started across. Something was up. And then he saw a black Intrepid pull up as the light changed. He pulled out his cell phone as he mingled with the throng of pedestrians on the street.

He dialed the room and after four rings a mumbled voice answered.

"Gant?" he asked.

"Yeah," the mumble continued.

It wasn't Gant. It sounded like a white guy trying to sound black.

Eric hung up and redialed Pablo's cell phone. The doors folded open for him as he entered the Palace. Pablo answered on the third ring.

"What the hell's going on?" Eric asked.

"What do you mean?" Pablo answered.

Eric was just about to answer when he saw Ladonna Purcell flanked by two tough-looking bastards, a couple of cops, and that Samoan ape bodyguard.

Oh, shit, he thought, and turned his head, continuing on into the casino. He turned right and went into an aisle of one-armed bandits, then zigzagged his way over to the far

Michael A. Black

other side of the expansive room.

"Eric? Eric? Are you there?" Pablo sounded frantic.

"Yeah, I'm here. And so is Ladonna with a bunch of cops. Hold on."

When he was far enough away he spoke in a low tone.

"Where you at? Is Gant with you?"

Pablo answered slowly. "Yeah, he's with me. A . . . we're—" The signal faded for a moment. "We're in a limo cruising the strip. Tell me where you're at and we'll come pick you up."

Eric looked at Ladonna talking to the cops. She was gesturing wildly. Some big, middle-aged hillbilly fucker was trying to calm her down.

"Lemme float here for a bit and see what's going on," Eric said. "How's the brat doing?"

"She's okay."

"Good." Eric thought for a moment. "You know, I just called the room, and somebody answered pretending to be Gant. Ladonna's probably put the cops on this, reporting her daughter as a runaway. We gotta lay low till we can get her cleaned up and to the big gala affair tonight." A waitress with one of those push-up bras and black tights came by and asked if he wanted a drink. Eric shook his head.

"Give me a location," Pablo said quickly, "and we'll pick you up and we can decide what to do together, okay?"

He was sounding frantic again. Eric stubbed out his cigarette and took out another one, glancing at his watch. It was close to four fifteen.

"No, I tell you what," he said. "You just hang loose for an hour or so. Take her to a beauty shop someplace and get her dolled up. What's she wearing?"

"A T-shirt and jeans," Pablo said.

"Okay, stop by one of the shops too, and get her a nice

274

outfit for tonight. And one for you too. We can't risk going back to the room till I get this sorted out. I'll be on damage control."

"Wait, Eric, how will I find you?"

"I'll call you on your cell. If worst comes to worst, we'll tag up in about an hour and go the Roman Holiday at around six or so." He drew on the cigarette and blew out a cloudy breath. "And if Corrigan or Moran call you, just remember, we ain't seen Rocky at all, okay?"

"Okay." Pablo's voice sounded like a squeak. "But I'd feel better if we could meet you now."

"I'll get with you later," Eric said. "Just do what I told you."

He ended the call.

That little son of a bitch is going to have to learn to fend for himself a bit, Eric thought. I've got to make sure that this all works out.

He considered his options briefly, trying to figure out whether to approach Ladonna or not. Better not, he thought. She looks pretty pissed. His mind raced. How could he work all this to his advantage?

If he called her and told her that Melissa Michelle was with Pablo, she'd probably go ballistic, but would she call off the cops? Better to wait on that. What if she demanded to talk to her daughter and the kid sounded all drugged up? Damn that fucking Pablo. Stealing another glance across the casino, he saw the Samoan gorilla looking around, like he was trying to spot someone. Eric sat immediately, feeling the seizing in his bowels again. After a few minutes, he stood, keeping his face turned away from their direction, and made his way toward the back entrance. When he was outside he literally ran down the alley by the parking area until he got to the corner. Then he slowed to a brisk walk.

He could smell his own body odor and knew he'd have to change shirts before tonight. Staying with the crowds, he took the walkways to cross Las Vegas Boulevard and headed over toward Caesar's Palace. He could get some new clothes in the interior mall portion and get cleaned up there as well. Then he'd call Ladonna, tag up with Pablo, and make the scene at the Roman Holiday tonight in time for the fading Latino Prince of Pop to announce his engagement to the only daughter of the dead King of Rock and Roll. And hopefully, the reporter that Spangler had told him about would bring the two Memphis fugitives and Corrigan could take care of that little loose end, too. Eric smiled in spite of himself. In his fantasy, he could see it all falling into place in front of him. It would all work out, and they'd never be able to put it together that he'd even seen Rocky since his relapse.

Harry had reread Buzzy's column about Graceful Valley Nursing Home several times when his cell phone finally rang again. He hoped it was Stockton with some news about a local hacker, but he saw by the Caller ID that it was a Nevada pay phone.

"Harry Bauer," he said.

"It's Marjorie Versette. We're at your hotel, in the lobby, if you want to come down and talk."

Time to see what this one's all about, Harry thought. It could be a wild goose chase, or it could break things wide open.

"I'll be right down. How will I know you?"

"We're going into the buffet. The non-smoking section. I'll tell the hostess we're expecting you."

She hung up.

Harry smirked. Short and to the point. He hoped their

conversation would be just as direct as he slipped the key card into his shirt pocket and went to the elevators. It was four thirty-five and Sonny Proper had told him to be at the Roman Holiday by seven. He'd have to wear a sport jacket. Or would he? It was so damn hot, and everybody in Vegas seemed to dress very casual. And Sonny had hinted to bring along Gabe and Marjorie and Willard as well. But why? Then again, maybe a face-to-face meeting between all the principals would be what he needed to sort this mystery out. Buzzy'd interviewed all these same people, and had made sense out of it. Gotten what he'd termed a "dynamite story." Or was he just exaggerating? His tendency toward hyperbole was legend. Harry smiled. Damn, he missed him.

Why hadn't I done more to stay in touch? he thought.

The elevator door pinged open and Harry stepped inside, hoping that whatever was waiting for him in the lobby would provide a few more answers. But that would depend on several factors, not the least of which was knowing what questions to ask.

Damn, he thought. If only Buzzy would have left a password with Linda or someone.

The elevator reached the lobby and Harry took a deep breath as he headed through the casino area and toward the buffet. The hazy smoke, the constant chimes of the slots, and the murmur of a thousand conversations mingled around him, but then traces of a familiar melody began drifting in. A Colton Purcell song, and Harry could swear that it was the original singing it.

"Don't ask the question . . ." Boo ba ba boo, the accompanying melody played, "if you don't wanna hear the answer."

Maybe it's a recording, he thought. But no, it wasn't, he realized seconds later, hearing the refrain again and glancing over at the small bar nestled among a cluster of artificial tropical trees. Adjacent to the bar a heavyset man with long gray hair and blocky physique crooned into a microphone, hitting every note with the utmost perfection, as a crowd of onlookers stood enthralled.

The big man pranced along the edge of the stage like a pro, smiling his half-crooked smile, the microphone held easily in his hand, as he pointed into the crowd and crooned the ending refrain once more, putting the customary Colton Purcell echoing finish on it. Hitting the final notes with accomplished ease, he smiled again to a scattered applause, to which he said, "Thank ya. Thank ya very much," and bowed. When the applause stopped, a middle-aged woman came up on the stage and gently tugged at the man's sleeve, pulling him close enough to whisper in his ear. His gaze immediately went to the floor and she guided him off the stage, profusely thanking the musicians and security guards who were standing in the wings.

Harry shook his head, and started toward the buffet, then suddenly stopped. The words of Buzzy's column suddenly came back to him and he turned just as the heavyset gray-haired man and the woman began to pass him.

"Nurse Marjorie?" Harry asked.

The woman froze, a look of terror on her face.

"I'm Harry Bauer." He smiled and looked at her male companion. "Is this who I think it is?"

Eric walked back across Las Vegas Boulevard at the intersection, carrying the bags with the new shirt, jacket, and pants he'd bought. No cop cars in front. That was a good sign. Maybe the heat was off once they figured out Pablo and Melissa Michelle weren't in the room, he thought. His mind raced over his last movements before he'd left. He'd flushed the remainder of his own powder, so any shit the cops might have found in the room, even Pablo's fucking syringes, would all be covered by one of his prescriptions. So they'd be okay on that part. And as for the brat being messed up, he had no more control over what she put in her mouth than Pablo did. He chuckled at the cleverness of his play on words as he moved forward, finally starting to relax a tad and hoping that this whole thing was on its way to getting worked out in his favor.

His cell phone rang as he moved up the block toward the Emperor's Palace.

Eric saw the Caller ID was blocked. He answered it anyway.

"Eric?" Spangler's nervous voice said.

"Yeah, what do you want?"

"Ladonna Purcell just called me. She's very upset. Melissa Michelle's disappeared."

"She ain't disappeared. She's with Pablo and Gant," Eric said. He paused at the entrance, letting the doors open automatically, and scanned the place. No visible police presence. No sign of Miss Bitch Ladonna screaming her head off. He stepped inside with a cautious gait as Spangler's garrulous voice continued to drone on.

"Well, she's reported the girl a runaway to Las Vegas Metro, so I would suggest that you get her back to her mother posthaste."

"That might not be such a good idea at the moment," Eric said as he continued to scan the casino. Everything looked good so far. "She got into some pill popping with Pablo a while ago. We're trying to let her come down a bit."

"Oh my god," Spangler said. "Is she all right?"

"She's fine." He headed for the elevators. "Just a little preview of the shape of things to come, is all."

"Does Ladonna know?"

"You nuts?" Eric was almost at the elevators now. He'd go up to the floor, take an easy stroll down the hallway, and maybe call the room as soon as he got this asshole off the phone. "Why don't you call her instead?" Eric said. "Tell her the brat's okay. That she's just out for some fun and games with the Latino Prince of Pop."

"You know I can't do that," Spangler said, his voice ripe with indignation. "Ladonna trusts me. I am her attorney, after all."

Eric smirked as he pressed the "up" button.

"Yeah, you've been a real loyalist where she's concerned, all right. Maybe I oughta clue her in on who really tipped me and Babcock to the blood test. Tell her that it wasn't that crazy fucking reporter."

"Don't you dare threaten me," Spangler said. "I should have never gotten involved with you."

"Maybe you shoulda thought about that before you put all that candy up your nose, counselor," Eric said. He was about to jam the knife in a bit farther when he saw a flash of dark hair moving quickly in the shiny chrome frame of the elevator jamb. Twisting, Eric glimpsed Samoan Joe about twenty-five feet away, moving toward him at a quick trot. Eric immediately turned on his heel and ran in the opposite direction. The hallway led past a small coffee shop and gift store and out to the rear parking area. An older lady ventured out the door of the gift shop and Eric pushed her down, stopping to check the burly Samoan's progress. He was closing the gap fast.

Throwing his bag in the direction of his pursuer, Eric pumped his arms and legs in an all-out sprint down the hall. The area opened up into a larger room housing another selection of stores and a larger restaurant. The doors to the rear parking lot and the alley were up a small section of steps. Joe had apparently slowed to avoid the old broad, but was resuming the chase and gaining now.

Shit, Eric thought as he caught the banister and whirled himself up the half-dozen steps. If I can get outside maybe I can make it to the strip and lose him in the crowds. At least till I grab a taxi or something. Another quick glance over his shoulder buoyed his optimism. The Samoan had to bounce off a wall to avoid knocking over two senior citizens strolling out of the restaurant.

Thank god for fools and losers, Eric thought, tearing open the first glass door. Two more steps brought him to the second, which he ripped open even faster. One more glance over his shoulder and he saw that he had increased the distance to an almost comfortable level, even though his breaths were coming in gasps now.

He went down the cement steps two at a time, curling his fingers around the black metal banister to swing himself around toward the alley and from there out to the street. It was all he could do to keep from yelling *Fuck you, asshole* as he ran. Then someone loomed in front of him and Eric reached up to shove the person out of his way. But the guy in front swayed away momentarily, and then moved with a panther-like grace. Eric felt a solid fist collide sharply with his heaving midsection. His momentum carried him forward for a few more steps on shaky legs. His chest expanded, but no air was coming in. It felt like someone had dropped a refrigerator on his chest from six stories up. Gasping for air, he went forward, managing to break his fall with his hands on the rough cement. The air still wouldn't come into his lungs, and he felt a pair of powerful hands grasping his arms, then lift him upward like he weighed no more than a rag doll.

"Take shallow breaths," a voice whispered in his ear. It had a distinctly Southern sound to it. "It'll help you get your wind back sooner." Eric felt his arms being forced together behind his back. "Then you and me are gonna have a little talk," the voice continued, "about a certain young lady by the name of Melissa Michelle."

Harry watched the big man sop up the gravy with the last of his corn muffins. Marjorie smiled at him and asked if he wanted another helping. A beatific smile stretched across his face, somewhat crooked, and showing a set of finely capped, sparkling teeth. He nodded. Marjorie took his plate and got up. Harry stood also, figuring he might as well grab another helping of those peaches.

"He's doing so well now that I've got him weaned off that Thorazine," Marjorie said, leaning close to Harry. Her voice was no more than a whisper among the ambient clatter of plates, spoken words, and drifting chimes from the slot machines. "I always told them they had him overmedicated."

"Just how did they decide on the name Willard Younger?" Harry asked. He scooped a few peaches and some juice into his bowl. Marjorie was busily perusing the steamed vegetables, mashed potatoes, and beef. Every few seconds she glanced back at the table, but Willard only sat there passively watching her every move. Harry thought of a pet dog he once had. The adulation was similar.

"You see, Mr. Bauer," she continued as they paired up and headed back to their table. "Colton Purcell's mother's maiden name was Younger. And Clayton's middle name is Willard."

Harry nodded, but his brow was furrowed. She must have noticed because she laughed as she set the heavily laden plate down on the dainty white tablecloth.

"Sit down and I'll go over it all for you," she said. "It sounds very complicated, but it's not, really."

Harry sat.

Marjorie waited until Willard picked up his knife and fork, then smiled in encouragement at him.

"Back in 1949 there were two boys born to Elizabeth and Wallace Purcell," she said. "Colton Gabriel and Clayton Willard. Identical twins. They were dirt-poor, and Wallace got caught peddling stolen car parts over to Texarkana. He served thirty-six months."

Harry raised his eyebrows. "I didn't know that."

"Not many do," she said, pausing to check Willard's progress and wipe his chin with a napkin. "After Colton got famous, he had Big Daddy Babcock pull some strings to get the records expunged and sealed. That Big Daddy, he knew how to work things." Marjorie compressed her lips into a thin line. "But even he couldn't change what couldn't be changed. When Wallace got out of prison, he came home and noticed one of his sons acting very withdrawn." She closed her eyes and swallowed hard. "That was Willard. In those days they weren't sure how to diagnose it. And being from such an impoverished background, they naturally thought of mental illness as something to be ashamed of."

Harry glanced furtively at the man across the table, silent and totally engrossed in eating his food.

Marjorie had been looking at Willard too, and reached over to squeeze his hand. He looked up and smiled again, showing hunks of food stuck along his gum-line.

"They managed to keep his condition pretty much unknown, at least till high school," she said. "The story was that he was away at a special school, but that wasn't always the case. Most of the time, he was shipped off to live with

Elizabeth's parents in the country. But they didn't know how to deal with his condition, and he got worse. More withdrawn. They came up with the story that he passed after Colton's singing career took off. They kept this secret, keeping him hospitalized under that other name, all these years."

"That's quite a story, Marjorie," Harry said. "But I'm still not getting it. Why, exactly did you . . ." He searched for the right euphemism. "Remove him from the facility and bring him here?"

"Mr. Sawyer told me. I called him. He'd given me his number back when he wrote that feature story on us. He said there was some real danger brewing and that I had to get Willard out. To bring him here and he'd get the truth about everything out."

"Did he say what the danger was?"

She shook her head.

"I could only guess it had something to do with the blood test," she said. "And they were talking about moving him to another place, and I couldn't allow that. I'm the only person that knows how to take care of him properly."

"Blood test?"

She nodded, pausing again to wipe some gravy and mashed potatoes from the gray-bearded chin.

"It was just a recent thing," she said. "I mean, we routinely do tests all the time to check the dosage and levels of the medicines, but this one was different. I came in one day and there was Big Daddy Babcock himself, standing there like an evil Colonel Sanders in that white suit and string bow tie, with a phlebotomist drawing out vial after vial. He had at least three of them, and was set to draw more when I asked him what they thought they was doing." Her lower lip drew up tightly. "Yes, siree, I stepped right up and put a stop to it. Big Daddy just laughed and said something real mean and nasty. Then, when the ward supervisor came to see what the commotion was all about, he said that Big Daddy had authority, and that neither me or Willard had a say in it. I put a quick call into the Purcell estate, trying to get them to do something, but by that time it was prit-near done. Ladonna Purcell's secretary called me the next day and asked a bunch of fool questions, saying Ladonna was very upset with the way the whole thing was handled. I said if she was so upset, she should come by once in a blue moon and say hello to him." She cast a warm look at Willard as he scraped the plate once again with a fragment of biscuit. "Then when word came out that they were going to transfer him someplace else, I just couldn't let that happen." She pursed her lips again. "I mean, there ain't nobody who cares about him as much as I do."

"I can see that," Harry said, smiling. He hoped he looked as sincere as he was trying to sound.

Marjorie smiled.

"Mr. Sawyer said he was going to talk to Ladonna," she said. "I can't believe, even though she and Colton divorced, that she'd want her brother-in-law, her daughter's only living uncle on her daddy's side, shut away someplace bad where people don't care about him." Her face looked pinched, as if her skin seemed to be suddenly pulled tight over her skull. "Would she?"

Harry glanced at Willard, who was now sitting quietly, his head jerking slightly to some internal beatitudes.

"I don't know," he said, reaching into his pocket and withdrawing the envelope with the guest passes to the Colton Purcell Imitator's Contest that Sonny Proper had given him. His cell phone rang just as he was about to ask Marjorie if she wanted to accompany him tonight. It was

Jan's number. Her voice had an undercurrent of excitement as she spoke.

"You'll never guess what's going on here," she said. "Those crime scene photos from Memphis of Big Daddy Babcock's demise? It was like déjà vu when I got here."

"Your autoerotic?"

"Right," she said. "Only we're thinking that things are not quite what they seem to be."

It's Vegas, he thought. Nothing is as it seems.

"There are all kinds of interesting surprises around here," she continued. "I'll probably be tied up for hours. The decedent is Pablo Stevenson's body guard."

"Wow," Harry said. "I'll bet he's a fun interview."

"Can't comment on that yet. Nobody's here and nobody seems to know how to reach him. And Ladonna Purcell's reported her daughter missing, too. It all might be connected to this incident."

Harry glanced down at the envelope in his hand and then over at Marjorie and Willard.

"Maybe," he said, "I can help."

Eric didn't know how long the van had been driving or where they were going. The vehicle's floor was carpeted, but it was still hard and unyielding. He lay on his side in a fetal position, trying to take the slow, shallow breaths, just like the big hillbilly guy had told him to do, all the time wondering what they were going to do with him as he fought the searing pain that still lingered in his gut. He rotated his head slightly, catching a glimpse of Ladonna sitting in the front seat, her face streaked with tears.

Ladonna Purcell, he thought. Who the fuck is she to kidnap me? And what are they gonna do, kill me? He tried

286

to force a laugh, mustered from false bravado, but it came off a coughing whimper.

"How's your gut feeling, boy?" the big hillbilly fucker asked, a grin spread across his face.

Eric ignored the question, not wanting to give the prick the satisfaction of knowing it still hurt.

"You wanna tell me just who you were talking to before we interrupted you?" the big guy said.

Eric didn't answer and the hillbilly prodded him with his boot. It was one of those pointed, fancy jobs, like they wore for horseback riding or something. The toes and heels had inset decorations of silver flourishes. God, he hoped the son of a bitch wasn't planning on kicking him.

"How do you know it was Montgomery, for Christ sake?" Ladonna asked, turning toward them.

The hillbilly looked momentarily upset.

"Because when Joe picked up this guy's phone, that's who was on the damn thing, okay?" he said.

Oh oh, Eric thought. These two obviously had history.

"So does that *mean* anything?" she asked, her voice lilting toward sarcasm.

"It means that you shoulda done what I told you a long time ago and got rid of that guy," the hillbilly said. "I told you—"

"Yes, yes, yes," Ladonna said, interrupting. "You were right, Sonny." Her voice sounded on the edge of cracking. "You're always right. I should have listened to you. Colton should have listened to you. Is that what you want to hear?"

The hillbilly was silent for a moment, then he said, "If he would've, he'd still be alive today."

Ladonna began sobbing softly.

"I just want my daughter back," she said softly.

Maybe this is my chance, Eric thought. He coughed as

loud as his sore gut allowed and managed a weak sounding, "Hey."

Sonny looked down at him.

"You wondering where Melissa is?" Eric said, somewhat pleased that his voice was coming out croaky. More sympathy that way, he figured. "I been trying to get that straightened out myself." He half sat up, and tried to manage a weak grin.

"Pull it over there, Joe," Sonny said, then turned back to Eric.

The van slowed and Eric felt the bumping shocks that meant they'd just gone off the pavement. They continued off road for a few minutes, then made a winding turn before coming to a stop. Eric waited on the floor, with Sonny looking down at him, until the side door jerked open and the sunlight and heat flooded in. Covering his eyes with his forearm, Eric tried to lie back down, but was suddenly jerked upward, finding himself nose-to-nose with the huge Samoan.

"Where's Melissa Michelle?" the ape asked.

"Hey, take it easy, wouldja?" Eric said. He could feel the other man's coiled strength waiting to explode.

"Hold on, Joe," Eric heard Sonny say. "Just put him down there."

The Samoan tossed Eric out of the van and onto the sandy ground. The ground felt hard and unforgiving as he got to his feet. He saw they were in the middle of nowhere. Nothing but cactus, sagebrush, and those reddish-brown mountains in the background. He brought his hand up and shielded his eyes.

"Where is she, Eric?" Sonny asked.

Eric waited a few beats before replying. No sense letting them know how scared he was. Shit, these guys were amateurs compared to being in a steam room with Ricardo Casio.

"She's fine," he said finally. Ladonna perked up at the words. "Her and Pablo just took a little pre-party trip, is all."

"So she is with him?" Ladonna demanded. "Where are they? I want her back with me this minute."

Eric shrugged slightly, trying to affect an air of confidence.

"Hey, they went to see the Grand Canyon or something," he said. "They're in a limo. I can try his cell, provided you let me use my phone, but they may be out of range. I mean, look at this terrain out here."

Sonny was leaning against the fender of the van, with a circular metal can in his left hand. He raised his leg and withdrew a knife from his boot with his right, flipped open the blade with one hand, and this made Eric a bit more nervous. Those good old boys always seemed to be carrying knives, and they knew how to use them.

But Sonny twisted open the can and used the silver blade to lift a dark section of tobacco from the tin. He stuck it in between his lower lip and gums, causing a grotesque-looking bulge.

"Eric, I hope you're not messing with this old country boy," he said slowly. " 'Cause I really ain't in the mood for it."

"I ain't messing with ya," Eric said, allowing a bit of petulance to creep into his tone. "Now get me back to my hotel and keep this ape away from me." He pointed at the Samoan who was staring intently at Eric's face now.

Sonny laughed slightly and spat a looping brown stream that splashed into the dry earth next to Eric's foot.

"Keep Joe away from you?" the hillbilly said. He

grinned. "Believe me, it ain't Joe you need to be concerned about at this point." The bulge shifted and he spat again, closer to Eric's foot this time. "When I was in the Marine Corps, back a couple of wars ago, I spent some time in a little place called Hue during what came to be called the Tet Offensive. While I was there, I watched some ARVN Rangers interrogate what we used to call some suspected Victor Charlies." He shook his head slightly. "Never thought I'd have any occasion to use any of the tactics I seen that day, 'specially back here in the States, but . . ." he let the sentence drift off, then sent another blast of spit in Eric's direction, this time splattering over his shoe and sock.

"We're gonna have us a little talk now, Eric," Sonny said, standing and moving forward. "Right here, right now, and you're gonna tell us anything, and everything we want to know, understand?"

Eric backed up slightly, looking around with a gut-wrenching desperation. But the problem was, there wasn't any place to run.

Chapter 25

Wedding Bell Blues

Corrigan leaned against the armrest of the stretch limo and stared at Pablo and Melissa Michelle who sat across from him about ten feet away. The air was hazy from Casio's cigarette, but Corrigan knew it would be a mistake to ask the boss to quit smoking. Not with him so worried about Rocky. The girl was curled in the corner of the seat next to the solid sidepiece. She hadn't stopped crying since they'd left the hotel. Her little shit of a boyfriend was crammed at the opposite end, not even making any effort to try and comfort her.

Some hero, Corrigan thought as he let the phone continue to ring. He was counting off the ninth time when Eric finally answered it. The guy sounded nervous.

"Where you at?" Corrigan asked.

"I'm in a meeting," Eric said.

"We need to talk."

"Yeah, I know." He sounded out of breath, like he'd been running or something. Or maybe punched in the stomach. "But I'm tied up right now. How about we tag up later on tonight, okay? I got a lot of things to set up here."

"Where's here?"

"Aaaa, at the hotel."

"Which hotel?"

"What is this, twenty questions, for Christ's sake. I told you, I'm in a meeting."

Corrigan was starting to get some bad vibes from this

conversation. He covered the mouthpiece and whispered to Casio. "Something ain't right. I think he might be getting ready to rabbit on us."

Casio's bottom lip tugged down at the corners, his entire face darkening with the scowl.

"I want that fuck. Alive, understand?"

Corrigan nodded and held up a massive index finger.

"When can we meet then?" he asked, trying to sound almost conciliatory.

"Um, I don't know."

"You talked to our favorite lawyer lately?"

"No, why?"

Vanshitberg was definitely nervous. On the edge. Corrigan made his tone sound almost friendly. "Just wondering if there was any news about that nurse."

"Word is that there's another reporter nosing around," Eric said. "He may be bringing them to the contest tonight. That'd simplify things, right?"

"Yeah," Corrigan said slowly, then quickly added, "You sure about that?"

"That's what I heard." He paused again and then asked, "Everything else okay?"

"Yeah." Corrigan purposely let the conversation drop to see where the other man would take it.

"Well, look, I've got to get with Pablo and we have to make an appearance at the Colton Purcell imitator's contest tonight. How about I call you after that and we'll get together?"

"Sounds good," Corrigan said. "I'll wait to hear from you."

When he ended the call he looked across at Pablo, then to Melissa Michelle, and back to Casio.

"I don't care about the money no more," Casio said.

"All I want is to get that slimy little prick that set up my boy."

"Boss, I got an idea," Corrigan said. "Maybe we can still get both."

Eric held his stomach to guard against another of Sonny's belly blows. He had already thrown up twice, and didn't think he had any more left to void. The big hillbilly fucker moved forward once more and Eric cringed as he raised his hand.

"No more, please," he said. "I already told you everything you wanted to know."

"Not everything," Sonny said through clenched teeth. "Where's Melissa Michelle?" He drew back his fist.

"No, no, please, you gotta believe me. I ain't sure where she's at, only that she's with Pablo."

The ringing of his cell phone again saved him. Whoever it was, he thanked God for them, because he didn't know if he could take another one of those gut punches. Joe held the phone out toward Sonny, who looked at the number and read it out loud.

"Who's that?" he asked.

Eric felt a flood of relief.

"It's Pablo," he said, holding out his hand.

Joe handed him the phone and Eric immediately answered and asked, "Where you at?"

"We're at a beauty shop. Melissa's getting her hair done."

"Is she all right?" Eric asked. Sonny was leaning in close now, twisting the phone so that he could hear it too. Eric's stomach turned over again. If Pablo mentioned anything about the drugs . . .

"Yeah, she's fine," Pablo said. "How about you? Where're you?"

"I'm getting ready to head over to the Roman Holiday. Why don't you meet me there?"

"Okay, how soon can you be there?" Pablo sounded nervous now.

Eric felt a hand clench around his upper arm, squeezing with enough force to raise him on his toes.

"I'll go there and wait for you," he said. "Just get there as soon as you can with Melissa."

After Pablo had agreed, Sonny reached across and almost gently removed the phone from Eric's hand. He pressed the end button, looked up, and smiled. The tobacco wad was still making his lower lip bulge outward.

"Guess it's all over but the waiting, now," he said.

Eric felt a wave of relief.

Thank God, he thought. Thank God.

Corrigan steered Melissa Michelle by the arm and Freddie had Pablo. The hooker they'd dialed up to be Ladonna at the Clark County Marriage License Bureau looked a bit too hot initially, so they made her put on a pair of dark sunglasses and a hat. All things considered, telling the guy behind the counter that they were concerned about celebrity security had the desired effect. He ran the license off with a minimum of questions and delay, smiling the whole time and reminding them that there was no blood test required in the state of Nevada. As they walked back to the limo Melissa Michelle started to go limp, but Corrigan snatched her arm just above the elbow.

"Keep walking, sweet cakes," he said, squeezing not so gently.

Freddie opened the door and ushered them inside, forcing Pablo and Melissa to their previous place on the far side of the compartment away from the door.

Corrigan paused, peeling off a hundred and an additional fifty for the prostitute and glancing around. The streets were crowded, but no one appeared to be paying much attention. No cops either. He slipped the C-note in the hooker's pants' pocket.

"Go buy her a blouse," he said, nodding toward Melissa Michelle.

"Okay, what size are you, honey?"

Melissa Michelle buried her face in her hands, saying nothing.

"Guesstimate," Corrigan said as he got back in the limo and slammed the door after him.

"You sure this is gonna work?" Casio asked.

"Positive," Corrigan said. "Like I told you, it's foolproof."

Casio took in a deep breath then exhaled slowly, nodding his head as he did so.

"Let's go do it," he said.

The small white chapel just off Las Vegas Boulevard had a large, flashing neon sign in front advertising twenty-four hour service, except on Sunday, when they closed at midnight. The limo pulled up in front, and Corrigan got out, followed by the hooker, still clad in her Ladonna outfit, Pablo, Freddie, and Melissa Michelle. She'd slipped the new blouse on over her T-shirt, but it was buttoned crookedly. Corrigan placed a huge hand on each of the captive's arms and squeezed, pulling them in close.

"Now remember," he said in a husky whisper, "don't even think about trying nothing, because then I'll have to hurt you both real bad."

Freddie grinned in commiserating fashion and pinched

Melissa Michelle's left buttocks. She jerked and inhaled sharply.

A third man got out from the passenger compartment of the limo.

"Roscoe, check it out," Corrigan said, nodding toward the chapel. Roscoe went through the small miniature white fence-way and into the chapel. A moment later his dark head appeared in the doorway and he nodded.

Corrigan eased everybody forward.

"You don't have to worry about me, man," Pablo said. Corrigan could feel the little creep's body trembling as he spoke. "I mean, I ain't gonna make no trouble. None at all. I'll do whatever you say."

"Good," Corrigan said. "Now look happy."

They moved through the doorway and Roscoe closed the door behind them, flipping the open sign to closed. The hooker took a seat in the back row, still keeping her dark glasses and hat on.

The minister, clad in a white shirt and vest, had been leaning on the small organ talking to a woman with bright red hair. She looked over at them from behind thick glasses and smiled.

The minister straightened up and smiled too. He looked to be in his early sixties with a face as round as a melon and a cleft of a chin set into a dollop of fat. His teeth looked denture-perfect and as false as his smile.

"Good afternoon," he said, glancing at his watch. "Well, I guess it should be good evening now." He gave an irritating little laugh that Corrigan thought sounded like a scared pig. "And whom do we have here?"

Corrigan, who was wearing his thin black leather gloves, handed the minister the marriage license.

The fat man took it, slipped on a pair of small oval

glasses, and scanned it briefly.

"Yes, everything seems in order—" He looked up as soon as he read the names, his eyebrows raising as he glanced from Pablo's face to Melissa Michelle's. "My Lord, look who we've got here. I was a big fan of your father's, Miss. Of your stuff too, of course, Mr. Stevenson."

"For security reasons, we want to get this done fast," Corrigan said.

"Oh, yes, of course," the minister said. "Of course. I understand." He licked his lips. "Ah, is this going to be a single or double ring ceremony?"

Corrigan shrugged.

"Do we need rings?" he asked. He realized that he'd forgotten about that part of it.

As if sensing his dilemma, the minister snapped his fingers at the woman and said, "Rosie, show this gentleman our ring selection." He laughed again. "We try to think of everything here." When Corrigan didn't laugh, the man busied himself inspecting Melissa Michelle's left hand. "Let's see, you look about a size five." Rosie held out a white board with a selection of wedding bands stuck into the slots. "Do you like any of these, my dear?" He glanced up at Corrigan and added, "Ah, it's a hundred extra for the ring. These are very fine stock."

Corrigan nodded and leaned toward Melissa Michelle. "I think this one suits you real good," he said, pointing toward one of the bands with a stylish design. "You got another for the groom?"

"Oh yes, yes, of course," the minister said. "Rosie, our masculine selections please." He reached down and grabbed Pablo's left hand, bringing it upward. "My, my, aren't we nervous," he said, pausing to wipe away some of the perspiration dripping from the hand. "Let's see, you look about a size five too. Same design, I assume?"

Corrigan nodded.

"Very well," the minister said, removing the ring and handing the card back to Rosie. He went to his lectern and removed his vestment, which had been draped over the top. He turned and looked at Corrigan with the practiced smile again.

"Ah, the young lady is under eighteen. We do have parental consent, do we not?"

"Yeah," Corrigan said, gesturing back toward the silent hooker. "Her mother signed off at the Bureau place."

A steady stream of tears began rolling down Melissa Michelle's cheeks.

"Very good, very good," the minister said, reaching for his Bible and moving toward them. He paused again. "Would it be possible for me to get a picture of this ceremony?" He emitted the nervous little laugh again. "We try to do that with all our celebrity ceremonies."

Corrigan smiled back at him.

"Sure, Reverend," he said. "Just make sure none of us undercover security are in the picture."

The minister shot back his patented grin. "No, no, of course. Rosie, the Polaroid."

Corrigan and Freddie stepped back and Roscoe, who was still at the door, turned his back. Corrigan motioned for the hooker to move to the side also. The pop of the flash and the mechanized ejection of the photo followed.

"Take one more for us," Corrigan said. "If you don't mind, that is." His lips stretched back into a Cheshire cat's grin as the Polaroid flashed again.

"Dearly beloved . . ." the minister began.

Chapter 26
Best Laid Plans

Harry craned his neck as he walked through the doors of the Roman Holiday with Marjorie and Willard in tow. Two large pillars framed the entranceway and a statue of Nero fiddling before an interactive backdrop of a miniaturized burning city was in the center of the huge hall. Beyond that Harry could see the ubiquitous rows of the casino's slots. He asked a uniformed security guard which way it was to the Colton Purcell imitator's contest, and the guard pointed down the hallway. As they proceeded forward, Harry glanced around, hoping to see Jan, who had said she'd meet him there to talk with Pablo Stevenson and his manager. But there was no sign of her.

They made their way through the narrow aisle lacing between the gaming tables and slot machines, each crammed with people placing coin after coin into them. Occasionally a groan or squeal could be heard over the constant pinging of the chimes. Harry turned to make sure he still had his companions and saw Marjorie leading Willard about twenty steps behind.

Slowing to allow them to catch up, he assessed his plan. Find Ladonna and company, confront them with what he now knew about the funny brother, the Babcock blood test request, and Buzzy's story. Act like he knew more than he actually did, and maybe, just maybe . . . something had to give tossing all those ingredients into the same pot. Plus, Jan had some very pointed questions she was going to ask Pablo Stevenson about the death of his bodyguard. This was shaping up to be one hell of a story, even without Buzzy's final encrypted columns and notes.

The strands of music and singing suddenly began to overtake the chimes of the machines as they rounded a corner, and a reasonable imitation of the original's voice was filtering over to them. A lighted marquee pointed the way to what was billed as THE SHOWROOM—FEATURING THE COLTON PURCELL IMITATOR'S CONTEST.

Must be getting close, thought Harry. He looked around. Willard seemed to be perking up at the sound. Harry chuckled and mentally added, I wonder what would happen if we got him on stage?

Several men walked by them clad in ersatz red, white, and blue jumpsuits and black, slicked back hair, with dejected looks on their faces. Two were carrying guitar cases. The music became louder as they approached the ballroom, which overflowed with people. And there were fans of all ages there. Middle-aged women with *I Love Colton* T-shirts and buttons on, younger girls with pierced eyebrows and lips wearing similar fashions. Men of various ages were in abundance, too, as well as a TV crew and reporter. The crowd grew denser as they moved down the hallway. Several security guards tried to focus people into a line to get photographed with a life-sized cardboard cutout of Colton Purcell holding a guitar. There were three incarnations to choose from: the early twenty-ish Colton, looking sullen in street clothes from *King Rebel,* the more toned down, moderate, blow-dried thirty-ish Colton dressed in a western outfit from *Ghost Town Blues,* and the late-thirties, stylized, jump-suited version who thrilled the world with a satellite concert broadcast around the planet.

Harry checked again to make sure he hadn't been separated from Marjorie and Willard. She was still about twenty-five feet behind him, but she had her charge well in tow, her arm hooked around his as they pushed through the masses.

Harry looked near the doors trying to see if Jan was there. Still no sign of her. He bit his lip slightly and took out his cell phone, dialing her number. It rang several times, or at least he thought it did, but the sound of the crowd hollering and the music blasting, drowned out any chance he had of hearing clearly.

Frustrated, Harry pressed the END button and put the phone back in his pocket. He'd have to get settled and try to find a quieter place to call. The next song filtered over from the stage and the crowd quieted immediately, its sound startlingly familiar. Harry glanced toward the stage and saw a young man dressed in regular street clothes, his hair slicked back in a greasy pompadour, strumming a guitar and singing "Please, Don't Drag My Heart Around," an early Colton Purcell song. But this guy had a voice. He sounded more like Colton than Colton, and he had the moves too. Suddenly the performer turned and Harry saw the man's face.

Well, I'll be, he thought.

It was Gabe.

Eric hadn't had a chance to change clothes and he knew that the ones he had on stunk badly. He could smell himself, for Christ's sake. But as he sat on the floor of the van watching the hillbilly fucker clean his nails with that big old knife, he knew better than to complain. They weren't going to let him change even if he had some clothes. The Samoan ape was driving and her bitchiness, Ladonna, sat in the front passenger seat. At least they could have gotten one with seats in the back. Or maybe they liked watching him get bounced around on the hard metal floor.

He felt the van slow to a stop, then make a turn. From the occasional glimpses he was able to catch through the windshield, he knew they were back in the city again. On the strip, most likely. Getting close to the downtown area. Maybe that'd give him a chance to get away. His best chance was to run if he caught a break, but where could he go? He knew Corrigan and Casio were looking for him, and maybe even the cops wanted to see him too.

Christ, it's hell to be popular, he thought, trying to give himself a laugh. But instead all he got was that familiar pull in his bowels. By now they have to know about Rocky, he thought, and that might mean they're looking for someone to blame. A flash of his conversation with Casio in the steam room made his intestines seize up so badly he gripped his stomach, afraid he might actually void himself.

"What's the matter, slick?" Sonny asked. "Your gut still bothering you?"

Eric looked up at him, his mouth hanging open.

"What do you expect, the way you were pounding me?"

"Sheeit," Sonny said. "That wasn't nothing, boy. If you don't lead me to Melissa Michelle at this here hotel we're going to, I'll show you what a real ass-whipping is all about."

Eric licked his lips and silently prayed that Pablo had been true to his word and had the little brat sobered up. He didn't even want to think about how they'd freak out if they saw her messed and high. But shit, they can have her, he thought. His first priority was seeing if he was in the clear with Casio. Then he'd let Corrigan take on the hillbilly. Then it'll be my turn to sit back and laugh, he thought.

The van made a right turn, and then slowed down to

make a left. Eric felt the vehicle slowing under him, and finally stop. Through the windshield Eric could see cement pillars and overhead lights. A parking garage?

The Samoan turned and looked back at them.

"We're here, Sonny," he said.

Sonny looked at Eric, wiped the knife on his pant leg, and flipped the blade closed with a deft movement. He slipped it into his right boot and grinned.

"Okay, Eric," he said slowly. "You and me are gonna go inside and find Melissa Michelle. You try and cross me and things will get real ugly."

"I'm coming too," Ladonna said, unbuckling her seatbelt.

"The hell you are," Sonny said.

She looked at him through the opening of the seats, her eyes intense.

"She's *my* daughter," she said. "You think you can keep me away?"

Eric saw Sonny meet her gaze, look down, and then slowly nod.

"Joe, stay here with the van," Sonny said. "In case we need to make a quick exit."

"Hey, ain't that the chick's mother?" Roscoe asked, lowering the tinted windshield that separated the driver's compartment from the interior of the limousine.

Corrigan looked out the window and smiled as he saw Ladonna get out of the passenger side of a nondescript white van.

Melissa Michelle twisted her head to look too.

"It sure is, and look who's with 'em," Corrigan said. He turned to Casio who was lighting another cigarette.

"Go get 'em," Casio said, his face darkening. "Roscoe,

you go take care of the driver." His cell phone rang and he answered it with a bark. "Where you at?" He paused, listening. "Who's with you?" Another pause, then, "Okay, get over here now. We're in the parking garage of the Holiday. Meet Corrigan and Freddie inside. Hurry up. We got the pigeons in sight." He hung up and said, "Moran's here."

After getting Marjorie and her charge seated at a table near the outermost aisle, Harry went up the side of the stage and watched as Gabe did an encore version of another Colton ballad, "It's Just a Matter of Time." Judging from the whoops and screams, Harry figured that the song was more prophetic than the kid knew. Squinting, he saw a pretty young girl who looked startlingly familiar standing near the stairs by the stage curtains. He blinked twice in the artificial lighting trying to place her. Then he had it. Jenna, the little intern from the newspaper. Harry grinned as their eyes met and she smiled an acknowledgement.

Yeah, he did say that he was seeing her, he thought.

Gabe was putting the finishing touches on the song when Harry's cell phone rang. He almost didn't hear it due to the thunderous applause that followed the final notes. Gabe smiled, looking more like a young Colton than all the other imitators put together, and took a bow.

Harry struggled to unclip the phone, then finally got it. He answered it just as the caller hung up. Looking at the number he saw it was Jan's cell and immediately began dialing her back. But Gabe and Jenna were suddenly at his side, Gabriel all smiles and a bit out of breath, holding his un-amplified guitar. The girl hanging on his arm and looking like she'd just won a ten million jackpot at the slots.

"Hi, Harry," Gabe said, stretching out to offer his hand.

Harry shook it and said, "Man, you were knocking them

dead. I didn't know you were going to enter this thing."

"I wasn't," Gabe said, his smile shrinking somewhat with a self-effacing shrug. "Jenna kind of talked me into it."

"It makes perfect sense," she said, looking up at Harry with clear blue eyes. "I mean, who better to sing like Colton than . . ." She let the sentence trail off momentarily, then added, "Gabe."

Harry nodded in agreement and went back to dialing Jan on his phone.

"And he's already in the top finals," Jenna said. "I think he's gonna win it, hands down."

"From what I just saw he should," Harry said.

Gabe shrugged and said, "Say, I was gonna call you. You still trying to crack that disk with Buzzy's articles on it?"

Harry gave a short, rueful laugh.

"Nah, I gave up on that a long time ago. Why?"

Gabe and Jenna looked at each other and smiled.

" 'Cause Jenna knows the password," he said.

Harry could feel his mouth drop open.

"What?"

Gabe nodded and turned to her with an encouraging look.

She shrugged and started talking with a sigh.

"Well, when I first got to the paper, Mr. Nash put me in the newsroom and told me to learn something. Nobody would even give me the time of day." Her lips curled up, as if she were remembering a bad smell. "All they wanted me to do was go get them coffee and cigarettes." She compressed her lips slightly. "Buzzy was . . . different. He was so nice. I started helping him, and he taught me so much. Him and his wife were going through kind of a bad time, on account of his child support and the kids he had with his other wives, you know."

Harry nodded in commiserating fashion, and trying to urge her onward.

Get to the password part, he thought.

"So, anyway, we used to go to dinner when we were working late together." Her eyebrows shot up. "It was nothing romantic, or anything like that. He just needed somebody to talk to, and I guess I've always been kind of a good listener."

"I'll bet," Harry said. *A lot better listener than I am right now.*

"So he told me about his password process," she said. "He used the first three numbers of his marine serial number, and then the first two initials of whatever story he was working on, and then the last two numbers of his marine number."

Harry was trying to remember what the number was and prayed that he'd saved whatever paper he'd scribbled it down on.

But Jenna beat him to it. "So for this story it would be 2-1-0-C-P, for Colton Purcell, and then 1-3."

"You're sure about that?" Harry asked.

"Sure," she said, shrugging. "Those other documents I downloaded to that disk had the same password. I just didn't know there were any more till today when Gabe told me." She looked up at him again and beamed like a schoolgirl in love.

"Gabe, you mind if I kiss your girlfriend?" Harry said, smiling.

"Go get your own gal, Harry," Gabe said, smiling back and pressing Jenna closer to him.

"I think I'll do that," Harry said, and finished dialing Jan's phone.

The next pair of finalists had taken the stage, wearing matching red, white, and blue jumpsuits. Harry glanced upward as he brought the phone to his ear and saw they were Lance and Powell Fabray. He immediately jerked his gaze away and motioned for Gabe and Jenna to follow him. Moving as far away from the stage as he could get without losing sight of Marjorie and Willard, he pressed the send button as Lance began warbling "My Way."

Jan answered on the second ring.

"Hiya," Harry said. "Where are you?"

"I'm in front of the Roman Holiday," she said. "I tried to call you."

"Sorry, I couldn't hear the phone in all this racket. You coming in here?"

"Yeah, in a minute," she said. "I have to meet a couple of feds first. They supposedly have some information on one of my homicides. They also want to talk to Pablo about some stuff."

"Oh? That sounds interesting. Anything you'd care to share?"

He heard her musical laugh come over the phone.

"Let's put it this way," she said. "You might be able to sweat it out of me, under the right conditions."

"I can hardly wait," he said.

"You sound very upbeat."

"Yeah, I am. I just discovered that I'm very close to breaking a big part of the story I'm working on."

"Well, be careful, okay?" she said. He could detect the note of concern in her voice. "All of a sudden these rock and roll dudes are starting to look like some very nasty people." She paused abruptly. "Oh, I've got another call coming in that I have to take. Stay where you are and I'll meet you in a few minutes, okay?"

Michael A. Black

"Like I said, I can hardly wait."

When he ended the call he was smiling, and both Gabe and Jenna were staring at him with equally big smiles.

"Is that your cop girlfriend?" Gabe asked.

"That's her," Harry said. "And you're about to meet her in a few minutes. In the meantime, I'd like to introduce you to someone else you may be interested in knowing." He glanced over and saw that Lance and Powell were blending in a harmonious declaration that they'd done things their way. Harry rolled his eyes and said, "If that's your competition, you got this thing wrapped up." He cocked his head toward the back. "I've been trying to dodge those two wackos since Memphis." Several members of the crowd leaped to their feet in jubilation as the song ended, just as Harry was trying to zero in on Marjorie and Willard's table.

Obviously Lance had paid some people off here, Harry thought, because they'd sounded like a couple of walruses.

He walked down the side aisle, trying to see where they were, but they weren't anywhere near the place he remembered leaving them.

Oh no, he thought. I hope the old boy didn't wander off anywhere.

He felt Gabe at his side suddenly, asking, "Anything wrong, Harry?"

"Everything," he said, and then he saw them. They were over by the doors, being ushered out by Sonny Proper and Ladonna Purcell. There was some other seedy-looking guy with them that looked like he was in need of a bath. Harry quickened his pace but the crowd seemed to all stand up at once, like seventh inning stretch at the ballgame. People sprang up in front of him, and Harry suddenly found himself pushing his way toward the doors in a mass of humanity.

"Ladies and gents," a voice came over the speaker system. "We'll be right back to announce our selection of the final winners. Go ahead and take five."

More people were getting up, making progress even slower. Harry looked back over his shoulder and saw that Gabe was several feet behind him, and Jenna even farther back. The small girl disappeared, swallowed by the crowd. But he was only twenty feet or so from the doors now. He redoubled his efforts, squeezing in front of and between the throngs, like a man possessed.

I have to be there for this reunion, he thought, wondering what Ladonna was saying at this very moment. It could mean the difference between finding out what the evasiveness and secrecy was all about, and being left in the dark again, like everyone's favorite mushroom.

The doors were only ten feet away now. Two very hefty ladies waddled from an adjacent aisle, each dressed in *I Love Colton* T-shirts and too-tight jeans. Harry had to stop so abruptly he went up on tiptoes to avoid a collision.

"Excuse me, ladies," he said, trying to push past them, which in the narrowing space was no easy feat.

"Watch it, buster!" one of them yelled.

The other shot him an indignant look and purposely stepped in front of him.

He slowed to a veritable crawl as the two sashayed the final few feet to the exit. Over their heads Harry could see more people filing out, but no sign of his quarry.

Swearing, he pushed his way through the door, muttering a string of "Excuse me's."

As he edged through the doorway, hugging the frame, he glanced about again, craning his neck. Suddenly he saw them, Marjorie, Willard, Ladonna, Sonny, and the seedy guy all heading down the hallway toward the back exit.

They were flanked by a quartet of rough-looking characters. From the expression on her face as she looked back over her shoulder, Marjorie didn't look very happy.

Harry called to her, but his voice seemed to get lost in the cacophony. He literally had to run to catch up and saw that the guy to the rear of Marjorie and Willard had to be at least six-six.

"Hey, wait," Harry said. "Hold on there. I'm a reporter."

The big guy slowed and turned to look back. A flash of recognition burst in Harry's memory. He'd seen this guy before someplace . . . or had he?

The guy held up a hand the size of a gallon milk jug.

"A reporter?" he asked. "What's your name?"

"Harry Bauer. I'm with Ms. Versette and her companion."

The big guy grinned.

"Is that so?"

The procession sort of halted, and an equally tough-looking, but shorter guy appeared beside the giant.

"What's the hold up?" the shorter guy asked.

"This is that reporter everybody's been telling us about," the big guy said.

"Beat it," the shorter one said.

"Yeah, beat it, Bauer," Sonny yelled. Harry detected a note of desperation in the tone.

"Moran," the big guy said. "I think he needs to accompany us. We have to find out how much he knows." With that he reached out and grabbed Harry's neck with a grip of iron, at the same time drawing him closer. Suddenly Harry felt something hard and metallic pressing into the small of his back.

"Keep moving with us or I'll blow your kidney all to hell and leave you laying here," the big guy whispered.

"Hey, Mr. Bauer," a voice yelled.

Harry managed to twist his head toward the voice.

It was Lance Fabray accompanied by his cousin Powell.

"I thought that was you," Lance said, moving forward with his hand outstretched. "What did I tell you? We're in the final five." His face twisted with a crooked Colton grin and he cocked his thumb over his shoulder. "Well, six, counting Powell."

"That's great, Lance, but I'm a little busy right now," Harry said, feeling the circular barrel pressing harder against the soft area of his back. He imagined a thunderous roar, then the bullet tearing through him.

"Well, shucks, we was hoping that you'd at least come see us win and do a write-up on us, right, Powell?"

Powell nodded, giving his best pouting, sultry look.

"Beat it, greaseball," the big guy said. "Can't you see the man don't want to talk to you?"

Lance's mouth dropped open and he stared back at the other man, having to cant his pompadoured head upward to look into the bigger guy's eyes.

"Say now, big boss man, you sound like you could use a lesson in manners," he said. The hanging leather fringes of his jumpsuit began to sway to and fro.

"Lance, beat it. Now, if you know what's good for you," Harry said.

"Mess with us and you're messing with trouble," Powell said, stepping up beside Lance. Harry expected the shot any second, but instead, the shorter tough guy, the one the giant had called Moran, grabbed both ersatz Coltons by their leather collars and with a quick, snapping motion, slammed their heads together with terrific force. Both men collapsed to their knees immediately.

"Corrigan, let's go," Moran said. "Move it."

"Here comes more trouble," the big guy, Corrigan, said, pointing at Gabe who was running toward them.

"I'll take care of him," Moran said, withdrawing a blue steel semiautomatic from his belt and slipping it into his coat pocket while moving in Gabe's direction.

"No," Harry yelled, but Corrigan was hustling him and the others down the hallway. "Please, don't hurt him."

Bobbling his head Harry caught a glimpse of Gabe being shoved into a nearby janitor's closet. He saw Moran's arm draw back, then the gun came out. They both disappeared into the closet and Harry thought he heard a muffled shot as they rounded the corner. The crowd had thinned out as they'd moved farther down the hallway, and it was suddenly devoid of other pedestrians. Corrigan shoved Harry roughly, so that he bumped into the seedy guy between him and Sonny Proper.

Oh, God, I hope Gabe's all right, Harry thought.

"Get moving," the big hood said.

A white van pulled up with a sinister-looking guy driving it. The guy with a huge head who'd been leading them reached out and opened the side door. Harry could see a man lying on the metallic floor, a puddle of dark blood seeping from his head, his brown eyes looking upward and slightly askew.

Corrigan pushed Marjorie and Willard forward and into the van and slammed the door shut.

"You stay with them, Freddie," he said to the big-headed guy, and then shoved Ladonna, Sonny, and the seedy guy toward a stretch limo. He grabbed Harry too. The windows were tinted with opaque, one-way glass.

"Everybody inside," he said, motioning for them to get in the open door.

"Mom!" Harry heard a young voice say as he was getting inside. "I think they killed Joe."

He saw a swarthy guy sitting in the far side of the seat smoking a cigarette, then a young girl and a freaky-looking guy he knew could only be Pablo Stevenson in the flesh. The girl embraced Ladonna, and they both began to cry. Corrigan pushed the rest of the procession into the capacious interior and got in himself, slamming the door. Sonny immediately put his arms around both the women, crowding Pablo out of the way.

"Ain't motherhood a beautiful thing?" the guy with the cigarette asked. He looked like a refugee from an old wise guy movie. A sudden familiarity struck Harry again. He'd seen this guy before too, but only on TV. He was Ricardo "The Hammer" Casio, last of the old-time Mafiosos.

Oh shit, Harry thought. No wonder Buzzy ended up with a broken neck.

"Eric!" Pablo yelled.

Harry saw the old gangster staring at the seedy guy, the one Pablo had addressed, next to Sonny.

"I been waiting till I saw you again," Casio said, crossing himself then kissing his thumb. "I been praying to God that he'd deliver you to me. Vengeance is gonna be mine, and you're gonna wish it was over long before it is."

"Mr. Casio—" Eric started to say.

Casio leaned forward and delivered a backhand blow to the seedy guy's cheek, splitting it open with one of the ornate rings on his hand.

Eric recoiled with the blow and then seemed to go pale in the dimly lit interior. A small trickle of blood ran down his cheek like a dark teardrop.

What's that mean for the rest of us? Harry wondered.

"Where's Moran at?" Casio asked.

313

"He's taking care of another shithead," Corrigan said. "Be along in a minute."

With that Casio surveyed the captives.

"Shit, this is turning into a fucking parade," he said. "What we gonna do with all them?"

"I got it covered, boss," Corrigan said. "All part of the plan. We got the spot all picked out. Moran knows where it is."

Casio grunted and suddenly there was a tap at the window. From the inside, looking out, Harry could see it was the shorter of the tough guys. The one they'd called Moran, who'd stuffed poor Gabe into that closet. God, he hoped that kid was all right, that maybe somebody would find him in time.

Corrigan opened the door, but as Moran began to get in, Casio's cell phone rang. He answered it with the immediacy of a man waiting for something. The lines in his face deepened as he listened without speaking. Finally he said, "Okay, I'll be there shortly." He slipped the cell phone into his coat pocket and turned to Moran. "You got a car here?"

Moran nodded.

Casio began to get up, moving toward the door, then stared at Eric. "You know where this spot is Corrigan was talking about?" he asked Moran.

Moran nodded.

"Drive me to the hospital," he said. "That was Alphonse. They're giving Rocky the last rites."

Chapter 27

Death in the Desert

They sat crammed into the extended interior of the limousine, all huddled up against the opaque screen sealing off the driver. Harry and Eric on the floor, Pablo hugging the left side armrest, Melissa Michelle and Ladonna, both being held by Sonny on the seat. Harry looked across from them at Corrigan, who now had the big, shiny Colt Python out and pointed at them. His face twitched into a grin as he saw Harry looking at him. He shifted his gaze to the other faces above him, all with a look of total and absolute despair. No one was talking, except for Pablo, who suddenly wouldn't stop.

"I don't even see why you kept me in here with them," he said. "I mean, haven't I cooperated? Haven't I said that I'd record any songs you want me to? Didn't I go through with that wedding thing?" His hands fluttered as he spoke and his eyes seemed like two white saucers with twin spots of black. "Have I ever denied you guys anything?"

Finally Corrigan said, "Shaddup, short eyes. I'm tired of listening to you."

The "short eyes" comment seemed to stun Pablo and his lips clamped together.

A sudden ringing broke the silence and Corrigan's head perked up.

"Who's ringing?" he asked, holding the pistol up.

"That'd be me," Harry said, reaching into his pocket and hoping to press the button to at least get in some message of distress if it was Jan calling him back.

"Give it to me," Corrigan said, his voice a growl. He leveled the pistol at Harry's forehead. "And don't answer it."

Harry tried to hit the SEND button to connect the call anyway, but as he did the big guy snatched the phone away with his left hand and ended the call. He smirked slightly, then pressed the button to lower his window and dropped the phone out. He moved forward slightly and used his heel to deliver a hard kick to Harry's shin.

Harry grunted in pain.

"Anybody else got any bright ideas?" Corrigan asked.

No one replied and Harry rubbed his leg, still feeling the burning pain. He saw Eric staring at him, then look away quickly.

How the hell did it come to this? Harry thought. Where did all these wise guys appear from? But hell, this was Las Vegas, wasn't it? They built the place. All the boys, Frank, Dino, Sammy, even Colton Purcell were rumored to have had mob connections. So, that explained the presence of the Latino Prince of Pop, but what about the rest of them?

And where are they taking us? he wondered. He watched the desert landscape slowly settle under a shroud of darkness as they moved farther and farther from the city's lights. Away from the safety of the crowds, away from Jan. Had he told her how he felt about her? He hoped she knew. He hoped she'd somehow come to rescue him and the others. Somehow suddenly appear on the horizon with a fleet of helicopters and a heavily armed tactical squad behind her.

But as they rode on in silence he knew that wasn't going to happen.

I should've tried to make a break earlier, he thought. Back at the hotel, when Lance and Powell stopped us.

Slices of the old boot camp lecture began to come back to him, and he could almost hear the DI's voice explain the tactics to them in that lazy Southern drawl.

You should avoid being taken prisoner at all costs. If this should occur, escape should be effected as soon as possible after the capture.

No shit, Sherlock, Harry thought.

Should you get captured by the enemy, remember that you are to give only your name, rank, and serial number. He remembered the DI's rueful, gap-toothed smile. *Also expect that in all probability, your captors will not abide by the rules of the Geneva Convention. Therefore, I say again, it is imperative to accomplish escape as soon as possible after your capture. The longer you are held, the farther away you will be taken from your lines. You should avoid being taken to an internment camp, if possible, at all costs.*

It's a cinch they ain't taking us to one of those, Harry thought.

Sonny must have had similar thoughts, because at that precise moment Harry's eyes locked with his. Dark eyes, Harry noticed, and not really expressing much. Just like their previous meeting in the bar.

Something suddenly hit Harry and he looked up, studying the eyes of the three of them, Melissa Michelle, Sonny, and Ladonna. Brown, brown, and blue. He remembered his research on the Colton Purcell article. How Colton's blue eyes had driven the girls wild. He'd even made a joke about it when he'd sung "Don't It Make My Brown Eyes Blue" on *The '82 Comeback Show.* Another voice from Harry's past crept into his memory, reciting another long ago lesson that had been filed away. It was the high-nasal voice of Mr. Cook, his high school biology teacher.

In genetics the matching of two recessive genes will only produce an offspring with the recessive trait. Two blue-

*eyed individuals who have a child together can only pro-
duce one with blue eyes, since they both are possessive of
only the recessive genes. The matching of two brown-eyed
parents, or the matching of one brown-eyed and one blue-
eyed parent, can, on the other hand, produce an offspring
with either the dominant or recessive trait.*

Harry smirked at the irony. He'd finally discovered what
in all probability Ladonna wanted so much to keep secret.
He'd gotten Buzzy's password too, and it was too late to do
anything about it.

The limo turned and went down over a bump. The en-
suing unevenness of the movement and the constant skit-
tering sound beneath them made Harry think they'd gone
off the roadway. He tried to look outside, to get some bearings as to where they were, but all he could see was darkness. In his mind's eye he knew the mountains were in the
background though, and he longed for one more chance to
see the sun come up over them.

The car slowed to a stop and the screen behind them
lowered slightly.

"We're here," the driver said.

Harry glanced up and saw the headlights of another vehicle, the white van, pulling in behind them.

Corrigan opened the door and held up the big pistol.

"I am a very good shot, so if any of you try to run, I'll
drop you in a heartbeat. Got it?" He started to get out, then
hesitated and addressed Sonny. "And if you cause any
trouble, shitkicker, I'll make sure to take it out real good on
the ladies."

Sonny didn't reply, but his stare looked ice cold.

Corrigan got out and slammed the door after him. Harry
watched him go to the trunk and open it, removing some-

thing. Then, leaving the hatch open, Corrigan moved back to the rear door of the limousine.

"Com'ere, short eyes," he said, opening the door. "The rest of you stay put."

Pablo's face had a look of abject terror on it as he curled up in the corner.

"I said, com'ere, bitch," Corrigan said. "Don't make me come over there and get you."

Pablo swallowed, and began his garrulous talking again, crawling over the laps and shoulders toward the door.

"I don't know why you want me," he said. "Like I told you, I cooperated. Haven't I? I told you guys whatever you wanted. I did whatever you wanted—"

Corrigan slapped him. He whimpered like a small dog.

"Get in the fucking trunk," Corrigan said.

"The trunk? What for?" Pablo's voice sounded several octaves higher than normal.

"Because I said so," Corrigan grunted and lifted the wispy figure to his feet, walked him to the rear of the limo, and then tossed him inside like a rag doll. He slammed the lid and came back around to the door.

"Okay, everybody but the broads get out now," he said, pointing the pistol inside the limo.

Ladonna cried out and Sonny quickly told her it would be all right and kissed her forehead gently. He, Eric, and Harry filed out and stood where Corrigan directed them. The highway was perhaps a hundred yards behind them, with the headlights of the two vehicles illuminating the rough-looking terrain of sandy dirt, crumpled, spider-like sage brush, and an occasional cactus through a floating patina of dust. Harry saw three shovels on the ground by the rear tire. Those must have been what he took out of the trunk, Harry thought.

The driver, a thin, rat-faced guy had stepped out of the limo, as well as the driver of the van, and the guy with the oversized head they'd called Freddie. Each held a revolver.

"Cut off the lights," Corrigan said.

Great, Harry thought. Four wise guys, all with guns. He looked over at the van and saw Marjorie and Willard holding each other on the metallic floor. The body lay a few feet from them, the pool of blood now running down the corrugated floorboards to leak out over the rear bumper like chocolate syrup.

"Roscoe and Theo, you watch them and the two broads," Corrigan said. "Freddie, you grab those." He indicated the shovels, then directed Harry, Sonny, and Eric toward the van. "Go get that body and carry it where I tell ya."

The three men moved to the van. Harry was going to try to say something comforting to Marjorie and Willard, as if he would even be able to understand, but Sonny beat him to it.

"Don't y'all worry none," he said. "Everything's gonna work out okay."

Harry figured Sonny knew he was lying, but just wanted to try and make it easier for them. They pulled the limp body out of the van, the blood smearing over the white metal. Harry saw where it was leaking from. An entry wound just below the man's left ear. He looked to be Hispanic or Oriental or something. It was Joe, he realized suddenly. The Samoan bodyguard who had accompanied Ladonna the morning they'd met in the bar.

"Hold it," Corrigan said, coming over and patting down each of them, going in their pockets and removing their wallets. He set the wallets on the hood of the limousine, then gestured for them to move down a slight embankment

320

and toward an arroyo. Their feet scuffed over the dry earth, the sage seeming to pull at their shoes like clinging hands. They went past a couple of tall cactuses, and the weight of the dead man began to feel heavier and heavier.

"How much farther, for Christ's sake?" the guy called Eric asked, his voice a pitiful whine.

"Just keep moving, asshole," Corrigan said.

Freddie laughed derisively.

After they'd gone about a hundred more feet, Corrigan directed them to stop.

"Put him down there," he said, pointing with the barrel of the gun. "Freddie, toss them shovels down. This looks like as good a spot as any."

"Hey, wait a minute," Eric said. "You can't do this to me, Corrigan. Please."

Corrigan smirked. "Pick up that shovel and start digging. I want to give this guy a decent burial." He gestured at the corpse.

"Hey, wait a minute," Eric continued. "It's me, remember? I've been with you on this from the beginning. I ain't said nothing about any of it. Not that reporter, not Big Daddy, not the nursing home bitch . . . none of 'em. You can trust me, Corrigan. You know that." The streak of blood had dried along his cheek, looking like an errant smear of mascara.

Freddie kicked a shovel toward Harry, who picked it up. Freddie stepped back quickly and pointed his gun at Sonny and then at the other shovel. Sonny slowly moved over and grabbed it.

"So how about it?" Eric asked. "You're gonna let me go, right?"

"Vanshitberg," Corrigan said, "I ain't gonna tell you again. Pick up that fucking shovel and start digging or I'm gonna come over there and break a couple of your fingers, real slow." He grinned malevolently.

Harry saw Eric's face go blank and the man grabbed at his gut. But he picked up the third shovel.

They began digging but the dirt was hard and un-yielding. Corrigan had produced a flashlight from some-where and shone it down on them as he and Freddie stood at the top of the arroyo. None of them worked very fast, and Harry reflected on the irony of being forced to dig his own grave. The fantasy of Jan somehow coming to his rescue flirted with his imagination. The other irony, of cracking the biggest story of his career, and not being able to tell anyone about it danced in next, replacing the tactically out-fitted picture of Jan, and he wondered if this was how Buzzy felt in his last minutes.

"She's yours, isn't she?" he whispered to Sonny, who was laboring slowly beside him.

The other man's gaze shot up, but he said nothing.

Silent to the end, Harry thought.

"Come on," he said. "Just tell me. That's what Buzzy knew, right?"

Sonny sighed.

"You don't ever give up, do ya?"

They were about ten feet away from Eric, and Harry whispered again.

"Please, just tell me if I'm right."

Sonny grunted, then nodded fractionally.

"I knew it," Harry said. "How'd Buzzy find out?"

"I don't know. Maybe Big Daddy tipped him. He was planning on trying to ruin things for Ladonna. Start some lawsuit. Do some DNA tests on Willard. Threatening to gum everything up. Him and his fifty-one percent. Guess he figured with Melissa about to turn eighteen, she'd inherit too much of what he felt was his." He stepped harshly on the blade of the shovel and tossed a load of dirt away. "Can't say that I was saddened by his passing."

King of the Hustlers, Harry thought.

"Yeah, well it sounds like he wasn't too crazy about it either," he said.

"Hey, quit your talking down there," Corrigan yelled. He shone the beam of the flashlight directly at them. "Remember, this is just business."

Sonny seemed to stiffen at the remark.

Harry felt a trickle of sweat drip down from his armpit. He slowed his efforts, taking only a half-full load each time.

No sense hurrying, he thought.

"Hey," he heard Sonny whisper. "You really an ex-gyrene?"

Harry nodded.

Sonny's eyes shot toward Corrigan and Freddie standing on the ridge above them.

"Them boys missed my knife in my boot," he said, keeping his voice low.

Harry glanced up at their captors. The incline was at least fifteen or twenty feet. A risky throw, at best, with a knife. Plus, there were two of them, both armed. Still, what were their other options?

"Give me a diversion and we'll rush 'em," Sonny said.

Harry nodded fractionally, knowing that their chances of success were a lot slimmer than being shot and left to die in the dirt. But they had to act before the hole they were digging got too deep.

"I thought I told you boys to quit socializing?" Corrigan said, grinning. "Just dig."

"Corrigan," Eric said. "You let me go now. I got something to trade." He glanced at Harry and Sonny and Harry suddenly realized that the little weasel must have overheard him and Sonny's plan.

"You got nothing, shitbird," Corrigan said. His lips curled up into a feral smile. "The old man's gonna wanna do you himself, but that don't mean that I can't start a little bit until he gets here."

Eric looked wounded. "Look, I had nothing to do with Rocky's relapse. I swear it. He just sorta showed up, and the next thing I knew him and that fucking Pablo—"

Corrigan extended the Python toward him, like he was going to shoot. Eric dropped his shovel and cringed.

"Pick it up and start digging," Corrigan said. "And don't say another fucking word."

Harry watched as Eric's hands slipped and fumbled with the shovel. Tears were streaming down his face.

The silence of the night was suddenly broken by the ringing of a cell phone. Corrigan unclipped his from his belt and glanced at it. Then he said, "Yeah, whatcha want?"

He frowned, held the phone away from his ear, and looked at it.

"Shit, this battery's going dead," he said into the phone after replacing it to his ear. He slapped Freddie's shoulder and said, "Give me yours."

"Hey, I don't carry one of those fucking things," Freddie said, cocking his head back in the direction of the vehicles. "Go get Roscoe's."

Corrigan frowned and said into the phone, "Moran, I'll call you back in a minute. This phone's going out. What? Say that again."

He held the phone away and scowled at it, then put it back on his belt. He glanced down at the three diggers, then to Freddie.

"Keep an eye on them," he said, handing over the flashlight and moving toward the cars.

Harry glanced quickly at Sonny, who nodded imperceptibly, fanning his fingers three times.

Fifteen seconds? Harry wondered. It has to be. Anything else would be too long. He saw Sonny's hand go low along his leg, working his pant leg upward as he dug. After a few seconds, he'd worked it up over his boot, and the shovel abruptly slipped from his grasp. Harry watched the other man's fingers dig into the tall boot and something silver seemed to glint in the moonlight.

"Hey!" Harry yelled, scooping up a shovel full of the dry dirt and hurling it upward. He ran to his left, hoping that Freddie would turn that way with the gun, exposing more of his chest.

A round exploded in the night and Harry felt something whiz by him. He glanced over his shoulder and saw Sonny charging up the embankment. Harry pivoted and ran up after him. The gun flashed again and he heard Sonny grunt. The knife was sticking out of the center of Freddie's chest and Sonny was up there now, twisting it with one hand and holding the other man's gun hand with the other. Another explosion from the barrel lit up the night, this time sending a rain of dirt over their twisting feet, and Harry was there now too, clawing and twisting at Freddie's gun hand. Then Freddie went limp. A series of yellow flashes erupted from the vehicles and Harry felt more rounds shoot by him. Harry managed to twist the gun from the lank fingers and he and Sonny ran down the embankment. Eric stood frozen in place.

Sonny stumbled to his knees and as Harry helped him up he saw the twisted expression of pain on the other man's face.

"Sonny?"

"Caught one," he grunted. "Let's get moving."

"Give me a hand," Harry said to Eric. "He's been hit."

Eric adjusted his gaze toward them, licked his lips, and then turned to run.

"You asshole!" Harry yelled after him. Then he pulled Sonny up and they started a fumbling stride up and over the other side of the arroyo.

Another shot rang out, missing them.

Harry paused, turned, and fired a shot in the direction of the cars. He was sure it went wide, but at least it might slow their pursuers down a little.

"Don't waste ammo," Sonny said. His voice sounded uneven and laced with pain.

Harry concentrated on moving low and to the left. Their shoes scuffed over every dry plant and uneven piece of ground imaginable, but finally he felt that they may have covered enough distance to stop and get their bearings.

He helped Sonny ease down to a prone position. The other man's breaths were coming in erratic gasps now. Harry concentrated on trying to get his own breathing under control. He was panting as well.

"How bad is it?" Harry asked.

"Bad enough," Sonny said. "Leave me and go on without me."

"I ain't leaving you," Harry said.

"You got to," Sonny grunted. "How many rounds you got left?"

Harry pressed the cylinder release and studied the cartridges. Four had expended primers.

"Two," he said.

"That's got to be enough," Sonny said. "You got to double back to the cars. Get Ladonna and Melissa and drive off."

"Sonny—"

"You're their only chance," he said. "Do it."

"I . . . I'm not sure I can," Harry said.

He felt Sonny's grip on his collar, pulling him close. Sonny gritted his teeth before he spoke.

"You were a fucking marine, for Christ's sake. You can do it. You got to."

Harry nodded, but in the darkness he wasn't sure if the other man could see it.

"I'll come back for you," he whispered, and took off on a low run, cutting diagonally toward the lights of the vehicles.

The beam of a flashlight swept in wide arcs, and Harry hit the dirt, stinging his face on some rough vegetation. The beam swung back over the area and he hoped that Sonny could keep low enough not to be seen.

I'd better start worrying about myself, he thought. I've got to get to those cars fast.

It looked like two of them were fanning out, looking for them. That left one by the cars. If he could get the drop on the guy, he'd have another gun. But that would leave two assailants who were also armed. And in all probability, they were better shots than he was. He hadn't fired a weapon since the Storm, and even that had been a sham. He'd been so far away from any one-on-one combat that he wondered now if he could shoot a man.

Shoot to kill, he thought.

Still, his instincts had taken over in the little scuffle on the arroyo just a few minutes ago. Survival of the fittest. Or the luckiest. But that left him with another problem. If he was able to take out the gangster at the car, would he be able to just drive off with the two women as Sonny had directed, and leave him? And what about Marjorie and Willard? It would take time to herd them into the limo. What if the keys weren't in it? He knew nothing about hot-wiring a car.

He lifted himself up and began a steady run for about fifty feet before dropping again. The flashlights seemed to be far to his right and he hoped that Sonny was on the move too, as best he could. The weapon he had was a snubnose revolver. A thirty-eight. That meant less accuracy at longer range. He'd have to risk getting close before firing, and even then, would he be able to take the guy down with just two rounds. None to spare, he thought. No misses.

He saw the rat-faced man by the car scanning the terrain. He looked alert. This wasn't going to be any cakewalk. The guy walked over to the limo and opened the door.

Oh, God, Harry thought. I hope he's not going to pull one of them out and use her as a shield.

Seconds later the guy was dragging a kicking, screaming Melissa Michelle out the rear car door. He held his gun hand high, and had his other hand wrapped in her hair.

Shit, Harry thought, and knew it was time to move. He got up and started a full speed run, zigzagging so that he might swing over and come up on the gangster's blind side. He had maybe thirty yards to go. His lungs felt like they were on fire. Twenty-five yards . . . twenty . . .

Rat face held the squirming girl and looked over his shoulder, directly at Harry. The man's expression twisted, and he swung his gun around. The fire seemed to jump a foot from the barrel, but Harry didn't feel anything hit him. He momentarily considered firing back but knew that would be a risky option.

Suddenly the car door burst open yielding a hell-cat, scratching and fighting and kicking. Ladonna jumped on the gangster's back, her fingernails raking the man's eyes. He tried to shake her off, then released Melissa and bought the gun up and pointed it over his shoulder at Ladonna.

Harry was there in two steps, before the man could fire,

and grabbed the pistol, twisting it upward just as it exploded. At the same time Harry pushed his own snubnose into the guy's gut and pulled the trigger twice. Rat face grunted with each shot, like he'd been punched in the stomach, then sagged to the ground. Harry was scrambling, tearing at the man's gun, but the gangster's fingers would not release it. He heard footsteps coming up behind him.

"Get in the car," he yelled at Ladonna. The gun came free from the man's hand and Harry whirled, firing it at the sound of the approaching footfalls.

Freddie's big head jerked into view behind a series of white hot flashes. Harry felt something sear his shoulder, his neck, and then side. He raised the dead gangster's revolver, aimed at the basketball-sized head, and began pulling the trigger. Freddie's head jerked backward, like it'd been struck by a poleax, and his legs twisted under him with his next two steps and he fell face-first about three feet away.

Harry knew he'd been hit. His shirt front was bloody. Very bloody. But nothing hurt.

Must be adrenaline, he thought. I just hope to God those keys are in the ignition.

"We gotta get outta here," he shouted, pointing to the open door of the limo. "Get in. It's our only chance."

"But the others," Ladonna said.

"I know. We'll have to go for help," Harry said.

And it was true. Get them out of harm's way, maybe far enough to regroup, find some more ammo, and then go back on foot for Sonny and the others. It was a plan, and it was all he had as he moved around to the driver's side of the limousine. He pulled open the door and slid partially inside, his fingers probing the ignition.

Keys, keys, keys, he thought. Please let them be there.

The space between the flat flanges was empty.

"Taking a trip?" Corrigan said, appearing out of no-where and clubbing Harry so hard on the head that he thought he heard bells after the initial crunch. "You don't think I'd be that stupid, do ya?"

Crumbling, Harry felt a powerful punch hit his side, followed by a series of two or three kicks. The whole thing seemed incredibly clear and lucid. Like he was watching it from above. The blows weren't actually hitting him. They were hitting this guy who looked remarkably like him.

I must be going into shock, he thought, and rolled over on his back, his head lolling to one side, as he looked up at the round black hole of the Python's barrel and beyond that at the man called Corrigan.

Two twin lights seemed to bounce along in the periphery of Harry's vision. As they grew larger and brighter he realized what they were. Headlights. They were car headlights.

The car pulled up and Harry adjusted his head slightly, watching a figure emerge from the vehicle. It was the shorter hood. The one with the mustache and goatee they'd called Moran.

"Corrigan, hold on," Moran said.

"About time you got here," Corrigan said. "You got the boss with you?"

"Un un."

Harry saw Corrigan cock back the hammer on the Python.

"Lemme just take care of this problem, and you and me'll do some digging."

"I don't think so," Moran said, and Harry saw that this guy was holding a gun outstretched too. He seemed to be talking into something in his other hand. A cell phone?

This is surreal Harry thought.

Corrigan looked back over his shoulder, his brow furrowing.

"What the fuck you doing?"

"Federal agent," Moran said. "Drop the weapon. It's over."

"Huh?" Corrigan said. "It can't be."

"It is. Drop it now, or I'll fire."

Corrigan seemed to consider it for a moment, then he smiled as he whirled, bringing the big barreled Python up in an arcing motion. The flame leaped from the barrel, but several quick bursts of fire shot out from the end of Moran's gun. Harry saw the window of Moran's car door shatter, then he felt a rain of glass from the one above him. The big man towering over him took a long stride, his gun hand lowering the Python, and letting it slip from his huge fingers. It thumped down on the hard dusty earth a few feet from Harry's head.

Moran was standing over Corrigan now, his pistol pointed at the bigger man's face.

"A fucking cop," Corrigan said, the blood bubbling from his mouth as he spoke. "I shoulda known . . ."

"Yeah," Moran said. He reached down and searched Corrigan's body, then moved over and grabbed the Python.

"How bad are you hit?" he asked Harry. The ringing in his ears was slowly subsiding, but it still sounded like the man was talking from inside a tunnel.

"Don't know," Harry managed to say. "But my friend's out there, and he's shot too."

Moran took off his jacket, patted Harry's shoulder, and placed the jacket over him.

"Stay warm," Moran said. "Help's on the way." He stood and Harry saw him speaking into a small portable radio. "Use the infrareds. There's people spread out here.

And we'll need a dust-off too. Got some injured."

A dust-off? And then Harry heard it. The staccato sound of helicopter blades cutting through the night. Just like the medevacs in the Iraqi desert. Like the beating of a flock of angels' wings.

Chapter 28

New Family Values

When Harry woke up he felt the softness of the pillow against his head, and the cool fragrance of clean cotton sheets over him. He wondered if he was wearing any clothes, and if he should try to get up to go to the bathroom. Then he looked over and saw Jan sitting a few feet away from him.

"Hi," she said, getting up and moving over to rub her fingers gently across his forehead. "How's my hero doing?"

"I don't know," he muttered. "I'll ask him when I see him."

Suddenly a wave of pain swept over him. He grimaced.

Jan laughed.

"Oops, sorry," she said. "I didn't mean to laugh at your pain. It was for your joke."

"How bad am I?" he asked. "Will I make it?"

"The prognosis is good. In fact, you'll probably be able to go home in the morning." She smiled. "They just wanted to keep you for observation overnight."

"Observation? But I got shot. I know I did."

"Grazed," she said. "Several times. And you might have a mild concussion. That's why I'm here to wake you up periodically through the night." Her hand crept down his abdomen and she smiled wickedly. "That is, if you're up to it."

"Oh, God," he said. "You know how to pick the times, girlfriend." He blinked several times. "Did they find Sonny?"

"Yes, he should be fine. He's hurt a little worse than you."

"He's a tough son of a bitch."

"He's a marine," she said. "Just like you."

Harry actually felt a smile creep over his face. But it hurt too much.

"And Gabe?" he asked. "What about Gabe?"

"He's fine too. They all are, thanks to you. You're a real hero."

"Yeah, right," he said. "That and a dollar will get me a cup of coffee." He made an effort to sit up a little and then asked, "Do you think you could get me my laptop? I've got one hell of a story to write."

"I'll see what I can do," she said, standing.

Suddenly the floor to ceiling curtain next to the bed separated slightly and Sonny Proper's face appeared from an adjacent bed.

"You better be careful what you write, boy," he said. " 'Cause I'll be reading it real close."

"What are you doing here?" Harry asked. "Don't I even rate a private room?"

"Security concerns," Jan said. "They wanted you two near each other."

"Not too near, I hope," Harry said. He grinned. It hurt a little less this time. "It'll be our story, brother," he said. "I'm going to call it, 'Death in the Desert, or How I Outwitted the Mafia.' "

Sonny grunted an approval and shut the curtain, muttering, "Just remember . . ."

"Just remember what?" Jan asked Harry. "You're going to have to explain all this to me so I can finish my report, you know."

"In due time I'll let you worm it out of me," he said,

lying back and closing his eyes. "But right now, I've got to think how I can sum it all up in succinct and stunning fashion."

Gabe and Jenna came to see him in the morning, holding hands and looking like the ending to one of Colton Purcell's old movies where the guy gets the girl and they ride off happily into the sunset. Ladonna and Melissa Michelle were there too, and they drew the curtain back between Harry's and Sonny's beds.

"Well," Harry asked. "Did you win the contest at least?"

Gabe smiled the crooked smile.

"No, when that guy, Mr. Eagan shoved me in that closet and told me to wait fifteen minutes and then call Detective Jan Grey, I missed my last encore."

"Those two big fat guys won," Jenna said. "What were their names?"

"Lance and Powell?" Harry asked, grimacing. "The Fabulous Fabray Boys?"

She nodded. "Their legs were so shaky when they got back up on stage, everybody thought they were doing some superb Colton gyrations."

Harry shook his head in disgust.

"Sometimes there ain't no justice." He looked at Gabe. "Hey, did you say 'Eagan'? I thought the guy's name was Moran?"

"That was my U/C name," a voice said from the door. Moran, or Eagan, minus his moustache and goatee, stepped inside. "My real first name is Jack, though. I just came by to see how you're doing." Jan came in after him carrying Harry's laptop.

"Thanks for saving my life," Harry said, extending his hand.

"My pleasure," Eagan said, shaking it.

"How long were you undercover?"

"I'm not supposed to say," Eagan said, holding up three fingers, "but just know that I'm glad to be out from under."

"Plus, we've formed a joint task force to handle things," Jan added. "Two of my homicides have been cleared up, and Ricardo 'The Hammer' Casio is in federal custody as well."

"Wow, on what charge?" Harry asked.

"Kidnapping and conspiracy to commit murder, to name a few," Jan said. "Plus numerous other federal charges." She stepped forward and kissed Harry on the cheek, then laid the laptop next to him. "And we grabbed the Latino Prince of Pop, too."

"Really?" Harry said, regretting that he sounded so pleased when he saw Melissa Michelle drop her gaze to the floor.

"Acquiring child pornography via the Internet," Jan said. "It was on his computer that we found at the hotel crime scene."

"This is all working out so well," Harry said.

"Not all of it," Jan added. "Looks like that slime-ball Eric Vantillberg might skate."

"He's a great candidate for the Witness Protection Program," Eagan said. "It's either testify against the mob and get relocated, or don't testify and get rubbed out."

"I think I'd prefer the latter for that SOB," Harry said. "Hey, I forgot to ask about Marjorie and Willard."

"We're flying them back to Memphis on our private jet," Ladonna said. She smiled. "Gabriel and his friend are coming too."

"We all sat down this morning and had a nice long talk," Gabe said, looking back at her and Melissa Michelle.

"Guess I got me a new family now to get acquainted with."

He smiled again.

Harry stared at Ladonna, who returned his gaze with a look of knowing sadness. Like she knew that he knew what the real story was.

"Hell, this damn thing is turning out to have more sugar than one of Colton's old movies," Sonny said, his voice sounding tired and grouchy.

Harry pressed the button on his laptop, ejecting the disk that said, Colton Purcell's Greatest Hits. The one that contained Buzzy's last few articles. The truth about what he'd known, and what he was going to write. The story of a lifetime, he'd called it. And it had turned out to be a story to die for, too. Harry looked at it for a moment, then held it out toward Ladonna.

"Ms. Purcell," he said. "I believe this belongs to you. Buzzy Sawyer wanted you to have it."

Chapter 29

If You Ever Get to Chi Town

As they rode down Paradise Road, Harry silently wondered why it took so long to get to there when it looked so close on the maps. Jan was silent too, driving with an expert proficiency, her lips compressed in a tight line. Finally, as they passed Wayne Newton Boulevard, he saw the sign crop up: Welcome to McCarran International Airport.

Looks like the end of Paradise, he thought, savoring the irony. So this is it.

He fingered the return ticket inside his sport coat, and glanced over at Jan, who still had the intense look on her face as she made the turn and proceeded through the parking area. Pulling close to the departure terminal, she swung the Intrepid into a spot marked Police Parking Only and shoved the car into park. Turning, she looked at him and sighed slightly.

Harry looked back, then slowly moved forward, as did she, until their lips met. The kiss was lingering, but brief. A promise, or good-bye? He wasn't sure.

A plane banked and descended overhead.

"Maybe that's your plane," she said. "America West, right?"

He nodded. "Let's hope they take their time gassing and checking it out."

She smiled and opened the door, removed the keys, and then pressed the remote. The trunk lid popped open.

Harry got out and grabbed his suitcase and laptop. Jan grabbed his carry-on and pulled up the handle. She pointed the way and they strolled across the cement streets toward the chrome and glass of the building.

The line at the departures desk was long, and an attendant was showing people how to use the computerized check-in points. Harry tried it three times, misspelling his name once, before finally getting his boarding pass.

"Gate seven," he said. "Maybe that'll bring me luck."

Jan shrugged and handed him the carry-on after they'd checked his bag. They went up the escalator and down the long corridor toward the screening point. Harry could feel his feet moving slower and slower.

He'd been dreading this moment, and now it was here. As they came up to the feeder ropes channeling people through the metal detectors, he stopped and stepped to the side, smiling.

"Well, if you ever get to Chi town," he said, letting the sentence dangle. He was going to say, "Look me up."

But the fragment had already seemed to hit her like a slap.

"Jan, I . . . un . . ." The words failed him as he saw twin rivulets of tears roll down her cheeks. "I don't know what to say."

"Ironic," she said. "A writer who can't find the words."

He immediately took out his handkerchief and handed it to her. She dabbed her eyes quickly.

"Believe me, I've been struggling all night to find them," he said, embracing her. He felt her squirm and released her. "I'm sorry. It's just that I've got so many things happening in my life right now." He paused and licked his lips. "I mean, I have to make sure I have a solid handle on this sobriety thing. And there's my daughter. I have to make sure that I stay a part of her life. And my job . . ."

"This is Vegas, remember?" she said. "Pretty on the surface, but underneath, nothing's real."

More tears. She nodded again, bringing the handkerchief up and blowing her nose.

He wanted to hold her again, but they were suddenly in the midst of a crowd and people were saying, "Excuse me" as they brushed by.

"Harry, I hate long goodbyes," she said, reaching up to hug his neck for one more time. "Take care of yourself." Their lips touched briefly, and then he felt her disengage, turn and walk away. He stood there, people flowing around him, and waited, watching to see if she'd look around and wave. But she didn't. Someone knocked over his carry-on, and he stooped to straighten it. When he glanced up again, she'd disappeared into the crowd.

He'd gotten a window seat, and started typing on the laptop almost as soon as the plane took off, putting the finishing touches on the story of the Colton Purcell Imitator's contest, leaving out any mention of his brush with death in the desert. That would come later, after the indictments hit. He'd leave out the section on Melissa Michelle, and mention Sonny Proper only as his companion in arms in the desert. The gangster angle would be enough, especially with the pending charges against the Latino Prince of Pop.

The pretty flight attendant came by and asked if anyone would like a drink. The guy next to him ordered a martini, and for a moment, when she looked expectantly to Harry, he thought about the smooth taste of the vodka and vermouth and how it would give him that nice, familiar burn all the way down. He sighed.

"Just coffee for me, please," he said. "Cream, no sugar."

She nodded and went to the next row of seats.

Harry went back to typing. He'd come to the end and

was searching for the right way to end it. Thoughts of Jan began to filter into his mind, and he saw her face, first smiling, and then streaked with tears as he had at the airport. Above him, a row ahead, the television screen was showing a music video of Colton Purcell belting out a song from one of his old movies. "NOW AND THEN," the white block lettering below the picture said, "THERE'S A FOOL SUCH AS I."

Another comeback, he thought, then watched the silent video a moment more.

No second acts? he wondered. Then suddenly the ending lines of his article came to him, and he typed, *F. Scott Fitzgerald once said, "There are no second acts in American lives." Obviously, old Scottie boy had never heard of anybody named Colton Purcell.*

The guy next to him was staring at the laptop screen, and Harry saved the document and shut it down.

"You a writer or something?" the guy asked. Harry could smell that this wouldn't be the guy's first martini of the day.

"Or something," he answered, and closed the top of the laptop.

Chapter 30

Epilogue

"Ladies and gentlemen, we're beginning our descent to Chicago, and we should be landing at O'Hare International Airport in about fifteen minutes," the pilot's voice said over the intercom. "Please fasten your seatbelts at this time, and remain in your seats. The temperature in Chicago is 72 degrees, and it's 10:25 P.M. Please refrain from trying to remove any items from the overhead compartments until the plane has completely stopped moving and is in the terminal, in that they may have shifted during the flight."

Harry felt the plane bank and glanced out the window at the myriad of glowing lights below. They looked like a complex series of symmetrical blocks, each widening into a bigger and bigger grid of houses, buildings, and stores. Nothing like Vegas where you had the desert and the mountains, Lake Mead, and then bright cityscape out in the middle of nowhere. This looked unending and complex, just like the tapestry of his life. And somewhere down there it waited for him, just like he'd never left. But there'd be no one to meet him down there, either. No second acts. Still stuck in the first.

He thought of how much he'd been through in just a week. But that seemed like it had been a lifetime ago.

The plane canted slightly, shifting the lighted scene below to one of a completely dark sky. For a brief moment Harry's own reflection stared back at him from the window.

No second chances? he thought. How many do you get to make it right?

The vibrating sound of the landing gear being lowered meant it was tight sphincter time, and he braced for the final descent. The wheels bounced and skidded slightly, and the reverse hum of the big turbines seemed to physically push him back into his seat. Once they'd stopped, the plane taxied for a long several minutes, with the pilot reminding everyone to "Please stay in your seats until directed by the flight attendants, and refrain from using any electrical appliances, including cell phones, until you have departed the cabin of the plane."

The anonymous voice thanked them for their cooperation and for flying with the airline. Harry glanced at his watch. The second hand seemed to be moving in slow motion. Finally the plane came to a stop and he saw them standing to open the pressurized door to accept the canopy. Everyone around him began standing and removing their carry-on stuff from overhead.

It took him ten minutes to get out, even though he'd been at the front of the plane. First class had its advantages. Two swinging seniors, still dressed in Vegas-style shorts and T-shirts sporting the name of their favorite casino, puttered along in front of him at an interminably slow pace. But he was already punching the numbers into his cell phone as he walked.

Emerging into the large terminal area, Harry pressed SEND and listened to the rings. She answered on the third one.

"Jan?" he said. "It's Harry. You forgot to give me back my handkerchief."

She was silent on the other end, then he heard a slight laugh.

"Yeah, I guess I did. I can mail it to you if you want."

"Don't bother," he said. "I thought I'd pick it up next

week. Are you free this Saturday?"

"This Saturday?" Her voice rose an octave. "Un, I have to work."

"Okay, Monday, then. That's one of the neat things about my job. No time clock, and I can do it from any-where." He waited for her response, and not hearing one, continued. "Then I thought the next weekend I'd fly you out here to Chicago. I'd like you to meet my daughter, Lynn."

"Harry," she said, her voice hesitant. "Are you sure about all this?"

"Sure I'm sure." He smiled to himself.

This is the second act, he thought, and I'd say it belongs to us.

About the Author

Michael A. Black graduated from Columbia College, Chicago in 2000 with a Master of Fine Arts degree in Fiction Writing. He previously earned a Bachelor of Arts degree in English from Northern Illinois University. A former Army Military Policeman, he entered civilian law enforcement after his discharge, and for the past twenty-seven years has been a police officer in the south suburbs of Chicago.

The author of over forty articles on subjects ranging from police work to popular fiction, he has also had over thirty short stories published in various anthologies and magazines, including *Ellery Queen* and *Alfred Hitchcock's Mystery Magazine*. His first novel, **A Killing Frost**, featuring private investigator Ron Shade, was published by Five Star Publishing in September 2002 with endorsements from such respected authors as Sara Paretsky and Andrew Vachss. The novel received universally excellent reviews, and was subsequently released in trade paperback.

Windy City Knights, the second novel in the Ron Shade series, came out in March of 2004, followed by **The Heist** (June 2005), a stand-alone thriller set in Chicago during its great flood of 1992. He has also written two nonfiction books, **The M1A1 Abrams Tank** and **Volunteering to Help Kids**, which were published by Rosen Press.

He has worked in various capacities in police work including patrol supervisor, tactical squad, investigations, raid team member, and SWAT team leader. He is currently a sergeant on the Matteson, Illinois Police Department. His hobbies include weightlifting, running, and the martial arts.

He holds a black belt in Tae Kwon Do. It is rumored he has five cats.

Freeze Me, Tender takes readers on a rollicking adventure through the glitz and grime of Las Vegas, as loyal fans gather in sin city to celebrate the tenth anniversary of the death of the King of Rock and Roll, just as his daughter is set to marry the Prince of Pop.

Visit the author's website at www.MichaelABlack.com.